A lawyer for over thirty years, William J. Coughlin was a
prosecuting attorney in Detroit before becoming a federal judge.
He lives in Detroit.

The Twelve Apostles

William J. Coughlin

Pan Books   London and Sydney

First published in Great Britain 1984 by Pan Books Ltd,
Cavaye Place, London SW10 9PG
987654321
© William J. Coughlin 1984
ISBN 0 330 284940

Printed and bound in Great Britain by
Cox & Wyman Ltd. Reading

This is a work of fiction. The events, settings and characters
that are described are fictitious and not intended to
represent specific places or living persons.

To Ruth Bridget

The game ain't over till it's over.

– Yogi Berra

1

She studied her reflection in the mirror with the same objectivity she used in analysing a land development proposal. Basically, she liked what she saw, but not in a truly vain way. Luck or genetics – she really wasn't sure which – had blessed her with the strong, handsome features that men called beauty. But she felt the high cheekbones were a gift from her mother's Irish ancestors, and that her smooth skin and brown hair came from the Spanish strain in her father's side of the family. She looked for wrinkles, found none, and then made a face at herself, mocking the search.

Thirty-six, the mother of a fourteen-year-old son. Christina Stevens Giles was pleased with what she saw in the mirror. She looked more like her son's older sister than his mother. And with regular exercise and careful diet she had managed to retain her youthful figure. That was important to her, and it had always been important.

Even the best product needed attractive packaging. She had proved herself a successful attorney, an asset to her law firm, but nothing could be neglected now. Her career at Nelson and Clark was at a criticial point.

Christina quickly slipped into her clothes. She chose an understated grey business suit with modest skirt and a plain silk blouse with a large bow that suggested a man's tie. Her hairstyle was a compromise between a severe business cut and a fuller, softer, and more feminine look.

She walked from the dressing room into their bedroom. Although her own bed was sleep-rumpled, her husband's hadn't been slept in. It was the second time in a week.

As usual, he had called and breezily informed her of an emergency case that would keep him at the hospital during the night. He said he would bunk down there if necessary. It was in keeping with his usual pattern. First there were the medical emergencies, overnights, soon to be followed by the medical seminars, always for a few days, and always out of town. All it meant was that the always charming Dr Hank Giles had found himself another girlfriend. It was always the same: he would be whistling and singing, happy with himself for a few months while the affair went on at a torrid pace. What always followed was a snarling, snapping period of depression after he, or sometimes the girl, called it quits. His affairs never lasted more than a few months at a time.

She was just as glad that he had found someone again; it would free her from his fawning, half-drunken embraces, at least for a while. Getting a divorce was part of the plan, but not until their son went off to college, now only four years away. By then the boy would be strong enough emotionally to handle the situation. Besides, she knew the firm frowned on divorced women and she had the chance to realize a marvellous opportunity there. If one of the main partnerships opened up – and Abner Slocum was fast approaching the age of mandatory retirement – she knew she would definitely have a chance at the vacancy since she was already the head of an important department within the firm, the only non-Apostle with such a major responsibility. So marriage it had to be, at least until something was settled at the firm. She could wait. She just hoped that Happy Hank, as people called him, would continue to content himself away from her bed. Once she had loved him, very deeply. But he was a boy in an adult body, and his constant infidelities had long ago killed her love and respect for him.

Christina checked herself once again in the full-length mirror. She wanted just the right look, attractive but professional. Satisfied, she walked down the hall to the apartment's spacious kitchen.

Her son merely glanced up at her, then returned his attention to his book. A bowl of half-eaten soggy cereal sat before him. Although she loved him, she secretly rejoiced that he was going back to boarding school in a week. He was becoming too much for her to handle. The metamorphosis from child to man, that painful period of adolescence, was producing a truculent, pouting, growing pillar of pimply flesh; created it sometimes seemed merely for the purpose of irritating her. They used to call him Little Hank, but now he was Henry. He wasn't little any more. In the past few months he had shot up in height, more and more beginning to resemble his father, a factor she knew could influence how she felt about him – and for which she made conscious allowance. There was certainly no point in visiting the resentment she felt towards the father upon the son. But she did wish that the cute chubby little boy could have stayed that way for just a bit longer. But, she reflected, at least he didn't have his father's insinuating charm, now so offensive to her.

She poured some instant breakfast mix and cold water into a cup and stirred the lumps out of it. 'Well, what mad and exciting adventures do you have planned for today?' she asked.

He scowled up at her. 'Kenny Wade is coming over later. We're just going to bum around for a while. Can I have some money? We'll probably end up at an arcade and I want to play the games.'

'Why don't you boys drop over to the Museum of Modern Art. They're having a new — '

He sneered. 'That place is full of fags. Jesus, Mom, I'm safer over on 42nd Street than in there.'

She sighed. He'd been sent to the very best schools, but he'd also been brought up in the city. Although he was a typical 'rich' kid and lived on the posh Upper East Side, he was nevertheless a true son of New York, and in his own way, streetwise.

She fished out a twenty-dollar bill from her purse and handed it to him, attempting a smile. 'Be careful,' she said, more to super-stitiously assure herself than to really caution him.

Her son took the bill, and merely grunted as he went back to his book.

She gulped down the chocolate drink, then headed for a mirror to repair any damage. A chocolate ring above the lips was definitely out this season, and today it was important that she look good. It would be a long and tiring day, but it would be important to the firm and to her. She had arranged a meeting with the Japanese bank people today. If they approved participation in the transaction, their money would be the key to unlocking a series of mortgages she had set up to bail out the giant Thompkins Steel Company. It was what she did best – arranging the financing of intricate mortgage deals for large corporations, and thinking up legal schemes to convert corporate assets into usable money without really giving them up. She was good at it, she knew that, perhaps one of the very best in the business. She seemed to have a special knack for the work.

The Thompkins deal, if it went through, would bring in an enormous fee to the firm, and the triumph would ensure extremely high visibility within Nelson and Clark. She knew that despite her relative youth and sex – there was already one woman Apostle – that by continuing to pull off miracles like the Thompkins business she would have a real shot at the next opening for main partner. It wouldn't be easy, nothing good ever was. And when the opening occurred, several of the participating partners, like herself, would compete for it. Only one would win while the others, the losers, would leave the firm. It was a tradition, a life or death thing, not unlike the gladiators of old – a struggle where one lived and one died. But today she felt ready, confident, almost eager for that struggle to begin.

She left the apartment, every thought of her son and husband gone from her mind. Christina Giles was all business now: she was a warrior on her way to do battle.

He often wondered why she hadn't abandoned Scarsdale; it was just not the same any more, not after the invasion of the advertising types and insurance executives, people who obviously had money, but not real money, not old money.

He smiled wryly, looking at the wrinkled, almost transparent skin of his hands. The old crowd was dead, or at least most of them. Vanished like some mystical tribe of legend, remembered, and spoken of occasionally, but having left behind no vestige of their once glorious culture.

'Is this it, sir?'

The chauffeur's soft voice startled him into the present.

'Yes,' he replied. 'Turn in through those gates just ahead.' Well, he thought, at least she had held on to the land, despite all the pressures brought by greed-inspired developers.

The house, framed by a stand of trees at the end of the drive, was a Georgian palace, a monument to a life-style long dead. Although he hadn't been there for years, the sight of the house brought a flood of bittersweet memories into sharp recall.

The limousine pulled up in front of the mansion's tasteful entrance. The chauffeur, accustomed to driving Abner Slocum when the attorney needed transport outside New York, skipped around to the passenger side of the enormous Cadillac.

Abner Slocum at first resented the extended hand. But finding his legs cramped and stiff after the long drive, he reluctantly accepted the driver's help.

The beautifully carved front door swung open as Slocum climbed up the few front steps. There was something regal about the place, it was definitely a residence fit for royalty. The maid, a middle-aged and slightly stout woman, smiled hesitantly. 'Mr Slocum?'

'That's right.' The attorney nodded his acknowledgement.

'The other gentlemen are in the library, waiting for you.' There was a hint of disapproval in her tone, as if he shouldn't have made such important men wait upon him. But Slocum knew she had no idea of their relative importance – the others were the estate appraiser, the accountant, and the man from the IRS. They would expect to wait for a man like Slocum.

The maid led him into the front hall, so instantly well remembered with the baby grand piano still standing in its accustomed place. Slocum knew there were other grand pianos scattered throughout the house. She had never learned to play the piano, but she liked the shape and preferred to use them as convenient tables. It represented the kind of sweeping expensive gesture he always associated with her.

'Just a minute,' he said to the maid, as he stepped into the huge main room, his eyes drawn to the life-sized oil hung above the Georgian fire-place.

He walked over and looked up at the painting, vividly remembering when it had been commissioned. She had been thirty-nine years old and a startling dark-eyed beauty. He'd been just twenty-eight. Although the pose was meant to be demure, still the full curves beneath the silken gown were plain enough. He acutely remembered how her body had been, the athletic thighs, the alluring fullness of her hips that contrasted with her surprisingly small waist and flat stomach. His eyes moved up to the simple bodice where a large catch of lace failed to conceal the beauty of her breasts.

Abner Slocum studied the face. Her eyes seemed almost to stare back at him boldly, just as they had done that first day, the day he had been sent out by the firm to take care of a minor legal job for her first husband.

Slocum sighed. Age could be a terrible thing. Just recently she had died – in her eightieth year – and now he was sixty-nine. In the beginning they had been lovers for a few years, and then friends after that. Memories flooded his mind as he stared up at the painting.

You made me what I am today, Sylvia, Slocum thought to himself, suddenly grateful. It was true enough. She'd guided his legal career until the summit itself had been attained: a main partner in Nelson and Clark, he had become one of the Twelve Apostles. It took the full power of her fortune, every bit of force that her money had generated, but he had made it.

Well, he thought to himself, you saved me years ago, Sylvia, and now, even in death, perhaps you can save me again.

Slocum smiled at the face in the painting, almost hoping somehow it would smile back. But by just looking at her he felt a sudden surge of confidence, a warm sense of power. It was nearly sexually erotic.

The maid cleared her throat with a little cough. 'Mr Slocum, the others are waiting for you.'

'Of course, my dear. We must not keep them waiting any longer, must we?' He followed the maid towards the library. He felt like whistling. No, they wouldn't beat him this time, not ever. He would be ready. Sylvia Winship's death gave him just the weapon he needed. He would be damned before he'd let them throw him out of the firm.

'Let's go over it one more time,' Patrick Collins said.

'Jesus, I'm sick of talkin' about it,' the girl snapped.

Collins half smiled as he looked at her. Too much make-up and not enough clothes, he thought to himself – or enough brains. 'Look, you'll be damn sick of women's prison, too, unless you handle this just right.'

She pouted. Collins made a mental note to have her boyfriend, Manny, a small-time hood, buy her a new dress for the trial – something that didn't cling or ride up. She had good legs, but this wasn't the kind of criminal charge where legs would buy her anything.

He listened once again to her obvious lies. He wondered if she was so stupid that she thought he would actually believe her fairy tale of mistaken possession of nearly a half million dollars' worth of cocaine. A jury certainly would not.

It was hopeless. She would never be convincing no matter how he might polish her up. Perhaps he could work out a plea if they were lucky. A trial would be a disaster.

'You and Manny come back Tuesday afternoon, about four. We may want to approach the defence a bit differently. We can talk about the alternatives.'

She shrugged and stood up. 'Manny said maybe I should give you a blow job. He said you'd like that, or maybe a half and half.' Her eyes wandered over to the worn leather couch.

Collins smiled. 'Maybe some other time, honey. I'm a little busy right now. But tell Manny thanks.'

'Whatever you say.'

He watched her hip her way out of his office. He sighed. Well, he thought to himself, there were going to be some very happy butches up in state prison when she got there, but at least it wouldn't be going to waste.

Patrick Collins glanced at his watch. It was just past one o'clock. His son, Micahel, would be in the interview now, perhaps only halfway through lunch. Collins knew far better than his son the implication of being recruited by Nelson and Clark.

He looked at his son's picture, framed in silver, on his desk. Grinning back at him, looking like a young John Kennedy, his son had the Irish features, blue eyes and wild brown hair so typical of his ancestors from the Emerald Isle. Unlike the late President, Michael Collins was thickly muscular and possessed an almost delicate grace. He was a son to be proud of.

Nervously, Patrick Collins got up from his desk and walked to the window. He looked down on Broadway, watching its human and vehicular traffic. Crawling with cabs, the street was a continuing symphony of horns as cars and trucks jockeyed for position. Some brave – or foolish – people risked life and limb as they scurried through the moving river of steel.

It was his world. To Patrick Collins there was no street quite like Broadway, a mix of everything – from pervert to priest, from hooker to hard-hat. Matrons strode right alongside whores, and businessmen shared the sidewalk with pimps and muggers.

But it wouldn't be the world of his only son.

Michael Collins was different. The boy had chosen a different path. Although he had elected to become a lawyer like his father, his eye had always been on a different level of the profession. First, he had gone away to the law school at Notre Dame, and had done well there, having graduated with honours after serving as editor of the *Law Review*. In contrast, his father Patrick had worked his way through the city law school and had always been grateful for a mere passing grade.

Now Michael was being recruited by the country's number-one law firm, Nelson and Clark, the legendary Twelve Apostles.

Although Patrick Collins was regarded by many as one of New

York's best criminal trial lawyers, he had never been graced in even meeting one of the Apostles. They were as distant from him as the original twelve. Called the Twelve Apostles because they had twelve main partners, the élite law firm occupied six full floors in the luxurious Logan Building at Park and 58th, and maintained an enormous staff of lawyers and clericals to serve the nation's most prestigious banks and corporations.

In the law, having the chance to perhaps one day become an Apostle was on the same level as an Englishman having the chance to become a Baron.

Collins could think of nothing except the interview. It was as though he himself were the one being considered for the law firm. He was feeling increasingly anxious.

Patrick Collins walked to his office door and opened it.

Edna, his secretary, looked up from her typewriter. She had a cigarette dangling from her lips. 'Yeah?'

Collins looked down at her. When he had first hired her, so many years ago, she had become his lover. But that relationship was over, and had been for years. She had married and was a grandmother. And she currently treated him like an Irish mother might treat a loved but errant son.

'No calls, except if my son telephones.'

The cigarette bobbed up and down as she spoke. 'Relax. The way you're acting, you'd think he was being knighted. He'll get the job, although I still think he should come in and practise with you.'

'This is no business for him. I don't want him hanging around with the kind of bums I do.'

'Bums are bums,' she said, 'whether they're Broadway people or Wall Street bankers.' She went back to her typing. 'Go in and pace. I'll put Sonny Boy through if he calls.' Her machine clattered away as she went back to her work.

Collins stepped back into his office and closed the door. He desperately wanted a cigarette. He walked over to the portable bar and poured out a small jigger of Irish whiskey, tossing it down, then waiting for the comforting warmth to hit.

He had always been proud of his son, Michael. Now, if things went well, he would be able to slip into casual conversations the fact that his son was with Nelson and Clark. He could imagine the eyes widening, the awe of his fellow lawyers who, like himself, practised in the dim and dirty halls of criminal court.

Collins, pleased at the prospect, helped himself to another shot of the Irish.

Michael Collins would have preferred an interview in the offices of Nelson and Clark, but apparently that wasn't done. He had been invited to lunch at the Four Seasons to meet Ainsworth Martin, the managing partner of Nelson and Clark.

Although he knew that the recruiting of new associates was always important to any firm, and he had been approached by some of the best, he was still nervous, feeling more like an unsure job applicant than someone who had been selected for a possible offer.

He had been to the Four Seasons twice before, once when he had graduated from Notre Dame and again when he had been appointed as a law clerk to the US circuit court, each time as a guest of his father, in celebration of his achievements.

He disdained the 52nd Street entrance; his father said that know-ledgeable people preferred the Park Avenue entrance. New York had a number of such quirky pecking order symbols.

He told the headwaiter in the Grill Room that he was to lunch with Mr Ainsworth Martin.

The man looked him over, as if making some sort of profound judgement. 'Mr Martin will be detained. He called. You must be Mr Collins, Mr Michael Collins?'

'Yes.'

'Please come with me, Mr Collins.'

He was led past the outer tables, the 'no-man's-land' as his father had called it, that ring of tables for the customers who enjoyed no special notoriety or power. Only New York's own royalty were allowed to be seated there.

The Grill Room was the triumph of the architect, Philip Johnson, with its high ceiling and soaring windows, covered with the curtains of ever-moving glass beads.

He was seated with a quiet, understated flourish. At the next table was America's well-known ambassador to the United Nations, seated with a black man in an expensive and elaborate African gown. Beyond him Michael recognised a famous movie actor who looked much older than on the screen.

The magnificent and abundant shrubbery was always changed to reflect the season, lending meaning to the restaurant's name. Now it was the flaming browns and gold of autumn chrysanthemums. It was the first week in October, and the Four Seasons was saluting fall.

The waiter brought him a menu. 'May I bring you a drink, sir?'

Michael looked up at him. Drinking would be a tactical error in any job interview, no matter what the setting. 'Nothing now, thank you.'

He glanced down at the menu. A tourist might have cardiac arrest if he were not prepared for the prices. A hamburger and a few drinks would cost as much as a ticket to a Broadway show.

Michael fingered the distinctive white ashtray with its autumn tree. The ashtrays were a favourite souvenir and expendable, although none of the important people seated in his immediate vicinity would be interested in taking anything so mundane as a memento.

Although filled to capacity, the place was dignified and quiet. He tried to avoid gawking. He realized others were looking at him, wondering about the young man seated alone at this centre table of power and prestige. He rather enjoyed the feeling.

Judge Fitzsimmons, for whom he had clerked, had recommended him to Nelson and Clark. Most of what he knew about Nelson and Clark had come from an old *New Yorker* profile he had dug up at the library.

As always, the magazine's coverage had been incisive, catching not only the history but also the very inside workings and flavour of America's most prestigious law firm. It was a rare, inside view of a famous yet mysterious organization, a glimpse into an unknown world.

With the possibility that he might be asked to join that world, he had carefully studied the piece, committing the main facts to memory.

Although the piece had been written in the mid-sixties, Judge Fitzsimmons assured him that while the firm had grown larger, it had basically remained the same as originally reported in the magazine. Times had changed, the Judge had noted, but the Twelve Apostles had not.

The *New Yorker* had reported that Hiram Nelson and Asa Clark had started it all as a two-lawyer operation just at the time when New

16

York, as well as the rest of the country, had entered into an unprecedented growth period, with steam power supplying enormous industrial expansion. Soon, in response to the demand for their services, Nelson and Clark had grown to twelve men, all equal partners. It was a large law firm for the time, and all the partners had been handpicked, all men drawn from the best New York families, families who were taking sure control of the finance necessary to control the awakening industrial giant.

As reported in the *New Yorker,* Hiram Nelson had drawn up the first set of rules for his law firm. They had been amended just after the Spanish-American War, but they still constituted the Bible for the business.

Old Hiram had specified that there be no more than twelve partners. Since the original twelve had all been quite dignified, and were probably quite pompous, some turn-of-the-century wag had tagged them as the Twelve Apostles and that nickname had stuck.

Michael's thoughts were disturbed as he watched his favourite screen actress escorted to a table near him. She was thin, extremely thin, and she looked as if she were lost, despite the fact that she specialized in sexy roles portraying aggressive women. The Four Seasons Grill Room was quite a setting for recruiting anybody for anything, but then, he realized the men at Nelson and Clark knew that very well. A law firm was really supported on the backs of the associates, the paid young lawyers. The key for all the firms was to grab the very best, the smartest, and the most diligent. Recruiting the right kind of young lawyer had become a keystone in running a profitable law firm. Collins had been told that in their own way the leading New York firms were not unlike colleges selecting football candidates. The college team's future depended on picking the very best, the fastest, and the strongest. And a law firm's future also depended on the quality of young men and women brought in.

He looked away from the actress and forced himself to again mentally review the *New Yorker* article.

The magazine said old Hiram had foreseen the possibility of expansion, and although he had stipulated there could never be more than twelve main partners, he created another type of partnership, named by him as participating partners. Actually, as the article pointed out, a participating partner was no more than an employee who also received a share of the firm's profits at the end of the year; a share determined by a complicated business formula based upon business brought in and hours billed, all set off against basic salary. Hiram Nelson had been afraid of too much growth, so his rules specified there could never be more than two participating partners for each main partner. Thus, said the *New Yorker*, ever since the turn of the century, Nelson and Clark never had more than twenty-four participating partners. In keeping with the biblical nick-name, of the main twelve, these twenty-four participating partners had become known throughout the legal world as 'the disciples'.

The magazine had reported that old Hiram's rules made it mandatory that a main partner could be selected only from existing participating partners. It had become a tradition that when an opening for an Apostle occurred, two participating partners would campaign for the spot. The loser was expected to quit the firm. Hiram had, in effect, set it up as a life-and-death contest. Although a good position was usually found for the loser – perhaps as a house counsel to a large industrial firm or as judge on an important bench – these were only consolation prizes. The winner would become one of the Twelve Apostles, and there was no equal or substitute for that glittering prestige.

Michael noticed a tall, elegant man following the headwaiter. The man had silver-grey hair, carefully cut and combed. His clothing, although conservative, was expensive and perfectly tailored to his long, slightly stooped form. Only his eyes, shaded by bushy grey eyebrows, contrasted with his rather bland face. They were dark and alert. Collins speculated that the man was probably either an ambassador – he had the look of a diplomat – and if not that, surely a highly placed banker. He was surprised as the man was led to his table.

The bland face permitted a small smile. 'Mr Collins, I presume.' The man extended his hand. Michael almost knocked over his chair getting up. He grasped the extended hand. 'I'm Ainsworth Martin.' The voice was soft, but deep and with an unassuming authority. 'Please sit down.'

Michael decided that when he grew older he would copy this man, or at least imitate him in dress and manner. He had never before seen anyone quite so regal.

Collins again declined the offer of a drink. Ainsworth Martin smiled knowingly and ordered a very dry martini.

'We are delighted that you're considering joining our firm, Mr Collins. May I call you Michael?'

'Of course.'

'Michael, if I may be quite frank, Nelson and Clark has become a bit topheavy with the products of Harvard and Yale. We are very interested in you since you come from Notre Dame Law School. We feel adding young people like yourself will give the firm a bit more balance.'

'Not being a product of Harvard might be a detriment when it comes time for a promotion, Mr Martin.'

Ainsworth Martin sipped the martini that had been placed before him. 'Promotions aren't based upon what school you went to, at least not at Nelson and Clark. I know that isn't true in some law firms. However, advancement historically had depended on two main elements: one, how much work a lawyer can produce – the firm lives or dies by its billings – and two, the amount of legal business brought in. Sometimes these are often combined in a hardworking lawyer who had business connections bringing in profitable fees. We reward on those criteria only.'

'Merit only?'

Martin chuckled. 'Usually. However, if a man or woman happens to be the child of the owner of a multinational company who happens to throw its business our way, that doesn't hurt at all. Other than that very practical consideration, merit is generally the test for advancement.'

'Mr Martin, most firms, at least the ones I've talked to, usually give an estimate of the number of years it usually takes to make partner.'

Ainsworth Martin put down his martini. 'That's possibly the biggest stumbling block to our recruiting, to be honest.' He smiled the same enigmatic smile. 'Our firm rules specify only twelve main partners. We're called the Twelve Apostles, as I'm sure you know. The rules then set up another partnership level, called participating partners. They receive a salary plus a share in the firm's profits. There can only be two participating partners for each main partner. Thus, Michael, we really have only thirty-six partnerships available, much, much less than most Wall Street law firms. Promotion in our firm depends on the frequency of Apostle vacancies.'

'How many associates do you employ now?'

Martin arched an eyebrow. 'Over two hundred.'

'The odds of making partner aren't very good then, are they?' Collins said. 'At least not in relationship to the prospects at other firms.'

Martin slowly nodded. 'I can't argue that. However, there is one important difference. If a man or woman becomes a main partner at Nelson and Clark, it is generally regarded as the very pinnacle of our profession. By the way, that applies to money as well as prestige.'

'About the money . . .'

'Always an important consideration. We generally pay a new associate on a competitive basis with other top firms. At the moment, we are starting our new people at $47,500. Of course, depending on a number of variables, there is usually a bonus paid at the end of the year. It varies, but it is based upon the amount of work done by the associate, and it is voted by the partners. Each associate usually gets a different bonus.'

'There must be a great deal of competition within in the firm.'

'That's true, of course, in any law firm. Most firms, as I'm sure you're aware, are set up on a pyramid basis. Most of the work is done by the associates. The risk of loss is borne by the partners; they have to pay the bills and the associates' salaries, so they get the chance for the profits earned by the associates. It's simple, really: the more business, the more associates, the more profits for the partners. Sometimes it works, sometimes it doesn't. Of course, each associate is anxious to show the right stuff, not only legal ability, but the capacity for hard work that produces a nice fat billing list to the clients. It helps at bonus time, and it helps at promotion time. Nelson and Clark is really no different in that respect, except that since we can't promise quick partnership we do tend to pay our more experienced associates a great deal more than other firms.'

'So, as I understand it, the risk is greater, but the prize is better.'

Martin's little smile ghosted across his features. 'Well put.' He paused. 'Are you married, Michael?'

'No.'

'That's a plus, at least at the beginning. The law, as some profound jackass was fond of saying, is a jealous mistress. Most of us, regrettably, have little time for our families. Being a single person

20

may prove a distinct advantage.'

'If I accept.'

'Do you have any idea how many people we contact to become associated with Nelson and Clark?'

'No.'

The smile vanished. 'Perhaps a dozen a year. We select only the top, the very best. It pays off for the firm in the long run.' He signalled to a waiter. 'The people who nicknamed the main partners called the participating partners "the disciples". An interesting continuing biblical theme, don't you think? I don't know if it's because of that, or because we are so careful about who we invite to join us, but the associates are known in legal circles as "the chosen".'

'And you want me to become one of the chosen?'

'Yes. I think you will help the firm, and, in turn, membership in the firm will, among lawyers, bestow upon you a rather instant recognition and honour.'

'That's what my father tells me,' Collins said.

Ainsworth Martin nodded. 'Yes, a lawyer of many years' standing. Does mostly criminal work, I'm informed.'

'Do you know him?'

Martin's face showed no expression. 'I'm afraid not. We travel in different circles. Nelson and Clark does no criminal work.'

Michael Collins knew exactly what Ainsworth Martin meant. His father, although highly successful and competent, lived on the other side of the legal tracks. There was an invisible dividing line – to be crossed only upon invitation.

'I'm interested,' Collins said.

'When can you start?'

'I don't want to appear anxious, Mr Martin, but I'm through clerking and I could start today if necessary.'

'Good. Come back to the office with me after lunch. We'll have you sign the necessary forms, health insurance, that sort of thing. Then we'll assign you to something. Agreeable?'

'Yes.'

'Good. I'm famished. Let's order. The mustard shrimp are superb.'

She got up and stretched, her full young body still glistening from

21

the pleasant exertion of sex. She felt warm, fulfilled, as she padded across the thick carpeting of the master bedroom to the bath.

He was shaving.

She stopped to watch as he guided the razor, cutting wide swaths through the white foam covering his jaw. He wasn't a tall man, and he was scrawny, almost spiderlike. He too was naked. She looked down. It was amazing that such a small man, with such wiry arms and legs, would be built like that. He told her they called him 'Tripod' in high school. But he certainly knew how to use it, and he applied the same driving energy to making love that he was famous for in the business world.

'Like that thing, don't you,' he said without even glancing over at her, just sensing where she was looking.

'It will do,' she giggled.

'It will do a lot.' He scraped the sensitive area beneath his large nose. He wasn't handsome. His face was too thin in proportion to his nose. His eyes, small and narrow, seemed almost Oriental. Grey flecked his closely cropped curly hair.

'You don't think you'll get in trouble about all this?'

'All this what?' He ran water into a washcloth, then wiped away the remaining traces of shaving cream.

'My promotion.'

He shook his head. 'Hell, no. You deserve it. Besides, who would give me trouble? I run the damn company.'

She sighed. 'I hear there's been talk – talk about us.'

'So what?'

'It bothers me.'

'The talk?'

She nodded. 'When you announce the promotion, they'll all think you did it just because.'

'Well, fuck them!' he snapped, his eyes narrowing. 'I don't give a damn what they think. You have a degree in business, and you've done your job. You deserve to be recognized.' He vigorously towelled his face dry.

'I've been with the company less than a year,' she said, 'and I'm only twenty-eight years old. I checked: the youngest vice president you have in the company is fifty-two, and he's a certified public accountant.'

He grinned. His teeth always seemed to be somehow animal-like,

like a fox, or even a wolf. 'So now he's going to be the second-youngest vice president after today. So what?'

'People say we're sleeping together. They'll say that's the only reason you gave me the job.'

He came out of the bathroom and put his arms around her, resting his hands lightly on her buttocks. 'We *are* sleeping together, but that's not why you got the job, Nancy. You're a brilliant kid, and this company needs new ideas, fresh thought, if it's going to keep growing. You've got those ideas. I spotted that right off.'

'I thought it was my breasts,' she giggled.

He shrugged. 'Well, those too.' Then he laughed. 'Anyway, what do you care? As soon as my divorce is final, we'll get married.'

'That might make it look even worse. It would prove all the stories going around.'

'Ah, you worry too much.' He gestured towards the huge oil painting of Napoleon, a picture that occupied almost an entire wall of his bedroom. 'He never worried about the small crap. Win the big battles, that's what he did. If you do that, they can never touch you.'

He gently smacked her bottom. 'You better shower and get dressed. I want to make that announcement this morning.'

'I still think you should wait.'

He grinned, pressing his pelvis tighter against her. 'You better get in there quick or we won't be going anywhere today.'

She lithely slipped out of his arms and skipped into the bathroom.

He heard the sound of the shower as he stood looking up at the portrait.

Newsweek had called him 'The Napoleon of Wall Street', and he felt the description was accurate.

She was wrong about the announcement. There wouldn't be any trouble. If anyone opposed him, they would be crushed.

Everyone knew that. He had built a reputation doing just that.

He smiled at the arrogant face of the Emperor of France. He had always admired Napoleon, even as a young boy. He knew that his hero had let things get away from him at Waterloo. He had made a mistake, and he had paid for it.

For John Norman Scott, president of Lockwood Limited, one of the largest companies in the world, there would be no Waterloos . . . ever. There would be no mistakes.

He grinned as he listened to the water running. Hell, it was always fun in the shower. He pushed open the shower door and heard her little squeal as he stepped into the stream of hot water with her. Their bodies entwined in the water and steam.

The New York court of appeals was the state's highest tribunal. But even so, Frank Johnson always felt that its Albany building – imitation Greek revival – and even its courtroom, with the vaulted panelling and portraits of past judges, was overstated, despite the court's importance. Johnson likened it to a rich woman who wore far too many jewels and furs: there was an aura of unseemly ostentation about the place.

He shifted irritably in his chair as he half listened to his young opponent make a passionless plea to the seven stonefaced judges. Appearing before the high court was obviously a new experience for the young man from Dickerson, Loftus; his tense voice revealed his anxiety and stage fright. The Justices sitting in a row behind the long high bench could be a threatening sight to any new lawyer.

Frank Johnson, on the other hand, was a veteran of the high court. Fifty years of age, he had spent most of his professional life with Nelson and Clark, and almost all of that time in trial work. As a former co-editor of the *Harvard Law Review* he could easily have chosen other work, but Johnson had come to love the give and take of litigation. It was like a game, an exciting game, usually played for very high stakes. He liked it, very much.

The young lawyer droned on; his case was weak and that alone seemed to help unnerve him. Frank Johnson felt sorry for him. Johnson had taught evidence at Columbia for a while, early in his career, fitting the classwork into his schedule without sacrificing his commitment to the firm. As a former professor he always felt a twinge of sympathy for all young men and women who had to step before the bar and pay the painful dues that sometimes accompanied admission to the stark and demanding world of litigation.

Johnson felt he had everything a man could really want. He was rich, at least by most standards, and he was married to a socially prominent woman. Despite their problems, he had to admit that Muriel, his wife, remained a beauty. And his being a member of the President's Commission on Trial Law and Practice, in addition to his committee work for the American Bar Association, had given him considerable professional respect nationally in matters concerning trial and appellate courts.

Johnson listened as his young opponent continued, his words sounding rehearsed, which made them even more tiresome. The whole thing was dull. Dickerson, Loftus didn't stand a chance of winning the case.

As a main partner Johnson was the head of the firm's litigation department. Litigation was the dirty end of the law business. The other partners might conduct their business in fancy clubs of dignified boardrooms, but Johnson had to do the gritty work in the courts, the trench warfare of the law. He had a large staff of trial men – participating partners, associates, and law clerks. But they chiefly assisted him. Johnson carried the main burden, especially the appellate work. Others in the firm might have risen by dint of family connection, or by the ability to bring in business, or through just plain luck, but Frank Johnson had earned his place, clawing his way up to the top by long, hard labour. He felt he deserved his place among the Twelve Apostles.

'Your time is up, Mr Morris.' Although the chief judge smiled, his eyes were cold and unfriendly.

'In conclusion, allow me to — '

'Mr Morris,' the jurist spoke sharply, 'that *was* your conclusion. Your time is up. You had ample opportunity to see the warning light on the lectern in front of you.' The smile turned just a trifle more icy. 'Now please step down and allow Mr Johnson to have his time at the bar.'

The young man from Dickerson, Loftus was about to protest, but quickly changed his mind when he looked up into the challenging eyes of the court's chief. He glanced over at the other judges but found only unspoken agreement with the ruling of their chief judge.

'Thank you,' the young lawyer mumbled as he quickly gathered up the many notes and law books he had spread out on the lectern.

Johnson, as was his custom, used no law books, only a yellow notepad, and he tried not to refer to that. It was a piece of showmanship. As he stepped up to the lectern the small light blinked to green. He looked down. The device was familiar to him, a miniature traffic signal with the usual three lights. The green light went on when the lawyer started to speak. At two minutes before the speaker's time was up the amber light flashed on. The red light meant it was time to stop. The signal device was controlled by three buttons concealed on the bench and operated by the chief judge. Most appellate courts used the same type of device. It seemed more civilized than a verbal warning. Frank Johnson had become a master of timing. Seldom, if ever, did the chief judge have to hit the red button when Johnson was addressing the court.

'Good morning,' Johnson smiled up at the panel of stern judges. 'I am Frank Johnson of Nelson and Clark. We have the honour of representing the appellee, the Stern Chemical Company.'

He paused briefly for effect. 'I know you gentlemen have had the opportunity to fully review the briefs submitted in this matter, so I don't propose to rehash the law, but I would like to make a few observations about the logic of our position.' Frank Johnson, in fact, knew that the judges were far too busy to read the briefs. He knew the court clerks had extracted the main facts, issues and law, and then condensed the voluminous material into a few concise paragraphs.

'Allow me to mention just a few points that I think have rather persuasive merit.'

'Do you wish to reserve any of your time, Mr Johnson?' the chief judge inquired gently. The smile was sincere: they had known each other for years. Each side was allowed thirty minutes for argument, and could reserve any amount of that time to be used in rebuttal.

Johnson returned the smile, but quickly shook his head. 'I don't think that's necessary, given the facts of this case, but thank you for the consideration.'

'You're quite welcome, Mr Johnson,' the chief judge said as he leaned back in his high-backed leather chair. 'Please continue.'

'Thank you, your honour.' Johnson didn't need to refer to his notes; he knew exactly what he wanted to say.

It was basically a very easy argument to make. Although the chemical waste dumped by Stern in 1947 had been shown to have caused a number of radiation-based illnesses, birth defects, and even cancer, the testimony of most of the experts clearly showed that no one back in those days had any idea of what harm the chemical waste might do. Johnson knew what to expect from the court. Judge Farber, with a reputation as the court's resident wild-eyed liberal, would find against the Stern Company. But the rest of them, with the possible exception of old Judge Ballum, would go along with the logic and decision of the trial court below. It was a sensible decision. So Johnson knew what he had to do; he merely had to stay even, being careful not to offend any of the judges whose vote he felt he could already count on. And doing that, for a man of Frank Johnson's experience, would be an easy matter.

Johnson continued: 'As the court knows from the testimony, no one in 1947 had any idea that radiation really existed, or that it could continue to do long-range harm. Remember, the experts were just beginning to learn the lesson of what atomic energy could do. It was just after the bombing of Japan, the very beginning of the Atomic Age. Little was truly known.'

'Then you admit that the chemical waste did great harm to the residents who brought this suit?' Judge Farber interjected, open hostility dripping from his words.

'It was freely admitted from the start,' Johnson replied evenly, almost solemnly. 'If my client had had any notion of the possible harm, the whole matter would have been handled very differently, of course.'

'Even if it meant no profits?' Farber's white eyebrows arched to show he considered the answer obvious.

'The Stern Chemical Company,' Johnson spoke calmly, and with quiet dignity, 'has a proven record of being a company with a conscience, a good neighbour. No one regrets the resulting horrors any more than the appellee, but the fact remains there was no duty to inform anyone, because at that time no one could possibly have known the danger.'

The debate between the judges then began, but without direct confrontation, the exchange taking the form of questions directed to the attorney at the lectern. It heated up; Judge Farber grew red in the face as he battled for his position. All the heat was directed at Frank Johnson. It was like handball: the judges bounced the questions off the attorney at the lectern, trying to make the opposing jurists miss. They never even looked at each other as they struggled. It was the way of all appellate courts.

Johnson carefully fielded all the questions, both the hostile and the friendly, his only aim to merely hold the ground already awarded him in the lower court's decision.

The amber light went on.

'In conclusion,' Johnson said smoothly, 'let me assure the court that such a mishap as the 1947 chemical dump can never occur again. The Stern Chemical Company has gone to considerable expense to ensure against any repetition of what happened. However, since the Stern Company couldn't have known of the danger, obviously it had no duty to inform anyone else. The law never requires an impossibility. We respectfully ask that you affirm the findings of the lower court.'

Johnson nodded to the bench, just enough to show respect, then gathered his notepad and returned to his seat.

His young opponent had reserved two minutes for rebuttal. But by the time the inexperienced lawyer had begun to organize his presentation, those short minutes had expired and he was ordered to sit down.

The chemical landfill case had been the last appeal of the morning. The court officer cracked the gavel against the wooden block. 'All rise,' he snapped.

The lawyers and the few remaining spectators got to their feet as the judges filed off the bench and into their chambers.

Johnson was aware of a heaviness in his chest. Too many damn cigarettes, he thought. Despite that, as soon as he left the courtroom and stepped out into the hall he lit up. He inhaled deeply, and while it didn't ease the feeling in his chest, it did help relax him.

It would be months before the formal court decision was printed and handed down. The young inexperienced lawyer ambled by, revealing dejection in every movement. He wasn't a veteran but he knew he had lost. He was a nice kid, and from a good firm.

'You did a good job,' Johnson said, expelling a stream of smoke.

The young man glanced at him and his smile seemed sour. 'I didn't think so.'

Johnson laughed quietly. He could well afford to be magnanimous in victory. 'Well, you're only as good as your case. The next time you may have much better cards. You know, there are some cases that no one can win.'

The young man shrugged. 'Maybe.'

Johnson once again inhaled deeply. 'If you have time before catching your plane, I'll buy you a drink. I find that always helps, win or lose.'

The young man looked shocked. It was unheard of that a mere

associate lawyer be invited for a drink by one of the mighty Twelve Apostles. It would be something to brag about back at the office. His world brightened considerably.

'I'd like that. Thanks.'

'Let's go to Murphy's,' Johnson said, leading the way. A couple of quick ones would relieve the discomfort in his chest. It always worked. And he had plenty of time before catching the flight back to LaGuardia.

2

The bank was at Madison and 78th Street but Christina Giles decided to take a cab. She liked to walk, and it was a beautiful autumn day, but it was windy, and she wanted to appear in her best light, not trailing loose strands of hair.

It wasn't strictly a matter of vanity. The bankers and executives she dealt with were usually older and critical of young women carrying such heavy responsibility. She sought a balance, remaining attractive but demonstrating an appearance of businesslike competence.

Most of the people at the meeting would be new to her, and first impressions were always important. She was glad she had selected the navy blue flannel business suit with its conservative skirt. The ecru silk blouse was also a good touch.

She caught a glimpse of herself in the glass doors leading into the bank building and felt confident. She was ready to make the presentation. And confidence was at least half the battle.

The bank's vice president with whom she had been dealing met her in the tiled lobby. A middle-aged man with a combed-over bald spot, he managed a nervous smile.

'Everyone is waiting,' he said.

'I'm not late?'

He shook his head. 'Oh, no, not at all. But the other firms and banks are so anxious about this transaction that everyone showed up early. Very unusual, as I'm sure you know, for bankers.'

'Tough crowd?'

He grinned. 'Not when they see you, Christina. For a woman of your abilities and charm, this will be a piece of cake.'

'I hope so,' she said. Despite her modest words she felt sure of herself and ready.

Taro Kuragamo watched Christina with the eyes of a true connoisseur. Some men appreicated graceful sailing yachts, others preferred beautifully sleek reacehorses. Kuragamo's interest was women.

Her voice he found melodious, and so different from the usual shrill feminine tones he so disliked. It was obvious that she was extremely intelligent, and such intelligence was always a powerful aphrodisiac to Kuragamo. There were many different degrees of beauty, some superficial, some luxurious and deep. He found her most beautiful. Her high cheekbones were almost Oriental; her skin was darker than fair, but its silken quality was especially alluring. The expensive business suit she wore couldn't conceal her delicate but full figure. She was indeed a remarkable woman. He knew that he wanted her.

Taro Kuragamo also knew he was handsome. He accepted it as he would any other natural fact, although he was grateful for his looks. He took pride only in those things which he himself had accomplished. And there was much to be proud of. But his looks were merely the lucky blending of two races. His father, a tall gangling Englishman, had married a strong but lithe Japanese woman just before the outbreak of World War II. As a child in Japan, Kuragamo had been an outcast among his own people, which had given him the advantage of developing as a loner and an individual, and not as a team player, the usual Japanese pattern. He had no loyalty except to himself.

He had grown tall, just over six feet, and possessed that pleasant blend of Caucasian and Oriental features. His face was full and strong, like his mother's. He was thickly muscled, and his dark hair was soft and fine. People said his almond, nearly black eyes were almost hypnotic. A woman had once told him that his eyes glittered like a snake's. He rejected such romantic notions, but he did recognize that some people, with good cause, feared having those eyes turn their way.

Kuragamo was the name of his mother's family. An ancient house of samurai origin, the family then proceeded to reject the daughter who had married the tall Englishman. Despite that, Kuragamo, for business reasons, had adopted his mother's name, although he had no contact with any of her relatives.

Harris had been his father's name, a father not remembered except in those few old photographs, a father who perished with so many others in the roaring flames of World War II. Kuragamo felt some degree of kinship with his father's relatives, who had seen to his education. He was an Oxford graduate. But besides providing for his schooling they had shown him no other signs of love. All encounters had been formal, strictly proper, and very aloof. The contacts had been minimal, but he remembered their generosity, and because of that, many of the Harris family were now wealthy.

Kuragamo's official title was merely director of Tokyo's Sunray Bank. But the bank belonged to him, as did so many other businesses. Hardly a public figure, even among the Japanese, Taro Kuragamo kept a low profile and sought no personal publicity. Only a limited number of people knew he was one of the world's richest men. And few, mostly to their sorrow, had discovered that Taro Kuragamo was ruthlessly accustomed to getting what he wanted.

Now this tall Japanese wanted Christina Giles.

He was impressed by the cleverness of the financing package she had developed. Kuragamo knew only that he would be meeting with a lawyer from New York's famous firm of the Twelve Apostles, but he hadn't expected a woman, and especially such a beautiful one at that.

She had noticed him too. The other men in the conference room were either typical New York bankers, uniform in their expensive clothes, haircuts and demeanour, or ageing Japanese businessmen, short, polite, and equally conservative. But his physical presence seemed to radiate power. Clearly this Eurasian was a handsome man who would be memorable anywhere in the world.

But it was his eyes that compelled her to look at him. They seemed to hold some secret knowledge, a knowledge that she felt penetrated right through to her deepest soul. Although he'd lived with the financing plan and knew it better than she did herself, she lost her concentration several times during the presentation when, as she sought eye contact with the others, she would end up looking into his magnetic eyes. There was something almost reptilian about those eyes, not unpleasant or frightening, but more hypnotic and mesmerizing.

After her presentation, as she had expected, many questions were raised. The tall Japanese asked nothing, although several times she found the others looking at him for some indication of what he was thinking. Both the Japanese and American bankers treated him with respectful deference.

At one point he whispered something to one of the bank presidents, who then scurried from the room. When he returned he smiled at Kuragamo, who merely nodded politely in answer.

She had lost track of time as she fielded their questions. Finally the tall man stood up.

'Gentlemen, I notice that it grows late and we have not yet had lunch.'

'Mr Kuragamo,' she said, finding herself almost uncomfortable under his steady gaze. 'I've arranged for lunch to be sent in for everyone.'

He bowed, a hint of a smile on his lips. 'Most efficient, Mrs Giles. And perhaps these gentlemen won't mind going over some of their mutual problems, but I would prefer to lunch at Pocko's. It is a favourite of mine here in your lovely city. Regrettably, I get there so seldom. However, if you could come with me, not only would I be honoured, but I have several questions of my own. Not only would you assist me in indulging in a small measure of pleasure, but we could also discuss a measure of business. I trust you gentlemen will allow me to steal Mrs Giles away for a short time. I promise to return her.' Again, a ghost of a smile seemed to dance about his mouth. She was surprised by the suggestion of an English accent.

'Well, Pocko's usually requires reservations,' she said, 'and at this time of day . . .'

He nodded, almost bowing. 'I have arranged for reservations. They are expecting us.'

She glanced quickly at the others. There were no disapproving looks, only the expectation that she would obviously accept his invitation. For a moment she was tempted to remove that half-smile by refusing. But this was business, and this interesting man did seem to have some kind of hold over the others. Winning him over could be important.

'I'd be delighted,' she smiled.

'Thank you.'

As he escorted her to the elevator, she was surprised that she was nervous in his presence. He waited patiently, his dark eyes betraying no hint of what he was thinking.

Outside, a waiting limousine pulled up and his hand was strong but gentle as he helped her in. Then he climbed in beside her.

The driver was Japanese and Kuragamo spoke to him in that language. As the limo glided into the stream of heavy traffic, the driver adopted the challenging tactics of all New York drivers – matching wits and nerve against pedestrians and other drivers, avoiding accidents by only inches. They turned into 57th Street and pulled up in front of Pocko's.

Pocko's, one of the most expensive French restaurants in the city, attracted the rich and famous. Christina had gone there once with Katherine Thurston, the only female Apostle in the firm. The prices, she recalled, had been astronomical, although she had to admit it had been one of the best dinners in memory. It was understood that a reservation at Pocko's had to be booked several weeks in advance.

Kuragamo had made polite small talk about the weather and New York's traffic during the short drive. His voice was a deep, almost purring baritone, the kind of voice that audio producers search for when they make commercials for the women's market.

He helped her out of the limousine, and his glance at her legs as her skirt rode up for a moment had been open, appreciative, and not at all self-conscious.

'They say you have to wait weeks before getting a reservation here,' she said as the doorman opened the large red lacquered doors.

'That is true, fortunately.'

'Fortunately?'

For the first time he smiled openly and the effect was startling. His whole face seemed to change, becoming the face of a playful and perhaps mischievous boy. 'I own the place,' he said, laughing. 'Or at least I own the company that owns it. So the more crowded it is, the more profit for me.'

Even if he hadn't told her that he was the owner, she would have guessed by the attitude of the maître d', who, instead of assuming the usual half-sneering arrogance associated with his profession, was suddenly reduced to bowing subservience.

'A table in the back, Henri,' Kuragamo said, still soft-spoken, but now his voice carried the icy hint of command.

They were seated in a secluded alcove at a small table under which their knees touched. She shifted to break off the contact; he gave no sign he had even noticed.

She ordered a white wine; Kuragamo, Scotch. Waiters seemed to hover about just out of earshot but close enough to rush in instantly at any signal for service.

'Mrs Giles,' Kuragamo said, raising his glass in salute.

She heard the bell-like ring as their glasses touched.

'That was a most impressive presentation this morning. I have heard of your law firm, of course, but this is the first time I have had an opportunity to observe the quality of your work. Quite impressive. Are you one of the famous twelve?'

She shook her head, wondering at both her discomfort and fascination in being with him. 'No, I'm a participating partner. Some day I hope to be one of the main partners.'

'They're called the Apostles, correct?'

She smiled. 'Yes.'

He sipped his drink. 'I take it you are married.' He nodded towards her left hand and her rings.

'My husband's a doctor. We have a fourteen-year-old son.'

He idly played with his glass, his eyes still on hers. 'I am also married. I have two sons. However, I do not live with my wife. We maintain separate homes in Japan.'

'I'm sorry.'

The half-smile returned to his lips. 'Don't be. In Japan the ties between families are still often cemented in marriage. In a situation like my own, divorce is out of the question. My wife is of the Missihassi family, an ancient house, and financially extremely powerful. Our sons will inherit the power and prestige of both houses. Thus, unlike you Americans, we must remain married, even but for pretence. It is a matter governed by our culture.'

She laughed. 'Tell me, Mr Kuragamo, this isn't just an Oriental version of that old wheeze about how your wife doesn't understand you?'

At first he showed no change of expression, then the boyish grin reappeared and a rumble of delighted laughter came bubbling up from deep inside of him. 'Well, now that you mention it, Mrs Giles, I really can't say that it sounds all that different.'

She knew her financial agreement to save the steel company was of the greatest importance, and now she was suddenly confronted with an element that could undo everything she had worked on for months. Yet, she wasn't about to go to bed just to sell the merger agreement. It would never come to that. Still, she found it important, in an entirely personal way, not to offend this strange but attractive man.

'You aren't building up to making what we call a pass? A pass is a — '

He laughed again. 'I know what a pass is. Believe me, Mrs Giles, if I thought it had any chance of success I would certainly try it. No, I merely want us to know each other better. I find you most attractive, not only as a woman, but as a business associate.' His dark eyes seemed almost to sparkle; it was a definite change. 'I seldom make passes at business associates.' He sipped his Scotch. 'Besides, I presume you are happily married.'

She hesitated, and regretted it instantly as she saw the quick understanding in his eyes. 'As I mentioned, my husband is a doctor, very successful, very busy – we have our son. I have my career. Yes, I think our family situation is most satisfactory.'

He nodded, his face once again a mask. 'Before we discuss anything more, let me assure you that I am going to approve your agreement.'

'That's wonderful.' Her broad smile was genuine. 'Now if I can persuade the others . . .'

He sighed. 'The others all work for me, in one connection or another. So everything is arranged. I was most taken with your plan this morning and I had determined to approve it. You know, you are a most remarkable person, with an almost devious mind.' He smiled. 'Your mind, I might say, and this is meant as a compliment, is really more Oriental than Western. Perhaps in some other life you were Japanese.'

'Do you believe in reincarnation?'

He shook his head. 'No. I was raised in a number of religions as I progressed in age and was passed along to various surrogate parents. First, the Shinto priests filled my mind with their theories, then your Anglican ministers at Oxford led me into the mysteries of their Christian beliefs. I think there may be a God, perhaps, but I don't know. I believe in nothing except the present, and,' he added with a flash of his boyish smile, 'myself.'

'Oxford?'

'You wonder how I speak your language, yes?' It was a perfect imitation of a screen Japanese villain, then the throaty laughter again erupted, but softly. 'Yes, Oxford. I took a First at Oriel College, Oxford, and I rowed for the college. My father was English.'

'But, Kuragamo . . .'

'My mother's family name. I thought it better for business, so I adopted it. That is not at all unusual in Japan.'

'I didn't mean to imply there was anything wrong, Mr Kuragamo.'

He smiled. 'I know that. Believe me, I have been asked that question hundreds of times in my career. Do you know what they called me at Oxford?'

She shook her head.

'Apparently Taro, at least the way I pronounced it, sounded to my schoolmates like Tiger, so they started calling me that. Tiger Kuragamo. It really doesn't fit, but I somehow came to like it. All my close friends call me Tiger.'

'You seem far too gentle to be called Tiger.'

His eyes again seemed to become pools of mystery. 'Sometimes the name is more apt than you might believe.'

There was a sense of power about him, and she became aware of his thick and muscled shoulders.

'I'd like to see you tonight,' he said.

She started to protest, but he raised a hand and his smile was disarming. 'Mrs Giles, I don't propose anything other than dinner, perhaps a show, or maybe just a talk. I promise no passes.' He paused, but this time there was no smile. 'I can buy sex. I need someone to talk to, someone who is intelligent. In other words, Mrs Giles, you have no worry with me, but you would be doing a kindness for a very lonely man.'

36

She was surprised to find herself speaking the words: they just seemed to tumble out. 'I'd be happy to have dinner with you.' Suddenly she felt extremely flustered and she realized that she must be blushing.

He nodded slowly, his eyes dark and expressionless. 'I am most honoured. Shall I pick you up?'

She felt her heart beating wildly. She couldn't believe what was happening. 'It would be better if I met you somewhere.'

'The Algonquin at seven? We can have a drink and then decide where to go.'

She merely nodded.

'Oh, something most important,' he said.

She looked up quickly.

He smiled. 'May I call you Christina?'

She nodded. 'Of course. In fact, many of my friends call me Chris.'

'Christina is a lovely name – I prefer that. Shall we order?'

She had forgotten all about food. Her mind seemed to be totally without thought; she felt as though she had just pushed off from the top of a slide, a very long, mysterious slide, and she couldn't see the bottom.

Dan Spencer knew he shouldn't be trying the case. If he lost, it would be a black mark against him. The firm never forgot the losers. If he wanted to become one of the Twelve Apostles, a record of court losses could kill whatever chance he had, which was slim in any event.

'Mr Dixon, what kind of materials were used in the construction of the garage?' The voice of the opposing counsel cut into his thoughts.

'In terms of quality?'

Dan was about to object, but decided against it. He could predict what the man would eventually say anyway. He wanted him to say it.

'Yes, in terms of quality.'

'The very best.'

The testimony was completely predictable. Dan only half listened.

Dan Spencer, Massachusetts born and bred, was one of the Spencer family, Back Bay Bostonians. Not much money, but the bluest blood on the Eastern Seaboard. He could have snuggled comfortably into his uncle's Boston law firm and found safe harbour among the bank and brokerage house clients, but he wanted the challenge and excitement of trial work. So he had clerked in the court of appeals, then served as an assistant district attorney doing criminal and antitrust work. He had first been brought into Nelson and Clark as an associate. They needed trial men, and they definitely preferred blue-blooded people. He had used his trial skills to good effect, and now he was a participating partner, the second man in the litigation department of the firm. But he knew full well that litigation was the lowest ring in the firm's pecking order. Oh, they needed it done, but it was dirty work, something that real gentlemen avoided. The real money and importance was in the elite corporate and finance-desk jobs. Still, he was drawn to trial practice, and he had sharpened his skills, building a good record for winning cases. The main partner and head of litigation was Frank Johnson. Frank was only fifty, so it was unlikely that there would be an opening for years to become a fully-fledged Apostle. No two men from litigation had ever served as Apostles at the same time.

Still, to have any chance it meant he had to keep winning. He could delegate the tough cases, but that would soon become apparent. Even if Frank Johnson were to switch to another firm – most unlikely since there was no precedent for that – or, even more unlikely, die, Dan would have no chance at Johnson's slot unless he continued to run up an impressive string of victories. It meant risk, considerable risk.

'Mr Spencer,' the judge said, 'the witness is yours. Do you have any cross-examination?'

In New York the trial court is called the Supreme Court; it is the state's basic trial court. The final and highest court of last resort, called the Supreme Court in almost every other state, is called the court of appeals in New York.

Spencer stood up, taking his notepad in one hand. 'Just a few questions, your honour.'

They were in a typical Supreme Court civil division courtroom. Panelling covered part of the walls, but like the judge's bench, hadn't seen a coat of wax or any other attention in years. The tile floor was old and worn. There were thirty seats for spectators, but only a few were occupied. The jury members sat in worn, even torn, old theatre-type seats. There was a dingyness about the place, as if it had been deserted for many years and then only recently reopened but without being cleaned. But now it was in constant use and dingy or not, it was an arena, a place for battle.

The jury watched him make his slow, deliberate trip towards the back of the courtroom. He wanted to get their attention, because it would all be up to them. He was keenly aware that this witness would make or break his case. The witness had sounded good during direct examination; his quiet demeanour had obviously impressed the jury. Somehow, Spencer needed to find a way to reverse that impression.

Once more he regretted taking the case. He could have assigned it to a number of others in the office. They would have done an adequate job, but none of them had his experience. And a loss would mean ruin and bankruptcy for his client. And to get ahead in the firm it was unwise to take too many chances.

Dan Spencer was a tall, lean man. After having been a basketball player at Brown, he had had one season with the pros prior to entering Harvard Law. He knew that he looked much younger than his forty years, and his shock of sandy hair made him appear even younger. The small half-glasses he had to use for reading helped him look somewhat older. Juries always liked older lawyers. Extracting the glasses, he slipped them over the tip of his nose, glanced down at his notes, then up at the witness.

'Mr Dixon, how long have you worked for Consolidated Engineering?'

The man was heavy-set and had a leathery face. He looked like the type who was most comfortable out of doors. 'For almost thirty years,' he answered.

'Always as a supervising engineer?'

'No. I started out doing a variety of jobs, mostly construction.'

'Always on-site jobs?'

The witness nodded. 'Usually.'

Spencer half-smiled, keeping his manner friendly. 'And you were the supervising engineer on the Chesapeake Building and its attached parking garage, isn't that right?'

The witness nodded. 'I testified to that.'

'Yes, you did.' Spencer agreed. He stepped back as if studying the witness, as if the engineer were an interesting piece of sculpture.

'Were you at the Chesapeake Building when the parking structure collapsed?'

'No.'

'Where were you?'

'I was on a company job in Saudi Arabia.'

Spencer nodded. 'When did you hear about the collapse?'

The witness shrugged. 'I don't remember exactly. The communications out there aren't too good. Probably I read about it when they flew in the newspapers to us. The papers were always a few days old when we got them.'

'Didn't your company contact you?'

The witness shook his head. 'No.'

'Now, you do know that fifteen people were killed and many more injured when the parking structure collapsed, do you not?'

The engineer frowned slightly, then nodded. 'Yes.'

'Didn't your company fly you right back to the United States? You were the supervising engineer on that structure when it was built, weren't you?'

'Yes. I had been the construction engineer. But that job had been over for a long time.'

'So you just went on with your work in Saudi Arabia, is that right?'

'Yes.'

'Didn't you fly back two days after the accident? Didn't you fly to Rome and then back to your company headquarters in Atlanta?'

'Objection. Multiple questions. Let counsel ask one question at a time.' The opposing lawyer's voice was lazy, almost friendly.

'Sustained,' said the judge, ill-concealing his boredom.

'Did you fly back to the United States just two days after the accident?' Spencer picked up a paper and pretended to study it as he waited for the answer.

The witness looked startled, and glanced briefly over at the other lawyer. 'Well, I think I did fly home about that time, now that you mention it. But I had some family business to take care of.'

'And your fare wasn't paid for by your company?'

'No.'

'And you didn't return because of the collapse of the Chesapeake parking structure and your company wanted to talk to you about the quality of work you had done on that building?'

Spencer held his breath. The answer would decide the case.

'No. I came home for family business.'

Spencer exhaled slowly, carefully concealing his exaltation. 'And that was your only purpose?'

'Yes.'

It was really over. The witness had lied. It was a stupid lie, an unnecessary lie. And Dan Spencer could prove it false through telegrams, aeroplane tickets, and company memos. Spencer would now carefully strip away the man's credibility until the jury would refuse to belive anything the witness said. He would do it so expertly that the opposing attorney could never repair the damage.

It was up to the jury to decide if the building had been improperly built or whether the material provided by Spencer's client was defective. The entire case hung on this man's testimony. And the witness had made the mistake of lying about an unimportant point. It would destroy him.

Just as in a chess match, the opposition had committed a fatal error. And no matter how they might try to recover, the end was now inevitable: it would be check and match.

Spencer allowed himself a brief moment to plan through the next careful step. Destroying the witness would be like an elaborate dance, and each movement had to be precise. He would win the case, and winning was the only thing that counted, at least with Nelson and Clark.

Dan felt great relief, almost relaxation, as he slowly and deliberately began to verbally roast the squirming man in the witness chair.

Katherine Thurston did not like dictating machines. The advantages of using dictation equipment in conjunction with word processors had been pointed out to her, and despite the fact that she fully appreciated the efficiency of the new technology, she still preferred to dictate to a live stenographer.

Her secretary and stenographer, who was as short and thin as Katherine was tall and voluptuous, was careful to get every word, every comma. Katherine Thurston permitted no margin for error.

Although they were phsically different, with completely opposite personalities, the young secretary, an insecure woman afraid of almost everything, still admired Katherine Thurston. And although she feared her, she realized that this fierce woman had hammered her way to the top in a male-dominated world.

They were preparing the first draft of a complicated set of bylaws for a corporation being formed to protect the interests of several foreign-movie firms. Millions were involved, and the instruments had to be perfect. Katherine Thurston had a well-earned reputation as a perfectionist. She was an excellent all-around attorney, but it was her strict attention to intricate detail that had established her credentials. She had become the first woman main partner in Nelson and Clark, breaking a barrier and causing ripples throughout the legal world, not just in New York, but in all large firms across the nation. The Twelve Apostles had admitted a woman – at the time it had been big news – even the American Bar journal had reported the startling event.

She had earned the right: top of her class, editor of her law school law review, clerk to a US Supreme Court Justice. Before she was thirty Katherine Thurston had carved out a remarkable reputation as a hard-eyed, steel-nerved attorney with a legal mind like a cobra. Even her marriages had helped advance her career. The first, to Senator Sam Field, had provided her with public exposure and visibility. She knew she was a handsome woman, not quite pretty, but with an imposing presence and a strong body that seemed to photograph very well. She had worked for the government for a while; then, with her husband's help, she had secured an associate's position with Nelson and Clark.

But Senator Sam hadn't been equal to her appetites. He was relieved when she began to take a series of lovers. Sam was left alone in Washington to keep up with the committee work of Congress while his tall, sturdy wife found the freedom to indulge her growing passions among the men, of all ages and types, of Manhattan. Finally, her activities, although generally discreet, began to sift back to Washington in the form of nasty little gossip items. She was photographed at various public functions, always with a different man.

Finally, and most reluctantly, Sam Field asked for a divorce. It was done quickly, and while there was publicity, it was over so fast and without a hint of scandal that the item was quickly dropped from the newspapers. Senator Field's career survived, as did her own.

It was her second marriage that provided the real springboard for her legal speciality – entertainment-industry law. Noel Thurston was ten years her senior, a man of aristocratic bearing and manner. Tall, lean, with silver-grey hair, he was the picture of the perfect cosmopolitan man. And he owned a majority interest in a movie production and distribution company, a string of legitimate theatres, plus a winner's record as a top Broadway producer.

Noel Thurston, besides being magazine-ad handsome and magnificently rich, also possessed a quick intelligence with a rich and sardonic sense of humour. His mind was equal to her own and they genuinely liked each other. Plus there was no fear that Noel Thurston would ever feel exhausted or threatened by his wife's sexual appetites. Noel, very quietly and discreetly, was thoroughly gay. There was never a hint of his homosexuality, either in gesture, movement, or speech. Urbane and witty, he happily flirted with actresses and aspiring starlets who had no idea that they were completely wasting their charms if they responded in kind.

Katherine knew and understood her husband, as he did her. It was a perfect marriage. They doted on each other, enjoying many evenings together when they could discuss the complicated happenings in their personal lives – a pleasure they both looked forward to and enjoyed. Sometimes they would even compare notes on their current lovers. The only rule they had between them was that Katherine would never advance on any of Noel's companions, and he, in turn, promised he would never try to turn the head of any young man in whom his wife might have an interest. They both had spectacular sexual prowess, and they both sought out interesting men. Thus, by agreeing never to compete, they roamed the world like two happy hunting animals, each going for its own meal but grateful for the other's company.

Both were equally discreet. Katherine Thurston would never think of picking up with some young stranger, and Noel carefully kept away from making advances to any new and unknown chorus boys, no matter how attractive. They chose as carefully as a quality butcher selects prime cuts – never hurried, making important judgements on personality, emotional stability, and physical potential – and then they quietly made their selection.

Katherine knew that among the office staff she was known as 'Katherine the Great'. Her eye for a new male associate seemed unerring, and, like her namesake, she made sure her favourites received preferential treatment. Katherine looked much younger than her fifty-two years. In her years with Nelson and Clark she had been responsible for building the careers of a number of associates and participating partners. She knew the office staff jealously referred to this selected handful of young lawyers as the Palace Regiment.

Katherine paused in her dicatation. Her secretary looked up.

'Marie, I think I'll need some help in the provisions about foreign law. Isn't that new associate, Simons, supposed to be something of an authority on international law?'

'I really don't know, Mrs Thurston. He's new and I don't know much about him.' That was a lie. Marie made it her business to find out all about the new young men. Charles Simons, like so many others in the firm, was from Harvard. And to Marie's dismay, he was married and had a child on the way.

Katherine Thurston sat back in her huge, high-backed leather chair and swivelled around to look out her window on Manhattan, gazing down at the concrete canyons below. The scene seemed to throb with life. 'I recall we were told that Mr Simons had a background in international law. It was one of the reasons he was hired. I think I will consult with him before I go on further on this draft. Marie, step out and see if you can have him stop by to see me for a few minutes.'

Marie swallowed. 'Yes, ma'am.' She closed her notebook and left the office, returning to her own desk. She knew that Katherine Thurston was an expert herself in international matters. Much of her work with film companies concerned distribution rights and royalties in other countries. Marie wondered if Charles Simons would accept his new status. Marie, an attractive young girl, often wondered at the power of Katherine Thurston. Men always seemed to obey her. And Marie knew it wasn't just Katherine Thurston's power in the law firm. There was something primitive and compelling about her that men – all men – seemed to find irresistible.

Office legend had it that Katherine the Great always began the conquest my making oral love to her intended victim. The legend said she was very good at it, and that no man who had recieved her favour could ever completely forget the pleasure. Then, so it was said, Mrs Thurston took her time in perfecting the conquest, languidly leading her new lover in each subsequent encounter into all the various fields of lovemaking, encounters that took place not only in the office, but at her apartment, and on weekends at her summer place on Cape Cod. But eventually she always changed from a seductive temptress to a dominating iron mistress, conquering her prize and finally reducing him to her love slave, anxious and willing to carry out her whims in any way she found amusing or pleasing.

No one knew the origin of the legend. Marie presumed that some of the Palace Regiment had talked, perhaps after too much drink, or perhaps compared notes after they had all been drawn into the whirlpool of sex created by the insatiable Mrs Katherine Thurston. And none of them ever escaped her.

Mrs Thurston buzzed.

'Yes?' Marie answered.

'Marie, before you call Mr Simons, check and see if this is the night of the monthly partnership meeting. I believe it's tonight.'

'It's scheduled for tonight,' Marie replied.

'Good. The way things are heating up around here I'm actually beginning to enjoy those damn meetings. They're not nearly as boring as they used to be. Now get Mr Simons for me, please.'

'Yes, ma'am.' Marie tried to characterize the mood she heard in Katherine Thurston's voice. It wasn't just mere arousal. It reminded her of the pleasure one often sees in cats just before they are to be fed.

3

'Damn it, peak them napkins up like tents! Jesus, boy, can't you learn nothin'?' The busboy was new. The monthly partnership dinner was the worst possible time to introduce a new worker into the intricacies of the law firm's protocol. But they were shorthanded and there was no other option.

'I did peak 'em, but the things keep falling over,' the busboy pouted.

'When you speak to me, boy, you say Mr Smith. I runs things here.'

The boy's black face showed his resentment of the older man. 'Mr Smith.' He half growled the name.

'Look, maybe you don't get the picture here. This is Nelson and Clark. They maintain a complete kitchen and two dining rooms. This one is for the twelve bigwigs. They call them the Apostles, but don't you ever call them that, hear?'

The busboy merely shrugged.

'This here dining room is usually open only for lunch. There's just this one long table and twelve chairs. So all we have to worry about is keeping twelve people happy, you understand that? That's our main job in life, just making sure everythin' is perfect for them. That means food, service, and table,' he said, as he demonstrated how to peak the napkins.

'Downstairs they got the regular dining room. That's for what they calls the participating partners. Different menu down there. Although the food's good both places, up here is always better. They can have visitors downstairs – guests, you know. But never up here. This room is only for the Apostles.'

'So what?'

Smith's thick black face scowled in response. 'I been working here almost twenty years. The hours are real good, the pay's not bad, and the work is easy. Now these people they got a couple of cooks, and a staff of waiters and busboys for just these here two dining rooms. God knows they don't make no money off 'em. They tell me it's a matter of tradition and convenience.'

'Be better off if they went down to McDonald's,' the busboy said.

'These people, they don't eat at no McDonald's, boy. These are quality people. Now if they don't like the way this operation is run, they'll just close it up and start eating out at them fancy restaurants and clubs. God knows, they all got money enough for that. But if we make sure everythin' is just right, and we keep them happy, then you and me have nice steady jobs. Do you understand that?'

The busboy shrugged. 'Suppose so. But if this here room is only for lunch, how come we serving dinner here tonight?'

Smith, outfitted in a neat black waiter's uniform, nodded as if the question had great significance.

'These people' – he gestured at the twelve chairs – 'has a monthly meeting. The first Tuesday of every month. They has drinks, a nice dinner, then they sets to argue about the business of this here law office.'

'Argue, like in fight?'

'Oh, they used to be polite enough, but lately they have really been getting a little loud. This law firm is a big operation, boy. They makes millions every year. A couple hundred people work here. It's a big business. These people' – he again pointed at the empty chairs – 'they runs the business. And I guess things haven't been goin' too good between them.'

'You ever listen in?' The busboy grinned.

The other man looked shocked. 'This here is a private meeting. I help set up the drinks, then we serves the dinner and clears the table. Then everybody except the twelve of them gets out. Still, lately you can hear sounds like shouting, all the way down to the kitchen.'

'Maybe this job of yours, maybe it ain't too solid anyway?'

The older man chuckled, his face suddenly placid. 'Boy, if this firm breaks up, you can figure the whole country is going down the tube. This here is the most famous law firm in the country. No matter how they argue, ain't no way these people are going to be so foolish as to break this business up. They all got too much to lose.'

The young busboy looked over at the well-stocked portable bar. 'Maybe they get to drinking too much. Ain't nothin' to start folks fightin' more than a touch too much booze.'

'Naw, not these people. They all uptight at these meetings lately, so nobody drinks much. They got a couple who can really handle that stuff, but they never do any serious drinking at the meetings. Like I said, these are quality folk, they ain't about to fuck up no major business decisions because they been drinking themselves silly.'

The young man pointed at the bar. 'Still, that there is a lot of expensive booze.'

'Everything is always first class here. Each of these people prefers a special drink. After all these years, I know what each wants. They usually has one, maybe two, drinks before dinner, but that's all. Now, come on, you seen how I fixed that napkin. Get the rest set up. They'll be wandering down here soon.'

'They don't all come at once? Their offices are all on the floor above, right?'

The older man nodded. 'Yeah. But they don't socialize much together. Everything is pretty formal. They start coming in, usually one by one, then they breaks up into little groups and starts talking business. Then I starts serving dinner.'

'Doesn't sound like no friendly bunch to me,' the busboy said. 'Sounds like they don't really like each other much.'

'You don't understand about powerful people like this. They don't have time for no friendships. This is a big business enterprise. They don't have to like each other if they making money. Hell, I expect most of these folks belong to half the fancy clubs in New York. If they want friends they can go there. This is all business. Come on now, let's get busy.'

Christina stepped out of the shower and carefully dried herself. She had made up her mind not to meet Taro Kuragamo. She didn't know where to contact him, so she decided she would just stand him up. Despite his importance to the steel company deal, and its importance to her own career, she would take the risk of offending him and would make an excuse later. It wasn't that she didn't trust the cool-eyed Japanese businessman; it was rather her own motives in having accepted his invitation that she wondered about.

Besides, she was nervous about the meeting of the twelve main partners. Recently, following those monthly meetings, she sensed increased strife among the partners. If she hoped one day to become one of the Apostles herself, she knew she had to become aware of the ebb and flow of office politics, and the implications for the future. But lately it had all been confusing. Tonight was the meeting. She wondered what might happen.

She heard the telephone ring while she was towelling. At first she was afraid it might be Kuragamo, but she dismissed that as impossible. He didn't know where she lived: besides, her home telephone number was unlisted.

Henry, her son, who had been brooding about something or other ever since she had come home, apparently answered. She fluffed out her hair with a dryer, then slipped into a terrycloth robe.

'Who was that?' she asked as she stepped out of the bedroom. She had to shout above the blaring noise of the television in her son's room.'

'Huh?' he grunted.

'I said' – she really shouted this time, irritation rising in her voice – 'who was that on the telephone?'

'Dad.'

She waited for more information, but none was forthcoming.

'And what did he want?'

Again her question went unanswered.

She stormed down the hall to her son's bedroom. He was lying on the bed, his head propped up on one hand, his eyes riveted on the television set that blared forth the inane dialogue of an old rerun.

'*Henry, what did your father want?*'

Startled, he looked up at her. 'Oh, nothing. He just said he'd probably be late at the hospital again. He said not to wait up, that he'd grab a bed in the hospital if it got too late.'

His words hit her with the sting of a slap.

Her son waited for some additional statement from her. Failing to receive any, he once again directed his full attention back to the television.

Anna, their maid, had left dinner waiting in the microwave. Everything was set for another usual evening at home, with no husband – who was at that moment probably in bed with some nurse – and a rebellious, insolent son, despite her love for him, made his dislike for her more evident every day.

Christina went back to her bedroom and quietly closed the door. To hell with it, she thought, and started to dress for her dinner date. But she abandoned her usual conservative and professional attire. To hell with the firm, to hell with everything. She'd been saving a slinky and feminine black dress she'd bought to be worn for a special occasion. As far as she was concerned, this was it.

Roosevelt Smith had served the Apostles for fifteen years. He knew them all, their ages, their work assignments within the law firm, and, most importantly, in his mind, their drink preference.

Mr Abner Slocum, at sixty-nine years the oldest partner, would soon be forced to retire from active practice by the firm's rule. He was a small, distinguished man, with delicate crinkly skin and a shock of stark white hair. Although Roosevelt Smith knew that Slocum was a man of temperate habits, still he looked much older than his actual age. Mr Slocum had been an Apostle for over twenty years, but since his birthday was getting closer, this would be one of his last meetings. Roosevelt Smith quickly mixed a weak Scotch and water, Mr Slocum's favourite.

A number of the other Apostles were also nearing mandatory retirement age. Smith had provided a bottle of good Chardonnay for Mr Solomon, who was sixty-eight, although Solomon only had two glasses – one before and one during dinner. However, the remainder of that good wine would not go to waste. It was one of the side benefits that Roosevelt Smith enjoyed. A tall, dark man, Morris Solomon's soft brown eyes never missed a thing.

John Crim, the head of the firm's Washington office – its only branch – had as usual flown in for the monthly meeting. He was the only Apostle who didn't have an office in the sacred precincts of the top floor. Like Solomon, he was sixty-eight, and his main responsibility was to act as the firm's unofficial lobbyist to Congress and the Administration. Roosevelt Smith had heard that Mr Crim was very good at his job and had often persuaded the Congress to do what the courts had refused. Mr Crim liked his Scotch heavy, with a touch of soda, and usually had several drinks before dinner.

Francis Xavier Desmond, sixty-seven, headed up Nelson and Clark's probate and estate department. A short man, partially bald, he was almost as wide as he was tall. He preferred Bourbon and ginger ale, but often switched to imported beer. Roosevelt Smith always kept several chilled bottles of Mr Desmond's favourite beer on hand for the meeting.

Mr Asa Chamberlain, the head of the firm's large tax department, drank only orange juice. Like Desmond he too was sixty-seven years old.

Roosevelt Smith always took special pains with all the Apostles, but he was especially solicitious of Mr Ainsworth Martin, the Apostle who had been elected and served as the firm's managing partner. Mr Martin, age sixty-six, actually ran the business of the firm, performing the daily tasks of signing cheques, hiring and firing employees, and keeping the office manager and the management staff on their toes. One bad word from Mr Martin, and despite his long service, Roosevelt Smith knew he would be out on the street.

There were several others who required special handling. Mr Bennet Brown, sixty, who, along with Mr Solomon, handled the financial section of the firm – including representing banks and brokerage houses.

Roosevelt Smith liked Katherine Thurston. The big woman always reminded him of a queen when she made her usual grand entrance – always just a trifle too loud, but always with a graceful flourish. He'd heard all the gossip about her, and Smith suspected it just might be true. At fifty-two she was one of those women who seemed to radiate sex. She reminded Roosevelt Smith a little of his third wife, who had also been tall, thick but athletic, and who had been wonderful in bed but hell everywhere else. Mrs Thurston always liked a vodka martini, very dry.

Roosevelt Smith checked to ensure that everyone had been served. Mr Frank Johnson, the head of litigation, still hadn't come in. They said that he was on his way from the appellate court. Johnson, always overworked and anxious, was, in Roosevelt Smith's opinion, much too worried about his job. And although he usually drank only orange juice at the monthly meetings, like Mr Desmond, Roosevelt suspected that Johnson might be a secret drinker. And too much secret drinking could sneak up and kill a man. He kept a glass of orange juice waiting.

However, the rest of the partners were all there. The older Apostles referred to them as 'the kids'.

David Pratt, the international law specialist, was only forty-eight. And he always looked as if he had just stepped off the pages of a men's fashion magazine. Pleasant but quiet, there was an unconfirmed rumour that he was gay.

The two other 'kids' were Seaforth Russell and Philip Crawforth. Seaforth Russell, III, the heir to the Russell Oil fortune, had been made a partner, it was said, to keep the large and important Russell account with the firm. Always serious, he puffed on a pipe and seemed forever to peer out at a world that he failed to fully understand. Roosevelt Smith had heard that young Russell, who was forty-four, was considered something of a dullard, the only main partner not capable of pulling his own weight. But with the Russell money behind him, that meant very little.

Crawforth, the newest and youngest partner at age forty-two, was a breezy, brilliant young man who had been recommended by Mrs Thurston. Gossip had it that he had been brought in to handle the corporate work screwed up by Russell. But despite the rumour, Russell and Crawforth seemed not only to be close friends, but also allies in the wars that sometimes swirled about in the affairs of the partnership. Both drank the same thing – expensive whiskey, served on the rocks – and they always sat together at the monthly meetings.

Frank Johnson came hurrying in. Roosevelt Smith handed him his orange juice, and in so doing thought he detected the odour of alcohol on the trial lawyer's breath. But since there was so much opened liquor around him, he couldn't be sure.

Roosevelt Smith kept busy with a bar rag, doing useless little things, careful to appear to be a diligent, committed worker. But while he performed his make-work duties he was able to casually observe the partners.

As usual, they split up into groups. At first they seemed just to be colleagues, casually chatting together after a busy day. But it wasn't all casual. Roosevelt Smith noticed that several of the partners worked their way from group to group, apparently lobbying for something coming up at the meeting after dinner.

Smith sensed tension in the air even stronger than at the usual meetings. And tonight it seemed more than mere tension; everyone seemed unnaturally quiet. Despite the easy smiles and the small talk, the atmosphere felt charged with unseen forces about to explode.

Dan Spencer was making his final argument to the jury. He had carefully observed them during the trial, trying to detect any obvious reactions, any hint that would allow him to later touch on that exposed interest or prejudice during argument. But, as with most juries, these twelve people had remained stone-faced, not unlike good poker players, carefully concealing their thoughts and emotions.

As he talked he made eye contact with each of them. Spencer well knew that a trial lawyer was a salesman. Whether it was cars, soap or liability and damages, the same selling principles applied. You had to convince the jury to your point of view; you had to persuade them that your client's cause was just.

He had carefully planned his argument, keeping it brief, direct, and aimed at the truly significant points brought out in the trial. He prided himself on his ability to argue without using notes. An argument had more punch if the lawyer didn't have to refer to notes. It helped give the impression to the jury that the lawyer intensely believed in everything he was saying.

He felt reasonably confident of winning, after destroying the credibility of the opposition's most important witness, who had made the mistake of lying about a detail not really connected with the meat of the case. That proven lie had tainted the rest of his testimony, and, Spencer hoped, the jury's thinking on the whole case.

As usual he finished with a cliché about justice under the American system, then thanked the jury for their attention during the testimony, and especially during his argument. He was playing it safe, anything else might prove to be overkill at this point. He felt he had the case won, so there was no percentage in taking unnecessary risks.

The judge, noting that the time was late, announced he would charge the jury in the morning. Both Spencer and his opposing number had submitted a number of written requests for instructions to be given to the jury. It was the judge's duty to explain the law to them, and tell them, in a general way, how the law might be applied to the facts brought out at the trial. Juries pay a great deal of attention to what the judge says, so his jury charge was an important component in presenting a case.

It really hadn't been a long trial, despite the fact that millions of dollars were involved. The legal bills on both sides had run up into small fortunes. But, as with most lawsuits, the major expense was chiefly for work done prior to trial.

The computers were very efficient. Everything was carefully identified and billed. Every cost, including stenographers, video-tapings, investigation, preparation, and all the other charges connected with the case were fed into the whirling machine. The lawyers' time was billed on an hourly basis. At the end of each month the computer not only itemized the charges owing, but sent the bill on to the client company.

Spencer simply made sure his own time was submitted for accounting; he had no other interest or control over the billing. The firm's management people tallied up everything else. So the final cost to the client was of no concern to him, even though he was the lawyer in charge of the case.

The young associate who had been working on the case with him was tired and anxious to go home to his wife and young family. It was a matter of making a train, so Spencer allowed him to dash off.

Spencer made it a point to spend some time with his client's officers, who had come down every day and monitored the trial. They were worried. The company's future depended on the outcome of the case, as did their jobs. Although it was Spencer's honest opinion that they had won the case, he refrained from telling them. He was only cautiously optimistic.

After the company officers left the courtroom. Spencer exchanged some halfhearted banter with the opposing attorneys. They were obviously worried, so the usual gentle jibes seemed forced and hollow.

Soon he found himself alone in the courtroom with only the court clerk, a severe woman who seemed to eye the world with grave suspicion. Spencer put his notepad into his briefcase and said goodnight.

The elevator was jammed with lawyers and court personnel but he managed to squeeze aboard.

Although he was glad that his part in the trial was over, Spencer felt unfulfilled, overcome by a strange sense of emptiness.

He walked through the rotunda and glanced up at the murals celebrating the various historic systems of law. The Supreme Court's Civil Division Building had been someone's attempt to rival the structures and glory of Rome. In Spencer's opinion they had failed badly.

He stepped through the revolving door and paused at the top of the long set of stairs. The giant columns were marred by pigeon droppings and dirt.

The area around Foley Square was teeming with lawyers, court people, and federal workers homeward bound from the glass tower of the Federal Plaza. Spencer ran quickly down the stairs and then looked for a cruising cab. The street was alive with taxis but they were all occupied. He thought about taking the subway and going back to the office, but decided against it. First, he was sick of the case, and he knew Frank Johnson, the main partner in charge of the litigation department, would want to talk about it. Besides, the monthly partnership meeting was scheduled and he didn't feel like being around any of the Apostles tonight. There was something going on among the main partners. He'd heard rumours of the problems and he didn't want to be seen with the wrong people if a major fight was brewing. He was always in trail and away from the office too much to get a real feel for what was going on. Since he didn't know the issues, he didn't want to appear as though he were taking sides in an unknown dispute. Spencer felt he had little hope of eventually becoming an Apostle, but even a remote hope was worth protecting.

He spotted a cab and hailed it but the taxi sailed right past him. The driver either didn't see him or more probably was just ignoring him. New York cabdrivers were an independent lot.

Dan didn't feel like going to any of the usual lawyers' haunts, those bars clustered near the court area where attorneys gathered to salute the end of the day. He was tired of the law and lawyers. He was tired of talking, tired of concentrating. He needed some diversion, something quiet and peaceful. There were women in his life, three of them currently, all career ladies, all very pretty and bright, but that didn't seem to be the answer to the sense of disquiet he was feeling.

For the first time in months Dan Spencer thought of his ex-wife. She lived in California now, working her way through her third husband. His teenage daughter had become a stranger to him. They still managed their Christmas vacation together in the Caribbean, but like most young girls of her age, her mind was completely focused on boys, and limited to the narrow world of her boarding school. Perhaps, when she grew older, they could be friends again, as they had been when she was a little girl. He hoped so.

Spencer glanced at his watch. He had wanted to see several of the new Broadway shows but generally he'd always been too busy. But tonight he had plenty of time. The shows had been running for quite a while now and he felt sure he could easily get a single seat. Having made that decision, he felt much better, and his mood brightened considerably.

A taxi pulled up to the kerb just ahead of him. An ancient, well-dressed man was having an awful struggle trying to hoist himself out of the cab. Spencer lent him a helping hand, then slid into the cab before the driver could move away.

He decided he would kill the time before the theatre with a few drinks and dinner. A nice place within walking distance of the Broadway theatre district would be best.

'The Algonquin,' he said to the driver.

'Sa' what?'

Spencer glanced down at the driver's identification. He had a Spanish name, and it was obvious that English was not his primary language.

'The Algonquin Hotel,' he repeated, speaking slowly and distinctly. 'It's on 44th Street, between Fifth and Sixth.'

'Oh,' said the driver, as if some great eternal question had just been answered. 'For'y-four Street.' He put the cab into gear and they entered into the uptown traffic stream.

4

John Norman Scott decided he would make the announcement twice. First, the monthly board of directors meeting would act as the ideal springboard, to be followed up immediately with a company-wide memo, signed by himself. He felt a confidence that boarded on omnipotence. God help anyone who might have the nerve to object!

He grinned to himself as he imagined the reactions. The board of directors were fond of their many perks – such as frequent trips abroad – plus they certainly liked the money. He knew they would approve anything he wanted.

The top officers of the company's administration would be a different matter. They would grumble among themselves, he knew that they would, but none would be so foolish as to actually raise a question about the promotion in his presence. He could, and would, fire any executive, and they all knew it.

Scott felt his adrenalin pumping as he left his large office and strode down the richly carpeted hallway to the company's executive conference room.

They all looked up as he stalked into the room. Their credentials were impressive. At one time each had enjoyed a taste of power. Several directors had held positions as cabinet rank officers in government. One, a woman, had served in Congress. The board also numbered among its members two very tame bank presidents, plus a couple of older corporate lawyers who seemed forever locked into a contest as to who could look the wisest and say the least.

Scott slammed down his file on the smooth mahogany of the long conference table. The noise startled several members of the board.

Scott preferred to stand as he conducted his meetings. Short of stature, standing seemed to confer upon him an almost magical power, and make it possible, for a change, for him to look down at other people. Called the Napoleon of Wall Street, he knew that part of the title was bestowed on him because of his height, or lack of it.

'Well, let's begin, shall we? I trust we can dispense with a reading of the minutes of the last meeting?'

There was the usual parliamentary bluster of motion and second, thereby eliminating the minutes.

'I have a few items listed in this morning's agenda.' He began, as usual, with a crisp outline of the current problems facing the company. And, as usual, whenever the board's vote was required, it was quickly and cheerfully given. The matters were mostly routine and took only a few minutes.

'Now, I have an announcement to make. And although this doesn't require any action by the board of directors, you know I always like to keep you abreast of changes in key administrative positions.'

Several showed their appreciation by smiles and nods.

'These are turbulent times, and I believe we are weak in planning and development here at Lockwood Limited. It is my belief that if we are to fulfil our leadership role in this country's business we must aggressively plan ahead for tomorrow.'

His words were greeted with solemn nods.

'Therefore, to correct that weakness, I have created a new position to be known as vice president for planning. I have made a careful search of prospects, both within and without the company. I believe I have come up with a lucky choice, a choice of candidate who will infuse this organization with new and innovative ideas and creative thinking.'

Their faces were optimistically curious.

'Also, in making my selection, I noted that we have no women among our top executive officers.'

'That's a circumstance I have also noticed,' the ex-congress-woman said severely, then softened her words with an overly sweet smile.

'Yes,' Scott said, half bowing in her direction, 'I thought you might have.'

The others laughed politely.

'As I've said, we absolutely need a new planning approach and some fresh ideas. And we can use the intuition of a woman in helping steer this organization towards its destiny.' He paused. He could read their thoughts. Some of the board members suddenly looked very attentive, while others tried to mask their apprehension.

'After my careful search, I have today appointed Nancy Merriam to the new position.'

He was greeted by a puzzled silence.

'Nancy has a masters degree in business administration, and she has worked very closely with me. I've been most impressed not only with her intelligence, but also with her natural business instincts. I assure you, you will be hearing much of her and her work in the future.'

One of the bank presidents looked troubled. 'Is this young lady, Nancy Merriam, the same one I met in your office last week?'

John Norman Scott had forgotten introducing them, but now he remembered. 'Yes, that's the same woman,' he said quickly.

The banker's eyebrows seemed to knot, although the rest of his face remained tranquil. 'Isn't she . . . well . . . a bit young for such a position?'

Scott felt the rage rise up in him. Who did this damn fool think he was dealing with? Who was he to question his decision? Scott had doubled the company's worth in just a few short years, and all his decisions, even the wildest ones, had all proven profitable and correct. The company had large deposits in this doubter's bank which could be withdrawn, and would be if he made trouble. Scott fought against showing his anger.

'She is not only quite young, but very pretty.' He added the last with a smile. 'However, I believe this board has plenty of reason to know that I make company decisions on a strictly professional basis. This young woman has a great deal to offer Lockwood Limited, and we are damn fortunate to get her.'

His hard stare cut off one of the lawyers who was about to speak.

'In any event, you can expect to see a report from our new vice president at the next meeting. And I know you will be pleased and delighted at what she has in mind.'

'Allow me to congratulate you on appointing a woman,' the ex-congresswoman said, although there was little enthusiasm in her voice. She was an elderly, plain woman, and the good news that a woman had finally been appointed to the front office had been robbed of some of its significance for her by the fact that the new vice president was both young and pretty.

'Now, on to other business,' Scott continued despite the tension in the room. They would get over that quickly enough, he thought, and those who didn't wouldn't be re-elected to the board. However, next month when they saw the scope and immensity of what he had planned, they would soon forget any reservations they might have had because of Nancy's age and looks.

At the next meeting he would spring his plan to capture Brown and Brown, the largest chemical company in the world. It would amount to a declaration of corporate war. Like his hero, Napoleon, Scott had carefully planned every detail. He was organizing his troops, including heavy artillery and support. In a month he would be ready for battle.

It would be the largest corporate war ever. And he would win it.

Next month he would have Nancy present the plan as if it were her own. That would silence any critics.

She would win all the respect she deserved then. And it wouldn't matter to anyone if he was fucking her or not. Or whether she was the greatest fuck in the world.

A Napoleon needed an Empress.

'Do you know much about trust agreements?' Fred Calvert carried a mound of computer printouts in his arms.

Michael Collins shook his head. 'Just what I learned in law school, plus what I picked up from a few cases when I was clerking in the appellate court.'

Calvert carefully placed the printouts on Collins' empty desk. 'You'll be an expert in a matter of days.' He stood back and studied the pile. 'These have been through the rough draft stage of the word processors. I want you to copyread and check everything down to the last comma.'

'Sounds more like a job for a clerk.'

Calvert grinned. 'Don't be proud – everyone has to start at the bottom. At least here at Nelson and Clark. Besides, we can't bill for a clerk's time. Every minute you spend doing this will be charged against an estate.' He patted the pile. 'And these babies all come from very rich parents. We'll make a dollar or two. But this firm has a reputation for no mistakes. Everything has to be perfect, so don't take any shortcuts. If these things have so much as a simple typo, Francis X Desmond will have you for dinner.'

Michael Collins looked at the stack of paper. Just the prospect of having to read every word was appalling. 'Probate work doesn't seem much of a challenge to me.'

Calvert perched himself up on a corner of Collins' desk. He took out a cigarette and lit it. 'It can grow on you. I felt the same way when I started. But now I wouldn't leave it for the world. True, it's not exciting, not like litigation, but it is a gold mine. If I ever have to leave this firm I have a speciality that would be snapped up by any law firm in town.'

'I heard one of the girls call this section "The Kingdom of the Dead". Why's that?'

Calvert blew out some smoke. 'A sick sense of humour. The probate and estate section handles the property of rich people after they die. It's not very glamorous, but it's damn essential. There's no point in building a multimillion-dollar fortune just to have it all taken away by the taxman or accidentally left to a pimply cousin in Cleveland. And we also earn a nice fee from our deceased customers.'

'What kind of fee?'

Calvert shrugged. 'Depends. Usually we charge on an hourly basis. Since everything is carefully done and reviewed a number of times, the firm turns a pretty profit. However, if really big money is involved, and what we do is essential to the outcome, we charge a percentage of the total amount. It can add up. Besides, it's nice clean work. Usually there are no emergencies, no howling dissatisfied clients, just a nice quiet paperwork transaction, usually with a bank coming in as trust officer. And our kind of people always pay their legal bills.'

'Everything in this section is run by Mr Desmond?'

'For the most part. Francis X Desmond handles the probate stuff. We also do work for Asa Chamberlain. There's a lot of crossover legally between probate and the tax department.'

'Is Mr Desmond hard to work for?'

'He's an Apostle, a main partner. They are all hard to work for. Each one runs his section like a little king. And each thinks he's the most important man in the firm. There's a lot of quiet warfare between the sections.'

'Do you ever think you'll become an Apostle?'

Calvert shrugged again. 'Oh, I don't know. You really have to be in the right spot at the right time. I've been here five years. I make more money here than I would at most New York firms. If I don't make participating partner I can always hop over to another outfit and become a partner. As I say, I've acquired a marketable skill here.'

'You could leave now.'

'I could, that's true. The work here is demanding but the money is good. I suppose I just like the prestige more than anything else. It raises a few eyebrows at a cocktail party when you let it drop that you're with Nelson and Clark. I've come to like that.'

'Am I permanently assigned to this section?'

Calvert shook his head. 'No. The firm usually shifts a new associate around until they find a place where he will be useful. It's a little like a medical internship; they want you to do a little of everything. They'll decide later what you do best.'

'What are they looking for?'

Calvert chuckled. 'Just one thing.'

'What?'

'Perfection. If you're perfect, then the firm will find you adequate.'

'That's a pretty tough standard.'

Calvert stood up and grinned as he patted the stack of paper. 'Maybe, but that's the way it is. It keeps you on your toes, believe me. And don't expect any mercy. Every single Apostle is a tough son of a bitch.'

Collins pulled the papers over to him and started checking for mistakes.

He hoped he would never find out if the Apostles were as tough as Calvert said they were.

The dinner was finally over. No one seemed to have much of an appetite. Tension in the room had increased perceptibly. The help, including Roosevelt Smith, had withdrawn. Several of the partners lit cigars, including Katherine Thurston, who delicately held a long thin cigar daintily between her sensual lips.

Ainsworth Martin stood up and rapped his teaspoon against his china coffee cup. 'As usual, one of us had to kick this little gathering off, and as your managing partner I suppose I'm the logical candidate.'

Frank Johnson sipped a large Rémy Martini. He was feeling the chest tightness again. It seemed to come and go like waves. The brandy helped.

'First of all, although this isn't the annual money meeting, I did want to respond to a question raised last month. I had our people check on the liquid assets of this firm – and that doesn't include office equipment or even accounts receivable, just what we have in the bank or invested.'

Asa Chamberlain, the partner in charge of the tax department, scowled, as if any mention of money rightfully belonged only to him. 'Precisely how much?'

Ainsworth Martin smiled coolly. 'It is not precise. Because of the nature of the investments it shifts from day to day, depending on the markets. It comes to roughly eighteen million dollars.'

David Pratt, the partner in charge of international matters for Nelson and Clark, held up a tentative finger. 'I say, has anyone given any thoughts to what the entire firm is worth – that is, if you did add in all the equipment and accounts receivable?'

A half-growl emanated from Bennet Brown, who, with Morris Solomon, handled financial matters. 'It might add another five or six million. As of right now, I'd make an educated guess it would be six million, give or take.'

Pratt nodded thoughtfully. 'Then if you divided everything by twelve, each of our shares would come to about two million, correct?'

Morris Solomon smiled slowly, his soft brown eyes sparkling. 'David, my dear young friend, I will be happy to buy out your interest right now for that amount.'

Pratt frowned. 'Then I presume you believe each share is worth more?'

Solomon nodded. 'Since each of us earns almost seven hundred thousand a year as our individual slice of the profits from this law firm, even the most conservative banker would say each share was worth a bit under four million dollars, possibly more.'

Pratt looked properly impressed. 'I didn't realize just how rich I am.' He grinned.

Ainsworth Martin cleared his throat. 'Obviously, I don't have to tell you that this information must not leave this room. From time to time, a partner is divorced. I'd hate to have one of our wives' – he bowed towards Katherine Thurston – 'or one of our husbands, bring this little financial matter up in a divorce settlement action.'

Philip Crawforth, the youngest and newest partner, spoke up. 'What would a share be worth if the saints didn't receive any part of the annual income? They get a half-share now, what would it mean if we eliminated that?'

Suddenly the room was eerily quiet.

Crawforth, unperturbed by his question's effect, continued. 'I said,' he repeated, 'what would a partner's share be worth if the retired partners – the saints – didn't get their one-half annual share?'

Morris Solomon's eyes were now like the eyes of a gambler: there was no twinkle, nor did his eyes or expression betray any trace of his thoughts. 'If we were in court, Philip, I would object to that question as being speculative.'

'We aren't in court, Morris, and I think it's a fair question. I know you people have those figures available. Let's have them. This is strictly an in-house matter, so we shouldn't have to hide anything from each other.'

Morris Solomon's aristocratic face appeared to soften. 'Philip,' he began quietly, 'I think we all know what you're leading up to. And if each of us had purchased our way into the partnership, your question might have some validity. But each of us was voted in and we had to pay just a token amount as consideration.'

'One hundred thousand dollars, hard cash,' Philip Crawforth said. 'That's hardly a token amount, at least not to me. Some of you have money, but I had to borrow to come up with that.'

Seaforth Russell blinked in surprise. It had never occurred to him that anyone wouldn't have a spare hundred thousand or so lying about somewhere.

'Now the way I figure things,' Crawforth said testily, 'if we keep paying out a one-half share to each saint – and it's certain we are going to add more saints – we won't be working for ourselves, we'll be working for them. Look, something has to be done. I suppose this half-share business was all right years back when very few lived to retirement age, but that certainly isn't the case any more.'

There was an embarrassed silence. Ainsworth Martin finally spoke. 'I don't think the concept was basically a matter of charity,' he said. 'Most of the partners who did reach retirement age brought in a great deal of business into the firm.'

'Rainmakers,' Crawforth snapped.

Martin nodded solemnly. 'Yes, that's the term currently in use. A rainmaker is a lawyer who has the capacity to bring in considerable business. The firm is useless, obviously, unless we have clients to serve. The saints, as they're called, all contributed a great deal to this firm's success.'

'Ainsworth, you state that in the past tense, and properly so.' Crawforth seemed to warm to his topic. 'Look, let us at least be frank with one another. As soon as a main partner retires he doesn't give a damn what happens to Nelson and Clark. Most of these old boys haven't brought in a nickel's worth of business to the firm since the day they got the gold watch. They collect a king's ransom at the end of the year and they don't do a damn thing to earn it.'

Ainsworth Martin's eyes narrowed slightly. 'And what do you propose?'

Crawforth exuded confidence, as if he had anticipated the question with obvious relish. 'We can't do anything about the present saints; their rights are guaranteed by the partnership agreement. However, I would ask that we amend the partnership agreement to exclude this one-half-share provision in the future. We can always set up a pension fund or even finance a retirement annuity. I don't want to be unjust to any partner who has loyally served the firm. But each of us will end up supporting a large group of rich men who spend their time in Florida playing golf. This just isn't the way a business should be run.'

Without meaning to, almost every partner turned toward Abner Slocum. They all knew Slocum was about to hit the magic age of seventy and with it, automatic retirement. He would be the first to be affected. Solomon and Crim were only a year younger than Slocum, and Desmond and Chamberlain only two years behind. All five men stood to lose a great deal of money if Crawforth prevailed.

Slocum, so small and seemingly fragile, slowly rose from his chair. His gesture was particularly significant since the meetings were always informal and everyone usually spoke from a seated position.

His voice, as always, was firm and strong, in marked contrast to his delicate physical appearance. 'Since I am nearing the mythical mark of seventy, I suppose all of you might presume that I am about to speak in opposition to Philip's proposal. I must admit the prospect of languishing about some Florida pool and collecting a third of a million or better each year does have a certain appeal.'

The older partners laughed.

'However,' Slocum said, as he moved behind his chair and began to use it like a lectern, 'I think there is real merit in Philip's idea.'

Francis Desmond's head snapped up as if he had been struck. He glared at Slocum. Desmond had only three years to wait until he could graduate into the status of saint. And he looked forward to that day.

'Philip states, and correctly so,' Slocum continued, 'that the status of a retired partner was established in a time when life expectancy was rather brief in comparison to what it is today. With the miracles of medical science we now tend to live much longer. As you all know, we presently have a roster of eight living retired partners. We provide them with offices and secretarial help, seldom used, and they rarely contribute to the firm's affairs. I admit that most of them were great lawyers and business-getters in their day, but sadly that day has passed, and most have no reason or inclination to bring new business into the firm.'

'It's a tradition,' John Crim interjected, 'the firm has always provided for the retired partners. It's all part of the magic of this law firm. We care for our own. No main partner has ever left the firm. It's traditions like that which have held Nelson and Clark together and given us a certain flair.'

'A rather expensive flair,' Slocum commented. 'Last year we paid out, in cash, over three million dollars to eight men who contributed nothing to the business. As I say, I believe Philip has a point. It really doesn't make very good horse sense, does it?'

'I would endorse a sensible plan to compensate any partner who wished to retire.' Slocum went on. 'We have such a plan for our surviving widows – it would work as easily for partners. Obviously, it wouldn't pay nearly as handsomely as the present arrangement, but it would be fair, and it wouldn't tend to drain the income and resources of the firm.'

Crawforth had carefully noted the words 'who wished to retire' spoken by Slocum, and breathed a bit more easily. The old man didn't want to retire; that was it. That was the motivation for his surprising position. Crawforth planned to use that deduction as a lever to improve the prospects for his proposal.

Ainsworth Martin cleared his throat, his polite signal that he was about to enter into the discussion. 'One of the prime motives for creating the status of saint for a retiring partner, and to provide a half-share, was to make mandatory retirement a bit more palatable. As I have always understood it, the mandatory retirement age of seventy was set to ensure there would always be a regular infusion of new blood, and one would hope, fresh energy and ideas, into the ranks of the twelve main partners.' He glanced around at the others. 'It was a trade-off. Generally, I think the arrangement has worked out rather well over the years.'

Crawforth rose from his chair to speak. The meeting was slowly being turned into a confrontation. 'I agree. But that was in the past. It isn't working at all now. We shouldn't turn a valuable man out to pasture just because of a birthday.' His eyes met Abner Slocum's. Neither man gave any indication of communication, yet both silently pledged their allegiance to the other. 'Seventy years of age may have meant a person was truly over the hill years ago, but that just isn't so any more. I say we amend the articles of partnership to include mandatory retirement for age, but set up a pension plan for those partners who may elect to retire.'

'And just what age might you deem optimal to make such an election?' Ainsworth Martin's tone was frosty with disapproval.

Philip Crawforth thought for a moment. He knew he could lock up Slocum's vote with the right answer. 'I think seventy-five would be a proper mark. If a man, or woman, wanted to retire then, well, that would be their business.'

'This whole thing is outrageous!' Francis X. Desmond boomed, his voice barely concealing his anger. 'First, this is important firm business and we received no advance notice as required by our rules. It is customary to advise the partners if something of a major nature is to be considered and discussed at a monthly meeting. This retirement business is not on the agenda. Therefore, I don't think we should even discuss the matter at this time.'

'Well, ordinarily I'd agree with Francis,' David Pratt said. 'But the matter has been raised. And we've never been sticklers for hard and fast rules before. I consider the matter urgent. And since we're all here tonight, I would urge a vote on it.'

'I object to a vote!' John Crim snapped. 'First of all, we really don't know exactly what it is we are to vote on. All I've heard here are some pretty foggy proposals. I suggest we name a committee to look into the matter and report back to us.'

Slocum had remained standing. He knew that if a committee were appointed, and if it delayed action, his birthday – only three months away – would come, and no matter what happened, it would be too late. And he would be out as one of the Twelve Apostles. 'I think, in general, that the thrust of Philip's proposal is clear enough. I would like to have a vote on it, Ainsworth.'

Ainsworth Martin frowned. He recognized that the issue, harmless on the surface, had the potential to destroy the firm. It had to be handled very, very carefully. 'Before we go to a vote on the issue itself, allow me to request a show of hands of those who favour considering the matter at all.'

Slocum's hand went up. Martin noted that only four additional hands were raised, all belonging to the younger partners. He was about to declare the question failed when Katherine Thurston languidly raised her hand and smiled. It was an almost evil expression. Then to Ainsworth Martin's surprise, Bennet Brown's hand also went up.

Brown, a levelheaded man, noted Martin's dismay. 'I am against the proposal,' he said. 'However, if we don't consider it, and get rid of it, it will be a divisive cancer within our ranks. I say we should face it square on, settle it, and move on to other business.'

'I see seven hands,' Ainsworth Martin said evenly. 'I take it that the majority wishes to consider the proposal as Abner spelled it out. All right, on that proposal I will call for a show of hands. But let me remind you that this is only advisory, and not binding. Since this would constitute a major change in the firm, we will have to follow our own rules, give notice, and then later have a formal vote. That is, if approval is indicated.'

The tension in the room seemed to grow with every passing second.

'How many,' Martin asked, 'want to change the retirement age, per the proposed change?'

Only five hands went up: Slocum's, together with Crawforth, Russell, Pratt, and Johnson. Ainsworth Martin felt relieved.

'Well, I guess that answers that.'

'Ask for the hands against the proposal,' Slocum demanded.

Martin nodded. 'Certainly. All right, how many are opposed to any change in the mandatory retirement age?'

Four hands went up, and Ainsworth Martin raised his own hand. Katherine Thurston and Bennet Brown hadn't voted.

'I thought you said you were against the proposal, Bennet?' Ainsworth Martin chided the partner gently.

Bennet Brown nodded very slowly. 'I suppose I am. But we seem to have a pretty even split here. You know, we've always managed to work these things out so we've never had any lasting schisms within our ranks. I believe this is more serious than it first looks. I am inclined to withhold my decision until we have something more in depth to consider. Then perhaps we can work out a solution acceptable to both sides.'

'What about you, Katherine?' Martin asked. 'You seem unaccustomedly quiet.'

Katherine Thurston really didn't care about the financial implications. It would be eighteen years before she had to face seventy, if she lived that long. She had more money than she could use, plus the healthy income of her rich husband. But her power over young associates and participating partners depended in part on the promise of openings both at the Apostle and disciple levels. And that was a serious matter, a matter that would require serious thought to determine just exactly what course would be best for her. 'I haven't decided on how I might vote,' she said, 'but I agree with Bennet. This is an issue that could result in a lot of lingering bad feelings if it isn't disposed of properly. I will abstain until I know more about the entire picture, and the possible alternatives.'

Philip Crawforth smiled. He had been one of the original members of Katherine the Great's Palace Regiment, and he knew exactly the kind of persuasion it would take to win her vote.

Ainsworth Martin again cleared his throat. 'Obviously, the vote is five to five, with two abstentions. As customary, when we cannot come to agreement, I will appoint a committee to study the matter and report back to us.' Martin, his face serene, glanced down the long table. 'Abner is for the change. Francis is against it. I will ask both you gentlemen to serve. Katherine, since you are undecided, I'll ask you to chair the committee. Is that agreeable?'

All three nodded.

'All right then,' Martin continued. 'If you could report back to us, perhaps in a month or two – '

'Ainsworth,' Slocum quickly interjected, 'I think Bennet is right. This should be disposed of quickly. I would ask that the committee report back to this body at the next monthly meeting. Then we can take a formal vote.'

'That does seem to be rushing it a bit, Abner,' Martin replied.

Slocum nodded. 'I would ask this as a personal favour. I will turn seventy in a few months. I will be the first one to be affected by our action. So, at least as far as I'm concerned, time is very much of the essence.'

Ainsworth Martin nodded gravely. 'It's the firm's tradition to honour a personal request by a partner. We will expect the committee report next month. Are we agreed?'

Most nodded affirmatively, but while a few looked uncertain, no one objected verbally.

'Good,' Martin said. 'That's settled. Now let's discuss some of the more mundane problems facing this law firm.'

The partners tried to return to normal, but the split was there – and out in the open. Sides had been chosen. Everyone seemed to go out of his way to be extra cheerful, even jovial, but they all recognized they had come to a dangerous place, and the future of Nelson and Clark might well depend on what happened.

War had broken out among the Twelve Apostles. On the surface it appeared to be a quiet, friendly confrontation – but nevertheless it was war.

5

The cab slowed as it approached the Algonquin Hotel canopy on 44th Street. Although Christina Giles suddenly felt afraid and foolish and wanted to tell the cabdriver to go on, she did not.

The hotel doorman smiled as he helped her out of the taxi. She felt annoyed that his expression seemed to be so knowing.

She paused before going in, trying to throw off the unpleasant feeling that she was not unlike some kind of call girl on her way to turn a trick. She almost said it aloud: that it was only a dinner, just a matter of business and nothing more. Still, she couldn't shake off the feeling that what she was doing somehow smacked of sin.

The Algonquin, a landmark in Manhattan, had been made famous by the glittering writers who had populated it during the twenties and thirties – writers who worked at *The New Yorker*, men and women who set the literary taste for America. The hotel owners cleverly preserved it just as it was during its years of greatness. Like a time machine, the revolving door seemed to be a magical instrument propelling visitors back into those years when Robert Benchley, George S. Kaufman, Dorothy Parker and the others had made the Algonquin the headquarters for wit, gossip, and a style that was to become New York itself.

Customers sat in comfortable chairs in the crowded, large lobby as waiters glided about like ghosts taking orders and serving drinks. There was no music, just the happy, busy sound of conversation along with occasional muted laughter.

She tried to locate Kuragamo among the crowd, but he spotted her first. He moved across the lobby, gracefully slipping between people and furniture. As usual, there was no expression on his smooth handsome face, but she thought there was something about his eyes that suggested pleasure in seeing her.

'I'm late. I'm sorry,' she said quickly, as he took her arm and escorted her through the crowded lobby. He guided her to two vacant armchairs placed close together in front of a small mahogany coffee table.

'It is no problem.' His smile was polite. 'Since I am a confirmed people watcher it was no chore to wait. New York is a fascinating city with many interesting people, and this place attracts a number of intriguing men and women. What may I order for you?'

'Just a white wine.'

'Certainly.' He glanced around, and almost as if he had willed it a uniformed waiter appeared and took his order.

'Does that happen to you often?' she asked.

'What?'

'Having waiters materialize as soon as you want them.'

This time his smile held real warmth. 'Oh that. Well, it's not much of a trick, really. I told him I was expecting a beautiful young lady and I pre-tipped him to ensure attentive service.'

'Well, there goes another illusion shattered. You make it sound so easy, Mr Kuragamo.'

Kuragamo crossed his legs. She could see that although his legs were slim, they were powerfully muscled. He had the look of a lean athlete, strong and graceful.

'Obtaining good service is easy,' he said. 'Money talks in a rather loud voice, be it here in New York or Tokyo. It is truly a universal language. Do you mind if I smoke?'

'No.'

Kuragamo extracted a long, very thin cigar from within his coat. 'Don't be alarmed,' he said, smiling. 'These are quite mild and the smoke isn't at all unpleasant.' The ubiquitous waiter appeared instantly and lit the cigar. Kuragamo looked up and nodded his thanks, then the man disappeared.

'That must have been some tip,' she laughed.

He inhaled deeply, then rather delicately blew a thin stream of smoke from his lips. His eyes never left hers. 'It was sufficient.' He took the cigar from his mouth. 'Tell me about yourself.'

She accepted the wine from the waiter. 'Nothing much to tell, I'm afraid.'

'Most people live an odyssey of some sort. Sometimes they fail to appreciate the drama of their own lives. But please, I am most curious about you.'

His dark eyes held a commanding power, a power that was both dicomforting and yet compelling. 'Where would you like me to start?'

'You are an intelligent woman. Suppose I asked you to describe a witness to me? I'm sure you would know exactly what to do and where to start. I am interested in the history of a woman named Christina Giles. Be a lawyer and tell me about her.'

'A quick profile, Mr Kuragamo?'

'A complete profile. And I would feel much more comfortable if you would call me Taro, or as I prefer Tiger. I shall take the liberty of calling you Christina, if I may?'

Despite herself, she giggled.

'What's so amusing?'

She smiled. 'I think I'll stick to Taro. Calling a man Tiger puts me in mind of a professional wrestler or perhaps a rodeo star.'

'As you wish. Now do tell me about yourself.'

She sipped the wine for courage. There was something about this man that somehow seemed to unnerve her. 'I was born Christina Stevens in a small town in upstate New York. I have a brother who's a musician and a sister who's head of a West Coast public relations firm.'

'Older sister?'

'Yes. She's divorced and lives in Los Angeles with her two daughters. The girls are in their early twenties. My brother is younger by a few years. He plays the trumpet. He teaches and gives concerts.'

Kuragamo smiled. 'A most talented family. What about your parents?'

'Both are alive and well. My father did quite well in real estate. He and my mother live in a retirement village in Florida. They seem very happy.'

'Seem?'

She was flustered, the man had an uncanny intuition and seemed to zero in on the meaning behind key words.

She sipped the wine again. 'My father is . . . well . . . something of a womanizer. Their marriage hasn't always been the most placid. Apparently being retired hasn't slowed my father down, at least not as far as my mother is concerned.'

'How old is he?'

'Sixty-eight.'

Kuragamo smiled slowly. 'Ah, he still has a number of good years ahead of him. In Japan, many men remain sexually active into their eighties.'

72

'If he gets much more active my mother will see that he never sees seventy.'

Kuragamo shook his head slowly. 'No, I doubt that, Christina. We are all creatures of habit. I should imagine your mother has developed the wronged wife habit to a fine edge. She would probably be lost if your father suddenly changed his ways. But enough of your parents and siblings. What about you?'

She shrugged. 'The usual American success story, I suppose. I went to public high school and always got good grades. I did my undergraduate work at Columbia, then I went to Yale, to law school. I was graduated with honours, then clerked for a year with the New York court of appeals.'

'You say you have a fourteen-year-old son. I would guess you're only in your mid-thirties. Did you go through school ahead of the usual American timetable?'

Christina's empty wine glass was effortlessly replaced with a full one. The waiter disappeared like smoke in the wind, like an almost invisible genie.

'I met my husband when I was at Yale. He was a young resident surgeon in Boston. We married while I was still in law school. I was pregnant with young Henry when I was clerking for the court.'

'Young Henry?'

'Henry is my husband, although they always call him Hank. I don't know when we started calling my son young Henry, but it stuck. Everyone, at least in the family, calls him that.'

Kuragamo laid down the cigar and signalled the waiter. 'Scotch on the rocks,' he said. Then he turned to Christina. 'Another?'

'I'm not through with this, thank you.'

'Your husband has a medical practice here in New York?'

She nodded. It was strange. Suddenly she had a compulsion to tell this dark-eyed man everything about herself, her life. She wondered if it was the wine.

'Hank is an orthopaedic surgeon. His speciality is microsurgery. That's –'

Kuragamo laughed and held up his hand. 'Please don't explain. One of my companies makes most of their equipment. Quite soon I believe that most surgery will be done by laser. Does your husband enjoy his work?'

73

She glanced down at the wine glass, avoiding his eyes. 'Yes. He's active in medical circles, and his speciality is still somewhat of a novelty, at least in this country. He spends much of his time teaching his techniques to other doctors.'

Kuragamo nodded solemnly. 'Hank, I think you told me he is sometimes called Happy Hank, correct?'

'Yes.' Again she avoided his eyes. She watched a man reading a newspaper across the lobby.

'Christina, I presume that Happy Hank is a womanizer – perhaps not unlike your father?'

She was about to reply when he held up his hand. 'Please, I know this certainly is none of my business. However, I hate to think of a lovely woman like you destined to a future like your mother's. We seem to have a pattern of imitating our parents, don't we. But of course you know that. It's all in the standard American college work on psychology.'

She looked defiantly into his dark eyes. 'As you say, it certainly is none of your business.'

He boldly returned her gaze. 'You're quite right. It was presumptuous and rude. Excuse me. But please do go on. I haven't heard the full story of your life so far.'

She wanted to be angry with this unsmiling man, but instead she felt an irresistible urge to tell him about Hank, about the nights away from home and her almost pathological fear of ending up like her mother, a prisoner in a dull retirement village, locked in a loveless marriage with a charming but faithless husband.

'After the birth of my son I became anxious to practise law. I was able to get a job with the legal department of a large bank here. I think it was while at the bank that I discovered I liked setting up complicated land developments with mortgage and other financing devices, and I found out I was good at it. I was offered a job as an associate at Nelson and Clark, and I jumped at it.'

'And now you're a partner.'

'In other firms I'd be a junior partner. In my firm, I'm what's called a participating partner. I get a salary plus a percentage of the profits at the end of the year. And, of course, the possibility of advancement.'

'To one day perhaps become one of the Apostles.' His smile was almost formal.

'In my world, the legal world, being one of the Twelve Apostles is about the highest ambition a person could ever aspire to. I suppose it's basically a status thing.'

'More status than a Justice of the United States Supreme Court?' Kuragamo asked quizzically.

She laughed. 'Any Justice on that court would quit in a minute if he or she had the chance to become an Apostle. And it's not just the money, although that's quite substantial. As I say, it's how you rank among your own, I suppose. In the law, being an Apostle is like being . . . well . . . nobility.'

Kuragamo had accepted his drink from the waiter, but had not yet tasted it. He toyed with it as his eyes remained fixed on her. 'Do you have a chance? To become an Apostle, that is?'

She smiled. 'Until Katherine Thurston was admitted as a main partner there had never been a woman Apostle. I suppose if there was an opening I might have an outside chance. I'm one of the few participating partners heading up a main department within the firm. But I doubt if those men would really tolerate two women in their exalted male ranks.'

Kuragamo looked lost in thought. 'They might, I suppose, if such an appointment would mean a great deal of new business coming into the firm.'

She half smiled. 'Come on, Taro .' The name still seemed strange to her. 'You're not suggesting that you'd become my sugar daddy and see that I got my little heart's desire, are you?'

Surprisingly, he laughed heartily, his eyes dancing with amusement. 'Well, Christina, you must admit it has been done before. But I can see from your reaction that you would prefer another route to advancement. More's the pity.'

Again she wanted to be angry, but somehow she couldn't find that emotion in herself, at least not with this man. 'So far, everything I've achieved has been on my own merit. I'd like to think I can still do that.'

'Oh, I'm sure that you can, my dear.' He laughed. 'Although, to be frank, the other way is usually easier, and far more certain.'

She laughed too.

'Now how about dinner?' he asked easily.

'To another restaurant you own?'

He didn't reply at once, but seemed to be calculating what he

75

would say. 'I employ a certified *cordon bleu* chef at my New York apartment. I pay the man more than he could earn in his own business. But it is well worth it; he is a master. Would you object to having dinner there?'

'At your apartment?' Her expression hardened.

He nodded. 'Before you respond, allow me to assure you that I entertain no dark motives. It is hardly a secluded rendezvous. I have a butler and several maids, in addition to my prize chef and his helper. I can think of several commercial restaurants in this city where you would find far fewer people than in my apartment. Besides, I promise to make no unwelcome advances.'

She noted the word unwelcome, but said nothing.

'And, as you know, we Japanese are very big on honour.'

'But you're only half Japanese.'

'And therefore you think I will only be half honourable?' A touch of a smile played across his lips.

'You must admit, it is a possible construction.'

He nodded. 'Yes, I suppose it is. Well?'

'I'm not sure that I've ever been offered the table of a *cordon bleu* chef all to myself before.' She looked directly at him. 'And I do think you're honourable. Okay, Mr Kuragamo, you've got a deal.'

He laughed.

The waiter again materialized and departed happily with the bill slipped to him by the tall, powerful man. Kuragamo took her arm and easily guided her through the bustling lobby.

Christina didn't even see Dan Spencer as she passed by him.

But Dan Spencer had seen Christina Giles. He watched her walk out of the Algonquin, as the tall Oriental man took her arm and exhibited an obvious pride of possession.

In any of their contacts at the law firm, Christina had always been all business. Charming, but always within the proper limits of their relationship inside the firm. Both being participating partners, they were of equal rank. He had recently handled the litigation that had resulted from a challenged land-option agreement she had drafted. He won, and she'd been grateful. On several occasions in connection with that case they'd gone out for coffee together.

She was beautiful and he was strongly attracted, but he knew she was married, and, he presumed, happily. He admired her quick mind, her breezy manner, and especially her wit and sense of humour. She had no way of knowing that he had often thought of her while he was going through the painful progress of his own divorce. There was a haunting quality about her soft brown hair, her blue eyes, and her pert, devil-may-care attitude. Once, and then only for a fleeting moment, he thought he had seen something deep within those soft eyes, something that seemed to speak of deep inner turmoil.

Dan Spencer remembered meeting Dr Henry Giles at one of the law firm's cocktail parties. The doctor wasn't a tall Oriental. Spencer remembered the curly-haired doctor to be a rather silly, shallow man who was intent upon calling constant attention to himself. He hadn't liked him.

So the man with Christina was not her husband.

Dan Spencer realized he was feeling deeply resentful, as if somehow he had been betrayed. And that, he knew, was certainly illogical since there had never been anything between himself and Christina Giles. He cursed his own feelings. Her tall escort could easily have been a businessman, a client who was just putting her into a cab home. But in his heart he knew that was wrong. He had observed how the tall man looked at her, desire glittering in those dark eyes. And, sadly, he recalled how very excited she seemed to have been.

Dan gulped down his drink and settled the bill. Then he stalked out into the stream of people on 44th Street. He was jealous, and that was surely foolish. She had never encouraged him in any way, nor had he said or done anything to show his interest in her. They were merely business associates, and that was how they had treated each other.

Spencer walked towards Broadway. Show time was approaching, and throngs of people had begun to swarm through the theatre district. Spencer saw a young woman approaching, her jumpsuit cut so low that her breasts were almost entirely exposed. She stepped along with the crowd, oblivious to the glances and stares she attracted. He wondered if the girl was a prostitute, or a dancer on her way to her theatre. Suddenly he felt the need for the solace of a woman's company, but he didn't want a prostitute. He wanted something more than just sex.

He walked past the sleazy sex shows and porn shops on Eighth Avenue until he came to Downey's, one of his favourite restaurants. He liked their steaks. Downey's, like Sardi's, was a show business restaurant catering both to performers and the members of their audience. It was a place where people could come and drink or eat before or after the theatre.

Spencer felt like getting drunk, to really let loose and have a good time. But he knew he couldn't do that. He would have to be alert in the morning when the judge charged the jury – just in case the judge tried to stick something harmful in the charge to the jury – so even the solace of numbing alcoholic excess was denied to him.

As he sipped his imported beer he thought of Christina Giles. He hardly noticed the steak as he ate it. His thoughts were fuzzy, just disorganized memories of her and the times they had talked together.

Seats were still available for the long-running *A Chorus Line*. He went to the Shubert and tried to lose himself in the performance, but it was no use. His mind kept returning to Christina.

Even though it was beginning to drizzle when the show ended, he chose to walk all the way home. He wanted the exercise to help clear his mind.

He felt an aching sense of emptiness, a feeling that something was missing from his life, something not at all defined.

At home, trying to sleep, he kept seeing her face. And he kept visualizing that tall Oriental's proprietary air, and he kept deeply resenting it.

He got up, turned on the light, and began to review some law, reading several lengthy cases he planned to use in an appeal brief coming up. The familiar drudgery of work performed its miracle, and he was soon sleepy.

His last thought just before drifting off was of Christina Giles. He decided that if anyone was going to possess her, damn it, he was going to be that man. Not some tall Oriental.

6

Frank Johnson felt tired, very tired. After a day of combat in the courts, he really didn't appreciate the added conflict that he had found at the monthly partnership meeting. Having been a main partner for almost seven years, Johnson was aware of the changes taking place within the ranks of the Apostles during the last few years. When he had first been raised to a main partnership, it seemed like heaven. Everyone got along. He'd been picked, in part, because he was a workhorse, and they knew it. And they had come to rely on his abilities to win the day in court when needed. The firm then was almost like a gentlemen's club, at least among the Apostles, when he had been elevated to that rank. Every main partner had money – some more than others – and the annual income from the firm was a pleasant and welcome addition to whatever else each partner had coming in.

But the country's economic woes were far-reaching and had even seeped into their comparatively golden lives. A few weren't concerned – their wealth was so enormous and widespread that they were completely isolated from care. But the others, especially the younger Apostles – with the exclusion of Seaforth Russell, whose family owned half the world's oil – were beginning to feel threatened. They had become accustomed to Park Avenue addresses with alternate homes in Easthampton, Palm Beach, or in the Keys. The life-style meant the very best schools for the children, and the prestige of a chauffeur, if needed, plus several other servants. Now the main pressure point had become the disturbing loss of disposable income, despite shelters and other tax-evading devices. Money that should have been used for investment and building now had to be spent on maintaining the usual standard of living. Therefore the annual income from a main partner's share had become more important for those Apostles who were not already independently wealthy.

Frank Johnson lived like the others, and his own way of life was becoming increasingly more expensive. His wife, who came from an old-money family – but a family now mostly broke – expected to live in the splendid style to which she had become accustomed. It seemed to Johnson that she had also become the sole support of several furriers and jewellers. Muriel Johnson loved the social life among the very rich; it was her true element. Frank had no time for that sort of thing. In order to meet the ever-increasing demands made upon the litigation section, he worked long hours, including weekends. He vaguely knew that Muriel had been unfaithful to him. It was more or less expected in her social circle. The circle contained a number of men, carbon copies of each other: men who did no work but lived from generous trusts or family fortunes; men, who in another age, would have been perfumed dandies at a royal court, concerned only with their own appearance, the gossip of their own exclusive group, and their latest sexual conquest, usually in that order.

Frank really didn't care. His whole world was devoted to the firm and his assignment. Everything else, even his own pampered children, were nothing more than mere satellites circling about in his universe, the core of his existence – Nelson and Clark.

Johnson left the firm's offices, but he didn't head for home. He knew Muriel was out, attending some damn opening at the Museum of Modern Art. He wanted no part of that.

Johnson walked along the street, dimly aware of the discomfort of indigestion. He'd had lunch at a greasy spoon near the courts and now he was paying for it. Although he was exhausted, he didn't want to go home. He needed to relax, and now that need seemed almost desperate. Home to him meant a large brandy, a Valium, then a tormented sleep. The tension of the day, the battle in the court, and the icy confrontation at the partners' monthly meeting had combined to leave him feeling like a tightly wound spring, a spring that would snap unless the tension was released.

New York could be dangerous to a person who didn't know the territory. One street could be relatively safe; the next a menace for the unwary. The trick was in knowing. Johnson carefully followed a route that he considered a minimum risk.

Frank Johnson knew exactly where he was heading; he knew he would end up there when he started out, even if he consciously failed to admit the fact to himself.

Aware that he was now in a part of town where safety *was* a problem, Johnson began to walk faster. A taxi would have been a more prudent choice, but somehow he'd wanted the exercise of walking, even though he noticed now he was becoming a bit short of breath. He maintained memberships in several Midtown athletic clubs, and although he always had the best of intentions, he never quite found time to use the facilities.

He was near the Hudson River. It was an old, narrow street lined with ancient buildings that had long outlived their usefulness. It was a dismal place. He cautiously watched the shadows now, but he saw no one who looked particularly dangerous, although it was hard to tell. The city seemed overrun with babbling insane people who, while docile, still had the potential to explode and slash out at the demons whispering to them. Johnson knew they had been forced out of the hospitals partly because of the courts and the law. Society found it cheaper to pump these desperately ill people full of chemical straitjackets, than to toss them out into the streets, where they carried their madness about like backpacks.

Sometimes, especially during the rush hour, when New Yorkers jammed together in traffic grids and became pressed masses of steel and flesh, Johnson wondered whether madness might really be a communicable disease.

Finally he came to the small bar. He opened the inconspicuous door and walked in. The bartender recognized him and nodded. As Johnson took a seat at the bar, two women, seated at the far end of the bar, watched him in the mirror. He knew one of them.

In one of the small booths behind him, a man in old working clothes was laughing with a young woman. Her dress boldly revealed small breasts pushed up by a wired black bra. Her wig was red and cheap. A badly marred complexion showed through heavy makeup. The man in the booth was too drunk to care.

'Hi,' the bartender said as he approached Johnson. He was a dark man with a day's growth of beard. Though he looked bored, half-hooded eyes gave his fleshy face the suggestion of ultimate evil. 'I haven't seen you around here for a while.'

'Been busy,' Johnson replied as he took out a bill and placed it on the bar. He was careful not to show how much money he carried. Such a thing in such a place was an invitation to disaster. 'Double Bourbon on the rocks.'

The bartender performed a practised ritual as he poured out the drink with a flourish. A small diamond ring set on his thick little finger flashed in the dim light as he whipped the Bourbon bottle up, sending a stream of liquor splashing expertly into the glass. 'You're a salesman, right?'

Johnson nodded. 'Yes. I get into New York every month or so.'

The woman he knew slid off the stool and came over. She smiled her recognition. She was about thirty but looked older. Her full body was beginning to show the ravages of her profession. Her skin-tight skirt revealed the broad curves of her hips. The skirt, cut high, was allowed to fall open as she sat next to him. Her legs, although somewhat heavy, were still shapely. He remembered she'd told him she had originally come to New York to become a dancer. She said a knee injury had ended her career. They all had the same kind of story.

She blew in his ear and laughed. 'As I remember, you liked that.'

'Hello.' He tried, but could not recall her name.

She noticed but laughed. 'God, have you forgotten me so soon? I'm Candy.'

'Candy the Dancer,' he said, tossing down the Bourbon.

She smiled again, this time with real warmth. 'Say, you're all right after all, lover. Looking for a party tonight?'

He nodded to the bartender. 'Again,' he said, then turned to the woman. 'Want a drink, Candy?'

'The usual,' she said to the bartender. Then she faced Johnson. 'In town for long?'

'Just for the night,' he replied. 'I'm in sales. We have to keep moving to make money.'

'I like salesmen, they make the very best lovers. And the ones with a touch of grey hair are the best of all.'

'Why's that?'

She lightly ran her long red nails over his greying temple. 'They're gentle, baby. A woman likes a man who's gentle.'

He took the second drink and sipped it. 'I've always heard that you women like the rough stuff, the real macho men. They say all women have a rape fantasy.'

This time her laugh wasn't professional. It was cynical and harsh. 'Listen, babe, I've been raped. Jesus, you can take that fantasy and stick it. In my line of work, honey, we treasure a gentle man. Most aren't.'

'Who's your friend?' He nodded at the young girl seated at the end of the bar.

'If you want to party, you don't want to fool around with that young stuff, honey.' The professional purr was back in her voice. 'She doesn't know half the things I do.'

He smiled. 'You're pretty damn good.' Actually, as he remembered, she was like an automaton, going through the acts of love like a bored mechanic fixing a muffler. To her it was just another job. 'I just wondered who she was. I've never seen her in here before.'

Candy frowned. 'She's new. Comes from Jersey.' Obviously, Candy wasn't about to extol the virtues of her opposition.

He continued to drink his Bourbon. It was taking effect and he was beginning to enjoy himself. 'I was thinking, only thinking you know, about fantasies.'

'Yeah?'

He finished the drink and set it down. 'Most men have a fantasy of making love to two women, you know, at the same time.'

She smiled quickly. 'Oh, think you could handle two of us at once, do you?' She laughed. 'Of course, it might give you some memories of a night you would never forget.'

'Think your girlfriend over there might go for something like that?'

Candy put her hand on his thigh. 'Sure. She's young but she's willing to learn. We could have a lot of fun, the three of us. Of course, it would be expensive fun.'

'How much?'

Her hand moved slowly upward, her eyes calculating what he might pay. 'Depends on how much time you think it might take. We're working girls, honey.' She laughed. 'We're like lawyers, you know – time is money with us.'

Surprised by her reference to his own profession, he finally managed to force a laugh.

'Some lawyer give you a screwing, baby?' she asked, noting his discomfort.

He nodded. 'Yes. A couple, almost a dozen.'

'Jesus! How many times have you been married?'

'Too many.' The truth was that he had been married only once, but his answer was still correct. Being married once to Muriel was one time too many for anyone.

'Suppose it took a couple of hours?' he asked. 'What kind of money are we talking about?'

She nodded. Her hand was now on his cock. She lightly licked his ear, while her leg pressed against his. 'A couple of hours? Well, I like a gentle man, honey. It'll be sort of a bargain, but it'll cost you a hundred for each of us. Believe me, you won't regret it.'

'And I pay for the room, right?'

'It might be fun to get a bottle too.'

'Okay, Candy,' he said, now fully aroused by her attentions, 'you've got a deal. Get your friend and we'll go.'

The friend was a thin girl, not yet twenty, whose eyes were defensive even when she smiled. Her name, she said, was Sandi – with an 'i', she told him.

They walked a few blocks to the Hotel Costa Del Sol. It was an antiquated hotel, once luxurious but now used exclusively by drunks and prostitutes. A decrepit and dishevelled man in a soiled shirt manned the desk. He provided the key to the room for a twenty, and a pint of cheap liquor for another twenty. Frank Johnson guessed the old man would probably have to split his profits with the girls. There were other hotels that would welcome the business. Life was a constant competition.

He'd been to the hotel before with Candy. As before, the room was drab, with a single bed and a dilapidated small-screen television.

Johnson sipped at the whiskey as the two women went through a strip routine. Candy, older and more professional, moved slowly and seductively. Sandi seemed to be nervous, and somehow this almost virginal quality made her movements more provocative.

Once they were naked, they began to undress him. Again the two techniques varied. Candy worked her hands and lips at an almost set pace, with practised fluid movements. The young girl, however, was awkward, and seemed to have little experience. She had a slender but well-formed body. He found her infinitely more exciting than the much more fully endowed Candy.

And then the first pain hit. It came on slowly, like a cramp, starting in his back and moving through to the front of his chest.

'What's the matter, baby?' Candy purred. 'This getting too exciting for you?'

The pain was like a vice, and he found he couldn't speak. He tried to get up, but they pulled him back on to the bed.

The pain ebbed, although he found himself suddenly sweating.

'Hold it a minute,' he said, reaching for the bottle. 'I have to get my breath.'

Candy giggled and began to massage his buttocks when he doubled over with a new wave of pain, this time much worse than the first.

'What's the matter?' Candy asked. Now there was no seduction in her voice.

'Pain,' he managed to gasp out, trying not to move.

The pain increased and he fell to his knees. His breath would not come.

'A doctor,' he gasped in agony. 'Call cops.'

'Holy shit!' Candy jumped up. 'He's having a heart attack.'

'What should we do?' Sandi asked in panic.

He lay writhing on the floor, conscious but unable to speak. The pain seemed total now.

'Get dressed,' Candy hissed. 'Quick!'

He tried to talk to them, to beg them to get help, but he couldn't.

Both women dressed surprisingly quickly. He looked up as Candy grabbed his wallet. She extracted the bills. Then she paused as she examined his credit cards and identification.

'Fuck, this guy's a New York lawyer!'

'What'll we do?' Sandi's big eyes were fixed on the writhing naked man on the floor.

'Get our asses out of there. This is trouble.' Candy threw the wallet on the bed.

'Don't worry, lover,' she called softly as they left. 'We'll have the manager send help.'

But they did not. They raced out of the hotel without saying a word to anyone.

Frank Johnson lost consciousness.

His body was discovered the next morning. His empty wallet lay on the bed. The hotel manager slipped in a tenspot and placed the wallet back into the trousers draped over the chair. He wanted no more robberies reported in his hotel; they were having too much trouble with the cops already. Then he called the police.

It was routine, and it was handled that way.

The autopsy performed revealed that Frank Johnson had extensive arterioslerotic heart disease. He had died of a massive myocardial infarction. Death, the pathologist reported, had been almost instantaneous.

Despite the efforts of the family and the firm to conceal the details surrounding his death – the police had traced the prostitutes who had been with him – little amused whispers of scandal managed to be circulated in Muriel's social circles and in the blue-blooded world of the top law firms. The rumours provided the foundation for some extremely crude jokes.

But beyond the jokes – except in the offices of Nelson and Clark – the passing of Frank Johnson, main partner, was little noticed. Muriel Johnson arranged a small, tasteful funeral service at one of New York's fashionable small churches in midtown Manhattan. She had had the body cremated, so there was no coffin at the service. Afterward, she flew down to their place in Palm Beach. By that afternoon any remorse she had felt was dissipated in the arms of Sonny Van Ward. Sonny knew exactly what she liked, and he was very good at providing it. She forgot about Frank, and the ultimte insult that he had died in a fleabag hotel in the company of common whores.

But in the richly panelled offices of Nelson and Clark, Frank Johnson's death had enormous impact. An Apostle had died. Not only was there now an opening as main partner, but Johnson's death meant that the key vote taken at the monthly meeting had changed. Now it stood six to five to keep the old rules intact. That meant Abner Slocum was on his way out. He was through as an active partner unless two things happened. He would have to see that the vacancy was filled with a person who would agree and vote with his proposal. That, and he had to find a lever to somehow persuade an opponent to change his vote.

And time was running out.

He knew that Ainsworth Martin, a stickler for procedure, wouldn't do anything about the matter until the next scheduled monthly meeting. It was likely then that Abner Slocum's future could be decided in three short weeks. He would have to put it all together by then or he would be finished. He knew the other main partners would be busy, too. They would try to block the appointment to the vacancy unless they were assured that the new Apostle would vote with them. It was going to get sticky, very sticky.

Frank Johnson's death, perhaps unmourned, was certainly not unnoticed.

7

Christina Giles found her son draped across a living room chair. He idly played with a control instrument, guiding dots and dashes across the television screen. He was completely intent on the game and didn't hear her come in.

'I'm home,' she said.

He didn't hear her, or pretended he didn't.

'I said, I'm home!'

He turned languidly and looked up at her. 'You made me miss,' he said.

She felt anger rise and fought against it. 'Did you have dinner?'

He started the electronic game again. 'Yeah.'

'What did you have?'

'I ate out.'

His head weaved as he directed the dots.

'Where did you eat?'

'The Chinese place.'

'Did your father take you?'

Again his reply was slow in coming. 'No. He gave me some money. I went by myself.'

'Where is he?' she asked.

'Out. He had a meeting at the hospital. He came home and changed.'

'What kind of meeting? Did he say?'

He jumped up and glared at her. '*You made me miss again.*' His words snapped forth in anger. 'I don't know what kind of meeting.' He threw the control device down. 'I'm going to my room.'

He stalked away, his movements reflecting his anger.

She was just as glad to see him go. She loved him and she tried to understand the process of maturing he was going through, but it was difficult. She felt suddenly lonely.

Christina found herself dwelling on the evening with Taro Kuragamo. He was as good as his word; there were no advances, unwelcome or otherwise, and his servants seemed to be almost purposefully conspicuous.

The dinner had been spectacular – a delicate cold madrilene, superb Cornish hen, endive-and-watercress salad – ending with succulent raspberries, flown in from France. Each course had been served with a different and more impressive wine. She asked Taro to call the chef from the kitchen so she could express her admiration. A small, unimposing man, the chef was not Oriental, or even French, but an Irishman. He accepted her compliments with a becoming modesty, as though his rare skill were hardly worth the mentioning.

Taro himself had been a surprise. In the outside world he walked like a king, holding himself straight, displaying an almost regal bearing. A formidable force in international business, he had the air of a man who knew exactly what he wanted and exactly how to get it. But in his own home, he was unassuming and relaxed.

She was delighted to find that he had a delicate sense of humour. It flashed often during their evening together, always unexpectedly. But despite his quick and lively wit, he was essentially a quiet man who seemed to enjoy her company and her conversation. Although she found that she couldn't fully relax with this man with the dark piercing eyes, she wasn't uncomfortably anxious.

Kuragamo was a good listener, and he attentively urged her to talk. Christina found herself prattling about her childhood, her youthful dreams, and her law school days. He appeared to be genuinely interested.

She had savoured the wine he offered. Knowing more than a little something about wines, she shuddered to even think of the price of such an obviously rare vintage.

As the evening progressed, she recalled hoping that he would abandon his word of honour. For the first time in years she found herself sexually awakened, and powerfully so. Since her marriage to Hank, she'd met some interesting men. At times she'd felt a mild attraction, but never before had she allowed herself to feel desire.

She wondered if it was his eyes, or perhaps his manner. Whatever, she couldn't help wondering what his arms would feel like, what kind of a lover he would be. These tantalizing questions, she realized, were obviously dangerous.

Taro had taken her home, escorting her into her apartment house. He had paused a moment at the elevator, then he had taken her hand, gently brushing it with his lips as he looked directly into her eyes. She felt a rush of excitement, like a schoolgirl being kissed on her first date.

The contrast between her reception at home and the admiration of Taro Kuragamo was painfully sharp, and she felt guilty at having enjoyed his attentions. But she couldn't help thinking about the tall man.

She read for a while, then went to bed. She felt lonely and empty. She fell asleep thinking of those dark, sure eyes.

Her secretary rushed to meet her as she approached her office the next morning. 'Mrs Giles – did you hear what happened to Mr Johnson?' The girl was tense with excitement.

'What?'

'He died last night.'

'My God. How?'

'How? Heart attack.' She started to giggle.

'I really don't think that's funny.'

The girl tried to be serious, but it was a losing cause. 'Oh, it's *terrible*,' she said. 'But they say he was with some prostitutes, you know, when it happened.'

'Who says?'

'The police, I suppose. It's all over the office. He died in some old hot-pillow place near the Village.'

Christina felt revolted. 'Gossip is often wrong. I wouldn't spread it around.'

Her secretary nodded, still having trouble controlling herself. 'Oh, I'm sorry about it, of course.' The giggle came unbidden. 'It's just so fun – well, he was an Apostle; it's just such a peculiar way for one of them to go.'

'He was a very nice man, and he has a family.'

The girl coloured. 'I'm sorry, Mrs Giles. I didn't mean anything.'

Christina nodded and walked past her into her own office. The shock of the news erased any thought of the circumstances. Johnson's death meant there was a vacancy for Apostle. Her own future was suddenly at stake.

She wasn't ready for such a happening.

If the rumour was true, she was sorry that Frank had died in such squalid circumstances. She like Frank Johnson, and everyone who had ever been associated with him knew, as she did, that he had truly worked himself to death. It was a pity that he hadn't died at court. Somehow it would have been much more fitting.

Everyone at Nelson and Clark recognized that as a head of a major department Christina Giles was a logical candidate for Johnson's vacancy – despite her sex and comparative youth.

But there was another, equally logical candidate. Dan Spencer was certain now to become head of litigation. He was recognized as the firm's number-one trial lawyer, an astute veteran who really knew his stuff. Spencer had won some surprising victories for several clients whom Christina Giles had handed over to him. She'd been grateful for his help. Like Frank Johnson, he was a hard driver, although he seemed to be much less tense, more relaxed.

Unless there was an unknown factor, or if either of them decided not to try for main partner, they were destined to become opponents.

Christina Giles wanted the job, more than anything else in the world. To be one of the Apostles was now her only dream. It would be much more than just a friendly contest. If she lost she would have to leave the firm; that was the time-honoured custom. She would be offered something, an executive position with a large, prestigious company – perhaps even a seat on the Federal bench. One defeated former candidate for Apostle now sat as an Associate Justice of the Supreme Court. But it just wouldn't be the same. To be one of the twelve main partners in Nelson and Clark meant power, prestige, and status unequalled anywhere else in the legal world.

She wondered how Dan Spencer felt. The fact that she liked him would make the contest all the more difficult. And indeed he would be formidable. A man like Spencer would do well at anything. She wondered if being an Apostle meant as much to him as it did to her. She wondered if she should approach him about it. Perhaps they could settle the matter so that neither one of them would have to move from the firm. If he would announce that he was withdrawing in her favour, that would mean he wouldn't have to leave. Of course, if being an Apostle meant as much to him as it did to her, such a thing would be out of the question.

And even if he did withdraw, getting the next opening wasn't all that certain. There were other participating partners who were coming up, displaying their abilities in their important specialities, or their talents as rainmakers – bringing the big money into the firm. And then there was a handful of others, the heirs to vast fortunes, who, because of astronomical fees from their family businesses, were always potential partners. So nothing was ever sure, except that if she and Dan Spencer opposed each other, it would be winner take all.

Christina decided that she should meet with Dan, but not to openly strive for any resolution to their problem. It would be better for both of them if they approached the situation as adults, if they remained friends even though they would be rivals. She wondered if she really should be so solicitous of the feelings of a rival. That had never been her style.

The intercom buzzed.

'Yes?'

'There's a Mr Kuragamo on the line. Do you want to speak to him?'

She felt herself blush. 'Yes. Please put him through.'

'Hello,' she said.

'Good morning, Christina.' His well-remembered voice was, as usual, deep, steady and businesslike.

'This is a pleasure, Taro. I meant to write you a note. I enjoyed dinner the other evening. Now I can save the stamp.'

'I, too, enjoyed it,' he said. 'I read of your Mr Johnson's death. It is regrettable.'

'Yes,' she replied. 'He was only fifty, but he worked long, hard hours. I think Frank just worked himself to death. His heart couldn't stand the strain, I suppose.'

Surprisingly, she heard him laugh. 'I've heard one or two things on the street that seem to indicate it wasn't all law work that brought about his untimely demise.'

She resented his remark. 'I've heard the same thing. Damn lies, if you ask me. Frank was a good man, a moral man. It seems a shame to talk about him like that after he's dead and can't defend himself.'

'I didn't know he was your friend. I am truly sorry. Please excuse my rudeness. Quite unforgivable.' The Oxford accent suddenly crept back into his voice for just a moment.

'We weren't special friends, we were colleagues. He was a very nice man. And you don't have to apologize, Taro. I suppose that story about Frank and the prostitutes is all over town by now.'

'Unfortunately I'm afraid that you're right. I'm sorry that he died. Nevertheless it is because of his death that I called.'

'Oh?'

'As I remember from our conversations, you have a chance to become a full partner in Nelson and Clark, am I correct?'

'Well, yes. We call it a main partner. I head up a separate department in the firm. That's really my main qualification to be made an —'

'Apostle.' He said it for her, a half-chuckle in his voice.

'That's funny?'

'My beautiful Christina, no matter what slang term they call your head people over there, you simply do not comform to any picture of any Apostle I could possibly imagine.'

'Because I'm not a man?'

There was a pause. 'Because you are so beautiful.'

She felt her pulse rise, and the feeling surprised her. 'I don't think this is going to be a beauty contest, so even if that were true, which I'm afraid it isn't, it wouldn't help me very much.'

'Never discount beauty,' he said softly. 'There is too little of it in our world as it is. Can I help you in this contest?'

She hadn't expected the question and hesitated.

'Christina,' he continued, 'I am not without some influence in the ways of the world and its commerce. I don't want to meddle, but if you think of any way that I might help, please call on me.'

'Thank you, Taro, that's thoughtful of you. But this is really an intra-firm matter. But I do deeply appreciate the offer.'

'My assistance is yours for the asking. May I have the pleasure of dining with you tonight?'

She realized that she desperately wanted to say yes, a fact that surprised her. 'I'm sorry, Taro. I'm having dinner with my husband and son tonight.'

'Ah, that should be pleasant. Perhaps another time?'

'Of course,' she said, then realized the implications of her answer. She had unintentionally revealed her interest. But despite this she said nothing to correct that impression.

'We'll stay in touch,' he said. 'Good luck, Christina. And if you need help, please let me know.'

The line went dead before she could answer.

She sat back and tried to analyse her emotions. She was developing a schoolgirl crush on the mysterious Mr Kuragamo, that was obvious. Well, she decided, as long as it went no further, it was all right. She wasn't happy in her marriage, but she wouldn't use that as an excuse for any excursions beyond the marriage bed. It was just a crush, and that was all it would ever be.

She called home and talked to her son. Not surprisingly, he reported that his father would be tied up at the hospital again for the evening. She invited young Henry out for dinner, but he declined, saying that he already had plans to go out with one of his friends.

Once again she would be alone.

She was becoming accustomed to it. Next she phoned her housekeeper and asked her to prepare a light salad and leave it in the refrigerator.

When she hung up, the anger began to rise inside her. Damn them, she thought, they treated her like some unwelcome boarder. She felt betrayed. If Taro Kuragamo called again, she'd jump at the chance to see him. For a moment she debated calling him. But she knew that could be interpreted by him in only one way. She was a capable lawyer, respected and honoured in her own profession; she would be damned before she would become some rich man's plaything. And although she didn't really think of Taro in just that way, she couldn't bring herself to make the call.

The intercom buzzed, and her heart began to pound. She hoped Taro was calling back.

'Mr Spencer wonders if you might have a few minutes to see him?' her secretary asked.

'Certainly. Tell him to come in.'

As he walked in, Christina noticed that he moved with his usual surprising grace. His reddish hair had been brushed back in a youthful style that she found attractive.

'Christ, I don't have much time. I'm running between courts. Things have sort of piled up on me since Frank's death, but I thought you and I should sit down and talk, rush or no rush. Would you be free for dinner tonight by any chance?'

Christina looked up at him. He showed no signs of anxiety. She wondered if she did.

'I think you're right, Dan,' she said. 'I was thinking exactly the same thing. We should talk. And, as a matter of fact, I've just discovered that both my husband and son each have plans for this evening, so dinner sounds fine.'

He nodded, a half-smile played upon his lips. 'Maybe we could meet somewhere? How about the Algonquin?'

She knew he noticed the surprise on her face. And the panic. 'Ah . . . well . . . how about just picking me up here at the office?'

'You don't like the Algonquin?'

'Very much. But I have some work to do. If it's convenient for you, meeting here would be better for me.'

She was sure she saw mild amusement in his eyes.

'Okay,' he said. 'I'm not sure when I'll get back. I have a judge who thinks his court should be opened around the clock. If I really get stuck I'll give you a call. Otherwise I'll come by here about eight. Okay?'

'Sounds terrific. I look forward to it.'

'So do I. Very much.'

After he left she wondered if that business about the Algonquin was just coincidental. In any event, she hadn't handled it very well. But she was afraid that Taro might be there, and even though it really wasn't any of his business, she didn't want him to think she had lied.

Later in the day when she received a call notifying her that the Thomkins Steel contract would be concluded at the International Bank in London rather than at the Chase in Manhattan, she didn't think it particularly unusual.

It would be inconvenient to fly to London for just one day's business, but she'd done it before. It was a nuisance, but part of the business. She didn't even think about Taro Kuragamo, or that he might in any way be connected with the request that she go to England.

Her thoughts wandered, equally divided as she tried to concentrate on some proposed mortgage documents. She thought about Taro Kuragamo, and his dark eyes. And she thought about Dan Spencer and what they might talk about at dinner. The paragraphs of the legal papers spread before her couldn't hold her attention.

Time passed very slowly.

Peter Kipling walked into his office. 'How's it going, Collins?'

'Not bad, Kipling. How about you?'

'Getting by. Do you want to get in on the office pool?'

'For what?'

'Each of us is throwing in ten bucks. It's all going to be decided by computer.'

'What is?'

'You can pick a name, a date, and a time. If that person is selected on that date, and you have the closest time, you win the pot. The computer is programmed so that no two people will have the same choice.'

'I still don't know what you're talking about.'

'The vacancy for Apostle,' Kipling replied. 'The speculation says it's between Dan Spencer and Christina Giles. It could be someone else. You can pick anyone you want.'

'I hardly know these people, or who has the best chance,' Kipling had been with the office for six months. Collins figured he would know who would win, or who had the best chance. 'There's no point in me throwing away ten bucks.'

'Hey, it's a gamble no matter who gets it. You still have to call the day, and even the time. Look, there's almost two hundred associates in this firm. You could win almost two thousand dollars, if most of us get in the pool.'

Collins nodded. 'Who's the favourite?'

Kipling grinned. 'Like I said, Spencer and Giles.'

'Who did you pick?'

'Christina Giles.'

'Okay.' Collins pulled out his wallet. 'Put me down as betting on Spencer.'

Kipling made a note. 'What day? You have to pick the day and the time when they make the selection. It's usually in the morning or early afternoon, they tell me.'

'I'll take two weeks from today. Make it noon exactly.'

Kipling wrote the information down, then took the money from Collins.

'Any special reason you think Spencer will get it?' he asked

Collins.

'None. I just bet against you.'

Kipling looked startled until Collins smiled. 'Hell, I don't know the secretaries' names yet. I haven't the foggiest who might be picked. If I win, it will be blind luck.'

Kipling laughed. 'Well, if you do get any inside information, share it with me. I know where we can do some heavy betting.'

'Sounds like the world series or something.'

'A vacancy for Apostle is a rare thing. They tell me the whole office goes a little nuts until a replacement is selected. I suppose this is the most exciting thing that can happen here. At least it is since I came here.'

'I can tell you who isn't going to get it,' Collins said, lowering his voice.

Kipling was immediately interested. He leaned closer. 'Who?'

'You and me.'

Kipling laughed. 'Yes. They may dip down in the organization, but they'll never get this far. But our day will come, eh?'

'We'll see,' Collins replied.

John Crim idly looked out the jet's window as the aircraft swept in low, following the twisting path of the familiar Potomac River below. It was getting dark and the capital's lights were coming on.

After Frank Johnson's funeral, he'd stayed in New York for a few days to take care of some odds and ends of firm business, but now he was coming home.

The shuttle run between Washington and New York had become an almost weekly ritual for him. He was a main partner in Nelson and Clark, and in charge of their Washington office, the only branch office the firm had ever opened. He was a full-fledged Apostle of many years' standing, but because he was out of the main New York office he felt he had never been completely accepted by the others. And that had always bothered him.

The pilot was making his final approach, and Crim glanced at the lighted buildings and monuments without really seeing them.

All of it could have been different if they had only seen the true potential of the Washington office. Other firms, national firms, maintained large Washington branches. The capital was a city sensitive to displays of power and prestige. It was a politician's town and it lived by political rules. Ostentation meant a lot in Washington, just as it did in Hollywood. So law firms with huge offices and large staffs were generally accepted as prestigious and powerful.

Nelson and Clark had never allowed him to expand the Washington office. He was the head – the Apostle in charge, as he knew the others called him. He had only two participating partners, although one was a former assistant secretary of commerce and the other a former congressman. They had a staff of ten associates plus the usual ratio of office help. But by Washington standards it was a rather small law office.

Of course, the national reputation of Nelson and Clark did extend to the capital, but he felt he and the Washington office never really got the deserved recognition.

The runway markers flashed by as the pilot set the plane down smoothly. John Crim was sixty-eight and, by present firm rules, had less than two years to go until they retired him.

He would have a substantial income, in addition to the considerable dividends and interest he already received from prudent investing – much of it done on quiet tips from high government officials. From the standpoint of earning power, staying or leaving the firm meant nothing to him. In either event he was financially secure.

The prospect of puttering around in a lush Florida golf course held little appeal for him. He was a poor golfer and played the game only for business reasons. He had no real hobbies, certainly nothing that would fill the great void left if he were no longer an active member of the firm. He did enjoy hunting and fishing, but only as occasional pastimes.

What John Crim wanted most was recognition of his special status from the community in which he lived and worked. Nelson and Clark could easily challenge any of the capital's leading law firms. The Twelve Apostles could be on top in Washington just as they were in New York. All that was needed was the mere expedient of maintaining larger and more lavish offices, with an appropriate increase in the number of lawyers employed. And it would certainly pay for itself in terms of increased business.

The death of Frank Johnson, Crim thought, might just make change possible within the firm. Abner Slocum's almost maniacal fear of retirement could provide the necessary lever. If the new Apostle – the one selected for Johnson's vacancy – could be pledged to change the retirement rules, and if Crim could get a commitment from Abner Slocum to build up the Washington office, Crim would offer to change his vote. And that would be sufficient to alter the rules on retirement. Slocum and he would each get what they so desperately wanted.

It would all turn on the lawyer to be chosen for the vacancy.

National Airport was old – a product of the New Deal building programme under Roosevelt – but it had character. It was dangerous, everyone agreed, but it was convenient for the congressmen, and they were the ones who paid the bills. So the airport stayed right where it was, on the banks of the Potomac, right in the centre of a heavily populated area. If a plane went down, as they sometimes did, they went into the river because that was the only route allowed in or out. Congress didn't want any front-page pictures of a hundred former homes smoking in flames.

John Crim bypassed the baggage depot. He had only a small carry-on flight bag. He walked out into the airport and searched until he saw the familiar blonde head. He smiled. It was nice to be home.

They walked out into the parking lot, past the circle of shouting cabdrivers, to the comparative peace of the short-time parking spaces. Crim was a man who prided himself on keeping in shape. Abner Slocum was only a year older than he, but Abner looked like an old man. John Crim, on the other hand, looked younger than his years, a lot younger. He had the spring of youth in his step and he possessed the lean body of an athlete.

'Been waiting long?' Crim asked as they walked to the car.

'No. I like airports anyway. I love to watch the people. You know that.'

Crim nodded, smiling. 'I remember.'

'Shall we go home or would you like to have some dinner?'

Crim laughed. 'Don't tease me. You know I want to go home.'

She answered with a seductive smile. 'That's what I thought you'd say. I have some cold cuts at the apartment.'

Crim sighed. It was good to be home. It was comfortable and it was nice to be loved.

He glanced around. No one could see them. He grabbed a quick kiss.

'Let's wait until we get to my place.'

Crim laughed. 'Whatever you say, darling. Whatever you say.' He admired her strong young body. She was a beautiful woman. He considered himself very lucky to have such a lover, a girl almost forty years younger than himself. She was his fountain of youth. When he was with her, as if by magic, he felt restored and renewed.

'When do you have to be home?' she asked.

'Not until tomorrow night. I told my wife I'd have to spend an extra day in New York.'

'I wish you were really mine. Then we wouldn't ever have to be apart.'

He tousled her blonde hair. 'We'll work on it, honey. You never know what the future might hold.'

8

John Norman Scott picked up the newspaper from the floor, where he'd thrown it down in rage. He could feel the blood pounding in his temples. His breath came in short, angry rasps; his jaw was clamped tight.

It was just a two-bit gossip column. Some damn fool writing under a cutesy name – Miss Kiss-and-Tell – probably some idiot fag and not a woman at all. Scott wouldn't have seen the article – he never read the column – except that Nancy had telephoned. At first she was sobbing so hard that he couldn't understand a word she said. Finally, although she was nearly hysterical, she did manage to get across to him that her unhappiness stemmed from an item in the second section of the morning newspaper. He told her to go home, to his home, and not to answer the telephone. He told her he would take care of the matter and would soon be there to console her.

He tried to calm himself. What was the old saying? Don't get mad, get even. Well, he would see that he did get even, very even.

The item itself was just a short teaser:

Kiss-And-Tell hears that a certain Napoleon-about-town has a new Josephine. And although he hasn't given her a ring or made her his Empress, he has her second-in-command of his corporate army. We hear the army is rather unhappy, even the generals. The generals have nothing against love (sex) but they just don't like it mixed in with their business. Watch out, Napoleon, don't let them send you to Elba. For heaven's sake, marry the lady and do it at home.

Scott's hands shook slightly as he reread it. Hell, everyone in town knew they called him the Napoleon of Wall Street. It had to be one of his top people who had leaked that item. They resented Nancy, all of them. They didn't take the time to know her or her abilities, yet just because she was young and pretty they hated her. And some coward had taken this sneaky way of exacting revenge. When Scott found the source, that person, he promised himself, would regret the day he was born.

He flicked on the intercom. 'What's the name of that guy who runs the *Morning Times*?' His secretary seemed to have that kind of information at her fingertips. The woman had a remarkable memory.

'*The Times* was just bought by Alexander Sobray, the one who owns all those European newspapers.'

'I want the guy who actually runs it. The guy who's responsible for what goes into that rag.'

'Oh, that would be John Laker, the managing director. He has a column every Sunday.'

'Get him on the phone.'

'Certainly.'

He sat back and closed his eyes, gently rubbing his temples, trying to regain his composure. He could buy and sell men like this Laker. He could easily have Lockwood Limited buy the damn newspaper from this fellow Sobray. Then he could fire everyone even remotely connected with that damn article, especially Miss Kiss-and-Tell, whether woman or faggot. He hoped this Laker had enough smarts to appreciate the power of John Norman Scott. If he didn't, he would regret it.

'I have Mr Laker on the telephone,' his secretary said, her voice crisp and businesslike.

'Laker,' he snapped the name out as if the man were already on his payroll. 'What the hell is this Napoleon business about?'

'Pardon me?' The voice was a deep bass, and completely relaxed.

'In this shitty column of yours – this Kiss-and-Tell thing – there's a dirty crack aimed at me. I want that corrected and whoever wrote it fired.'

For a moment there was no reply. 'Mr Scott.' The voice now sounded amused, which made the anger rise anew in Scott. 'I presume you are the president of Lockwood Limited, correct?'

'That's right. One of the largest companies in America.'

'Yes. As I recall, we ran a feature piece about you in the Sunday magazine about two months ago, didn't we?'

Scott's eyes narrowed. 'Yes. But that was after the articles in *Newsweek* and *Time*.'

'Hold on a minute. I'll take another look at the Kiss-and-Tell column.' There was a pause. 'I've reread it and I don't see anything in the column that refers to you.'

'*Newsweek* _ and even your own newspaper – called me the Napoleon of Wall Street. That's who is named there – me! Goddamn it, don't play games. You know that and so do I. The whole damn city knows it. You're trying to ruin the good name and reputation of a very talented lady and I deeply resent it.'

'What young lady is that?' The question was asked politely.

'Look, don't play the innocent with me. I appointed Nancy Merriam as my vice president in charge of programme planning. Some people in my company seem to resent that, and they've used your newspaper to take a cheap shot at one of my best executives.'

There was another pause. 'If I understand you correctly, you feel this item intimates that the girl got the job only because of her relationship with you – is that what you're claiming?'

Scott felt the pounding at his temples again. 'There's no other way of saying it, Laker. That thing is an underhanded, rotten attack upon an extremely capable young woman, and, by the way, upon me. I don't intend to stand for it.'

'Well, let's see what we can do about that, Mr Scott. We can't very well print a retraction without some basis. Would you possibly consider giving us a statement about the matter? It could really help straighten things out.'

'Will it get printed?' Scott snapped.

'I can assure you that it will, Mr Scott.' The voice sounded contrite and apologetic. Maybe this fellow Laker wasn't such a bad sort after all, Scott thought.

'I'll make a statement. I'll give it to you right now if you like.'

'No, Mr Scott. We may have caused you a great deal of pain and trouble. And if that is so, I sincerely regret it. Please allow me to send a couple of our best people over there now. It will only take a few minutes. I know you're a busy man, but we do want to handle this correctly.'

Scott nodded. 'I have a meeting in ten minutes, but it shouldn't go on for more than half an hour or so. Suppose you have your people come here to my office at eleven sharp?'

'Don't worry, Mr Scott, they'll be there. Anything else I can do?'

Scott relaxed. 'No, I think that will do for now. Look, I may have sounded a little hostile, Laker, but I think you would agree I had cause. However, you've handled this like a gentleman and I appreciate it.'

Miss Kiss-and-Tell was actually two people. Most of the writing was done by Gloria Weber. Gloria was a stocky woman, thrice divorced, who could outdrink and outswear any truck driver – but she wrote with a fine touch, using words like a great swordsman might use his flashing rapier. The other part of the team was Sam Walsh. Sam had been the paper's nightlife writer for years, building up a string of sources ranging from busboys all the way up to the owners of the fanciest restaurants. There wasn't a bartender in town who didn't know Sam Walsh, or hadn't helped him into a cab whenever he had had a bit too much, which was most of the time. Sam still wrote a weekly saloon column, but it was only a cover for his real work as the tip man for the popular Kiss-and-Tell column, now one of the most widely read items in the newspaper.

Laker called both members of the team into his office. It was morning, so Sam Walsh was still sober.

'If we get sued by John Norman Scott, can you back up this Napoleon and Josephine item in the K and T column this morning?'

'I just write that shit,' Gloria snapped, her ever-present cigarette bouncing on her lips as she spoke. 'Ask the alcoholic here. He's the legman.'

Walsh just grinned. 'Legman has two connotations. I plead guilty on both counts. Of course, not your legs, Gloria. I haven't seen anything like them since they shaved the zoo's gorilla.'

'As I recall, that was your girlfriend, right?'

Laker held up his hand. 'Knock it off. I want to know what you have, exactly.'

'Napoleon pitched a bitch, did he?' Walsh asked.

Laker nodded. 'And he wants to make a statement refuting everything in the article.'

'You're kidding! Nobody's *that* big an asshole!' Gloria laughed.

'I want to know exactly what you have.' Laker directed the question to Walsh, who suddenly looked more alert than his editor had seen him in years.

'I got tipped from a guy at the Book Mark, that saloon over near 57th Street, the one where some of those literary agents hang out.'

Laker nodded. 'I know the place.'

'I was in there and I see this guy I know, a guy who once wrote a book about the advertising business. Good reviews, lousy sales. The guy's still in advertising but he likes to hang out with the literary types.'

'And what did he tell you?'

Walsh paused to gather his thoughts before speaking, as if testing the accuracy of his memory. 'We were chatting about things in general. I think we were talking about the new sex scandal in the Senate. Anyway, he says that sort of thing happens in private business too. Then he tells me that this guy Scott had the balls to appoint his bimbo – a young bimbo in her twenties – as vice president of Lockwood Limited. This guy I was talking to handles part of the Lockwood account for his agency. He said he had heard about it from one of the vice presidents at Lockwood and that all the company officers were pretty pissed off about it.'

'Did he say what kind of qualifications the girl might have?'

Gloria snorted. 'Probably gives great head.'

Walsh grinned at her. 'Boy, you sure would never get a job at *that* place, Gloria.'

Laker's patience was wearing thin. 'Get on with it,' he commanded.

Walsh nodded. 'I didn't think much of it until a waiter at Maguire's said he'd seen Scott playing kneesies with some pretty little broad. Young girl. And Scott's what? Fifty, maybe fifty-five, something like that. Anyway, the waiter figured he was a dirty old man fooling around with a kid. He thought it was disgusting.'

'So?' Laker asked.

Walsh grinned. 'I checked it out. I called Lockwood Limited and asked for the broad. Her name is Nancy Merriam. That's what the ad guy told me. She wasn't there but her secretary said she'd just been promoted to vice president for planning. I pretended that I wanted to talk to her about a possible company project. I said I thought I had met her, then I described Gloria here.' He chuckled. 'An old broad, fat, with a little moustache.'

Gloria was about to snap a response but Laker's stern glance restrained her.

'Of course,' Walsh continued, 'the secretary had to correct me, right? She said the new vice president was twenty-eight, had brown hair and was very attractive. I told her the woman I knew had gone to Boston University. Again she set me straight. The little bimbo has a masters in business administration, but from Farmington University.'

'Did you ask her about Scott?' Laker inquired.

Walsh shrugged. 'Naw, that would have given the game away. What the hell, I figured I had enough to support a blind item. Gloria here cleaned it up a bit, and that's how it got in the paper.' He paused. 'Is he honest-to-god going to make a statement?'

Laker nodded. 'At least that's what he told me. Of course, when his public relations people get wind of it they'll stop him, even if they have to tie and gag him. But you never know. So we'll take a shot at it anyway.'

'God, that would sell a few newspapers: *Tycoon Denies Screwing His Bimbo*.' Gloria's cigarette ash fell down her blouse as she laughed.

'Can I go out on the interview?' Walsh asked. 'Let me take a crack at him. Hell, I found the story, by rights it should belong to me.'

Laker smiled as he shook his head. 'No, Sam, I'm sorry. I'm going to send out Harry Andrews and Mark Hertel.'

Sam Walsh half sneered. 'Christ, those two are financial page writers! What the hell do they know about love? Let me go – I'll bring back the story.'

Laker leaned back and studied the ceiling. 'They look harmless, don't they? Like a couple of accountants, complete with three-piece

104

suits and thick glasses. If Scott is fool enough to talk, he'll talk to them. They won't scare him off.' Laker sat up quickly. 'Besides, both of them came up through the ranks – police beats, the courts, the whole magilla. They're real reporters and they'll do all right. We just might have some fun with this.'

'Want us to do anything?' Gloria asked.

Laker nodded. 'Start digging into Scott's background. As I remember, he's divorced. Just recently. There might be something there. Check the files, dig up everything, Gloria.' He turned to the disappointed Walsh. 'You go out and start making the rounds of the fancy bars around Lockwood. You might pick up a few more items. It's worth a try. I have a feeling we're going to get lucky with this one.'

'It doesn't seem possible,' Gloria said. 'I mean Lockwood Limited is one of the world's largest conglomerates, doing billions every year. Christ, what kind of egomaniac would have the gall to install his young girlfriend in as a major corporate executive?'

Laker grinned. 'The original Napoleon would. He had just that kind of nerve. Remember, he put his brothers and sisters in as kings and queens of conquered countries. He had chutzpah. And, from what I read, this guy Scott likes to think of himself as Napoleon. In his own way, he might be doing the same thing as his hero. Chutzpah is chutzpah. I think he might just have the balls to talk about it.'

'And if he decides not to give a statement?' Walsh asked.

Laker shrugged. 'We don't have a story.'

'He'll never talk,' Gloria said. 'He'll think about it and wise up. The man can't be a complete fool.'

Walsh stood up and patted her on her ample back. 'You may be right. Oh, yeah. Listen, Gloria, about that crack I made about you not being able to get a job at Lockwood. Forget it, will you? Hell, a couple of the night janitors here say you give great head.'

'In any event, Sam, you're never going to find out.'

'Cut that stuff and get going,' Laker said. 'We all have work to do.'

John Norman Scott was elated. They both had been perfectly nice young men, pleasant and cooperative. He had allowed them to tape the interivew. They hadn't asked many questions. But then he'd planned out exactly what he was going to say, so after making his statement there hadn't been any real need for additional questions.

Andrews and Hertel, they were newspapermen, but they reminded him of serious students of business. He was impressed. Scott planned to drop a note to their editor. It was always nice when someone told the boss you had done a good job.

He was glad he had decided against consulting with the company's department of communications. They were just a bunch of old ladies down there anyway – all holdovers from the previous administration. He was going to replace them with new, young people, go-getters who could come up with vital ideas. These old men, mostly former newsmen, cut the crap out of everything until it was almost meaningless. He was pleased with himself. He had done a much better job than any of those hacks.

Scott debated about waiting until he got back to the apartment to tell Nancy of his triumph. But he had a meeting with the heads of several subsidiary companies that afternoon. And, as delightful a prospect as a quick roll in the hay seemed, he just didn't have the time. He decided to call her, to soothe her concern and ease her despair. The phone rang several times before he remembered that he'd told her not to answer. He glanced at his watch. He would have just enough time, if he hurried, to get over there and then make it back to the meeting.

One of the company cars, complete with driver, was always on standby. Scott rushed to the car and gave the driver directions. The car sped through the Midtown traffic as fast as the anxious driver could make it. It wasn't a comfortable task to drive the big boss himself, so he made every effort to get to the address as quickly as possible.

Scott opened the apartment door. He found Nancy sitting in the darkened living room. The stereo and television were silent. He took her in his arms. She'd been crying; her eyes were red and swollen. He felt her tremble as he held her.

'Everything's all right now, Nancy,' he whispered.

She looked up at him.

'I fixed everything,' he said. 'I put a stop to all that nonsense. You won't have to worry about that sort of thing ever again.'

She sighed and stepped back. A relieved smile flickered across her full lips. 'How did you manage that?' Her eyes spoke of her grateful respect for his genius.

'I gave a statement to the *Morning Times*. They were really quite decent about it.'

'What!' Her eyes widened.

He grinned down at her. 'I told them all about you, your background and your qualifications. I even hunted up a photograph of you. I think they'll probably run it on their financial page. It'll make a nice addition to your scrapbook.'

Her mouth hung open. She seemed to be in shock. But Scott knew that good news sometimes did that to people. 'So, as you can see, there'll be no more crummy cracks about Napoleon and Josephine.'

Her voice, when she finally found it, came out low and trembling, sounding to Scott almost like anger. 'What did you tell them?'

He shrugged. 'Oh, just your background, how talented you are, why I chose you for the job, the usual stuff.'

'And did they ask about our relationship?'

'They didn't have to. I told them we were good friends, that we dated once in a while, but that we were all business in the office. I think that should set the record straight.'

She shook her head in disbelief. 'Didn't you *think*?'

'About what?'

Her nostrils flared in anger. 'They didn't have a story until you opened your mouth. Oh Jesus! How could you get so far in business and be so fucking stupid!'

'Now, Nancy . . .'

Her teeth were clenched in a half-snarl. 'You've ruined me! You asshole – I'll be the laughing stock of the whole country. That story will be on page one, you damn jackass, and you'll look like the stupid fucking asshole that you are!'

'Baby, I can certainly understand a little hysteria, but you really should try to get a grip on yourself — '

'Get out!' she shrieked.

'But this is my apartment.'

'I don't care who it belongs to, you asshole! *Get out!*'

He left, hurt and puzzled by her reaction. He knew she would feel foolish later. And she would have plenty to apologize for when she saw a nice little story on the financial page, just as he had predicted. She would regret her outburst then.

But the next day her picture and his statement, plus backup

articles with quotes from former Lockwood Limited employees, were on the front page of the *Morning Times*. It was the lead story.

Nancy Merriam didn't apologize, nor did she show up for work, nor did she answer her phone.

John Norman Scott knew he would have to do something really dramatic to win her back.

He actually wasn't fully prepared to launch the attack, but the time had come to make war on Brown and Brown. It would be the largest corporate war ever fought. But, he reasoned, there was nothing like all-out war to unite people.

To him it seemed the only answer.

9

Christina Giles finally manged to become so engrossed in her work in preparation for the London closing that she even forgot she had agreed to go to dinner with Dan Spencer. While her mind had been on Taro Kuragamo and Dan Spencer, several paragraphs in the complicated mortgages had caught her attention. They would require careful alteration in preparation. Not only did the basic language need to be changed, but all the other parties had to be contacted to reach agreement on the changes.

Her secretary had worked along with her, staying late until the essential work was all done.

Christina was tired, but she forced herself to go through the whole package once more. It paid to be thorough. The wrong placement of a comma could destroy the legal meaning in an instrument. She put her full concentration into proofreading the documents one more time after her secretary had gone home.

The tapping at her office door startled her. Like most New Yorkers, she felt that night carried with it a certain primal apprehension. The offices of Nelson and Clark occupied six full floors. and many of the lawyers worked late at night. Still, as she glanced at her watch, she wondered if she might be alone on her floor.

'Yes, what is it?' she called.

'I think we have a dinner date,' came the answer and Dan Spencer's familiar voice.

She jumped up and hurried to the door.

He was grinning down at her as she flung it open.

'Forget?' he asked.

'I'm sorry. I got carried away. I have a closing in London in a few days, and I found some mistakes when I looked through the papers. It took most of the afternoon to straighten it all out.'

'You look tired. We can always make it another time, Chris.'

She shook her head. 'No, I really am hungry. But I must look a mess. Will you make yourself comfortable while I freshen up?'

He had changed clothes and wore a freshly pressed suit. He was an attractive man and he wore his clothes well. His usually unruly hair had been carefully brushed into place.

'Would you like me to go over the paperwork and give you a second opinion? I can do it while I wait.'

'That's kind of you, Dan, but I just finished proofreading it. Besides, it'll only take me a minute or two to get ready.'

He nodded and took a seat on her long leather couch. Each participating partner had a couch – it was one of the badges of rank within the firm. An original oil on the wall and a couch delineated the lair of a participating partner. Associates had offices of the same approximate size, but a mere print and a simple easy chair were the lesser symbols of status. Each Apostle was entitled to fix up his grand office on the top floor in whatever manner he or she preferred. Some were spartan, others looked like throne rooms. It depended on the personality of each Apostle.

Participating partners were entitled to small private washrooms adjoining their offices. Associates had to share the employee rest rooms. It was yet another perk that helped to establish the pecking order within the law firm.

She closed the door to her washroom and looked in the mirror. 'Tired' was too kind. She looked like a wreck, at least to herself. She hurriedly went about trying to repair the damage, thinking as she did so of how she might tactfully approach the subject of the competition for main partner. It would be an extremely ticklish thing. She decided the best course was to subtly sound out Dan on how much he actually wanted the partnership. Perhaps he didn't really care. But she dismissed that thought as wishful thinking.

Her Calvin Klein tweed suit, so fresh that morning, looked battle-worn, and she wished she'd made arrangements to change clothes. Compared to Dan, she would look haggard. The day and its labours, almost twelve straight hours, were wearing on her. She was exhausted, but she didn't want to go home – not to an empty apartment, to an emptiness that would only underline the sense of rejection she so strongly felt. Christina determined to find a second wind somehow, and complete this business with Dan Spencer.

She stepped out. 'Well, I may look like something washed up on the beach, but I'm ready to go.'

He stood quickly. She'd forgotten just how very tall he actually was. He was taller than her husband and even taller than Taro Kuragamo.

'You look lovely,' he said.

She was surprised that he sounded so genuine.

'We better go dutch,' she laughed. 'I'm starving and I might end up bankrupting you.'

He grinned easily. 'Look, I hope I'm not treading on sensitive feminist toes, but I prefer to pay. It makes me look macho to the waiter. You can slip me a little something later, of course, if it makes you feel better. Just leave it on the dresser on your way out.'

She laughed. 'Only if you're really good.'

'Do my best.' He took her elbow and escorted her towards the elevators.

His lighthearted manner seemed to defuse her purpose. Suddenly she wanted no more than just a pleasant dinner date, just some laughter and talk, nothing serious. But, like it or not, it was going to be serious. She knew that, but she really didn't feel up to it.

'Chris, do you have any special place you'd like to go? Or do you want to be surprised?'

She thought of Pocko's and again of the Algonquin. She certainly didn't want to go to either place.

'Just someplace quiet,' she said. 'Someplace where a tired lady can have a relaxing drink.'

He signalled and a cab pulled over to the kerb. He helped her in, then folded his long form to squeeze into the close quarters of the cab's interior.

He gave a Third Avenue address to the driver.

'What's that?' she asked.

'A place you probably don't know about. It's quiet enough except when the fights break out.'

'God, it certainly doesn't sound like the Plaza.'

'It's Igor's, a half-Hungarian, half-jock place.'

'You're right, I haven't heard about it. New place? It seems half the restaurants in New York change hands and names every six months at least.'

He laughed. 'You're right about the turnover. It seems that just when I get used to a place it gets turned into another kind of restaurant, run by somebody else. But Igor's has been around for years. I first started going there when I played for the Celtics. Of course, that was long ago, and my career, if you can call it that, was short-lived.'

'I've heard that you played basketball, but I didn't know you played for the pros.'

Dan shrugged. 'You're not alone. No one ever heard of me. I played only one year and I spent most of that on the bench.'

'What happened?'

He turned and smiled. 'I had everything except one thing – talent. Oh, I did pretty well at Brown, but it's a much faster league with the money boys. I wasn't quite quick enough. They didn't offer me a second year. I took the hint and then enrolled in law school.'

'What's all this about fights? Igor's sounds a little tough.'

'Not really. Oh, once in a while the fists fly, but it's usually just football players. They always seem to be seething with aggression. I don't know why, but there's never a problem with hockey players, or even boxers. But the football players will occasionally have at one another, though they never bother the patrons unless they try to interfere.'

She laughed. 'Great! Couldn't we have gone to the Plaza instead, or the Four Seasons? I just wanted a nice quiet drink.'

The cab moved quickly through the early evening traffic.

'You'll like Igor's. It's quiet enough. Sometimes they even have a couple of gypsy violinists. But generally it's peaceful. If you don't like it we'll go somewhere else.'

'That's a deal.'

They were driving past a seedy part of Third Avenue. The street-lights lit up a scene of urban desolation. Although elegant high-rise

111

apartment houses were only a block away, this part of Third was the kind of New York place – dirty, desolate and cheap – that frightened out-of-towners.

The cab pulled up in front of a small place with a small neon sign saying IGOR'S in a stamp-sized front window.

Dan paid the cabby, then took her inside.

It was much larger inside. Adjoining walls had been removed to make it bigger. She could see a full bar-room on one side, a large dining room in the back, and a row of snug little booths running along one wall.

'Wha'd'ya say, Dan.' They were greeted by a thick, powerful man who except for a grey fringe of hair around his ears was completely bald.

'Hi, Eddie. We'd like a booth at the back, okay?'

Eddie beamed, leering down at Christina. 'My, with a sweet thing like this in tow, I'd want a back booth too.' A little diamond set in one of his front teeth flashed in the dim light. 'Come on.'

He led them down the length of the place to a booth set against the back wall.

Dan Spencer waited until she slid in one side before sliding into the other. It was a two-person booth, small, intimate.

'You want a drink, of course.' The big man laughed.

'Chris, have you ever had Agrana?' Dan was quite at home, completley relaxed. 'It's a plum brandy. Very nice. A Hungarian speciality, or so they tell me.'

'I'll try it,' she said.

'The same, Eddie.'

Eddie lumbered away.

'You're certainly well-known here,' she said.

He nodded. 'I'm a creature of habit. I get in here at least once a week, sometimes more. The food's good and I like the people.'

'So this is your hangout?'

He grinned. 'You make it sound like a gangster joint. I live near here. It's convenient, that's all. How about you? Don't you and your husband have a special place you generally favour?'

The reference to Happy Hank caused her pain, for reasons she was unable to determine. 'No,' she answered quietly. 'He's busy most of the time. We seldom have the chance to get out much together.'

112

He said nothing, and she had to look away from his inquiring gaze.

Eddie brought the drinks. The liqueur was deep plum in colour, even in the dim light. It was served in a small brandy snifter, nearly half-full.

Eddie growled 'Enjoy,' then lumbered off again.

There weren't many customers in Igor's. She could hear some men laughing in the bar, concealed from their view. Another couple, half-hidden in their booth, was having dinner.

'Not much business,' she said.

'It's quiet tonight. No games. The basketball and baseball teams are all out of town. As I said, this is primarily a sports joint. On game nights the place starts to fill early. Sometimes if you get here after an important game you can't get in at all.'

She tasted the liqueur. It had a smoky plum flavour that she found delicious. 'Say, that's very good.'

He nodded. 'Yes. I like it. But be careful. It doesn't taste like it, but that stuff has the kick of a mule.'

She sipped again. It didn't even taste alcoholic.

'Well, should we eat first and then talk, or vice versa?' she asked.

'Whatever you'd like.'

She liked his eyes. 'I'm sorry that we should be the ones in competition for Frank's opening,' she said.

'Why?'

She studied her glass, not wanting to look at him directly. 'Oh, because I've always liked you, Dan. You're an excellent lawyer and you've always been ready to help me on any of my cases. There are a few people in the firm that I don't really like. I'd much rather be competing against them.' She felt uncomfortable and finished her drink in one long gulp.

'Be careful, Chris,' he laughed. 'I'm not kidding – that stuff can be dynamite.'

'Don't you feel anything?'

He grinned. 'You mean about this?' He too drained his glass. 'Or do you mean about the situation at the firm?'

'The firm, Dan.'

He signalled Eddie, who quickly brought another round without exchanging a word.

Dan leaned back, resting his head against the dark wood of the

113

booth. 'The reason I helped you, Chris, was because it was part of my job. You had cases that came into the litigation department; they were assigned to me. Oh, I must admit I enjoyed working with you; you're a very pleasant person to be around. But it was my job.' He sipped at the fresh drink. 'I guess I too wish that you weren't my rival, although I'm not altogether sure either of us is really in the running.'

'Oh?'

Spencer looked straight at her. 'If it was strictly on merit, I think we would be in competition. And if the selection depended on our relative importance – and I mean how much money is brought into the firm – I think you'd probably win.'

'Oh?' she repeated, then laughed nervously. 'I'm quite a conversationalist, am I not?' She drank deeply from her glass.

'I think I surprised you.'

'Somewhat. The way I see it, it's strictly between you and me.'

He nodded. 'You head the corporate development division. It's important to the firm and brings in huge amounts of money. You're the only non-Apostle to head up a separate department. That's what makes you think you're in the running, right?'

'Something like that,' she agreed. 'And you think not?'

'Well, look at my situation. Now that Frank's dead, I'm running litigation. One of the Apostles has always headed up the litigation department. Usually it's been the successor in that slot, and at the moment I'm the successor. That's the reason you think I have a shot at the opening, isn't it?'

A relaxing warmth was beginning to spread throughout her body. 'Of course – don't you?'

He swished the Agrana around in his snifter. 'Ordinarily I would. But there's more to it this time.'

'You obviously possess information that I don't.'

He grinned. 'Tell me, lady, if you truly are my rival, why should I tell you?' His eyes, picking up the soft lights in the restaurant, almost seemed to twinkle.

'I'm fun to be with.' She was surprised at the flippancy of her own answer.

He laughed. 'As a matter of fact, you are.'

She felt a little fuzzy as Eddie brought still another round of drinks to the table.

She giggled. 'Are you making a pass?'

His smile was almost sad. 'You're a married woman. A very lovely, nice lady. No, I'm not making a pass. If things were different, maybe I would.'

She couldn't suppress another giggle that was bubbling up from inside her. 'Which different? If I wasn't married, or if I wasn't nice? Do you make passes at not-so-nice married women?'

He grinned. 'I think we better get something to eat. You're not used to this stuff.'

'You're evading the question, counsellor. I'm not a trial lawyer, but even I can see that. Tell me, what do you know that might eliminate us as contenders for the vacancy?' She paused, becoming serious. 'Dan, you really don't have to tell me, you know. I would certainly understand.'

He reached across the table and touched her hand. She felt a sensation like a chill, but it was pleasant. He didn't take his hand away, nor did she.

'The Apostles are engaged in a war among themselves. Some of them want the mandatory age retirement provision eliminated as a firm rule. Some of the others don't care about that so much, but they do want the slice of profits now paid to the saints either cut down or eliminated altogether. Some of them are protecting the retirement and half-share provisions like tigers. I think merit is going to have damn little to do with who gets the job. It'll come down to politics. It will all depend on how you say you will vote and what side you commit to. And if you pick the wrong side, the eventual losing side, you'll be out. I think the Apostles will start buttonholing every participating partner to find out how that person will go, if selected. So that, and not merit, is going to be the deciding question, at least in my humble opinion.'

'How do you know all this?' Her words sounded slightly slurred even to her own ear.

The first thing she noticed was the pain. It seemed to throb through her entire body, beating steadily, like a drum. It took her a few minutes until she mustered up the courage to open her eyes.

A wave of dizziness came and went. She moved her head and looked about her. She was in a very large and rumpled bed and it wasn't her bedroom. The drapes on the windows had been pulled closed. She couldn't tell if it was night or day. A spasm of nausea swept through her, then slowly abated.

Slowly, cautiously, she sat up. She was wearing the top of someone's pyjamas, a man's red and blue striped pyjamas.

Light streamed in through a doorway from another room. She barely managed to swing her legs over the side of the bed, but she couldn't quite gather the courage to stand up.

She became aware that someone was standing in the doorway.

She was almost afraid to look up.

'I sure hope you feel better than you look,' Dan Spencer said.

'Where am I and how did I get here?' Chris's mouth felt as if it were full of cotton.

He disappeared for a minute, then returned with a wet, cold cloth. He held it against her temples. It felt wonderful.

'You had a tad too much of that Hungarian brandy.'

She felt her stomach churn at the mention of the liqueur. 'You should have taken me home.'

'First of all, you wouldn't go. Secondly, you got sick all over yourself in the cab and I had to find someplace to clean you up. This is it – my place.'

She looked down at herself. 'My clothes?'

'I was able to clean them up pretty good. They're in the bathroom drying. It wasn't so much that you made a great mess – you just seemed to manage to hit everything you had on just a little bit.'

She looked down at her bare legs and thought of her pantyhose. 'Who undressed me?'

'Would it make you feel any better if I said my mother?'

She felt another wave of nausea, but it passed. 'Your mother?'

He didn't laugh, and his face was uncharacteristically solemn. 'No, I was trying to make a joke. There's no one here but me, I managed to get you out of everything. I sponged off your things after I got you to bed.'

'You undressed me?' She looked up at him. 'Did we . . .'

'Obviously you don't remember anything.'

She felt a tear start down her cheek.

He quickly sat next to her and put his arm around her. 'Chris, I didn't touch you except to get your things off. What the hell kind of man would do a thing like that? You were dead drunk.' He squeezed her. 'In a manner of speaking, you're still a virgin.'

116

She looked up at him as if to test the truth of his statement.

He grinned. 'I won't say I wasn't tempted. You're . . . well. . . a very beautiful woman, Christina. But, believe me, if we ever do go to bed together, it will be only when you have full possession of your faculties, okay?'

She nodded. 'Thanks.'

He stood up. 'I'm going to whip up the famous Daniel Spencer hangover cure. Don't look so alarmed, it's mostly tomato juice. Then you can grab a shower and dress.'

'Dan, what time is it?'

'A little after six.'

'In the morning?'

'Yes.'

She wondered what she was going to tell her son. There were no medical emergencies in the law. She would have to think of something. She again looked up at Dan Spencer.

He looked exhausted, drained.

'Have you been to sleep?'

Spencer shook his head. 'No. I wanted to make sure you were all right.'

'That wasn't necessary, but it was very thoughtful, Dan.'

He grinned. 'No problem. I'll go whip up the hangover cure now, and then you'll be as good as new, maybe even better.'

Christina Giles, alone in the bedroom, looked down at her naked legs and wondered why she felt so disappointed when Dan told her that nothing had happened.

10

Clogged traffic impeded John Norman Scott's limousine, causing it to crawl along with more plebeian vehicles whose drivers provided no special deference for his big, tinted-window car. This, plus the possibility of being late, caused angry frustration to bubble up within him. Scott had allowed plenty of time, but he knew somewhere in the Manhattan street grid some idiot had caused a traffic accident and it had had an effect like a cork plugged into a flowing bottle. Rich or poor, it didn't matter – every driver was caught in the steel grip of the car-locked streets.

Scott took his ire out on his driver, commanding him to squeeze the huge grey limo through impossibly narrow spaces or to drive through a moving line of pedestrians.

Despite the car's air conditioning and the coolness of the day, the driver was sweating. John Norman Scott could be unpredictable, and a regular job was becoming a very precious commodity. The driver pretended to obey and restrained himself from any show of annoyance.

'Christ, we're locked in like sardines in a can. What the hell am I paying you for? Can't you get us out of this?'

'Sorry, Mr Scott. Everybody is caught in this gridlock. Eventually they'll send out an army of traffic cops to get things moving, but until then we're stuck. New York just wasn't built for this many cars.'

Scott snorted, implying that it was really his driver's fault. 'I'll get there quicker if I walk.' He yanked open the rear door and stepped out into the street.

'I'm sorry, Mr Scott,' the driver called. 'Do you want me to wait for you at the Logan Building?'

Scott looked back and sneered. 'No, I'm better off walking.'

The driver's face reflected his anxiety, but he said nothing more. Sometimes the little man was like a snapping terrier, and then it was best just to stay out of his way and avoid his bite.

Moving quickly, Scott shouldered his way through the crowd as if the people had all been purposely placed there just to try to stop him. New Yorkers are used to being jostled, so all he drew was an occasional angry stare or curse.

The limo driver watched him go, then relaxed, shoved his uniform cap back and lit a cigarette. Someday, he hoped, the little bastard would shove the wrong person. The thought made him smile. He'd love to see that.

Scott felt more at ease as he walked. At least progress was in his hands now and he wasn't the pawn of unseen forces. Scott firmly believed that things went wrong when he didn't personally handle them. He was always supremely confident when he took total command.

He didn't like losing control of Nancy Merriam. She had come to his apartment only twice since the announcement, and then only to pick up a few articles of clothing. But she hadn't removed everything of hers and he felt that was a very good sign. Although he had had a new office prepared and decorated just for her, she hadn't come by to see it. Even if she wasn't there, he saw to it she was still on the payroll as the new vice president. Ultimately he was confident she couldn't resist the power and prestige he had provided for her.

But he did miss her, and it wasn't just because of his sexual needs, although he was seriously considering finding a surrogate until she came to her senses. He missed her company. She was a good listener and he enjoyed the adulation. He was determined that they would recapture what they once had, whether she liked it or not.

He strode into the offices of Nelson and Clark as if he owned the place. It was a habit. Scott stared down at the receptionist, forcing her to speak first.

'Can I help you?'

'I have an appointment with Ainsworth Martin.'

'And your name?' she inquired pleasantly.

He tried to stand a bit taller. 'John Norman Scott.' He spoke his own name as if it were a title.

But it seemed to mean nothing to her. 'Just a moment, Mr Scott,' she said, again with reserved pleasantness. 'I'll give his secretary a call.'

Scott listened as she repeated his name, but when she said it, it was just a name; there was no drama.

Her smile was constant, apparently given in equal measure to commoners or kings. 'You're expected, Mr Scott. Just go through that door. Mrs Reilly will meet you and take you to see Mr Martin.'

He nodded, strode across the reception room, threw open the door with force, and found himself in a long hallway. A stylishly dressed older woman came towards him. She had the exact same smile as the receptionist, pleasant but without real warmth.

'Mr Martin is expecting you.' She made it sound as if somehow the lawyer were doing him a large favour. Scott knew most attorneys would kill to get a chance at the legal business of a giant conglomerate like Lockwood Limited. He had expected a much more enthusiastic reception.

She guided him to a large office furnished in a style more suited to the turn of the century. A large mahogany desk, its thick wooden legs carved to resemble animal paws, dominated the sombre room. Old-fashioned wooden bookcases lined the walls, all crammed with ancient leatherbound volumes, testaments to the thoughts of judges and lawyers long dead.

Ainsworth Martin arose from his worn leather chair and extended his hand in greeting. He towered over Scott.

'It's good to see you, Mr Scott.' He spoke with quiet dignity, echoing the attitude of his secretary. His manner seemed to imply that his law firm had all the business it could handle, and Scott would have to sell Nelson and Clark on taking his case. Scott found this most annoying.

'Please sit down.' Martin indicated a large leather chair facing his desk. 'Can we get you something to drink? Coffee perhaps – or something stronger?'

Scott didn't like to drink during business meetings. But he felt that Martin was indicating coffee was the only acceptable choice, so he wanted to demonstrate that he couldn't be intimidated.

'Bourbon on the rocks,' he snapped.

Martin smiled and nodded, but Scott thought he saw disapproval in his eyes as he spoke to his secretary. 'Mrs Reilly, please bring Mr Scott a Jack Daniel's on the rocks.'

Ainsworth Martin sat down and offered a leather-covered box of cigars to Scott.

'No, thanks,' Scott said. 'I don't smoke.'

Without asking if Scott objected, Martin extracted a long black cigar and clipped off the end with a small pair of silver scissors. 'We have a device in the ceiling,' he said without looking up, 'that whisks away the smoke, so it won't bother you. My partners insisted I have it installed. I am one of the few in the firm who likes cigars. I'm getting to the age where a good cigar is almost the only pleasure left to me.'

He puffed the cigar into life. As predicted, the smoke swirled about his head for a moment, then was immediately sucked up towards the ceiling. 'Now what can we do for you, Mr Scott?'

Ainsworth Martin's eyes seemed supremely confident, as if he somehow knew the future. Scott found that also annoying. He decided he would make the white-haired old bastard sit up and take notice.

120

'I'm here in my capacity as president and chairman of the board of Lockwood Limited.' He spoke the words crisply, as if announcing a royal edict.

'One of the largest companies in the world,' Martin responded quietly, as if anticipating Scott's next words.

'Exactly. And before I'm through I plan to make it *the* largest company in the world.'

Martin studied his cigar as if quite indifferent to the subject at hand. 'From what I read in the *Wall Street Journal* and the *Times*, you are moving towards that goal at a very rapid pace.'

'That's why I'm here,' Scott said. 'I want to retain your firm.'

Ainsworth Martin inhaled thoughtfully on the cigar, letting the smoke curl from his mouth when he finally spoke. 'I thought you were represented by Jannis, Markwin. That is, in addition to your company's own rather substantial army of in-house lawyers.'

Scott nodded. 'We retain Jannis, Markwin. They come in handy, especially with the Washington crowd. My own people handle most of the day-to-day legal business.'

Martin's eyes seemed almost half hooded. 'And you wish to drop Jannis, Markwin and substitute Nelson and Clark?'

Scott shook his head. 'No. I want to hire you people for a special job.'

Martin reflected no great interest as he watched the smoke swirl up towards the ceiling. 'And that is?'

Scott didn't smile, although he felt like it. What he planned to say would shock this disinterested old man into complete attention. He paused, to give his words more dramatic effect. 'I, that is, Lockwood Limited, want you to represent our company in a hostile takeover. I have decided to buy up Brown and Brown.'

Much to Scott's surprise there was no reaction at all. Martin merely looked at him, registering no discernible response.

'Brown and Brown.' Scott repeated the name irritably. 'It is the country's largest drug manufacturer.'

Martin nodded, seemingly unimpressed by the information.

'I have heard that your firm handles that type of work,' Scott said, feeling now just a trifle uncomfortable.

Martin inhaled deeply on the cigar, savoured the taste for a moment, then let a large cloud of smoke drift up above his head. 'We don't specialize in hostile takeovers, although we have handled some

121

rather large hostile acquisitions in the past. Nelson and Clark do handle mergers, but we generally prefer to represent companies who wish to join with each other.' A small smile played on his lips. 'More a matter of marriage than rape.'

'I've checked,' Scott said. 'I'm told your firm is the tops in the country. They call you the Twelve Apostles and they tell me you people have more legal clout than any other law firm going. True?'

Ainsworth Martin smiled gently. 'Our firm is very old and very respected. We are careful workmen, and we take pride in the quality of our work. I think our reputation is built upon that, rather than, say, clout.'

'Whatever. I want you people to handle this takeover.'

Martin sighed. 'I know your business reputation, Mr Scott, and it is quite outstanding. Remarkable, really. So I appreciate that you must have carefully thought out all the possible consequences of such a proposed action. But allow me to caution you as to the risks, and, of course, the costs of such an undertaking.'

'I know what I'm doing,' Scott snapped. 'This isn't the first company I've taken over.'

Martin's expression somehow seemed more thoughtful, wiser. 'But it is certainly the largest, isn't that right?'

'A hostile takeover is the same, large or small. The principle, as well as the law, is the same.'

'Unless I miss my guess, such an acquisition will cost you well over a billion dollars, perhaps much more. Is your company prepared to risk that much? It may well amount to much more than the Brown and Brown stock is worth. That happens in these hostile acquisitions, or can, as I'm sure you know.'

Scott frowned. 'Lockwood Limited is prepared and ready. We have the money necessary. And if we need more, we know where to get it. Don't worry about the costs, that's my concern, not yours. All I want to do is win.'

'Everyone wishes to win, Mr Scott. But sometimes people lose. Are you prepared for that?'

Scott's frown turned into a scowl. 'I'm not in the habit of losing, Martin,' he growled. 'Look, if you don't want the business, just say so.'

The tip glowed again as the tall lawyer puffed at the cigar. He seemed to study Scott, as if trying to make up his mind about the man.

Martin again exhaled smoke as he spoke. 'Please don't mistake me. I know and admire your business sense, but if a massive corporate battle develops, Nelson and Clark may have to put aside all other legal work and enlist most of our lawyers to help in your matter. Believe me, Mr Scott, that would be most expensive. We don't work on a contingent basis. Lockwood Limited would be billed by us as the matter progressed, monthly.'

'Christ, is that all you lawyers ever think about, your goddamned fee?'

Ainsworth Martin showed no reaction. 'Ours is a business, the same as any other, Mr Scott, the same as yours. You wish to purchase our services. I am informing you as fairly as I can that the cost will be considerable.'

'Name your price.'

Martin shook his head. 'We don't work like that here, Mr Scott. We don't set a flat fee. You will be billed according to the man hours spent. This promises to be a large undertaking, so we have to agree on an exact hourly rate.'

'What do you mean?'

'If a senior partner, what you call an Apostle, works on your matter his time will be billed at five hundred dollars per hour.'

'Five hundred?' Scott sneered. 'Who the hell do you people think you are? I'm hiring lawyers, not rock entertainers. Maybe if you had a good act and you were in Vegas you could get that kind of money, but with me . . .'

'Something we never do with our clients, Mr Scott, is haggle over fees. We tell the prospective client what our fee is, and then he can take it or leave it. But we never bargain. It is a Nelson and Clark rule.'

Scott felt anger rise within him. Any other law firm in New York would jump at the business. He wondered if Martin wasn't just putting on an act for his benefit. He felt blue-blood types were just as capable of running a scam as anyone else.

'I'm not going to pay anyone five hundred dollars an hour.'

To Scott's surprise, Martin stood up and extended his hand. 'Then I wish you luck, Mr Scott. And please don't be concerned that

123

I might divulge your plans. I'll consider our conversation as covered under the protections of the lawyer-client privilege.'

Scott did not get up or take his hand. 'That five hundred figure is just for senior partners, right? The Apostles themselves?'

Martin sat down, his expression bland and unchanging. 'Quite correct. Participating partners will bill their time at three hundred dollars an hour, and the associates at one hundred an hour. Most of the work will be done by associates, so the overall bill will reflect that hourly fee in the main. Obviously we'll bill for expenses: transportation, outside stenographers, court costs, and so on, in addition to the hourly charges.' He inhaled on the cigar, looking quite unconcerned whether Scott should agree or not. 'Be advised again that if this takeover effort results in a major legal battle, the fees could run into the millions.'

Scott just nodded. 'You get what you pay for. This will be the biggest conflict to ever hit American business. I want the very best. Given the total amount we'll have to sink into buying up Brown and Brown, a few million in legal fees is, after all, just a drop in the bucket.'

Ainsworth Martin said nothing for a moment, then he spoke, even more deliberately than he usually did. 'Mr Scott, everything depends on just how much legal work has to be done. These things can turn into wars. Intense, but usually of short duration, and costly nevertheless. You say those words – a few million dollars – as if it were merely a tip you were leaving for a waiter. Our fees may run even more than that.'

Scott's eyes narrowed. 'Are you with me or not?'

Martin leaned back in his chair. 'If you are determined to go ahead, we will be glad to assist in any legal way we can. As you say, we have some experience in these matters.'

'Battle tested.' Scott's words carried just a hint of mockery.

'Seasoned, perhaps, is the better choice,' Martin replied. 'If you wish us to represent you in this takeover, we will require a million-dollar retainer.'

'That's a bit high, isn't it, even for something like this?'

Ainsworth Martin looked at Scott. 'Not really. As I say, these things happen rather quickly, in weeks sometimes. We will bill against the retainer until it is depleted, then we shall expect a like sum to be paid to our firm's account.'

'You should have gone into business and not law. You certainly know how to get a good price.'

Martin ignored the comment. 'If you agree to those terms I'll have my secretary step in and I'll dictate a short agreement covering the work to be done and the fees to be charged for our services. Then, as soon as we receive the retainer, we will go to work.'

Scott shrugged. 'Whatever you say. I can have my company's cheque over here this afternoon.'

Ainsworth Martin allowed himself a slight smile. 'That will do nicely.' He pushed the button summoning his secretary. He was good at drafting. It would be just a short memo spelling out the fee schedule and method of payment. However, as soon as Scott signed it, it would be just as binding as the longest and most complicated contract.

In Ainsworth Martin's opinion, John Norman Scott hadn't put up much of a fight over the fee of retainer. But, then Martin reminded himself, Scott was dealing with a real expert.

If all went well, Nelson and Clark could afford to hire a small army of associates, not only for this matter, as Martin figured it, but for all the work it might bring in.

A victory, especially a big public victory, always increased the firm's business.

Ainsworth Martin smiled benignly at John Norman Scott.

Michael Collins climbed the circular stairs to the sacred precincts of the main partners. He could have taken the elevator but he knew Francis X. Desmond was in hurry for the law citations he had found in the firm's library and the stairs were quicker.

Collins almost collided with the fast-moving John Norman Scott as he came out of Ainsworth Martin's office. The little man's pace was nearer a run than a walk. Collins jumped aside as Scott hurried by him.

Collins instantly recognized him. John Norman Scott's face had decorated the covers of the country's news magazines, and his photo was seen frequently in the pages of the *New York Times*.

Scott, according to the articles, was a millionaire, running a company worth billions. They called him the Napoleon of Wall Street. Collins was impressed. It was like seeing a movie star up close. And the small man seemed to give off an air of command, a certain intensity of purpose.

There were no clients like John Norman Scott in his father's law practice. An occasional bank embezzler or a dope dealer was as close as his father ever got to clients with money. Mostly, he was the attorney for people who wore worn clothing and lived in the farthest ring of the city's economic life. Michael Collins reflected, as he walked toward Francis Desmond's plush office, that it was much better to have wealthy clients, people who were rich and famous like John Norman Scott. There would never be a problem about being paid with clients like that.

Michael smiled to himself. He was beginning to like the rarefied air of his new silk-stockinged world.

'Sit down, Dan,' Ainsworth Martin said, smiling slightly.

Dan Spencer eased himself down into the big leather chair. Ainsworth Martin, the firm's managing partner, smiled infrequently; it was an expression that apparently didn't come easily to him, at least not at the office. When he did smile it usually meant something significant was about to happen. It could be good or bad, Ainsworth's cryptic smile seemed to cover all eventualities.

'You're head of litigation now,' Martin said, lighting a cigar.

Everyone had presumed that Dan Spencer would be selected. He was the natural choice, but nothing had been said. Spencer's elation was tempered with a tinge of wariness. Martin usually wasn't so direct. Spencer guessed Martin had something additional on his mind.

'I'll try to do a good job, Ainsworth.' Spencer had been awarded the honour of calling the managing partner by his first name for almost a year. It was considered a good sign that Dan was being seriously considered for main partner. Very few lawyers in Nelson and Clark enjoyed that privilege.

'Hmmm,' Martin mumbled as he puffed the cigar into life, sending up billows of smoke. 'You always do a good job, Dan. Dependable, that's the word for you.'

'I don't know if that's entirely a compliment, Ainsworth. Dependable sort of implies a lack of imagination, a hardworking drudge.'

'If there's a choice between, say, brilliance and dependability, I'll take dependable any day. I've seen brilliance. It's usually a transient condition, inspired by some lucky happening. Brilliance is more a temporary public relations thing than lasting reality. When I say dependable, believe me, it is one of the highest compliments I can pay a brother lawyer.'

Spencer watched the smile fade from Martin's face. Spencer felt a sense of relief. He was more accustomed to the sombre, sometimes menacing face looking at him from across the desk.

'You've worked on some of our mergers, as I recall.' Ainsworth Martin made it more of a statement than a question.

Spencer nodded. 'I've had very little contact in the friendly mergers, except for defending the occasional lawsuit by some outraged stockholder. But I have worked on every one of the hostile takeovers we've had, at least since I've been with the firm. God knows, there's plenty of red-hot litigation work to be done then.'

Ainsworth Martin nodded silent agreement. 'Let me tell you what we are about to undertake. It concerns you and your department.'

Spencer waited for Martin to explain. He knew it wasn't just accidental that he had been made head of litigation. He sensed he was about to pay his dues.

'You are, I presume, acquainted with Lockwood Limited?'

Spencer shrugged. 'Who isn't? I think it owns half the companies in America.'

Martin's face became even more masklike. 'Are you acquainted with Lockwood's head man, John Norman Scott?'

'I don't know him personally. However, I've read those magazine articles about him. Quite a character, if those articles are correct.'

Martin took the cigar from his mouth. 'Let me assure you, based on my observation, that they are most accurate.'

'So?'

'Mr Scott was in to see me this afternoon. His company has become a client of the firm.'

Spencer whistled. 'That's a really big account, Ainsworth. Congratulations.'

Martin tapped the cigar on the rim of a large ceramic ashtray. 'We didn't pick up the account, not as such. He has retained us for a special job.'

'And that is?'

Martin pursed his lips before replying. He continued to tap the cigar. 'He wants to acquire Brown and Brown.'

'The chemical company?'

'Yes. The largest chemical manufacturer in the world, as a matter of fact. Or so he tells me.'

'Friendly takeover?'

Martin shook his head. 'Unfortunately, no.' He sucked on the cigar but it had gone out. 'Scott has made no formal moves toward buying the company, but he anticipates they will resist.'

'And he wants Nelson and Clark to handle the takeover.'

Martin looked at the dead cigar as if it were traitorous. 'Exactly. They call him the Napoleon of Wall Street, and I think he quite possibly merits the title. He is going after the chemical company like the original Napoleon did Austria. He wants war.'

'Perhaps they insulted him. These fellows can be quite touchy.'

Martin quickly shook his head. 'No, I think not. I didn't detect anything personal in his attitude. He has something in mind, but it doesn't sound like revenge. He is determined to seize the chemical company and crush its officers, but I think he means it to be an example for others, to frighten anyone who might be so bold as to oppose him in the future.'

'So what do we do?'

'I suggested to Mr Scott that we would need several weeks to prepare for the flurry of lawsuits, both ours and theirs. Scott seemed to be a most impatient man. Of course he's been through a number of these takeovers before, so he knows the steps and is anxious to proceed. Perhaps too anxious. I worry that he might tip our hand before we're ready.'

Spencer's expression matched his puzzlement. 'If he's done this before, and successfully, why does he need us? Why doesn't he use his usual law firm? It seems strange that he would suddenly want a new bunch of boys to do his dirty work.'

Martin relit the cigar. 'I thought of that too, of course. And I put it to him directly.'

'And?'

Martin watched the smoke twist upward. 'This will be the largest takeover he has ever attempted. In fact, based on the amount of dollars, this may turn out to be the largest takeover in history. He said he wants the very best.'

'And you believed him?'

'That we are the best? Of course. I consider that given. Of course we don't specialize in takeovers the way some firms do. However, we do them, and I believe Mr Scott wants to purchase his firm's, ah, reputation with the courts. Scott called it clout. And apparently he is quite willing to pay a pretty price for that honour and privilege.' He inhaled on the cigar. 'We will make millions on the takeover, win or lose. No matter what happens the firm will do quite nicely. However, if we win, and if it's an impressive win, we just might pick up all the legal business of Lockwood Limited, and that would be a very tasty plum indeed.'

Spencer experienced a sinking feeling. Obviously it would all be up to him.

Martin seemed to have read his mind. 'I'm sure you're aware of the procedure in selecting a main partner. Frank Johnson's tragic death leaves a spot open. The partners have a committee looking into several aspects of the selection. It will take some time, but not long. Of course, the takeover, by law, will take only a very short time once the legal action starts. Your chances of being selected for main partner will be greatly enhanced if Nelson and Clark is able to pick up the Lockwood legal business because of your efforts. I hate to put such a burden upon you, Dan, but it is a fact of life.'

'Grim reality. If I win, and Scott is pleased, I become a full partner. What if I lose?'

Martin's ghost of a smile flickered across his lips. 'You know the firm's abhorrence of defeat, Dan. I can't say it would cost you the partnership, but it certainly wouldn't do you any good.'

'Ainsworth, aren't you being a bit like the Spartan mother? Aren't you basically telling me to come back with my shield or on it?'

'Rather dramatically put, isn't it? Although I suspect that's very close to the reality of the situation, to be frank. However, I have absolute trust and confidence in you, Dan. I'm sure you'll carry this off with flying colours.'

'Considering what's at stake for me, obviously I'll do my very best. Which I think was in your mind all along.' Spencer looked for some reaction from Martin but found none. 'Now to business. This will probably turn into an enormous legal fight, Ainsworth. What kind of support can I expect from the firm?'

'You'll get top priority. However, it will be quietly done. Until we spring this trap the whole matter must be conducted in absolute secrecy. If even a hint of this gets out, Brown and Brown may escape the trap we eventually set.'

'Full priority is a nice phrase, Ainsworth, but let's discuss a few details, okay? If landing a huge account like Lockwood's, to say nothing of my becoming full partner, is dependent upon winning, then we better damn well leave nothing to chance. I will need lawyers, stenos, money, and space to do this job.'

Martin's smile again vanished. 'You see, Dan, I was right. Dependable is a word that suits you very well.' He pointed with his cigar. 'I want you to form a team. Use Andy Perkins and a few of your top men as a nucleus. I would suggest both Rowe and Chasen. They are rather outstanding trial men in my opinion.'

'I agree.'

'But keep the team small to begin with. Mainly, at this point, you'll be concerned with planning strategy and tactics. We can assign an army of drones to get out the paperwork when the time comes. But I want this whole takeover mapped out right down to the last detail. Allow no margin for error.'

He paused. 'Oh, if you don't mind, I'll assign young Michael Collins to your team, at least temporarily. Do you know him?'

'I'm not sure that I do. Is he that new kid, the one who looks like a muscular John Kennedy?'

'Yes, that's him. He's from Notre Dame. His father, I understand, is a rather flamboyant criminal lawyer, but I'm impressed with the son. In addition to that, his presence may come in handy if you come up before any Irish judges. I think young Mr Collins may eventually become one of the firm's rising stars.'

'Brilliant?' Spencer asked, smiling.

Martin didn't smile. 'Dependable.'

'Then how can I refuse?'

'Dan, at the risk of repeating myself, remember this whole matter must be kept entirely secret. I know this may sound like something out of a television melodrama, but I would suggest that you use a code name for our little operation and for the names of the principals. No memos or letters should ever refer to either Lockwood, Scott, or Brown and Brown by name, even in-house memos. We can't risk a leak at this point.'

Spencer was tired. He had spent a full day in court and now he would have to spend the evening organizing for a job that would either make him a full partner or end his career at Nelson and Clark. 'We'll run it like a military operation,' Spencer replied. 'Everything will be on a need-to-know basis.'

Spencer continued. 'Perhaps it might be wise if we rented an office in another building. If our little team is seen working together here it could cause talk, and worse, speculation.'

Martin shrugged. 'Do what you have to do. You have an absolutley open cheque book on this one. Whatever you need, get. Just keep an accurate record. We'll bill Lockwood.'

'Anything else?'

Ainsworth Martin paused for a moment. 'The need for secrecy is paramount, Dan. Please inform the members of your team that this matter, or any part of it, can't be discussed with their spouses. If Brown and Brown gets wind of what's happening they'll have time to throw up their defences.' The little smile returned. 'That secrecy rules goes for their sweethearts too.'

'I'll tell them.'

'One more thing, Dan. This John Norman Scott is a self-made man. You know the kind, all bustle, self-importance, and filled with a sense of curious omnipotence. I warned him that we would need weeks to prepare, but I sense that he's very much like a high-strung racehorse, and we may have a hard time holding him in the gate before the race. Given that circumstance, I can't guarantee you any time, so be guided accordingly.'

'We'll work around the clock if we have to.' Spencer stood up. 'Don't worry, we'll help Scott gobble up Brown and Brown like it was a Christmas turkey.'

'Let us fondly hope so. Good luck, Dan.'

As Spencer left the office, Ainsworth Martin once again lit the cigar. The word 'dependable' seemed to echo in his mind. But he wondered if being dependable would be good enough. Perhaps, before they were done, they might really need a touch of brilliance in this explosive situation.

'We'll see,' he said to himself as he watched the cigar smoke being drawn up towards the ceiling fan.

11

'Well, my dear, I was beginning to wonder if you were ever coming home.'

Christina Giles was startled. Her husband was out of sight, his sarcastic voice coming from the darkened living room.

'I had to work late. I'm due to fly to London tomorrow.' She didn't know why she felt so defensive. After all, it really was work. 'I'm closing a big corporate financing arrangement there. The paperwork is enormous.'

She walked into their large living room. He had opened the drapes, and the skyline of the city of New York cast its usual spell. She had always found the view dazzling at night when the buildings sparkled like Christmas trees. The sky was now a deepening purple. It was a magic time of night.

Half visible in the reflected light of the city, Hank Giles was in his lounging robe, an imitation Arab cloak she had bought for him for a past birthday. As always, it was becoming to his long figure. His bare legs were crossed on top of the coffee table. His hair, towelled dry, had been carefully combed. She detected the faint scent of his aftershave lotion.

'Have a drink,' he said lazily. 'I made a pitcher of vodka gibsons, very dry, just the way you like them.' He sat up and slid an empty glass across the table top towards her.

'Maybe later,' she said. 'I really have to get packed. This trip came up so suddenly I haven't had time to prepare. The banks at the last minute decided on a London closing.'

In the shadows his smile was only half seen. 'Com'on, Chris, let's take a few minutes to be together. Surely you can afford that? We really have some serious things to discuss.'

'Is anything wrong?' Suddenly she thought of little Hank. Perhaps something had happened at school.

'God, you're getting paranoid. Nothing's wrong. I just want to talk to you, husband to wife. We haven't done that in a while.' His voice had a low timbre, a sexual quality. His words were spoken with care, a sure sign he had had too much to drink.

She was annoyed. Although he kept the robe tightly wrapped

around his midsection, it was obvious he wanted to make love. The tone of his voice was unmistakable. When they were first married, that whispering timbre had always thrilled her. But that had faded as his infidelities increased. At least he wasn't displaying himself as he usually did. Once, long ago, that always aroused her, but now it seemed crude and irritating, like seeing some old man in a bus station exposing himself. The thrill was definitely gone. At least he had finally learned to cover himself.

'Chris, just one drink. I'm not going to bite you. Please.'

She sighed, took off her jacket, and sat down opposite him, avoiding joining him on the sofa. With a flourish he filled the large cocktail glass and handed it to her.

She sipped. It was almost straight vodka, the smooth Russian kind that he knew she liked. He obviously had something in mind.

'You know, you still have wonderful legs.'

'There isn't much light to see by.'

He laughed. 'I've been in here awhile. Your eyes will adjust. There's plenty of light from the city. I can see you quite well. You know, Christina, you're one of those rare women who improve with age.'

She sipped the drink again. It tasted good and she did feel the need to relax. Lately his company, even in the rare instances when they were together, made her nervous. She realized she was drinking a bit too fast.

'I've been thinking,' he said, looking out at the city. 'We really have allowed ourselves to drift apart. It's been mostly my fault, I'll admit that. But we really had something great once. I think we can find it again if we really try.'

Despite herself Christina felt a stirring of the old regard she had had for this handsome man. If he really meant to change, perhaps there was a chance for them. She suddenly realized she had not closed her heart to him entirely.

'The other evening you were gone all night,' he said quietly. There didn't seem to be any challenge in his tone.

'I stayed with a friend, a girlfriend,' she lied. 'Things got hectic at the office and I decided to get what really amounted to only a short nap.' She felt guilty in having to tell a lie; the words left a bad taste as she spoke them.

'Hey,' he said, laughing. 'I'm not accusing you of anything. God

133

knows I'm in no position to throw stones. But you being out like that did cause me to do some heavy thinking about our situation.'

'And?'

He drained his glass, leaned over and filled both glasses from the pitcher. He leaned back, pulled the robe tight about him, and sipped his drink. 'Chris, I think we'll have to change the way we live or our marriage is headed for the rocks.'

'I know,' she replied.

'You're a lawyer, perhaps you should be the one saying this. I just cut up people for a living. But despite that, I think if we both made a real effort, especially me, we could make this thing work again.'

'I don't know, Hank. I really don't think you can change, do you?'

'In what way?'

She took a healthy gulp of her drink. She fully realized that this conversation could easily end up in an ugly, bitter argument if she chose the wrong words or took the wrong tack.

'Hank, I may have failed you as a wife. Perhaps I did. But I cannot tolerate sharing you with other women.'

'I can understand that,' he said softly.

'I know you can, you're an intelligent man. But, unfortunately, I think something in you needs other women. Whether it's the male ego or whether I just haven't measured up – whatever it is – I don't think you can resist the normal temptations you doctors seem to be subject to.'

'Well, I don't know about that.'

'Please,' she said softly. 'You know what I'm talking about. There's always some nurse around, whether at the office or the hospital, who is available and has eyes for any handsome doctor. And then you have the lady patients, and even the wives of your male patients. I know about these things.' She laughed, surprising herself. 'I've seen them, and doctors' wives have been known to compare notes. It's common knowledge. There are temptations aplenty in your world, Hank, and I don't know if you can withstand them. And I'm not saying that in any mean or vindictive way, believe me.'

He took a long drink, then chuckled. 'You're right, of course. I'd be a fool to deny it. There is something in the female's psychological makeup, at least some females, that seems to make doctors irresistibly attractive.'

'I know. I used to suffer from that disease myself, at least where you were concerned.'

He reached over and gently patted her knee. 'Maybe we can see you catch the bug again, eh? It wouldn't be too difficult, Chris. We were deeply in love once. I think there might be enough of the old spark left to restart the fire.'

'Maybe.' She finished her second drink. He casually refilled her glass.

She giggled. 'Hank, are you trying to get me drunk?'

He didn't laugh. 'Just relaxed. I really want to save our marriage, Chris. And I think we can, together. If there were no more late nights or overnights at the hospital, I think that would cure a lot of the problems. I really didn't realize how devastating that was until you were gone all night long. I felt, well, betrayed. And hurt.'

She sipped the drink, feeling slightly dizzy. 'Do you know how many nights I have felt like that, Hank? Over the years, can you imagine how it has been for me? Finally I just stopped caring. It hurt too much.'

He again reached over. She half hoped he would embrace her, but he merely patted her hand, very gently. 'That's all in the past, Chris. I've done some deep thinking about this and I believe if we put all that behind us, we can start again. I'm willing if you are.'

She felt almost giddy. 'And what happens, honestly now, when some young blonde RN starts making eyes at her great hero? Hank, good intentions are one thing, but I wonder what might actually happen.'

'I said that sort of thing was over.'

She studied the city lights. The night sky was turning a clear dark blue and now stars were blinking about New York. 'I can't allow myself to be hurt again, Hank. I have managed to build up some defences. It keeps me sane. I've built a life apart from you. If I open myself up to you and something happens' – she stopped: even the thought held terror for her – 'I think I'd actually die.'

He nodded, his profile catching the light from the window. He was right, her eyes had adjusted to the gloom and she could see quite well with the help of the outside illumination.

'I know it must be a tough thing to put your trust in someone who has hurt you, and hurt you repeatedly, Chris, but I think it's worth the risk. I'm not saying that I'll merely try – we've been through that before. This time I promise you I will do it. You have to admit that's different.'

She tasted the drink and nodded. 'Yes.'

'Well?'

She thought for a moment. He had been drinking, but his words made sense. Perhaps there might be a possible redemption of their sad and empty lives. 'It would take time, Hank. After all I've been through, I just can't abandon my defences. Trust doesn't come overnight. It's a slow thing, usually, built on successful experience.'

He nodded, then looked at her. His face caught the light and he looked even more handsome in the shadow than in full illumination. A slow, boyish smile spread across his features. 'We have nothing but time, lady. I'm not going anywhere. I think I can prove to you that I love you. I can win your trust, Chris. At least I'll try damn hard.'

She finished the drink. She had taken too much too fast, and on an empty stomach. She knew she was getting tipsy. She experienced a wild, almost irresponsible feeling. 'This is all happening very fast, Hank. I'm surprised, frankly. I really didn't think you valued the marriage at all. But if you are honestly serious, I'm willing to take a chance.'

He was a graceful man and he stood up easily. 'Christina' – his voice was just above a whisper – 'I love you.'

The robe fell as he moved towards her. He was fully erect. Her eyes had adjusted to the light and his groin area seemed to be stained or marked.

He reached for her, but she pulled away.

'What is that? On your legs?'

He quickly pulled the robe around him. His easy smile flickered into a half-embarrassed expression. 'Just a rash. I get it from time to time. An allergy, I think.' He again reached down to give her a kiss, but she moved away and flicked on the lamp next to her chair.

Both of them blinked in the sudden burst of light.

'Hey, you'll ruin the romantic mood!' Although he laughed, his words carried a hint of irritation, even anger.

Without asking permission she pulled at his robe. He was losing the erection. In the harsh light she saw his thighs, lower abdomen, and penis were speckled with small ugly sores.

Horrified, she stood up and backed away. 'What the hell do you have? That's no rash!'

He stood there awkwardly, then he once more drew the robe around him. 'Just an allergic reaction. Probably something in the laundry soap.'

Her stomach churned within. She felt as if she might vomit. '*Damn you*,' she snarled. '*You have herpes!*'

The boyish grin again emerged, but this time it was almost a sneer. 'So it's herpes, so what? Practically everybody has it nowadays. It's fashionable.'

She stepped back, revolted, as if he were a leper. She felt herself shaking with rage. 'You were going to give it to me, weren't you? You were going to get me drunk, make love to me, and infect me with that hideous disease.'

He walked back to the sofa and flopped down. 'So what? You've probably been fucking half the men in that law firm of yours, or blowing them. Don't kid me. You don't fool me a bit, Christina. All I wanted was a little fuck, that's all.'

She had never felt the desire to kill before, and she was suddenly glad she didn't have access to a gun. The man sitting on the sofa was a monster, a monster who had tried to do a terrible thing to her. She wanted to destroy him.

'I can understand why you'd need a "little fuck", Hank.' She spat out the words. 'No nurse, no normal woman, would have anything to do with you in that condition. I imagine that little rash has put a big crimp in your sex life, hasn't it? I know hospitals and I know news there travels fast. Everybody knows by now that the handsome Dr Hank Giles has an active case of herpes. So you were desperate – you had no one left but me.'

'You're my wife,' he said petulantly.

'Oh yeah, your wife – only you don't give a damn about me. You even talked about rebuilding our marriage, you rotten . . .'

He poured himself another drink. 'You're over-reacting.'

His patronizing tone was like a sharp slap in the face. Suddenly the rage left her, replaced with a cold and ferocious determination.

'This is truly the last straw, Hank. It may sound trite, but this time you have really broken the camel's back. I'm moving out of here tonight!'

'Suit yourself.'

'I'll file for divorce as soon as I return from London.'

'Big fucking deal.' He turned and looked directly at her, smiling once more. 'Is that some kind of threat? Shit, I've already checked it out with some lawyers I know. You make damn near as much as I do. You've got a career. I may be on the hook for Little Hank's support, but outside of that, you won't get a nickel out of me.'

'I wouldn't want anything you've ever touched, especially not now, you bastard.'

'All you bitches are alike. You say that now, that you don't care about money, but soon that little cash register mind of yours will start ringing. Well, you're out of luck. Hell, all we own is a small amount of stock and this apartment. We'll probably have to split that down the middle. You've got your own bank account and I've got mine. Whether you care or not, you still won't get much.'

'I want custody of Little Hank,' she snapped.

'You've got it, baby. Shit, that kid is an emotional cripple anyway. I don't need some whining teenager hanging around me. You've got him, lock, stock, and barrel. I realize I'll probably have to pay for his education even if it won't do that little pimple a bit of good.'

'You're about as good a father as you are a husband.' She turned and strode out of the room.

'You always were a lousy piece of ass, Chris,' he called after her. 'Thank God you're a lawyer – you couldn't make it as a whore.' He ended his words with a drunken giggle.

She made it to the bathroom just as her stomach gave a final lurch. After she lost the liquor she felt better, although she realized she was still a little woozy. Although she hadn't touched him, she had accepted the glass he had prepared, and she washed very carefully. She knew washing wouldn't do any good, not if she had been infected, which was unlikely. Still, Christina used mouthwash to gargle. She washed her face in cold water, then looked up at her reflection in the mirror. She had never looked so terrible.

Hank was drunk and it was a risk to spend any more time in the apartment. There was a possibility he could turn violent and try to rape her. She had always felt there was a deep streak of cruelty in him, carefully hidden, but there, nevertheless.

She took no time to put on makeup. Grabbing her purse, she

headed out of the apartment. There was no time to try to pack for London. She would buy what she needed new, either in New York or London. She was determined never to return to the apartment. In her mind it had become a pesthole, a leprosarium. Her husband, she decided, did have a form of leprosy – not of the body; that was herpes. But he did have a terrible wasting disease deep in his very soul.

She shuddered when she remembered she had almost let him make love to her.

Christina Giles got a taxi right away.

The hotel desk clerk, seeing her stark face and noticing she had no luggage, was reluctant to give her a room at the busy St Regis, but her credit cards and bar association identification allayed whatever fears he had.

It was a nice room. She took a quick shower. She had no desire to eat. She telephoned for an early wake up call to allow time for shopping before catching the plane for England.

Lonely and depressed, she cried into her pillow, muffling the sound of her sobs. Her mind raced with fleeting haunting images, a thousand painful memories of her life with her husband. No matter how she tried, she could think of nothing else. She did not fall asleep until only a few minutes before the desk rang her room and wished her a cheery good morning.

Dan Spencer had arranged a meeting of the lawyers who would form the embryo of his team for two o'clock. He was about to leave but took a few minutes to review the overall plan for the takeover. It was very much like a chess game. Everyone knew the moves; it was really a question of when to make them. But paramount to the planning was the ability to make those moves quickly and effectively, to be able to score without being destroyed.

The Brown and Brown lawyers, whoever they might turn out to be, would probably be experts at defending against hostile take-overs. He had to assume they would launch a variety of lawsuits, both state and federal, and try to throw up a protective screen. The Nelson and Clark team would have to be ready with pre-typed prepared answers – answers which would anticipate every possible allegation in the coming attacks. They would have to work around the clock, and they couldn't afford the luxury of any wasted motion.

Spencer was the general, and he had to anticipate everything and plan for each eventuality down to the last comma.

He was startled by the soft knocking on his office door. Usually his secretary telephoned if he had visitors or if she wanted to see him. The closed door meant he was working.

'Yes?'

The door opened and Abner Slocum stuck his head in. 'Can I have a word with you, Dan? It will only take a minute.'

Abner, like the other Apostles, could command anyone in the field at any time; it was an unwritten rule. Although Dan desperately wanted time to prepare for his meeting, he knew he had to give some time to Slocum.

'Please come in, Abner.'

'If I've come at a bad moment, I can always . . .' He didn't finish the statement. He didn't have to. It was only a show of politeness. Slocum was clearly invoking his right as a main partner.

'No problem, Abner. Do sit down.'

Slocum eased his thin form into the chair facing Spencer's desk. His ancient skin creased into a friendly smile. 'You may be moving out of here and up into God's country,' he said, his tone matter-of-fact.

'You mean into Frank Johnson's vacancy, of course?'

'I trust you'd like to join us on the floor above?' Slocum laughed.

Spencer leaned back and smiled. 'It had entered my mind.'

Slocum nodded. 'I would think it would.' He glanced around the room. 'When I became a main partner, I could think of no greater ambition. It was the biggest thing in my life. It still is.'

'It's an honour, not to mention the additional income.'

Slocum's face grew serious. 'It's more than money, or just an honour, Dan. It's a bit like entering the priesthood. Among lawyers, the ones who really count, being a main partner in Nelson and Clark is something like becoming a cardinal, or perhaps more realistically, one of twelve popes.'

Although Spencer thought Abner Slocum overstated Apostle status, he had to agree that it was the pinnacle of the legal profession.

'As you may know, Dan, I'm the oldest Apostle.'

'Young in heart, though.'

Slocum smiled wryly. 'That's one way of looking at it. You know the rule of the firm – they turn you out at age seventy. I've only a few short months to go.'

'Well, Abner, there are worse fates. You'll be making a fortune for doing nothing, and you'll have all the time in the world to indulge your interests and hobbies. Not so bad, really.'

'Do you know what my hobby is, Dan?'

Spencer shook his head.

'The law, pure and simple.'

'Then you don't want the retirement, obviously.'

Slocum nodded. 'Oh, I suppose I could always find other things to do. A man like myself can always become active in the bar association, get myself named to this committee or that. Perhaps I could sit on the board of some poverty-law agency, rubbing shoulders with people I have avoided all my life. That is hardly the law I know and practise, Dan. My specialty is counselling businesses, conducting company offices and directors through the maze that constitutes the American legal system today. And I'm good at what I do. If I retire, or even quit so I can practise, I would never be able to attain anything equal to the rank of a Nelson and Clark main partner, nor would I be able to attract the type of business client represented by this firm.'

'What alternatives do you have, then?'

'You want to become an Apostle, correct?'

Spencer nodded.

'And I wish to stay on as an Apostle. That's all I want, understand?'

'So?'

'Dan, I like you. You're a hell of a good lawyer, and now you're head of the Litigation Department. In ordinary times I would vote for you without thinking twice.'

'And these aren't ordinary times?'

Slocum smirked. 'Not for me they aren't. I'm fighting for my very life here, Dan. That's what being an Apostle means to me. And I am prepared to do whatever I must do to stay on.'

'Abner, I know you've sounded out some others in the firm, possible candidates as to how they might vote to amend the mandatory retirement rule, if named a main partner. I take it you will only support someone who promises to vote your way?'

Slocum nodded. 'I like you, Dan. You come right to the point. And that is precisely the point. If you vote for me, for what I want, I'll vote to have you named Apostle.'

'Tit for tat.'

'Precisely.'

'Do you propose a gentleman's agreement, or something more formal? That is, if I accept.'

Slocum held up his thin hands. 'I know you, Dan. If you give your word, you'll be bound by it. I think you can say the same for me.'

Spencer realized he was being edged into dangerous territory. He had to be very careful about what he said. 'I take it the Apostles must be split on the retirement issue. Otherwise you wouldn't be hustling after one measly vote. Right?'

Slocum seemed almost to slump as he spoke, his low voice reflecting his desperation. 'There are a number of older partners who actually look forward to leaving all this. They want their rights protected. They are as anxious to see the rule preserved as I am to see it abolished. The question is heating up into a very big issue in the firm.'

'Now, if I promise to support you, Abner, but you don't have enough votes, what happens to me then?'

'I'll still vote for you. I would be committed. You must know that.'

'But what about the other side? I doubt if they would want to vote in someone who has pledged to cut their throats. If you can't swing this retirement thing, Abner, the other side will prevail. They won't want to elect any candidate of yours. It would be self-defeating.'

Slocum's eyes narrowed. 'Are you saying you want to see who will be the ultimate winner before committing yourself? I suppose there's some wisdom to doing that. However, if you should choose wrong . . .'

Dan Spencer laughed. 'Com'on, Abner. You know me better than that. Let's be frank. You're not about to cut your throat for me, and I'm in the same boat. I may end up voting to change the rule. I haven't studied it. Since Frank's death I haven't had a minute for myself, let alone office politics. Abner, the only promise I can make at this time is to consider the problem. When the time comes I won't fence-straddle. And I won't say one thing and do another – you know me better than that. I'm not cut from that kind of cloth. I'll tell you where I stand on the rule issue after I've studied it, and before there's a vote for the vacancy. That's fair, isn't it?'

'Fair, but perhaps not too smart, Dan. I may have another candidate by that time. I too won't go back on a commitment. If I were you, I'd get aboard now. But of course I'm speaking from a position of self-interest.'

'I understand, Abner.'

Slocum stood up. If he was feeling any strong emotion, he didn't show it. He smiled the thin, wan smile that was so typical of him. 'Let's hope all this works out well, Dan. It could end up getting pretty rough. Keep my words in mind.'

'I will, Abner.'

Slocum left, shutting the door behind him.

Dan Spencer sat motionless for a moment. He had expected the proposition from Slocum, but not the threat.

Spencer wondered if Slocum's vote was really that important. A big win in the takeover effort would mean he wouldn't need Slocum's vote. A loss would mean he was out, no matter how Abner might vote. Still, even with those circumstances, Abner Slocum's vote could cost him the main partnership.

'Mrs Giles, you look like a lady who could use a nice Bloody Mary before dinner.' The young flight attendant grinned down at her. He was a handsome young man with coffee-cream skin. He had braced his hip against the seat in front of her, his posture an advertisement for his masculinity. He had the lithe build of an athlete, and his manners were impeccable except for a veiled challenge just below the level of his civility.

She looked up from the papers spread on top of the briefcase in her lap. 'Tony' – his uniform jacket displayed a prominent nametag – 'I never drink when I'm working. But maybe a diet soda if you have it.'

His smile widened as he looked her over. 'You don't have to watch your figure, Mrs Giles.'

'I'll still stick with the diet soda.'

After setting down a Diet Coke with a wedge of lime in the glass, Tony moved across the aisle to talk to an elderly woman, who, despite glasses perched on the end of her nose, held a magazine out almost at arm's length.

Christina was amused, and a shade disappointed, as she heard Tony use almost the same patter on the lady across the aisle. The woman ordered a double vodka.

Christina always found people interesting, and she stole a closer look at her fellow passenger. Although time had had its ravaging way with the woman's skin and figure, her high, delicate facial bones echoed the memory of a past beauty. She looked intelligent, and Christina idly wondered if a number of lovers could have been enthralled by the lady. Perhaps even husbands. Christina was tempted to start up a conversation despite her usual distaste for talking with strangers. She wondered if the woman might have a few practical tips on divorce and how to handle the devastating feelings boiling around the breakup of a marriage. But then it was mere speculation – the woman might never have had any romantic adventures, and she would consider such questions upsetting. Christina decided against speaking.

They were well out over the Atlantic, which was obscured from sight by a thick cloud cover. Above those clouds, at the plane's high altitude, the sky was a clear blue although they would soon be flying into the darkness of Europe's night.

It would be after midnight, London time, when they would touch down at Heathrow Airport. But her body clock would still be set at seven o'clock in the late afternoon. There would be no jet lag to blame this time; she was already exhausted, although all attempts to sleep on the aeroplane had failed. Her night at the St Regis had been nothing but wide awake anguish. Now, a London bed sounded very good, no matter what time it might be.

As Christina sipped her soda, she wondered if she might have problems with the British customs people. All her clothes, every piece of baggage, was brand new, purchased earlier at Bloomingdale's. She wondered if that fact alone might elicit suspicion. If she were a customs officer, she decided, she would wonder about a woman, travelling alone, who had all new clothes from the skin out, and with new luggage, all purchased the day of the flight, all from one shop. It sounded very much like the beginning of a mystery story.

To even manage to get aboard the flight on time had been almost chaos. Christina had had to make a flurry of international telephone calls to nail down some loose ends in the London closing. She had managed to break away for a few minutes to do her hurried and frantic shopping at Bloomingdale's. It was a woman's dream, really. Price didn't matter. She just picked out what she liked as she raced through the place, commanding a small army of salespeople as she put together a basic wardrobe. She wasn't pleased at the less-than-perfect fit of some of her purchases, but they would just have to do. She wanted nothing from the apartment, not even her clothes. She wanted nothing that she connected with her old life with Hank.

Somehow she had managed to call Earl Levine, an old classmate who specialized in family law. She wanted a low-profile divorce if possible. She knew she didn't dare use anyone in the firm. The less known there the better. The divorce could possibly spell the end of her chances for a main partnership at Nelson and Clark, but it had to be done. She knew that Earl Levine would keep everything low-keyed and dignified. She hoped such discreet action would appeal to the main partners, despite some of the prejudices of some of the older members. She hoped she would still have a chance.

And she had made one more personal call before leaving, a call she had to make. Young Henry had sounded resentful at being summoned away from his friends merely to talk on the telephone to his mother. But she could hear the hurt in his voice, and somehow that had caught her unprepared. She spoke a few awkward words of consolation, but his only replies were irritable grunts. She wanted to explain, to tell him the truth about his father, to cry out in anger and expose the man for what he was, but she held her tongue. He was confused enough and her words would only sound like the screechings of a vengeful woman. It was an unsatisfactory communication. She hoped perhaps in time he would realize just how much she loved him. But that was in question. She looked down at the clouds and the growing darkness. As the aeroplane sped towards Europe she felt very much alone.

12

Dan Spencer had rented a suite at the Gramercy Park Hotel for the meeting. It was comfortable and very private. He had asked the hotel to supply a full bar, something usually never done at a business meeting, especially an in-house meeting of Nelson and Clark lawyers. It was a pleasant room, looking out on the stately autumn beauty of Gramercy Park itself, tucked away, like a small emerald, among the towers of concrete and brick. Seen by few tourists, the small private park with its locked iron gates was a calm oasis in a city filled with sirens and noise.

Andy Perkins and Charley Manning, both participating partners assigned to the litigation section, arrived in a cab. They greeted Spencer when they came in. Perkins, who always seemed quite relaxed, fixed himself a light highball. Manning, who always seemed nervous, impatiently declined anything alcoholic. He paced while they waited for the others.

As though the time of arrival had been dictated by the firm's pecking order, next came two senior associates, both rising stars in the litigation department. Bruno Chasen, whose family name had been Charsanowski, but who had it legally shortened, and who had in a few short years become more waspishly Yankee than even the most blue-blooded members of the firm, walked in with regal dignity. The other associate, Jeffrey Rowe, a shorter version of Chasen, both blond and thickly built, came from a genuinely Wasp Yankee background. Yet Rowe was as breezy in manner and dress as one could be in Nelson and Clark without drawing fire. Opposites in so many ways, the two men had nevertheless become inseparable friends. And both had proved themselves excellent trial lawyers, displaying good minds and cool heads.

Jeffrey Rowe had a straight vodka over ice, while Chasen sipped daintily at a clear glass of seltzer water.

Michael Collins, the last man to arrive, came into the room at a half-run. 'Sorry to be late, Mr Spencer,' he said, looking embarrassed. 'My cab got caught in a jam on Broadway.'

'It happens,' Spencer remarked, glancing at his watch. He was anxious to begin.

Collins declined a drink. Spencer mixed a weak whiskey and water for himself. All eyes were on him as he leaned against the top of a highback chair, using it like a lectern.

'There are six of us here,' he began softly. 'Each of you has been hand-picked for a very special assignment. Now, before I begin, I want to impress on each of you the need for absolute secrecy concerning what we are about to commence.'

He made eye contact with each of them. 'Not one word of what is said here can be told to anyone, and that includes members of the firm, and even wives or girlfriends.'

Perkins laughed. 'What are we going to do, build a hydrogen bomb?'

Spencer ignored the jest. 'This assignment will take up every moment of your time. That can cause a great strain on family relationships. If anyone feels they can't keep this secret, of if they aren't prepared to give over their time from morning to night, just raise your hand and you're out.'

Manning looked troubled. There had been rumours that his wife was complaining about the time he was spending at the office. Spencer continued. 'By the way, I fully discussed this point with Ainsworth Martin. If anyone wants out at this point it won't be held against them in any way. There will be no sanctions of any kind. We really want nothing but volunteers on this project.'

He looked at each of them for a moment as though they were members of a jury. 'Well, does anybody here think he might have some problems with those conditions?'

There was no response.

'Will taking this assignment screw up anyone's personal life?' Spencer looked at Manning. 'Let me rephrase that. Is each of you prepared to put this job ahead of your personal lives and problems?'

Manning slowly raised his hand. 'Dan, how long do you expect this assignment to last?'

'At the very least, one month. Up to three months, although I doubt it would go on that long.'

Manning bit his lower lip for a moment. 'Weekends?'

'If you accept this, Charley, and this goes for the rest of you, kiss weekends goodbye. This is going to be an all-out thing.'

Charley Manning frowned as he seemed to consider the matter, then he looked up at Spencer, his expression one of determination.

'Okay.' He spoke the word slowly. 'That doesn't sound too long. You can count me in.' He thought about the awful scene his wife was sure to make about his time away from home. She was always threatening divorce. He balanced his marriage against the possible enhancement with the firm by becoming a volunteer. Eventually, some time in the future, he might have a shot at one of the top twelve jobs. The risk was well worth it.

'Anyone else?' Spencer asked. 'Everyone here except myself and Mike Collins is married. Think it over before you jump.'

'I'm in,' Perkins said, grinning. 'Hell, I'll do it just to satisfy my curiosity. It sounds immoral or illegal. I'm fascinated.'

Bruno Chasen scowled. 'Will this involve litigation?'

Spencer nodded. 'Yes. In all probability there will be one hell of a lot of fast and furious court action.'

Chasen nodded. 'All right. You know I like that, Dan. I'm in.'

Jeffrey Rowe laughed. 'It gives me a chance to get away from my old lady. Sign me aboard.'

Spencer turned to young Collins. 'This could make a monk out of you, Mike. I doubt you'd even have time for drink dates. Think it over.'

Collins shrugged. 'You must have a better sex life than I do, Mr Spencer. All it means is that I'll be passing up rejections at the singles bars for a while.'

Everyone laughed. Even Bruno Chasen managed a smile. Collins grinned at them. It wasn't true. He had a girlfriend, but it was none of their business. And he wouldn't allow that to stand in his way. He wouldn't be like his father. Michael Collins was determined to rise to the very top of the legal profession. Spencer said he had been specially selected. Perhaps he had, and if so, he might be being given a rare opportunity to climb up Nelson and Clark's golden ladder.

Spencer took a sip of his drink before continuing. 'Okay, one last call. Does anyone want to reconsider?'

It was a corny thing to do, but he waited silently for a moment. He wanted them to be impressed by the fact that they were committed to the end.

'All right,' he said slowly. 'That's it then. We've just become a brotherhood like the Mafia. I don't want to hear any whimpering about the time you are required to spend on this job. As they used to say in the Marines, you volunteered, you weren't drafted.'

Perkins stood up and mixed himself another drink, this time a bit stiffer. 'Do we have to take an oath or give a secret sign?'

Spencer and Perkins were natural rivals within the firm, about the same age, with almost the same time invested. It was a recognized fact within the firm. The others in the room realized that Perkins was establishing his standing in the small group's pecking order. As number-two man he would be subject to Spencer's leadership, but just barely. If anything went wrong, Perkins knew it was essential that it occur under Spencer's solo leadership. He wanted to escape responsibility, yet remain close enough to pick up the pieces. As second in command he felt he could pull it off. He liked Dan Spencer, and he would help him, but he had to be ready in case things did go wrong.

Spencer made a point of waiting until Perkins had finished pouring his drink before continuing. 'I'm sure you're all familiar with Lockwood Limited?'

All of them nodded, some more positively than others.

'Then you know that Lockwood Limited is one of the largest conglomerates in the world. It packs an enormous economic punch in several industries and in many of the major markets in the world. We have agreed to represent them in a small matter.'

Spencer smiled to emphasize he really meant just the opposite of small.

'John Norman Scott, the president of Lockwood, has decided he wants to go into the chemical business, and he wants to start at the top.'

'He usually does,' Manning volunteered. 'At least that's what the magazines say.'

Spencer nodded. 'He attracts publicity. He's the current boy wonder of Wall Street. And he wants us to pick up the largest chemical company in the world for him. Cheap.'

The surprise registered on their faces reflected the realization of the enormity of what they were being asked to do.

'Scott wants to acquire Brown and Brown,' Spencer said.

'A hostile takeover?' Perkins asked, no longer laughing.

'I'll come to that,' Spencer replied. He, too, wished to establish the pecking order. Until he made a major mistake, he wanted the others to know who was in command. Perkins might be number-two man, but Spencer wanted it clearly understood that Daniel Spencer would be calling all the shots. He had the responsibility if they lost; he wanted the credit if they won.

'The six of us will form the nucleus of the firm's team. Each of you will be given an area of responsibility. Later, as needed, we'll add other lawyers and clerical staff. But we constitute the starting varsity for this operation.'

Spencer paused for effect. 'We are literally dealing with billions here. I think you can see now why there is an absolute need for secrecy. The stakes are enormous. Even among ourselves I will often deal with you on a need-to-know basis. If you need to know, you'll be told. If not, don't ask questions.'

Manning was up and pacing again, his nervous anxiety finding release in quick little steps. He spoke as he walked, something he would never do in a courtroom since it was distracting. 'Dan, how can we possibly keep something this big a secret? God, as soon as the typing pool gets wind of a special operation within the firm, they'll start comparing notes. They're pretty good at that. They'll have it all figured out before we can even get off the ground.'

Spencer nodded. It was a point he too had considered. Nelson and Clark, like most large offices, was a beehive of petty gossip. 'We will open an office downtown in the Village. It will be completely outfitted: furniture, phones, word processors, everything we'll need. As far as secretarial help, I have asked for some of the senior women to be assigned, ones who can keep their mouths shut. Even so, we'll try to keep things fragmented sufficiently to conceal what's really happening. Much of the non-essential typing work can be sent out to secretarial services. If we take reasonable precautions we should be able to keep this thing under wraps until it finally explodes publicly.'

'And when will that be?' Bruno Chasen asked.

Spencer was reluctant to reveal the basic strategy, but it wouldn't make any sense to the others unless he did.

'I spent most of yesterday evening with Scott. We reviewed all aspects of the matter. He wants to open things with a proxy battle to take control of Brown and Brown that way.'

Perkins frowned. 'Those things can turn into real pissing contests. Does he honestly think he has a chance to pull it off?'

Spencer was tired of standing. He walked around the chair and sat down. 'No. Andy, as a matter of fact, he knows damn well he won't have sufficient stock proxies to win.'

'Then why do it? It tips his hand,' Perkins said. In the past, he had been assigned to proxy fights and had found them ugly and distasteful.

'Scott told me he will use it to undermine stockholder confidence in the present management at Brown and Brown. He plans to raise hell about their losses, claim that the company will be ruined under inept leadership, all the while getting front-page coverage. He plans to scare the stockholders so that they will jump at the chance to sell to him later when he goes for the actual takeover.'

'Dangerous business,' Perkins said. 'That mud can be slung both ways. Scott's liable to end up with a lot of brown stuff all over him. It could backfire – the stockholders may be turned off by his antics.'

'He knows that,' Spencer replied. 'I guess he feels the game is worth the risk. Anyway, the time spent in the proxy fight will give us some breathing room to prepare tactics and pleadings for the flurry of lawsuits they'll drop on us when Scott goes for the main target. If you boys have been neglecting your legal research, believe me, you're about to get a nice refresher course.'

Jeffrey had stretched his legs out in front of him. He played with a fresh drink. 'Dan, what do you think of this guy Scott?'

'In what way?'

Rowe shrugged. 'My old man think he's a freebooter, just a lucky guy with a MBA who happened to be in the right place at the right time. In his words, my beloved father thinks he's a lightweight.' Rowe's father was vice president of an international bank.

'Did your father say why he feels that way?'

Rowe grinned. 'My old man thinks most of Scott's deals were, well, sorty of splashy. More for the drama than for profit, if you get my drift. This Scott, my father says, is the P T Barnum of the business world. He never makes a move without having it announced by a brass band.'

'A showman,' Spencer said.

'More than that, at least according to my father. He thinks Scott is dangerous, a man who doesn't think things out carefully before he takes action. He thinks Scott takes too many risks.'

Perkins laughed. 'Like promoting the bimbo he's boffing? Have you guys been following that in the papers? It's a howl.'

Chasen looked over at Perkins. 'I've been tied up in trial. I haven't seen a newspaper lately.'

Perkins seemed to warm to the story of how Scott named Nancy Merriam as vice president at Lockwood and then gave the press an interview about the whole thing.

Spencer decided it was time to step in. 'Despite all that, Scott has an outstanding record as the man who guided Lockwood from a small company into a multinational giant. He's nobody's fool,' Spencer added. 'And, no matter what else you may think of him, he is our client, and we owe him some loyalty.'

He then went on to detail what each member of the team's specific responsibility would be.

'Mike Collins will work with me. He'll be my eyes and ears – and messenger when necessary,' he concluded.

Collins looked crestfallen. He had expected an important assignment. Now he was only the official flunky. But he also knew that a job was what one made of it. Before the battle smoke cleared he vowed he would show them he was more than just a flunky.

Finally Spencer held up his hands, palms out. 'That's it, fellows,' he laughed. 'This will be your last free evening, maybe for months. Make the most of it. Tomorrow we'll start the actual work.'

'Something like the Mafia going to the mattresses, isn't it?' Perkins laughed, but there was a hint of taunt in his tone.

'Not a bad analogy, Andy,' Spencer replied, not laughing. 'This will turn out to be a war when all is said and done. And whether we win or lose may depend on just how effectively we utilize the time remaining before the lid blows off.'

Dan Spencer waited until everyone had gone, then he took the elevator. He walked down the tree-lined street towards Third Avenue. He had a chilling foreboding about what was about to happen.

It was to be a corporate war, but like in any war, there were bound to be casualties.

'Good evening, Mr Scott.' The headwaiter's smile was practised and waxen. 'We haven't seen you for a while.'

Scott looked around the room. It was early, few people were seated. 'Henry, give me a table in the back, one where I can do a little talking without being overheard, got it?'

Henry frowned. 'Well, let me see . . .'

'How about that table back at the windows? It's away from everyone else.'

The headwaiter shrugged. 'It's quite warm back there, Mr Scott. The late-afternoon sun heats up that little alcove. The air conditioning hardly touches it. I'm afraid you wouldn't want that.'

'I like to sweat once in a while, henry,' Scott said, slipping a twenty into the man's moist palm. He hated doing that; it smacked a lack of sophistication. But, sophistication or not, it always seemed to do the trick.

'If you become uncomfortable, Mr Scott, I'll be happy to move you. Just let me know.' The fixed smile was now replaced with a conspiratorial grin. 'Follow me.'

'A young lady will be joining me, Henry.' At least Scott hoped she would.

'Miss Merriam?'

Scott felt a rush of anger. Everyone had read those damn newspapers features. 'Yes, as a matter of fact, she is.'

'I'll personally escort her to you.' He held the chair for Scott, signalled a waiter, then moved away.

Scott ordered a martini, then sat back and looked out on the restaurant's back lawn. It was a pleasant, sunny day. The headwaiter had been correct; the sun did act like a furnace, but the heat wasn't unbearable. The table was well away from the other diners, and he considered that essential.

Nancy had finally returned his phone calls and had icily agreed to meet him. He felt like a young boy, very unsure and very anxious. Scott wished the woman didn't hold such an attraction for him. Life would be so much easier. But he could think of nothing else but her, and with the coming battle, things had to get settled. He would need all his wits about him for the tasks ahead.

She came in, following a fawning Henry. She moved with the sensuous grace which had always excited him. She made the simple act of walking an almost erotic dance, without ever intending to do so.

Nancy had tied her long, light-brown hair behind her, fashioned into a businesslike bun. But rather than looking severe, it seemed to accentuate the beauty of her face. She looked soft and vulnerable.

She had dressed in a tweed suit with a catch of purple silk at her throat.

Scott noticed more than one male head turn to follow her journey across the dining room.

He stood up and extended his hand. She merely nodded and allowed Henry to help her into her chair, facing Scott across the table.

The headwaiter again signalled another waiter, then moved away.

Nancy Merriam's eyes avoided Scott's as she ordered a glass of white wine.

'You look splendid,' he said, trying to keep his excitement from being reflected in his voice.

'Thank you.'

'Really, you do. You're beautiful, but I never really remember just how beautiful you are until I see you. It's always a thrill.'

Her eyes now met his. 'You proposed a business meeting, John. I doubt if you'd talk to any of the other company officers like this.'

Although he felt like responding in anger, he nodded meekly. 'You're right, of course, Nancy. It's just that seeing you after all this time . . .'

'It's only been a few days.' Her tone was cold and without emotion.

'Seems like a year to me.'

'John, if you wish to discuss company business, I'll be happy to do so. If you want to talk about . . . well . . . personal matters, I might as well leave.'

He quickly shook his head. 'No, it will be business. I promise you.'

The waiter brought her wine, then left them alone.

'Well, what's going on that's so important?'

He had told her the company's future depended on their talk; that it was that important. Flattery and an appeal to her curiosity was the only way he felt he might lure her into the meeting with him.

He sipped his martini before continuing. 'Your office is fully furnished and waiting for you.'

'I'm not coming back. I'd look like a fool.'

He wanted to reach out and grasp her hand, but he knew that would be a tactical mistake. 'You might look like more of a fool if you didn't come back,' he said quietly. 'You know, staying away like this just gives credence to all those stories they're spreading about us.'

'Thanks to you.'

He nodded slowly. 'All right, you've got a point. I made a mistake. Like the man says, I don't often make mistakes, but when I do they are really lulus. Still, if you don't come back we'll both look worse than we do now.'

'You will, not me,' she snapped. 'You're the one who loves to see his name in the paper. You got me into this – you live with it.'

'Look . . .' He was getting angry but he controlled himself quickly when he saw the matching anger in her eyes. 'Nancy, when I promoted you to vice president I told you it wasn't because we were sleeping together. I told you then it was because of your business talent and your ability to come up with fresh and innovative ideas.'

'You told me a lot of things.'

He sipped the martini again. 'But you must admit, I did tell you that your promotion was not personal but for the good of the company, am I right?'

'That's what you told me. So what?'

'I meant it.' He cleared his throat, then continued in a low voice. 'Look, I don't mean to be crude, but you must admit I was already getting into your pants. What the hell could I have had in mind, if not business? I was already getting the milk, I didn't have to buy the cow, if you see what I mean.'

She snorted. 'Crude is a good word for you, John. I haven't the foggiest idea what you really had in mind. I told you I didn't want the job, I told you what people would say, but you ploughed right on, making damn sure the gossips would have the front pages of the country's newspapers to spread their scandal.'

Again he felt enraged. Few people talked to him like that. Few dared. But Scott could understand her anger. He felt he knew her, knew what she really wanted. Like a good cardplayer, he felt it was time to play his ace.

'Nancy, I'm not asking you to come back for my sake.'

'I'll bet.'

He signalled the waiter for another martini. Nancy had yet to touch her wine.

'Your concept for taking over Brown and Brown is under way.'

'Oh?'

'Look, you were the one who spotted their weak position. This is your baby, Nancy. I hired Nelson and Clark to act as Lockwood's counsel in the takeover.'

For the first time the guarded, resentful look left her eyes, replaced by surprise. 'You did? Really?'

'Yes. They have agreed. They'll set up a team of lawyers to handle the whole thing. They expect it to be a major corporate war.'

She nodded. 'Yes, it will be that.'

'And you're the one who thought it all up.' He took his drink from the waiter. 'This thing is all yours, Nancy. I should think you'd want to see it through to completion.'

Her anger was definitely gone now; interest seemed to sparkle from within her. 'I didn't think it up, John,' she said softly. 'I studied the company and brought my findings to you. The takeover was your idea.'

This time he reached over and gave her hand one friendly pat, then he quickly withdrew. 'Our idea,' he said quietly. 'This is the big time, Nancy. I'm going to need you. More importantly, the company needs you.'

She took a tentative sip at her wine.

'John, I don't know if I have the experience to take responsibility for such an enormous undertaking. With me, it was just a theory, but actually doing it is . . . well, something else.'

'It's in the works, Nancy. I've hired the country's number-one law firm. I have an investment banker, one of the best, helping with financing. I've got the army, but I'm short of a general. I can't trust the other company officers. You have to be in charge of this or it will all come crumbling down. Surely you can see that?'

She drank the wine, almost finishing the whole glass in one long gulp. 'If I come back, you'll actually trust me to run the whole show, the entire takeover?'

He smiled and nodded, looking at her over the edge of his glass. She was bright and she would come in handy. But there would be only one Napoleon leading the army, and that would be John Norman Scott. She was trustworthy and would be useful as a sounding board and runner. He'd let her think she was running things, at least in the beginning.

'Nancy, you're much younger than I am. You have a wonderful future ahead of you. Perhaps soon you'll be the most famous businesswoman in all of America. I wouldn't be surprised. This is your chance of a lifetime. I hope to God you don't kick it away because of a personal beef against me.'

The waiter brought her another wine, then departed quickly. Scott made a mental note to leave the man a substantial tip.

She sipped the drink, then looked directly at him. 'If I come back it will just start the stories up all over again. I don't think I could stand that. I feel like a whore.'

'When the war breaks out, when we go after Brown and Brown, it will eclipse everything else, believe me. This scandal sheet crap about you and me makes great reading in the cheap tabloids now, but you'll be on the cover of *Time* and *Newsweek* as businesswoman of the decade before this is all over. Nancy, this is where it's at – this is your line of departure. If you have the right stuff you'll shrug off all this and show them what you're really made of. Don't let this slip by.' He paused for effect. 'It's important to both of us.'

She nodded. 'Do you really think this will take people's minds off . . . us?'

'I guarantee it.'

'What has your wife got to say about all this?'

'I don't talk to her, you know that. She lives in Florida, and her lawyer talks to my lawyer. That's our only communication. Since all the flap in the newspapers, her lawyer can sense the jugular, so he's upped her money demands. It's a crock, of course, but it'll delay the divorce for a while until my attorney can bring her man to reason. If we show real power in the takeover, maybe it will scare the bitch and she'll cave in. You never know.'

'If I come back, we can't live together, not until all this is over.'

'Does that mean I can't see you?'

She thought for a moment, then hesitantly shook her head. 'No, I suppose not, not as long as we're discreet. But we'll have to be careful. They'll be watching us; the people at the office, the newspapers – everybody.'

He took her hand now and held it. 'Look, honey, we'll be as discreet as can be. It'll be all right, you'll see.'

'I can't come to your apartment any more,' she said, almost in a whisper.

He could see where this was going. 'Of course you can't. And I can't come to yours. We'll meet in hotels or motels, places really out of the way. Trust me, everything will be handled very prudently.'

She smiled, finally, and squeezed his hand. 'I trust you, John,' she said. 'And I'm excited. I can't wait to start.'

He relaxed. 'Nancy, would I be pushing my luck if I invited you to a small motel just a few miles from here? It's a tiny place, really out of the way. If I'm pushing, just say the word.'

She hesitated, then spoke. 'Well, I suppose if it's really out of the way . . .'

'Good. Let's just take a few minutes to finish our drinks. You see, I'm a changed man already. None of the old charging rush any more. Okay?'

She nodded.

He damn well wanted to run to that motel. He was as horny as he could ever remember. He was taking his time not because of any new approach to their love life, but to allow time for his intense erection to subside. It wouldn't do for him to try to walk across the crowded dining room now.

He smiled at her.

The wait would be worth it.

The main offices of Brown and Brown looked more like the setting for a dismal Dickens' boys' school than the headquarters of the world's largest chemical company. Red brick buildings, all constructed at the turn of the century, formed an almost fortlike square. In the early days, a railroad spur had run into the centre of the square. But all that belonged to a different era. Behind the ancient structures, glistening modern chemical plants had been constructed, complete with giant metal holding tanks spanning a distance of almost a mile. And it was just the tip of the iceberg. All over the country and in many parts of the industrial world, similar Brown and Brown complexes worked at producing a complete line of industrial chemicals and medical drugs. Laboratories, sprinkled across the world, contained an army of researchers ever on the hunt for new chemical miracles to increase the company's profit.

But none of these new structures upheld the tradition of the square of red brick buildings. Their picture made up the logo of the company, and in every executive office of Brown and Brown throughout the world a lithograph of these institutional buildings graced totally modern walls, a reminder that headquarters, no matter how far away geographically, was always as close as the telephone.

The square's railroad spur had been removed long ago. Although the square was certainly large enough to be a parking lot, it was forbidden that this space be used for parking except for two cars – the president's and the chairman of the board's.

Usually, only the president made use of the space. He was a working executive and came in every day when he wasn't travelling on company business. The chairman of the board, on the other hand, was seldom seen. He was one of the last members of the original Brown family, although his name was Edwards. He was a watchdog, set by the distant shadowy family owners to see that their precious investment was protected. Most of them had never worked and none of them relished the prospect.

Edward Simpson Edwards was old, approaching eighty, and despite his years he seemed in good health. A dour man who never seemed to laugh, he was as sharp as ever mentally, even though his hearing was beginning to fade. Arthritis made it difficult for him to walk, so he generally had to be assisted by his driver or anyone else who happened to be handy. He accepted help as though it were his just due, and never thanked anyone, ever. Only a fringe of white hair remained, wisped around his ears. His eyebrows were patches of dirty grey. His skin was as wrinkled as an elephant's, and looked to be about as tough. Like little steel balls, grey eyes shone forth from his wizened skin. There was never a hint of pathos, or even humanity, in those eyes; they sparkled with an air of animal cunning.

Edward Simpson Edwards was a man to be feared – especially if you were the president of Brown and Brown.

Augustus Murray was the president of Brown and Brown, and he was terrified of old Teddy Edwards.

For a quarter of a century no president of the company had ever served more than three usually stormy years. Brown and Brown changed presidents the way a losing pro football team changes coaches. The rewards were substantial: a salary fit for the king of a small country, a pension plan – although no president ever made it to the five-year vesting mark – and stock options, perhaps the juciest plum of all.

But Brown and Brown was no losing football team. Even in the

159

worst of times, the company had always turned a nice profit. They relied on their research to come up with winning combinations that had always bailed the company out in bad times. The firm was respected worldwide for the advances provided not only in industrial chemicals, but in lifesaving drugs – drugs always produced and sold at an enormous profit.

The company had been started by the brothers Brown – both Civil War veterans – in a small basement in Hoboken, New Jersey. They made a single elixir, guaranteed to cure almost anything afflicting mankind. It was three parts sweet syrup, five parts good alcohol, and two parts cocaine. While it might not have cured anyone, no one was ever unhappy after taking the stuff.

Both Browns had passed away by the time the great tides of social reform swept over the nation. They were spared seeing the Congress pass laws banning narcotics in over-the-counter medicine. Fortunately, by that time, Brown and Brown was not only a successful drug company possessing good managers with shrewd foresight, it had also broadened its product base. Although its famous cocaine-laced elixir was still the mainstay of its business, Brown and Brown had branched out into research and other chemical-related fields. During the period of social reform there was also a great wave of technological advances. The elixir company had kept pace.

When deprived of the capability of tossing a little opium into their otherwise worthless products, many of their competitors had gone under. Although Brown and Brown had experienced some rough weather financially, like a storm-battered ship it emerged into the sunshine of the twentieth century, a few rips in its corporate sails, but still under way, and, with a few patches, better than ever.

The descendants of the Brown brothers managed to hold on to sole ownership through the turbulent Twenties, and even through the depths of the Depression. When taxes made such sole ownership painful, they still managed to hold on to a considerable slice of the company, even though they had to sell the majority, go public, and put the stock on the open market.

They had all been rich to begin with, and with the sale of the stock, they became even richer. Nevertheless, for most of them, their slice of Brown and Brown constituted the main source of income, the real foundation of their fortune.

Edward Simpson Edwards was a relative – the chairman of the

board had always been a relative – and although of distant relationship to most of the stockholding family, they all called him Uncle Teddy.

And they all rested very well in their luxurious beds at night knowing that Uncle Teddy was on the job. He was heartless, mean to the point of cruelty, and as crafty as a jewel thief – an attribute they considered absolutely necessary for the watchdog selected to guard their fortunes.

Augustus Murray, the current president of Brown and Brown, was a hardworking executive, a technician who carefully supervised every aspect of the chemical company's far-flung empire. He was tall, lean, well-dressed, and came from a good family. He had attended the country's very finest schools, and his track record at every company he had served was excellent. Always comfortably self-assured, except when the chairman of the board came to call, Gus Murray looked forward to Teddy Edwards' visits the way a French aristocrat might have looked forward to the guillotine.

Whenever the old man's chauffeur-driven Rolls-Royce came gliding through the archway into the company's historic square, Murray knew it might be simply a routine visit, or it could mean that the car and its occupant were carrying the warrant for unemployment. In addition, he detested the old man.

Murray realistically knew he couldn't hold on forever as president of the company. He hoped to last at least long enough to see the old man die and attend the funeral. It had become his main goal in life.

Gus Murray watched the dreaded Rolls-Royce slowly drive into the square. The old man was assisted from the vehicle by his driver. Murray became aware that his heart was beating faster and that he was beginning to perspire.

He shook off the dread and quickly moved to get downstairs and greet the old man. If he was late, he would be chastised like a schoolboy.

Gus Murray took over for the driver, gripping the old man by his bony elbow and guiding him towards the ornate office set aside for the chairman of the board.

Employees respectfully stood aside as Murray helped Edwards walk down the ancient high-ceilinged corridor. A nervous but smiling secretary opened the chairman's office door as Murray assisted the old man to the high-backed leather chair behind the long

161

mahogany desk. Edwards irritably shook the helping hand away as soon as he was safely seated.

Murray sat down in the lone chair directly in front of Edwards' desk.

'You are looking quite well, Mr Edwards,' Murray said.

The metallic eyes glittered malevolently. 'I look like hell and you know it. I hate people who lie, Murray.' The words were spoken in his usual tone of voice, a sound somewhere between a growl and a whine. 'Besides, my damn health has no bearing on what brings me here today.'

The words had a funeral ring to them, the tone suggesting something final. Gus Murray felt his stomach muscles tighten involuntarily.

'What seems to be the problem?' Murray asked quietly, careful to keep the fear out of his voice.

'The pharmaceutical division is showing another annual loss,' the old man said. 'Although that certainly isn't anything new.'

'It's been that way for several years. I think our research people are on to something quite good. The FDA is trying out a new drug . . .'

'I know, I know all about it,' the old man said testily. 'A surefire haemorrhoid cure, or so they say. What the hell difference does it make? There aren't enough people with haemorrhoids to bring the division into the black, even if every damn one of them went out and bought the product.'

'Still, you must admit it would help. And we have other —'

The old man irritably waved his hand, shutting him off. 'I know everything about this company, Murray, every damn thing. We lose money on the drug business, break even on almost everything else, and make money on industrial chemicals – enough money to balance out the others and give a small company-wide profit at the end of the year.'

Murray nodded. It was an accurate assessment.

The old man wheezed as he talked. 'I've had some people checking our land holdings. How much do you know about the value of our real estate?'

Murray felt sure of his ground. He knew every inch of ground the company owned. 'We have our factories, our warehouses. We own

162

docks and disposal sites. And we have reserve land for future development.'

The old man slowly nodded. 'And what value do you attach to this land you say we are holding for future development?'

Murray calculated for a moment before answering. 'I'm not sure to the penny, but combining the American and Canadian holdings alone, we pay taxes based upon a valuation of approximately fifty million dollars.'

Edwards' thin face seemed to grow almost translucent. 'How about the land in California and the Texas tracts?'

'We've owned that land for a long time. I'm not precisely sure what the current market valuation might be.'

The old man's face twisted into a snarl. 'You aren't, are you? Well, let me tell you what my people found out. There's been a tremendous explosion in land values in both areas, each for different reasons. Guess the value?'

Murray felt himself colouring but contained his voice to sound merely curious. 'You obviously know.'

'Yes, I do,' the old man snapped. 'And so should you. That land could bring this company crashing down.'

'Oh?'

'It's now worth over two billion dollars, Murray.'

Gus Murray managed to force a smile. 'Come now. I don't think it could be worth quite that much. I know that land value fluctuates— '

'Over two billion, and that's conservative. Do you know what that means?'

Murray was tempted to snap back, but he knew that such impudence would mark his last day as president of the chemical company. He waited silently for the answer.

Edwards let his frail body sink back into the chair, his head barely visible above the desk. His steely little eyes seemed as dark as coal.

'It means that we have an enormous asset that can be turned easily into liquid cash,' Edwards said. 'It means, my friend, that this company is worth one hell of a lot more than the price of its stock reflects. At the moment, our stock is a tremendous bargain. It means, Murray, that if an ambitious company finds out about our little treasure, they will come after us, snap up the cheap stock, and make a very nice killing. It's our land they will want.'

Gus Murray realized he would have to handle his response carefully. The old man had obviously already decided on a course of conduct. He would have to fence a bit to see which way the wind was blowing. Old man Edwards liked to trap people.

'You're worried about a hostile takeover, obviously.'

The little eyes never blinked or left his face. 'Of course. We are the ideal target. My friend, this company has been in the hands of my family for over one hundred years. Those of us who still hold stock have a special interest in its future. For many of us, the company's future is our future. If it dies, so do we, in a manner of speaking. Therefore we have to protect the company. We must do something about that land immediately.'

Murray nodded, as if agreeing, but he still had to see which way the old man was headed. 'If we sell the land, we'll still have the cash. And if we invest the profits, it will still be an asset.'

Old Edwards nodded. 'That's right. Two billion dollars in the bank won't help at all. Cash will draw vultures even quicker. And a profitable investment will do the same thing.'

'So?'

'Murray, when I hired you, you came well recommended for the president's chair. You had a good track record at the other companies you worked for, now let's see if that's really worth anything. Tell me what we should do, given the present situation.'

It was a test. The wrong answer would mean he would be out of the company by day's end. Even the correct answer was no guarantee of continued employment, but it would help.

'We would have to invest the money either in a losing business or invest it in such a way that it couldn't be quickly liquidated.'

The old man nodded, almost imperceptibly. 'Perhaps both,' he said at last. 'It's peculiar, isn't it? Most companies in the past would be delighted by such a grand windfall. But the times make it imperative that we get rid of the land as quickly as possible, loss or no loss. I want you to arrange to sell that land, quickly but quietly. Then hunt up some marginal businesses into which we can pour the proceeds. Buying these assets is the only way we can prevent one of those financial pirates coming after us.'

Murray still suspected a trap. 'If we hold on to the land, even if we were the subject of a hostile takeover, wouldn't your family be enriched by a sizable increase in the stock?'

The old man paused for a moment before answering. 'These things are done quickly, Murray, as you probably know. The tender for sale of stock is made at a high price. Those who oppose the takeover lose selling at the inflated price. The company is raped of its assets, broken up and sold. A stockholder who doesn't sell may take a loss on the stock he holds if the takeover is successful. And believe me, that isn't going to happen to Brown and Brown or to the stock owned by myself and my family. I trust you understand?'

'Of course.'

'Speed is of the essence. If you don't sell the land and protect the proceeds quickly, one of those pirates will spot us and that could be the end.'

'We'll get on it right away, Mr Edwards. Is there anything else?'

The old man's head jerked up. 'Jesus, isn't saving the company enough?' He struggled to get out of his chair.

Gus Murray hurried around the desk and helped him to his feet. He escorted the frail man all the way to the square, where the chauffeur took over.

The automatic window on the Rolls slid down, and Edwards' worn old face peered out for one last word.

'Do it fast, Murray. Fast.'

Murray nodded his understanding as the huge limousine rolled silently away. Murray shook his head. The old man was losing his marbles, that much was clear.

It would take the formal action of the full board of directors to divest such major holdings. Back in his office he dictated off a notice of an emergency board meeting. Later he would call the board members individually to let them know what was coming. No use in making any unnecessary enemies. Teddy Edwards was all the enemy any one person needed.

13

The captain's smooth, cultured voice interrupted Christina's sleep. They were about to make the approach to Heathrow Airport. She pushed the seat button and sat up. Outside the plane's window she could see only moonlit clouds. The captain described the weather waiting for them in London: 48 degrees and overcast. Showers were expected.

Christina stood up for a moment. Her stiff legs protested the unaccustomed position. She removed the blanket the flight attendant had provided, smoothed down her skirt, then sat down and snapped the seat belt around her hips.

Glancing at her wristwatch, she realized she hadn't been asleep for long. And in those few minutes of sleep she had suffered through anxiety dreams, violent dramas associated with both her personal and business problems.

She felt more than tired, as though somehow she were burnt out – physically, mentally, emotionally. It would be a matter of just putting one foot ahead of the other for a while. The London closing was really no problem. Although huge fortunes would be changing hands, all the real work had been done. All that was left was mere formality. She had presided over hundreds of similar transactions, and this one would be no different.

But her life had changed completely. She had no home. And, in a way, she had no family. Her relationship with her husband had been severed forever. Her son, in his callow youth and insensitivity, was lost to her, at least temporarily.

Even Nelson and Clark, the anchor in her life, was now chaotic. Frank Johnson's vacancy had to be filled. And she was a natural contender. But if she lost she would have to leave the firm. And her great quest – to become one of the Twelve Apostles – would be all over for all time.

They were descending now. The plane was coming closer to the carpeting of clouds, and the change in pressure blocked her ears.

Heathrow was always a madhouse. She dreaded the effort of having to go through customs, and the trip into London.

As the aircraft glided down through the clouds, she could see the twirling lights of the English countryside below.

The aeroplane banked gently and began its final approach towards the lights of the huge airfield. Although the landing was smooth, they seemed to taxi forever before disembarking.

English customs people were generally more friendly and less menacing than their American counterparts. Christina pushed her new bags ahead of her in the baggage cart as she stood in line with her fellow passengers. The tall young man in uniform requested that she open only one suitcase. He too looked tired, even though he was quite friendly in an impersonal way.

She didn't even see Taro Kuragamo until suddenly a firm hand took the bags from her hand.

'Taro!' she exclaimed, as, throwing her arms around him, she hugged him closely for a moment.

Christina drew back, embarrassed, surprised at her own reaction. 'I'm sorry, Taro,' she said. 'I didn't mean to get carried away. Airports have that effect on me, I guess.' She tried to make a joke of it, although she knew it was the result of the terrible loneliness she felt.

'I shall make it a point hereafter to meet you only at airports,' he said, his stony expression changing instantly into that remembered boyish grin.

She laughed. 'I didn't expect to see you. How'd you know I'd be coming to London?'

'The closing with Thompkins Steel,' he said, as if that mere fact explained the whole thing.

'I don't understand.'

The boyishness vanished, and his expression reverted to the usual half-amused look. 'I own Thompkins, or at least I own a controlling interest. So you see it was only natural that I should discover which American lawyers was coming over to handle the transaction.'

'But if you own . . .'

'Com'on, Christina. My chauffeur is waiting in a no-parking zone and he's rather nervous about it. Follow me.' He strode off as if her heavy bags weighed nothing at all. She had to run to keep up.

A powerful man with wide shoulders and a trim, lithe body, he moved with the easy grace of an athlete or dancer.

She wondered if, as the owner of Thompkins, he might have set up the London closing just to be with her. But she discarded that as simply a flattering notion. Businessmen, or at least the ones with whom she dealt, were never romantic when it came to their company balance sheets. She seriously doubted if the mysterious Mr Kuragamo was any different.

A hefty driver, dressed in a suit that could double either as a uniform or ordinary clothes, looked relieved to see them. He quickly took the bags from Kuragamo and placed them in the trunk of the enormous Mercedes.

Kuragamo helped Christina into the luxurious interior, then climbed in next to her.

The driver took off without any additional instructions. As she remembered, London was several miles from Heathrow. The traffic seemed light.

'You were booked at the Hilton,' Kuragamo said. 'But it's so . . . well, metal and plastic. Nice, of course, efficient but not really European. I took the liberty of moving you to a suite at the Savoy. I think you'll prefer it.'

She felt some resentment about his easy assumption that she would agree with whatever he decided.

'I'm an American, Taro. Perhaps I prefer a hotel with typically American convenience and efficiency.'

He nodded. 'Yes, Christina, but you are also a woman, a very beautiful woman. I think the Savoy will be more your style.'

'Mr Kuragamo . . .'

He held up his hand. 'Please, my dear. I thought you would be pleased. Honestly. If you like, I can change things back.'

She sighed. 'You were trying to be kind, Taro. I'll only be here tonight, anyway, so it really makes little difference. I suppose I can pretend I'm Queen Victoria and let the Savoy treat me accordingly.'

Kuragamo was not smiling now. 'Ah, there's a small problem. The closing has been postponed a day. The Netherlands bank won't be able to clear its participation with their board until tomorrow. We tried to reach you, but you'd left the office. My people tried you at home, unsuccessfully.' The last word was spoken almost as an afterthought.

'I don't live there any more,' she said quietly. 'My husband and I have decided on a divorce.'

She was looking away but she felt his eyes on her. 'And where do you live now, Christina?' he said just as quietly. 'This has been rather sudden, has it not?'

'Yes, very sudden. And very private.'

He patted her hands. She hadn't realized that she'd been grasping them so tightly together that her knuckles were white.

'We Japanese hold privacy in high regard. I won't pry. I am sorry to hear of your trouble, however.'

She relaxed her hands and sat back. They were flying down the motorway, speeding toward Europe's greatest city.

'I fly a great deal,' Kuragamo said, 'and the biggest problem I have is adjusting to the time change. I seldom suffer from jet lag, fortunately, and I find that I can sleep almost instantly on aeroplanes. But waking up in a completely different time zone is always so odd to me. Here in London it is just a few minutes past midnight. Yet it is only seven o'clock in the evening in Manhattan. Christina, your inner body clock must be telling you it's seven o'clock. This must be the dinner hour there, am I correct?'

'Most people in New York eat later. It's not the Midwest, you know.'

He laughed. 'Thank God. I have spent some time in your Midwest. Kansas may be heaven for people born and raised there, but I found it profoundly boring. Nice in the way a billiard table is nice – very green and very flat. No, I'll take London, New York, or Hong Kong any time.'

'I think you might turn out to be the secret owner of Kansas. You seem to own just about everything else.'

The boyishness returned as he began to laugh. Her comment seemed to have amused him. 'I do own rather a large farm there. Several thousand acres, mostly wheat. If I owned the entire state, I'd sell it. I don't care to own things I really don't like. The wheat eventually makes good French bread, but that's as far as my sentimental attachment extends to Kansas.'

They were driving through the outskirts of London now.

Kuragamo gestured at the passing scene. 'Unlike Kansas, I love this city. It's one of my favourite places in the world. I used to come here at weekends when I was at Oxford. You can spend your life in London and never really see it all. It changes. Perhaps not dramatically, but it does change: like a beautiful woman who gets better as

169

she approaches mid-life, or like a delicate wine.'

'Do you live here?'

'I have a home here. I have homes in many places, Christina. The convenience far outweighs the expense. And it gives me a sense of belonging. This is important, no?'

She felt her own sense of isolation. 'Yes, that is important,' she said, her words barely above a whisper.

'Would you like to have dinner, Christina? It's late here but I could . . .'

'Dinner was served on the plane,' she interrupted him. She didn't add that she had no appetite then, and even less now. She had picked at the salad, but that was about all.

'Then we will get you settled at the Savoy. Perhaps then I can persuade you to have a nightcap.'

She turned and found his dark, intense eyes on hers. 'I'm tired, Taro,' she said, and then quickly saw his disappointment. 'But perhaps one drink . . .'

'It is settled,' he said, beaming. Kuragamo leaned forward. 'Stocker,' he said to the chauffeur, 'take us directly to the Savoy.'

As they got deeper into metropolitan London, Christina recognized more landmarks.

Kuragamo's enormous power and wealth were evidently quite persuasive at the hotel. Everything had been arranged. They were led to her suite by no fewer than three porters, each apparently more anxious to please than the other.

She gasped as he escorted her into the lavish suite. Everything seemed delicate. The fireplace was marble with intricate carvings in the stone. The decor was definitely period but there was no limit to the modern conveniences. A concealed bar was opened by a solicitous middle-aged porter. It seemed complete except for ice. Even the television was artfully concealed in a bureau.

Exquisite antique figurines adorned the glass shelves of a fabulous étagère. The bedroom, the huge canopied bed turned down and inviting, was fit for royalty.

The porters retreated as though they'd merely been smoke sucked away by some magic machine. Christina found herself alone with Kuragamo.

'Shall I have dinner sent up?'

'Not at this hour. I'm sure the kitchen's closed.'

He smiled and nodded, now looking more Japanese than British. 'For me, I think they might be able to manage something.'

'I suppose you own the Savoy, too?'

He laughed quietly. 'Hotels have never been my speciality. The profit margin isn't high enough. I don't own this lovely place, but I am quite close to those who do.'

'I really am very tired, Taro,' she said.

'I believe I was promised a nightcap, or is that a problem?'

She laughed and sat down on the comfortable couch. 'No, I think I can stay awake through one drink. And,' she added, 'I think I'd like the company.'

He bowed. 'Allow me.' He walked to the portable bar and opened its doors to reveal an array of fine liquor. 'What do you prefer, Christina.'

'I'd love a Vodka Gibson, very dry.'

'By very dry, you Americans usually mean all vodka and pass the vermouth cork gently over. Correct?'

She was beginning to relax. 'You catch on quickly.'

'Music?' he asked.

'I thought the BBC went to bed early.'

He smiled. 'This suite has a superb stereo, replete with tapes.' He flipped a switch, and the rooms were filled with a soft, sensuous melody.

'I'm impressed.'

Kuragamo laughed as he quickly and expertly fixed the drinks. He handed the Gibson to her. 'Just a touch of vermouth.'

She sipped it. 'Perfect.'

He sat opposite her, extending his long, muscular legs before him, quite at ease and at home. His drink was in a tall glass and amber in colour.

'What are you drinking?'

He looked at the glass. 'I suppose I should drink only saki, which I do like, by the way. But I'm also quite fond of Scotch. I have a number of schizophrenic preferences. I learned about Scotch from my fellow students at Oxford. Saki, I suppose, is a taste acquired at birth for all Japanese.'

'But you're only half-Japanese.'

'The body is British,' he said, indicating his tall form, 'or at least much of it. My mind, however, I think is mostly Japanese.'

171

Christina sipped her vodka slowly. She remembered all too well the perils of drinking on an empty stomach. One drink would be her limit tonight. Although she knew she should politely usher Kuragamo out, she suddenly felt the desperate need to be with someone. The loneliness was almost physical, palpable like a pain spreading slowly throughout the body.

'I'm surprised that you consider yourself Japanese.'

Slowly he raised an inquisitive eyebrow.

'I mean, you were educated in England,' she said. 'I would have thought you would be more at home here, than, say, in Japan.'

He shrugged. His shoulders, she couldn't help noticing, were strong and broad. 'As a boy I was raised in Japan. The formative years, as they say. All that came after, Oxford and so on, merely broadened my education. My soul had been formed. No matter what the degree of blood, no matter what genes I've inherited from my father, I am Japanese.'

She slipped off her shoes and brought her feet up under her. His eyes were on her legs. She wished her skirt weren't so rumpled from the long flight.

'You do look tired, Christina. Perhaps I should go?'

It was a crossroads, and she realized it. He was right. Now was the proper time for them to part. If she asked him to stay, he could only interpret it in one way. Still, the idea of being alone was unbearable.

'I am tired, Taro, but I'm not sleepy. Perhaps you wouldn't mind spending a few more minutes with me. I feel like a little girl – I'm afraid to be alone, at least for a while. It's been quite an experience, these last few days.'

His eyes seemed to darken, even more intensely, though there was no apparent emotion in his expression. 'Of course,' he said simply. 'I'd be delighted to stay, Christina.'

'It's silly, Taro,' she said, feeling herself colour. 'Just let me finish this drink and you're a free man.'

'As long as you like, I'll stay.'

He stood up, towering over her as he approached. There was that indefinable aura of power surrounding him. He looked down, again without expression. 'You've been through a great deal,' he said quietly, taking her hand. 'The trauma of breaking with your husband is understandably painful, but these things have a way of working out. It generally ends up for the best.'

She didn't pull her hand away. 'You sound as if you've been through the same thing.'

He shook his head in denial. 'No. As I told you, my wife and I live in a different world, an Oriental world. We were never really close. I felt no loss when we went into our separate houses.'

'What about your children?' She felt suddenly intimidated by him as he stood over her. He continued to hold her hand, but didn't move. She was at eye level with his belt buckle.

'They are true Japanese. I am their father, a person to be respected and obeyed at all times. They know they are being trained to take my place one day. The bond is strong between us on that count alone, but even if I were a humble fisherman, they would honour me. It is our custom.'

'And their mother?'

He smiled down at her, a gentleness in his face. 'Oh, they honour her, too. I doubt if they even think about our reasons for living apart – they know it is none of their business. We are their parents, each of us to be respected equally. Of course, the fact that my sons will take over my interests probably makes them closer to me, but they take pains to show their respect for their mother. Anything else would be unthinkable.'

'Too bad that sort of thing hasn't caught on in America,' she said, the words ending up in a kind of half-sob – much to her surprise.

He squatted until his eyes were level with hers. Dark and mysterious, his eyes gave no hint of what he was thinking. He took her other hand and held them together.

'You are unhappy,' he said softly. 'You deserve to be joyful. You were made for that. Forget what has happened to you, Christina. Never look back; you can do nothing about the past. It's gone forever. But the future belongs to you.'

Christina felt a small tear slowly creep down one cheek. She couldn't brush it away. Now he held both her hands tightly. She found that she didn't mind at all – at least it was an expression of some kind of human warmth, something she needed very desperately at the moment.

'Your son,' he whispered, 'is very young. He knows little of the real world, or people. You'll see, he'll come around in time. You

173

haven't lost him. He'll see his father in a true light one day.'

She looked away, her heart aching. 'I'm not sure, Taro. Not at all.'

'Do you love your husband?' he asked gently.

She looked directly at him, her eyes awash. 'At one time I did, very much.'

'But no more?'

She shook her head, unable to form the words.

'Then you are much better out of a loveless marriage, is that not so? Perhaps in Europe or my country such things are tolerable. Each seeks other avenues of love. But in America, the Puritan ethic still lingers. The spouses live together, locked in silent hate. Christina, that is no life for anyone, especially not a warm and loving woman like yourself.'

She didn't answer, conscious not so much of his words as the touch and firmness of his sure hands.

'Stand up, Christina,' he said, rising. He held her hands tightly as he did so.

She blinked away the tears and stood up.

He was close, very close, and his presence seemed the only reality. He placed her hands against his chest, released them, and circled her with his strong arms, pulling her close against him.

'Taro, we shouldn't . . .'

'Christina, my dearest, it's the only thing we *should* do.' His words were a whisper as his mouth closed over hers. She was surprised that such strength could be blended with delicate gentleness. Suddenly there was no world except the man who held her. She felt a surge of life, a budding desire calling her back from desolation. Slowly and tentatively she responded to his kiss.

As if intoxicated, she was only partially conscious of what was happening to her. His mouth was insistent, his tongue probing, awakening a fire within her. She felt his fingers expertly unfastening the buttons on her blouse.

She considered resisting, protesting, but found that she really didn't want to do so. Her skirt fell away to the floor. Awkwardly she managed to step out of it. In contrast to her unsure movements, he was like a gifted dancer, moving, yet clinging to her with a smooth effortless grace.

The air of the room felt cool to her bare breasts. Taro delicately caressed them, his hands like messengers carrying the urgency of his desire. He gripped her tighter as his mouth moved to the curve of her throat. The tip of his tongue felt like fire as he flicked it against her skin.

His mouth moved slowly to her breasts, his tongue circling each nipple.

'Taro, don't,' she whispered without meaning it. She knew she was losing all perspective.

Kissing her quickly on the mouth he scooped her up as if weightless and carried her to the altarlike bed. She watched as he quickly stripped, his movements fast but graceful.

'Taro, we shouldn't. I never have — '

He came to the bed. 'I wanted you from the first moment I saw you,' he said quietly. 'You are the most attractive woman I have ever known, Christina.'

'Taro, this isn't right.' Her words trailed off. He stood before her like a young bull, strong with smooth rippling muscle, a man fit for sculpture. He was fully erect and surprisingly large. She felt a general throbbing just in looking at him.

He kissed her repeatedly as he swiftly and skilfully removed her pantyhose and slip. His hands were like the wings of a soft bird, fluttering, gentle, yet exciting as they moved over her body. She felt as if she might burst into flame.

'You are lovely,' he whispered as his mouth closed over hers.

Stimulated, she was fully ready for his thrust. His strong muscular body joined hers in quick decisive rhythm. She abandoned all restraint. Her consciousness contained no thought, except awareness of the throbbing world of his embrace.

'Oh, Taro,' she whispered as he finished.

He was breathing hard, his skin glistening. She opened her eyes and looked at him. His face was smooth, his eyes half-closed, his jaw set. Rather than an expression of joyous possession there seemed to be the look of a conqueror in his dark eyes.

But she was really only conscious of the echo of pleasure, the touch of his hand, his strong back and smooth skin warm and moist. He lightly kissed her eyelids, then her mouth. This time the kiss was almost languid.

'I wanted you,' he said in a normal voice. 'And now I have you. You belong to me, Christina.' His words did not have the soft sound of a satisfied lover, but rather rang with a hint of arrogance, as if he had, in truth, conquered her.

Then he smiled widely, boyishly. 'Besides,' he grinned, 'you are really a great lay. I wouldn't want to lose you.'

She laughed. But his eyes hadn't changed.

'I can't,' she said, pulling his hand away.

'What do you mean, you can't?'

'It's my time of the month, Michael. I started yesterday.'

Michael Collins felt irritated, rejected. 'Other women make love during their menstrual period, Mary,' he said, allowing his disgust to be reflected in his voice.

'Maybe they can, and do,' she snapped. 'But I don't. Even savages regard that as a taboo. You make it sound as if there was something wrong or weird with me.'

He sat up and pulled out a pack of cigarettes. He lighted one and looked over at her. Mary Quinn had been his sweetheart since high school. They had first made love during his senior year at Notre Dame. She was lovely, even seductive, with her long black hair and pert, sexy figure, but even when they did make love it was always fast and accompanied with a silent sense of shame. They had discussed marriage and both had agreed to wait until he was established in the law. Or at least established enough to support a wife and the certainty of childen, something that Mary Quinn held very dear to her heart.

'Michael what's wrong with you? You've never minded before.'

He inhaled deeply, letting the smoke out as he spoke. 'Mary, I've been given an assignment by the firm that will take up my evenings and weekends for a month, maybe two. This is my last night free.'

She giggled. 'You make it sound like you were a soldier going overseas.'

'Maybe it's funny to you, but I have certain needs, physical needs.'

'This keeps getting worse, Michael. You think you're the only one suffering? Haven't I waited for you? All that time you were away as an undergraduate, and in law school. I was your girl. I think sacrifice has been at least a two-way street. I've kept my part of the bargain. I've been faithful, and I've even slept with you. And now you pout like a spoiled child when I refuse.'

'I'm not a spoiled child, Mary. I'm a healthy twenty-four-year-old male. I didn't take a vow of celibacy, I'm not a priest. I am going to be tied up for at least a month, working my ass off. This is my last chance . . . Oh, forget it!'

She flounced up. 'Do you really think you'll change after we get married?'

'I wonder,' he said quietly.

'Michael, you're just being difficult. I can understand your being edgy. This is your beginning with a prominent law firm. You're worried about your career. But you'll see, everything will settle down soon. In a very few months we'll be married.'

He turned to put his arms around her but she quickly stood up. 'No, not the way you feel tonight. It would only cause more trouble.'

Michael Collins shook his head. 'No, I'm going to go.'

'So soon?'

'The new assignment will take all my energy, so I might just as well go home and get some rest.'

She arched an eyebrow. 'It's nothing, well, illicit, is it?'

He laughed. 'Nelson and Clark would never touch anything illegal. It's all above board.'

'Nothing like what your father does?'

'Criminal work, you mean?'

She wrinkled her nose as if detecting something bad. 'Yes. All that is so shoddy. I wouldn't want you to get mixed up in anything like that.'

He was about to reply, but stopped himself. Nothing would help. In a way she was right, the firm had become the most important thing in the world to him.

'I'll be tied up for quite a while,' he said. 'I'll try to find time to give you a call, but don't worry if I don't.'

She pursed her lips for a parting kiss.

Collins walked towards the bus stop, feeling resentment towards the girl he was going to marry. She was so rule-oriented, so un-yielding. He was thinking of a singles bar someone had told him about. It was his last evening.

14

Dan Spencer could think of nothing else to do except return to the office. He checked his mail. His secretary, like most of the other clericals, had gone for the day. But he knew why he had really come back. He left his own offices in the litigation section and walked through the halls.

If anyone did happen to see him, it would have appeared that Spencer was just wandering around, but he did have a purpose. He arrived at Christina Giles' section. The door to her office was closed.

One of her staff was typing away, her gaze fixed on what she was transcribing.

'Is Mrs Giles in?' he asked.

Startled, the girl looked up. 'Pardon me?'

He smiled to reassure her. 'Is Mrs Giles in?' he repeated.

She shook her head. 'No, she isn't. She flew to London earlier today. She'll be back tomorrow.' Her tone carried a note of wistful envy.

'Thanks.'

'Mr Spencer,' the girl called after him, 'do you want to leave a message for her?'

'No. It's nothing terribly important. It'll keep.'

For Spencer, the offices of Nelson and Clark now truly did seem empty and lonely. He realized just how much he had wanted to see her.

Spencer returned to his office and looked out at the Manhattan scene below. Darkness was descending earlier every evening, or so it seemed. The city's buildings glowed like banks of diamonds; the sky was a deep purple. He felt very alone.

He debated calling one of his select lady friends, but the prospect wasn't even tempting. Even the thought of the awesome responsibility placed upon him by the firm failed to keep visions of Christina from occupying his mind.

Spencer stood up, deciding that he would walk for a while, perhaps grab a cab to a favourite restaurant. He waited for the elevator.

As the elevator's doors opened, Spencer was met by Morris Solomon.

Solomon greeted him with a smile. 'I've been hearing a lot of good things about you, Dan.'

'Glad to hear it.' Spencer always found himself just a little unsure when he was around any of the Twelve Apostles, at least the older ones.

'Ainsworth's told me what's planned,' Solomon said.

'Then you know it's essential that nothing leaks about the project.'

'Of course. That goes without saying. But I'm always interested to see that a new client gets the very best treatment. Ainsworth tells me you even have a code name for the adventure.'

'That's true.'

Solomon laughed. 'I'm not a spy. Dan, I'm on your side.' He took Spencer's arm. 'I think it might be profitable if we had a quiet drink.'

It would be unthinkable not to accept the invitation of one of the Apostles. 'Sure, be happy to,' Spencer replied.

'It's early. We'll go over to the Blue Dolphin. The bar will be jammed with young people, but the tables at the back will be nicely secluded. We can talk there.'

Solomon addressed the headwaiter by name, and was in turn rewarded with the fawning respect paid a regular customer who tips well. They were guided past the crowded bar to a group of tables surrounding a postage-stamp-sized dance floor. A small stage was cluttered with an organ and a set of drums, both currently not in use.

A waiter took their order and they were left alone.

'They have a pretty good jazz combo here at night. I often come in after closing the shop.' Solomon talked softly, just barely audible above the noise coming from the distant bar. 'It's really quite relaxing. Although I'd bet that probably I'm the only person over thirty in the place, except for the musicians. They've been around for a while. If you like progressive jazz, you'll love it. If you don't, it's just so much discordant clatter. I happen to like it.'

The waiter returned with their drinks.

'Dan, sometimes Ainsworth Martin is somewhat tight-lipped. I don't know if you've been fully informed.'

'Oh?'

Solomon sipped tentatively at his drink. 'As you know, this Lockwood matter is going to blow up into a major financial war.'

'That's obvious.'

'Yes, it is. But I don't think you fully understand the scope of what is about to happen, Dan. You'll be handling the litigation end of this thing. I'll be in charge of the financial arrangements.'

Solomon rolled the ice in his drink with such force that the liquid nearly spilled over. 'What kind of money do you think will be involved here, Dan?'

Spencer shrugged. 'Millions.'

'Billions. The figures are so astonishing that even a man like me who deals with those kinds of numbers all the time has a hard time imagining just how much real money will be involved.'

'This is scheduled to start with a proxy fight. That's not too expensive, is it?'

The older lawyer shook his head. 'Cheap, if you win. It's only the beginning. But even that will cost millions. It's no child's game. I tell you.'

'I didn't presume it would be.'

Morris Solomon took another small sip. 'This war, just like the real thing, must be financed from somewhere. We will try to prevent the Brown and Brown people from borrowing money, and they'll be busy doing the same thing to us. I spent most of the day today trying to line up the main people at First of Boston.'

'First of Boston?'

'One of the largest investment bankers in the world. They love to see a battle like this. They plan strategy and lend money by the tons, then giggle as they collect their fee. There's really no risk for them. They always get paid.'

'There are lots of banks. What's the problem?'

Solomon slowly nodded. 'Yes, my friend, there certainly are many banks. But you tell me, how many banks do you know who are in a position to lend, say, two billion dollars, and on short notice?'

'Two billion?'

'That's exactly what we're talking about. If Scott really wants to buy Brown and Brown, a majority block of stock will cost him almost that much. The rest is for legal fees and other costs.'

'What's the use of trying a takeover? It sounds like a terrible gamble to me. If you win, you're out money, and if you lose, you die. Hardly the game I'd like to play in.'

'Or me,' Solomon agreed. 'But the prestige to Scott will be priceless. With it, he can pick up other companies at a dirt-cheap price. They'll be afraid of him and of the power he commands. It's a question of power and prestige.'

'I didn't realize the huge sums involved.'

Solomon chuckled. 'I know you didn't. That's why I wanted to have this little talk, Dan.'

Solomon grew serious. 'Then there is the very real importance of this matter to our firm.'

'The fees?'

'Usually law firms get their fees in these matters, no matter what happens. If your client wins, he's glad to pay. If he loses, the other side usually is happy to pay to get rid of you. No, it isn't the fees, although they'll add up to a quite healthy sum before this is all over.'

'What then?'

'Reputation. Nelson and Clark is the country's number-one business-law firm. We have held that reputation for decades. But if we take the lead position in the biggest corporate war this country has ever seen and lose . . . well, it may not mean a great deal to the man in the street, but the men who run the big boardrooms will take note of that fact and we won't be number one any more.'

'Aw, com'on, Morris. This is, after all, just a job. We are lawyers, not magicians.'

Solomon finished the last of his drink. He was staring at the empty bandstand. 'You're younger than I am, Dan. Allow me to give you a tip, a real piece of ancient widsom. Clients don't want a lawyer, they want a magician. If you can keep pulling the rabbits out of the hat you're okay, but the day when the trick doesn't work, you're in trouble.'

'The law isn't a trick. Morris, it's a body of knowledge applied to society . . .'

Morris snorted. 'Good heavens, Dan, we're talking about the real world now. Nelson and Clark has to win this goddamned Lockwood thing.'

'And you're saying all this is my responsibility?'

Solomon turned and faced him squarely in the eye. 'In some ways, yes. Oh, some of us will share the burden. But you're the field general, Dan. Win and you're a hero. Lose and you will be hung.'

'Meaning?'

'I can't promise you anything, Dan. I'm just one of the twelve. But there is Johnson's opening, isn't there? It will all turn on how you do.'

'Jesus, Morris. Is there any other word of encouragement you might have for me?'

Solmon stood up. 'I like you, Dan. And I wish to heaven we had never taken Lockwood on as a client.' Solomon sighed. 'Well, we can't turn back now. We've accepted the challenge. I have to go, Dan. I hope our little talk has been instructive?'

'Frightening,' Spencer replied.

Solomon smiled and left. Dan hadn't touched his drink now he downed it in one gulp.

'Take a look at what my public relations guys whipped up.' Scott tossed copies of a three-page handout to Dan Spencer. 'Shit, this will really rock those chemical boys.'

Spencer handed a copy to Michael Collins. He had brought Collins along to introduce him to John Norman Scott. Collins would serve as unoffical runner during the battles to come, and it would make things go more smoothly if Scott knew him by sight.

'I really get a kick out of the part where they accuse the present board of poisoning children for experimentation. That's real dynamite. I love it.' Scott grinned. 'Hell, I didn't know my own people were this good. If I had used them, I wouldn't have put my foot into it over little Miss Merriam.'

Spencer didn't reply. The words on the page seemed to fly out at him. It wasn't a news release, it was a scandal sheet, an indictment, an outrageous horror story. 'I hope to God you can prove all this,' Spencer said quietly. 'Otherwise this will be the best case of libel ever seen.'

Scott laughed. 'We can prove most of it. Look, just between us, those board members and corporate officers were doing just what any practical businessman would do – testing a product here, cutting some losses there – we all do it. Of course, they were dealing in medicine, so it makes them easy targets for this sort of attack when things go wrong.'

Spencer looked up. 'You accuse them of wholesale murder.'

Scott shrugged. 'It's not quite worded that strong, but it comes down to that. Hey, we're in a pretty good position legally. The Federal Drug Administration wouldn't let them market a childs' pain-medicine in this country; the feds felt it was untested and potentially dangerous. So Brown and Brown, who had a lot of the stuff on hand, shipped it to Africa. They used it as a donation for tax purposes. The FDA boys were right. The damn stuff blinded several hundred little kids and even killed a few, just like the FDA warned it might.'

'Jesus,' Spencer swore softly.

'Hey, like I said, it's standard business practice. You have to find a market for your product – but I can hang them by the balls anyway. What do you think a jury might do if facts about poisoned children were presented at a libel trial? We'd win.'

Spencer made no comment. He handed the paper back to Scott. 'What do you plan to do with this?'

'I have a press conference scheduled for this afternoon. Should be all over the front pages in tomorrow's editions.'

'If you publish this, the people at Brown and Brown will know you're after them, Mr Scott. I thought it was agreed you'd hold off until we had time to prepare the legal pleadings necessary for the takeover before you went public with anything.'

'Hey, this is only the opening gun of a proxy fight.'

Spencer felt the anger slowly rising within him, but he controlled it. 'The people at Brown and Brown aren't dumb, Mr Scott. They'll realize what you really have in mind. That will give them adequate time to prepare their defences against a takeover.'

Scott coloured. 'I'm not in the business of making life easy for lawyers. I hired Nelson and Clark because you guys are supposed to be the best in the business. This is the big time, Spencer. If your outfit can't handle it, you just let me know and I'll get someone else.'

'We are quite capable of handling anything legal, Mr Scott.' Spencer's voice was taut. 'You seem to plough right ahead without seeking advice from your professionals. I'll wager you haven't had any lawyer look at this handout of yours to see what the ramifications could be, have you?'

Scott grinned toothily. 'Didn't have to,' he said as he lit a thin cigar.

'I got the bastards by the short hairs, like I told you. I don't care if it's libel or not. They can't scream; they don't dare. I'm ready to roll on this thing.'

'Have you checked out the regulations concerning the stock you've purchased in Brown and Brown?' Spencer asked.

'Sure. The outfit I had on retainer before you people advised me what to do. I'm in technical violation, but it doesn't mean much.'

Spencer's eyes narrowed. 'What do you mean, technical violation?'

Scott shrugged. 'Don't get your hair in a braid. You have to file one of those goddamn schedules with the Securities and Exchange Commission if your corporation owns more than five per cent of another. We've been quietly buying up Brown and Brown – the price is really good – and I've got maybe five or possibly six per cent of their outstanding stock. I'll file the damn schedule one of these days.'

Spencer didn't reply at once. He paused in order to plan his words carefully. 'Mr Scott, the attorneys for Brown and Brown will get a court order stopping you from voting your stock and voting any other proxies.'

'Bullshit!'

'I'm afraid not,' Spencer said. 'You're in violation of the law; it's as simple as that. Maybe it's only a few percentage points, but I imagine the number of shares and the total price is substantial, right?'

Scott simply nodded. For the first time he appeared to be just a little unsure of himself.

'Any lawyer worth his salt will waltz into either a federal or state court and stop you dead. By the time we get the court matter settled, the annual stockholders' meeting will be a thing of the past.'

'You're kidding.'

Spencer sat back, almost enjoying himself. 'Definitely not.'

'Jesus, I've got everything keyed to that stockholders' meeting! The whole campaign depends on starting there. I've got millions sunk into that stock. How come that other law firm didn't tell me about this shit?'

'They probably did.' Spencer's words crackled with a sense of irony. 'Of course, at that time they probably didn't realize you were going after Brown and Brown. But I'll bet you have a letter in your files pointing out the illegality of buying more stock than allowed.'

Scott slapped his hand down on the desk, his face reddening. 'I don't need any brothers-at-the-bar shit, Spencer. If what you say is true, what can I do to correct it?'

Spencer turned to Michael Collins. 'Make a note to call John Crim and have him let the SEC know a proper schedule is on its way.'

'We'll have the right forms in the mail tonight, Scott.' He purposely dropped the 'mister'. 'One of our main partners runs a branch office in Washington. He can square things with the SEC, but that doesn't mean you're out of the woods.'

'Why the hell not?'

'Because you have given the other side an opening. They can go to court and argue that you were in violation and shouldn't be allowed to vote the proxies. They can muddy up the waters, maybe even kill your proxy campaign.'

'If they do that, I'm dead,' Scott said, his voice low and shaken.

'You can always call off the press conference.'

'It wouldn't do any good. I told a couple of newspapers what I had in mind. They wouldn't come to the conference if I didn't.'

'We'll do the very best we can.' Spencer said briskly. 'I'll need all the information on the stock, the amount you own, the dates of purchase, and so on. We'll need to borrow a company officer, one with authority to sign the schedule we prepare. This has to be done today. If we start now we can have it carried on the shuttle to Washington tonight and filed tomorrow. Then we'll all have to prepare to fight the other side in court. It's the only thing we can do. But time is of the essence.'

'I'm not a detail man,' Scott said, trying to laugh but failing badly. 'Nancy Merriam is assigned to the probject. She likes working the computer; she'd be the one to provide the information you need.' He paused. 'Hell, she's vice president. That would give her the power to sign the forms, too. You can work along with her, okay?'

Spencer remembered the pictures of the young woman that had occupied the front pages recently. He wondered if she had any brains. Certainly Spencer doubted that her diminutive boyfriend did.

'We'll take whoever you say,' Spencer said cripsly.

Scott flipped on his intercom and had his secretary send for Nancy Merriam.

There was a strained silence among the three men as they waited. Scott relit the cigar, sending forth clouds of acrid smoke.

Michael Collins, seated with his back to the door, heard it open. Scott greeted her, but didn't stand.

Spencer turned and stood, then Michael followed his example. Michael Collins was startled. There was a subtle, glowing beauty about Nancy Merriam. An elegant, well-tailored suit failed to conceal her provocative figure. Collins quickly stole a glance at her legs and classified them as first class.

'Nancy, this is Dan Spencer . . . and, what's your name again?'

'Collins,' he said, the name coming out like a squeak. 'Michael Collins.'

'Right, Mike,' Scott said. 'Anyway, these guys are from the Twelve Apostles. They tell me I've stuck my foot into it by not filing some goddamn government form about the Brown and Brown stock.'

'I sent you a memo about that,' she said quietly.

Collins liked the musical sound of her voice.

Scott shrugged. 'Jesus, I get a storm of memos every goddamned day. There's no way I can read them all. Anyway, these guys will need someone to gather the information they need, help fill out the goddamned form, and sign it when it's done.'

She smiled an acknowledgement. 'Of course.' She turned to Dan Spencer. 'What's best for you? We can provide all the secretarial help you might need right here, or I can go to your offices?'

Spencer nodded. 'I think our offices would be best. We have similar filings and the proper forms on hand. All we need is the information relative to the stock purchased, the amounts, dates, and so forth. Could we get that?'

'No problem,' she answered brightly. 'It's all on computer. I can run it off in a minute.' She stole a glance at Scott. 'I had supposed we would need that information some time, so it's all ready to go.'

'That's fine, Miss Merriam,' he said.

'Please call me Nancy.'

'Okay. I'm Dan and this is Mike. In order to expedite this, perhaps I should get back to the office and start things rolling there. Mike, you stay with Nancy until she's gathered what we need, then both of you join me. Okay?'

'Sure.' Michael Collins felt his heart rate increase. He liked the arrangement very much, but he carefully kept his enthusiasm from showing. John Norman Scott was looking directly at him, perhaps trying to guess just exactly what Collins was really thinking.

'Now, listen, you people,' Scott broke in sharply. 'This has got to work. So everybody put their best efforts forth, right? Let's give it everything we have.'

Spencer didn't bother to respond. The whole takeover was in trouble because of Scott, and now he tried to make it sound as though someone else had caused it. He seemed good at it, and Spencer decided he had had plenty of practice. Maybe his reputation as a whiz kid was a fraud, a smokescreen held up to conceal the incompetence of the man.

'Give me a call before you leave,' Spencer said to Collins. 'I'll double-check with our corporate people to see we have everything we need at this end.'

Collins had been looking at Nancy Merriam. He was startled, and nodded quickly. 'Right. Don't worry, we'll take care of that.'

'Remember, people,' Scott said as he stood up. 'This is war. No prisoners and no mercy.'

Spencer merely turned on his heel and walked out of the office. His career in the firm depended on how he handled this matter, and he had a self-centred madman for a client, a madman who had violated basic trading regulations. If it wasn't handled like a live bomb, it could explode – destroying the future of many people, but especially his.

Other than that, Dan Spencer thought to himself, things were just swell.

Abner Slocum knew something was up. Although the firm had grown to hundreds and had employees spread through six floors of the Logan Building, still there was a special excitement in the air. He had spent so many years with Nelson and Clark that he was like an old seaman: he sensed things before other people became aware of anything unusual.

And he instinctively knew something was happening now. He could smell it. Morris Solomon had rushed out after a feverish morning of dictating to alternating secretaries, something that Solomon never did unless there was an emergency. Usually quiet, dignified and unhurried, the financial section was currently abuzz with activity. Today was indeed different.

So Slocum made it his business to drop down a floor and see what was happening in the litigation department. Dan Spencer was locked away in conference with Andy Perkins, the second man in litigation. And the clerical staff were busy at their word processors, spilling out reams of paper.

Abner felt the eyes of the staff on him as he surveyed the other floors. For the staff to actually see an Apostle was a rare occurrence.

Slocum's slow tour revealed that almost everything else was normal, routine law office business proceeding along at a nice, steady, but unhurried pace. Only in the finance, corporate, and litigation sections were the staffs engaged in almost maniacal behaviour.

He retraced his steps to the top floor and sought out Ainsworth Martin.

'Some people seem to be quite busy.' Slocum sat in a chair facing Martin's desk. 'Something big going on?'

'Just the usual,' Martin replied, trying to force a little smile. 'It's annual meeting time for some of the clients, and the corporate officers are getting a little hysterical. Nothing uncommon, just the usual annual stockholder meeting anxiety.'

Slocum said nothing for a minute, then spoke slowly. 'I've been a member of this firm for almost forty years, Ainsworth. And I've worked in the corporate section almost all of those years. I'm familiar with the stockholder willies, but I've never seen anything like this.'

'Merely a minor setback, Abner. One of our people forgot to file one of those damn SEC schedules. It could really cause a fury at the meeting. Our people are just bashing away at getting it in. We'll have it done and into John Crim's hands in Washington before the commission opens for business in the morning. We can be inordinately efficient in a crisis.'

Slocum nodded in assent. 'Yes, that's a fact. We have a reputation of staying ahead of possible crises. The firm can respond quickly when it is necessary.'

'True,' Martin said, selecting a cigar.

'What client is it, one of mine?'

Martin shook his head. 'Ah . . . no, Abner. This is a new one.'

'So, what company?'

Martin puffed the cigar into life. 'I'm afraid that information is on need-to-know basis, Abner.'

Slocum sat quietly for a moment, then spoke. 'I'm one of the main partners, Ainsworth. Surely there's nothing that has to be kept from me. In my almost forty years in the firm I have *never*, never had information withheld from me.'

'In point of time,' Martin responded, articulating each word as though it had no connection with others. 'It's a delicate situation, Abner. We are on the lip of a major corporate war. At the moment we have no need of your considerable talents or experience, so it's just as well that you don't know. I'm trying to limit things so that there won't be any leaks.'

'Do you seriously think I'd leak something to damage one of our clients?' Slocum snapped.

'Don't be offended, Abner,' Martin replied evenly. 'It's nothing personal. But I am limiting information to only those connected with the matter, and even then they learn only what they need to know to carry out their job.'

'What about the other partners?' Slocum demanded. 'Who is in on this very special project of yours?'

'It's not my special project, it's the firm's.' He relit the cigar. 'Only Solomon, and myself are connected with it at the moment. We are the only main partners involved.'

Disbelief illuminated Slocum's small features. 'It's not because you think I'm going to be let out to pasture in only a matter of a couple of months, is it?'

Ainsworth Martin gave up on the cigar. He laid it down in his marble ashtray. 'No, Abner. A special unit has been set up to handle this matter. As things progress I suspect all the main partners, including you, will be involved. As a matter of fact, I called John Crim in Washington and have him standing by, although I haven't told him why.'

'Juvenile,' Slocum snapped. 'No one elected you king! You're the managing partner, Ainsworth, that's all. It seems to me this flies directly in the face of firm procedure.'

Martin shrugged. 'Perhaps it does, Abner. But when it comes time to reveal what we're up to, I'm sure you'll agree with me that this was absolutely necessary.'

'So you're really not going to tell me,' Slocum said incredulously.

As he shook his head, Ainsworth Martin again attempted a smile. 'I'm afraid I can't; not at this time. At the moment it would only be gossip, and dangerous gossip if it somehow got out on the street. You're being treated exactly the same as everyone else, let me assure you.'

Abner Slocum felt anger, but determinedly fought against showing it. 'Perhaps.' He paused, then continued. 'How is the committee on the retirement question coming along? Any progress?'

Martin shook his head. 'I believe they've met. I'm waiting for a memo from Katherine Thurston, but I haven't received anything so far.'

'You don't seem to be in any great hurry to resolve the issue.'

Martin looked him in the eye. 'Abner, I know how important it is to you. I'm against changing the rules, as you know, but I wouldn't ever sabotage the committee. Relax, they'll come up with something soon. Perhaps favourable to your point of view, who knows? I'm really tied up with this other thing, but I'll make an effort to touch base with Katherine first thing in the morning.'

Slocum stood up. Outwardly he maintained calm, but inside he was seething. 'I'd appreciate it,' he said.

Slocum walked briskly back to his office, unmindful of the pain in his arthritic legs. The other partners were already cutting him out of the firm business. There was something ghoulish about it, like giving away the clothes of a sick man who hadn't yet died.

Never had he been treated like that before. Abner Slocum slowly began to formulate a plan to ensure that he would never be treated like that again. Ever.

15

The ringing of the telephone awakened her. As in a dream, she was at first completely disoriented by the foreign sound of the telephone, and then by her room. Panic seized her until she finally realized she was in her room at the Savoy.

Christina quickly sat up and looked at the other side of the big bed. It was empty. She then located the source of the sound and picked up the receiver.

'Yes,' she said.

'Mrs Giles, this is John Forbes, Mr Kuragamo's London secretary. He asked me to call you.' His accent was very definitely upper-class with just a hint of an effeminate inflection. 'It's two o'clock here, Mrs Giles. Mr Kuragamo asks that you join him for tea this afternoon.'

'What time?' She still felt as though she were half in a dream.

'Now, or tea time?' The man's voice was civil, but there was a hint of exasperation.

'Now.'

'Two o'clock. In the afternoon, British time, Mrs Giles. Allowing for the five-hour time difference, it is nine o'clock in the morning in your city of New York.'

'And what time is tea?'

'Four o'clock. Mr Kuragamo asks that you join him downstairs. The Savoy is a favourite place to take tea.'

'In the restaurant?'

'No, madam.' Again the voice was just barely civil. 'Tea is taken in the foyer.

'That's at four?'

'I presume that I can inform Mr Kuragamo that you'll meet him then?'

'Is he there? May I speak to him?'

There was a momentary pause. 'I'm afraid he's at a meeting at the moment, Mrs Giles. I can see that he gets a message if you wish.'

'No, that won't be necessary.'

'And you will meet him for tea?'

'Yes.'

'Very good.' She heard the click as he hung up. Replacing the receiver, Christina lay back on the crisp, linen sheets.

She wondered if she had dreamed it. She hadn't been with many men: two young men, both college lovers, then Henry. There had been no one since, until now.

And the lovemaking itself had been dreamlike, too, although satisfying. Kuragamo was a powerful man, sure of himself. She had given herself completely.

She looked at the ceiling and wondered what was happening to her. It all seemed a blur: her break with Henry, the encounter with Kuragamo. She wished she felt the warmth of love for the tall Japanese, but her feelings were more complex, a mixture of affection and awe. She wondered if somewhere along the way she had lost the capacity to feel unreserved love.

She sat up and swung her feet over the side of the bed. She still felt groggy. Why hadn't Kuragamo himself called? He'd always been so courtly. Perhaps he really was tied up in a meeting. His secretary had probably been trained to keep people away from him until he wanted to speak to them.

The bathroom was solidly handsome in design but completely modern, including a shower. She enjoyed the sensation as hot water sprayed down from the golden shower head. Staying in the shower much longer than usual, she let the soothing heat drive away the lingering fatigue.

She towelled herself dry, but didn't dress. Parading around the suit in the nude made her feel sinful, and she liked the feeling. Her empty luggage had been stored in a cupboard and her few clothes had been carefully hung up.

Christina located her handbag and took out her address book. The hotel operator placed the call to the London bank for her. The closing officer assured her that everything was ready for the scheduled closing tomorrow.

That meant that she would have a whole day in London, or at least half a day. She loved the city, its order, its quiet, at least in comparison to New York. She liked the London underground – always safe and clean – so unlike New York's subway system, a form of transportation she always avoided. She would now have time to visit the shops in Knightsbridge. She would do that, perhaps after tea. Even if the shops were closed, it was always fun to window-shop.

Helen felt the first stirrings of hunger. She really couldn't eat now, it would ruin tea. From experience she had learned that English tea could mean more than simply a cup of amber liquid. It would be impolite to eat first. She decided she would wait.

Scenes of the previous evening kept creeping unbidden into her mind. She could almost feel Taro's hands, so strong and yet so sensitive. He was a practised lover. Yet, there seemed to have been little real passion or emotion. He was a competent lover, but a silent one, whose facial expression never seemed to change.

192

She chose one of the outfits she'd purchased at Bloomingdale's. She used a nail file to remove the still-attached price tags from the simple navy blue wool crêpe suit and burgundy silk blouse.

When she had finished dressing, checking again to make sure that the new outfit was correct, she took the elegant elevator to the street. In the lobby waiters were busy setting tables. She walked out to the entrance overlooking the river and was pleasantly surprised by the mildness of the day.

Apparently it had rained. The pavement was still wet, but everything seemed clean and fresh, as she walked through the Embankment Gardens admiring the flowers.

Her depression began to lift. The atmosphere was relaxed here, so different from the frenzied, hectic pace of New York. If the British were anxious or in a hurry, they didn't seem to show it.

Although she had no home, and really had no idea which direction her personal life might take, or, for that matter, her professional career with Nelson and Clark, she began to feel again as if she had some control over her eventual destiny. She had had some sleep, and her spirits seemed to rise with every step she took.

Her stroll took longer than she'd expected, and she returned to the hotel at ten minutes past four. Although it was jammed with people, everyone seemed quite relaxed and untroubled as waiters moved like ghosts among the guests.

A huge trolley of pastries, its tiers taller than a man, was being wheeled from table to table. She was delighted to hear a talented violinist playing the music of Cole Porter while a pianist accompanied him. It was the sprightly music of a time when romance and adventure were the rage.

Taro Kuragamo wasn't hard to find. He sat at a table by himself, looking much like a king surveying his court. Elegant and dignified, he rose as she approached the table.

'I'm sorry to be late, Taro,' she said. 'I went for a walk and it took longer than I'd planned.' A waiter helped her with her chair. 'I hope you haven't been waiting long.'

He wasn't smiling. His dark eyes again betrayed none of his thoughts. 'I don't mind waiting, within reason. As I think I've mentioned, I enjoy watching people. I make a game of it, trying to guess their occupations, or perhaps, if it's a couple, their relationship.' He gestured to the waiter, who responded immediately.

Without consulting her, he ordered tea and sandwiches.

As if in answer to her thoughts, he spoke. 'I rather doubt that you've had time to get anything to eat. I thought a light snack might be welcome.'

'I am hungry.'

He nodded. 'Any problems about last night?'

'In what way?'

He studied her for a moment before replying. 'Many women might have feelings of guilt, Christina. After all, I rather doubt that you do this sort of thing on a regular basis.'

She felt herself colour. 'Did it show that much?'

He laughed quietly. 'No, not in that way. You are a perfect lover. I meant that you are obviously a chaste lady. I fancy that this may be the first such experience you've had since your marriage. Am I correct?'

'That's rather personal, isn't it, Taro?' She could almost hear her mother's words counselling her that a woman should always remain mysterious to a man.

'I hope I haven't offended you.'

The waiter served the tea.

She waited until he had gone before responding. 'You are quite right, Taro, that was the first time. There were other men, but that was before I met and married Henry.'

He nodded solemnly. 'Ah, the American woman. So liberated, yet so bound by feminine ethics.'

'What do you mean by that?'

'Not an insult, dear Christina. But this is the age of the modern woman, is it not? I have some personal knowledge in that department. This is the age of sexual equality. A woman can have just as full a sex life as a man, or at least that's what's proclaimed by the feminist revolutionaries. You don't seem to have measured up to that degree of liberation.'

'And you find that unattractive?'

He smiled. 'Quite the contrary. Loyalty, physical and spiritual, is greatly prized by the Japanese. Our women are expected to behave in that manner, revolution or not.'

'And subservient, too.'

'There are compensations, Christina.'

'Oh?'

194

Kuragamo managed a slight smile. 'Security, of course – a valuable consideration in our turbulent world. And the predictability of one's future. True tranquillity demands there be no surprises. There is much happiness in an orderly existence, my dear. Japanese women, or at least most of them, find that such an Oriental world holds the true meaning of contentment.'

'Does your wife agree with your philosophy?'

He nodded solemnly. 'Of course. She knows what every day will bring. She has her children; she has their respect. She is honoured as my wife. I think she enjoys her situation.'

'And what about love?'

'Ah, the romance of American and European women. You must have it, mustn't you? It really is just an illusion, Christina. Respect, or honour, if you prefer, plus tranquillity, is the key factor in life. My wife understands that.'

'And sex?'

He shrugged. 'Like the blossoms of spring, it is to be enjoyed in a woman's early years, for the production of children. In maturity – and a respectable woman understands this – it passes, as does the spring.'

'That doesn't seem to apply to you.'

'Ah, but I am a man. There are different biological forces at work within my body, different needs. The Japanese culture recognizes this. We are a practical people.'

'It's called the double standard in the United States.'

He chuckled softly. 'That's the battle cry of the feminists, is it not? Do away with the double standard? Yet, my dear, the sexes are different. In our society, they are equal, but in a different way. We Japanese follow the dictates of nature and common sense.'

Her irritation was rising. At first she thought he was joking, poking fun to see if he could get a reaction from her. Now she began to see that he meant everything he was saying.

'And if your wife took a lover?'

A sudden scowl, which he quickly tried to hide, crossed his features. 'That would be a great mistake on her part. It would dishonour me.'

'So you'd get a divorce?'

He shook his head. 'No. She would be . . . well . . . disciplined for her transgression.'

'That sounds positively medieval.'

'Hardly. I don't mean any force would be used. But she would feel the sting of certain financial sanctions. Life would suddenly become rather difficult. And her lover would rue the day he ever saw her. But he would have known that to begin with, of course. He would be destroyed, but only in a financial sense. Everyone who knows would understand.'

She sipped her tea, suddenly not hungry any more. 'My God, Taro, for a man who has been educated in the English system, you sound like some kind of ancient warlord.'

As if complimented, he bowed slightly. 'You are right, of course. But please understand, I am the product of my heritage. I had the choice to embrace either the European way of behaviour and thought or the Japanese. I have made the correct choice; the choice dictated by cold logic. My life is quite tranquil, serene. That is the ultimate test.'

Christina felt oddly disturbed. His words she found offensive, against all principles in which she believed; yet she was unaccountably stirred by his overwhelming arrogance. There was something almost hypnotic about this man's confidence.

'You should eat something,' he said quite gently. 'Even American women need to eat in order to live.' His face was guarded, but the dark eyes seemed amused.

Despite herself she picked up a sandwich and took a bite. Suddenly she was ravenously hungry.

'This is pleasant, is it not?' He gestured at the courtlike setting. Other people were talking quietly or just listening to the music. 'I take tea here often. It is most relaxing.'

She nodded.

'When you're finished, perhaps we can go up to your room for a few minutes?'

She looked at him. Again, his expression gave no clue as to what he was thinking.

'I have tickets for tonight's Royal Shakespeare Company's performance at the Barbican Centre. But the curtain isn't until eight.'

'And you want to go up to the room and make love?'

He reached across the table to take her hand. Despite herself, his touch was like electricity. 'If you don't feel like it, my dear, then we can talk.'

196

The conflicting emotions of annoyance and attraction were disquieting.

'Isn't it still customary for a woman to invite a man up to her room? Not the other way around? Or have things changed that drastically?'

Kuragamo's immobile expression remained unchanged. 'As I said, Christina, I deal only in reality. Last night we were lovers. You found me attractive and acceptable then. Surely I haven't changed all that much in less than a day. We could of course perform the usual ritual courtship dance – perhaps have a few drinks and then go up to the room by "accident". But that is a foolish waste of time. I am only being honest, Christina.'

He suddenly stood up, his tall form towering above her. He held out his hand.

Once again she was caught up in a tumult of emotions. She didn't want to go, to sacrifice her pride, and yet his attraction was so strong, in a way quite irresistible.

He helped her up and guided her towards the elevators.

'I feel like a whore,' she whispered.

He looked down at her and smiled. 'Ah, but surely a very beautiful one.'

16

'Mr Murray,' his secretary whispered, 'there's that white ring around your lips again.'

Augustus Murray nodded, turned on his heel, and returned to his office. As president of Brown and Brown, his large office had a modern bathroom, complete with shower, a perk of his corporate position.

He examined himself in the mirror. She was right. A thin white line, not unlike a highway divider, lined both his lips. He wet a towel and dabbed away the telltale marks.

Lika many other American business executives, Murray suffered

197

from stomach ulcers. He existed on a bland diet except for brandy, which he drank with milk. He also consumed an unending supply of chalky liquid medicine, which, no matter how carefully he swallowed it, always seemed to leave its residue on his lips, a badge of the businessman's disease.

He took one more critical view of himself in the glass, straightened his tie, then marched forth, his stomach burning.

His secretary looked up and smiled her approval. She was a good woman, efficient to be sure, but aging and unattractive. He had selected her himself.

Murray walked down the long hallway to the corporate boardroom.

An emergency meeting of the board of directors had been called by Edwards. Calling a meeting was usually the responsibility of Gus Murray, but Edwards hadn't even consulted him. All the members of the board had been hand-picked by the old man. They did exactly what he told them, no matter who called the meeting. They were all assembled in the boardroom and waiting.

Reluctantly, Murray opened the leather-covered doors and walked into the meeting. The room originally had been used as the main mixing room for Brown and Brown's magic elixir; now the long, windowless vault served as the board's base of operations.

They were all seated, including the company's four vice presidents plus a stranger. An equal number sat on each side of the very long, antique, polished table. Teddy Edwards occupied the head chair. His old, wizened face looked, from a distance, like a skull.

'Sit down, Murray,' the old man commanded irritably, as if he were late, which he wasn't.

Murray took a chair next to Eleanor Baumgardner, the senior board member. Mrs Baumgardner was almost as old as Teddy Edwards. Her hearing was severely impaired, but she was a nice quiet woman, and Murray liked her. She was one of the few board members whom he did like.

'You've all seen the newspapers,' Edwards chirped in his high, crackling voice. 'It seems that Brown and Brown is under attack.'

'What's that?' Mrs Baumgardner asked.

Edwards stared at her angrily. 'I'll tell you later, Eleanor!' he shouted in his shaky voice.

She smiled and nodded, happy to be recognized and secure in the knowledge that whatever happened at the long table would eventually be explained to her.

'As I say, we're under attack.'

Edwards launched into a lengthy explanation of John Norman Scott's audacious scheme to take over Brown and Brown. He glared at Murray, who had raised his hand. 'What is it?'

'I don't belive Scott said anything about a takeover. He says he's going to try and make a proxy fight, to get enough votes to oust the present management.'

Edwards' eyebrows raised in exasperation. 'Is that all you think this is, Murray, a proxy fight?'

'Isn't it?'

The old man's eyes narrowed. His voice was taut with disgust. 'No, it is not a proxy fight. Oh, that's how he'll start it, but he intends a hostile takeover of this firm, lock, stock and barrel.' He sat back in the high-back chair and glared down at the others seated at the table. 'What makes us so damned attractive is all that valuable land we have. It is a bankable asset and Scott knows it.'

Murray felt himself flush. The burning in his stomach increased.

Edwards' eyes remained fixed on Murray as he spoke. 'Now, if you think your store is going to be robbed, what do you do? You hire a policeman to protect you – at least you do if you have any sense.'

He gestured towards the stranger. 'This is Mr Emerson Becker, of Becker, Sloan and Kettering, a law firm specializing in the prosecution and defence in hostile takeover matters. You may have read in the *Wall Street Jouranl* _ those of you who do read – that Mr Becker is called the "gunslinger of Wall Street". A reputation richly earned, I'm informed. This whole business is going to get very nasty before it's done,' Edwards continued, 'and I wanted our company to have the very best to protect our interests.' His eyes were distant, almost dreamy. 'I have been entrusted by my family to protect this firm – our firm – and I am not going to allow some half-ass interloping buccaneer like Scott to come in here and ruin everything it has taken my family almost a century to build. There is absolutely nothing I won't do to stop that man.' He fell silent for a minute, as if the energy expended in his passionate speech had greatly tired him.

The others at the table were uncomfortable. They looked at each other, but each, knowing his or her future depended on the whim of the old man, remained silent.

Emerson Becker slowly stood up. A man in his mid-fifties, Becker was thick-chested but athletic. His light-brown hair was receding, and he combed it over the bald spot; the effect gave him a theatrical appearance, as though he were wearing an ill-fitting wig. His expression was closer to a sneer than a smile.

'Good afternoon, lady' – he bowed towards Eleanor Baumgarden – ' and gentlemen. As your chairman said, your company is in a rather difficult position. I believe Mr Edwards is quite correct when he says Mr Scott's actions on behalf of Lockwood Limited are indeed the opening manoeuvre leading towards a hostile takeover of this company.' Emerson Becker's voice was a deep and rumbling baritone, good for the stage or courtroom. 'While your company is indeed the world's largest chemical company, for the last few years most divisions have lost money. Your stock is sadly low on the board. The land that Mr Edwards spoke about is extremely valuable and is worth upwards of two billion dollars.'

'How much?' Mrs Baumgarden asked, now really interested.

Becker glared down at her as though she had just committed an unpardonable social sin, a signal to the others that he did not relish being interrupted. 'Two billion,' he repeated sharply.

He took a deep breath and continued. 'Thus, you present the ideal target for a takeover. You have a cheap, undervalued stock, easily purchased, while your true worth is much more, making that stock an extremely good bargain indeed. Although the cost of a takeover is enormous, even when friendly, when it is hostile, that is, against the wishes of the present owners, a company such as yours can be seized, sold piecemeal, including the land, and a handsome profit made even after all expenses have been paid.'

'What kind of expenses are you talking about?' Gus Murray asked. He was resentful that he hadn't been consulted in the choice of a lawyer.

'In order to take over a company, you have to offer to buy the shares from stockholders at a good price, one much above market. Now, after buying that stock, you break up the company, selling what you must. You need to make up for all the money you spent in buying up those controlling shares, right?'

Several people at the table nodded.

'That's the biggest expense, of course. But there are others. Obviously we lawyers don't come cheap, and companies really need us. The fees paid to investment bankers for obtaining financing are huge. Then there are the public relations people and so forth. It can add up.'

'Shouldn't we, ah, vote ourselves what they call a golden parachute?' Murray asked hesitantly.

Becker looked at the others. 'You all probably know what he's talking about. It's a resolution, binding upon the corporation and its successor, that if the takeover is lost, the officers get a handsome salary and bonus for a few years, hence the term "golden parachute".'

Old Edwards seemed to come alive, his eyes two malevolent slits. 'Murray, there'll be no golden parachutes here. You people' – he included the four vice presidents in his sweeping glance – 'are going to be faced with a life-and-death situation. My family isn't going to finance your goddamned futures. This will be a winner-take-all situation for you company officers. Either you stop Mr Scott and his plans or you'll be out on the street without a job, and with no money coming in. In other words, gentlemen, you have your backs to the wall.'

Murray and the four vice presidents manfully tried to hide their bitter disappointment and panic.

'I'm informed,' Becker, completely unruffled, continued, 'that John Norman Scott has retained Nelson and Clark to represent him. In case any of you don't know, Nelson and Clark like to think of themselves as America's number-one law firm.' An almost sinister grin made Becker's face even more feral. 'When this is all done, we will not only take care of Mr John Norman Scott, we will leave the famous Nelson and Clark lying in the dust. Reputations like theirs are often just puff and collapse when put to the test. This will be something of a personal contest both for me and my firm.' His last words were spoken with great relish.

'John Norman Scott has built his reputation through these takeover actions. He has built Lockwood Limited into one of the world's largest conglomerates by doing exactly what he plans to do to Brown and Brown.'

Becker clasped his hands before him – an obviously practised gesture – looking now like a schoolmaster enlightening an eager class.

'Scott usually follows the same pattern. In the beginning, he tries a proxy fight. Of course if he can pick up enough votes to gain control, he gets the company very cheap and makes a far greater profit when he breaks it up and sells what he doesn't want.' He paused. 'However, most companies can withstand Mr Scott's proxy war. He does it mainly to discredit the officers of the target company. Stockholders get nervous and will be conditioned to sell their stock at the premium price he offers later on. In other words, he poisons their minds, sows the seeds of distrust, and then later reaps the harvest of suspicion. Like a burglar, he has developed his own modus operandi. We know what we can expect of him.'

'Shouldn't that give us the upper hand?' Murray asked, feeling the old man's eyes eating right into his skin.

'It helps, but in the final analysis it's money that talks in these matters. It's like a no-limit poker game – you have to have as much money as the other guy in order to stay in.'

'We can sell the land. I've already started the machinery,' Murray said.

Becker slowly shook his head. 'This will be a very fast track. As soon as the stockholders' meeting is over – and that's only a short time away – Scott will launch the takeover bid. By law he must wait a few days, and then he has only another few days to take tenders of stock. Because of the statutes and regulations, a takeover war is very fast. From what I understand from Mr Edwards, you'll never have a chance to sell that land in time. Even if you had a purchaser available, and that's big, very big, money you're talking about. You'd need banks to make loans, and that takes time. Then you'd have to reinvest to protect the profit. No, as a practical matter, you don't have time to sell that land and protect the asset.'

'Then what do we do?' Murray asked.

'We fight!' Edwards' squeaky voice cut in.

Becker's was a cold smile. 'Mr Edwards is exactly right. That's what you've hired me for. Scott will think he has taken a ride on a tiger when he tries to take Brown and Brown.'

Murray's face reflected his puzzlement. 'A ride on a tiger?'

Edwards almost twitched with anticipation. 'It's an old Chinese saying: It is easy to ride a tiger but you can never get off.'

'I don't understand –' Murray started to say.

'If the son of a bitch tries to get off, the tiger will *eat* him, you idiot!' old Teddy Edwards exploded.

202

Murray felt himself colour. The eyes of the directors avoided his. He didn't know if John Norman Scott was riding a tiger or not, but he felt that he, Augustus Murray, was, and perhaps this tiger would make him get off.

His stomach felt as though hot lava were exploding within it.

Becker ignored the exchange. 'Our first battle will be over the proxies. For the most part it will be fought in the newspapers,' he continued. 'I've hired Casey and Ambrose, a top-flight PR outfit. They'll have an exciting counterattack in tomorrow's papers. Mr Scott won't look so good when we're done with him.'

The attorney still kept his hands clasped, although he was apparently thrilled at the promise of battle. 'The real fight will take place when he makes the takeover offer for the stock. That war will be fought primarily in the courts.'

Old Edwards cackled. It was a sound not unlike crunching papers. 'It won't be all that hard. That Scott's a fool. Anyone who loses his head over a fancy piece of young pussy is a bumbling moron.'

'Piece of what?' Eleanor Baumgarden asked.

'Pussy,' Murray said, but she didn't hear him either.

Edwards' strange laugh filled the room. 'See, we aren't the only company with idiots running the show. We'll knock the crap out of Mr John Norman Scott.'

Becker's smile became a leer. 'And his Twelve Apostles, too.'

Michael Collins had returned to Nelson and Clark, bringing with him Nancy Merriam. Dan Spencer was pleasantly surprised to see how quickly the young lawyer had organized the clericals and attorneys to begin the frantic work ahead. Spencer was also impressed to see that Nancy Merriam wasn't just an idle spectator. She seemed to be everywhere at once, quietly taking charge, but carefully avoiding treading on any sensitive toes. Spencer noticed Michael Collins' obvious interest in Nancy. He guessed that Collins was fast developing a schoolboy crush, a dangerous thing when the woman belonged to one of the firm's important clients. He decided he would have to keep a wary eye on that budding relationship. There were more than enough complications to go around now, without adding anything so potentially volatile.

Spencer made his way to his own office, took off his coat, and sat in the large leather chair. He swivelled around and studied the Manhattan scene below as he began to plan the next step. There was so much to do.

He buzzed his secretary, who was being pressed into overtime work. 'Get John Crim in Washington, please,' he said. He idly massaged his temples while waiting. He circled the fingertips, trying to rub away the growing worry. Every minute counted now, every step was crucial, not only to Scott and his company but to the firm, and absolutely crucial to his own future.

'I'm trying,' his secretary said over the intercom, 'but I can't locate him. He's not at the office, and his wife thinks he was going to several business meetings.' She paused. 'Do they have business meetings this late in Washington?'

'They call them cocktail parties,' Spencer replied, 'but they are really business meeting. Crim tells me the truly important work of government is done there not during the day and not on Capitol Hill. Tell you what. Try the other men – either in the office, if they're still there, or at home. Maybe one of them knows where Crim is. Tell them it's an emergency.'

Dan Spencer leaned back in the chair. It was essential that he contact Crim. Much had to be done before the filing of the government form in the morning. It all had to be done this night. He fought against the panic. They would somehow locate Crim. An Apostle always stayed in touch with the office. It was a rule. Crim knew that. Especially Crim, since he was really the firm's lobbyist with the Washington establishment, and emergencies often called for his services.

His secretary poked her head in the door. 'Mr Krotz, the former congressman, says he has a number where Mr Crim can be reached, but he suggested that only you try it. I don't know why.' She sounded slightly irritated.

'Don't worry about it. Those Washington people are preoccupied with security. The whole lot of them is paranoid. Give me the number and I'll see if I can reach him.'

She gave him the note, retreated, and tactfully closed the door behind her.

Spencer dialled the number. It was a Washington area code. The telephone rang without response, and he was about to hang up when someone answered.

'Hello.' It was the voice of a young woman. She sounded as if she'd been laughing.

'This is Dan Spencer in New York,' he said. 'Is John Crim there by any chance?'

'Who?' she asked.

'John Crim,' he repeated.

'No, I mean, who is this calling?' Her voice was pleasantly melodious.

'Dan Spencer,' he said his name again. 'From Nelson and Clark.'

'Dan Spencer,' she repeated slowly, 'from Nelson and Clark.'

'That's right.'

There was a pause. He heard whispers.

'Just a minute,' she said, half-laughing.

'Hey, Dan, how are you?' Crim's smooth voice floated from the receiver.

'Busy. I hope I haven't caught you at a bad time. We tried the office and then your home.'

'No problem. How did you get this number, incidentally?' Crim sounded very relaxed.

'Joe Krotz had it. My girl told him it was an emergency.'

Crim chuckled. 'Listen, Dan, I'd appreciate it if you'd just forget this number. If anyone asks, tell them you contacted me at the Hungarian Embassy. There's a big party there tonight. Now, what kind of emergency have you got up there?'

Spencer wondered what she looked like. 'It's hot, John. We have a 13-D Disclosure Schedule to file with the Securities and Exchange Commission tomorrow morning. It's overdue, and that could ruin something very high in the wind if the commission balks or stalls.'

'What's going on?' Crim asked. 'The commission doesn't give a damn about small technicalities.'

'I'd prefer not to discuss it over the phone, John.'

He heard the exasperated gasp at the other end of the phone. 'Look, Dan, I want to be obliging, and apparently you want something from me, but I have to know what's going on before I know what to do.'

'We'll need you to contact the commissioners tonight and sort of prepare the way.'

He snorted. 'Hell, they'll get sore. They have private lives just like I once had.'

'I said I was sorry to bother you, John, but this is top priority.'

There was a pause. 'Look, I'm not just a flack down here, do you realize that? I'm one of the main partners, one of the Apostles. Now, as I recall the articles of partnership, if anyone gives orders around here, Dan, it's supposed to be me. Am I making myself clear?' The words were spoken pleasantly enough, but the message was clear.

'These aren't orders, John. It's firm business, important business.'

'Tell me the problem.'

'Our client has acquired over five per cent of a corporation. Approximately six per cent, perhaps a bit more. He neglected to file the disclosure statement. It's being prepared now.'

'Six per cent of whom?'

'Brown and Brown.'

'The big chemical outfit?' Crim asked.

'Yes.'

'Jesus, six per cent is one hell of a block of stock. Who's our client?'

'I'd rather not say over the phone.'

'If you expect me to do anything tonight, you'd better impress me as to the emergency.'

'Our client is Lockwood Limited.'

'John Norman Scott?'

'The same,' Spencer answered.

'Jesus.' Crim's voice was almost a whisper. 'Does this mean what I think it means?'

'Mr Scott announced his intention to take over the company today. He's soliciting proxies.'

'Holy Christ! His ass is hanging out if he hasn't filed the disclosure – that's what it's for. And he's acquired more than five per cent – that's illegal if you don't file. Doesn't the dumb bastard know that?'

Spencer was delighted by the new note of interest in Crim's voice. 'He isn't much of a detail man. But you can see the importance.'

Now Crim's voice did drop to a whisper. 'Have we been retained to handle the proxy matter and what's sure to follow?'

'You got it,' Spencer answered.

'Oh, boy, if this one gets blown we'll look like a bunch of fools. Who took this bastard on? Scott's dangerous.'

'Ainsworth Martin.'

'Damn. Old Ainsworth hasn't changed a bit. With him the money always comes first . . . cut that out, I'm busy,' he snapped at someone at the other end of the phone. 'This could be an extremely risky undertaking,' he said to Spencer.

'You're absolutely right about that, John.'

'Who's assigned to run the show?'

'I am,' Spencer replied.

There was a pause. 'Hmmm. A bit unusual. Nothing against you personally, Dan, but this sort of thing is usually reserved for one of the main partners.'

'I know. I didn't volunteer.'

Crim chuckled. 'Well, I'll bet you didn't. Christ, if you blow this one . . . well, let's just say I don't envy you your position.'

'I'm not wild about it myself, but it's an assignment, the same as any other. Will you try to contact the members of the commission tonight?'

Crim didn't reply at once. Then, when he did, his voice was once more smooth and relaxed. 'Right now, with the political winds of the moment, the chairman really runs the show over there. He's a good friend of mine. I think I'll be able to persuade him to help things along tomorrow morning. I'll feed him some cockamamy story about a clerk screwing us, something like that. Things should go okay if the chairman guides the thing past his legal eagles over there. It will have to be handled delicately, especially if our friend has announced his intentions. When can you get the schedule to me?'

'First thing tomorrow I'll have someone hand-deliver it. Do you want it at the office?'

'Yes. I'll make it a point to get down early. I think I can persuade the chairman to have one of his people meet me and we'll slip that sucker through like it was crap through a goose. If anything untoward happens, I'll let you know right away, although I think this can be handled without problems.'

'As this goes along, we'll need a great deal of help from you.'

Crim laughed quietly. 'You bet your ass you will! God, just think of all the agencies and legislative committees I'll have to cool down. You know, Dan, I've been trying to persuade the others that this office in Washington has to be expanded. It's crucial to matters like these. But I'll be damned if I've had any success. Maybe this will prove it to them.'

'We'll see,' Spencer replied, carefully avoiding getting into intra-Apostle politics.'

Crim chuckled. 'Don't be coy, Dan. If you handle this right, you'll end up as a main partner. If you do, can I count on your vote to expand the Washington office, or is that taking unfair advantage?'

The manner was offhand and the question was posed lightly, but Spencer knew that Crim was deadly serious. He had to play it just right. If he promised Crim what he wanted, he could be offending other partners. It would not do to get on the wrong side of partnership business at a time like this.

'John, if that ever happened, if I were ever elected as a main partner, I'd certainly give your idea very serious consideration.'

Crim laughed. 'God, not all the bullshit is stacked down here on the old Potomac. But I can see your point. You don't want to start making commitments before you get the job – in case they turn out to be the wrong commitments, right?'

'Something like that.'

'Good enough. I like a practical man. I'll get going now, Dan. If anything goes wrong, I'll let you know.' He paused. 'Oh, one other thing.'

'What's that?'

'Tell Ainsworth Martin just how crucial my help is, Dan. That's almost as good as your vote. And you won't be exaggerating, you know that.'

'That's true. I'll tell Ainsworth.'

'Good, and I'll get moving, too.' He chuckled. 'Although I did have other plans.'

Spencer could hear the playful slap of a hand upon bare flesh and a woman's equally playful cry.

'Sorry,' Spencer said.

'Me, too,' Crim laughed.

The boardroom of the London bank looked more like a government office than the headquarters of one of the world's most imporatnt financial institutions. The table and chairs, although expensive, were starkly plain. The walls were bare save for a small oil of one of the bank's royal patrons and the usual portrait of the Queen.

'Gentlemen, you see before you a number of documents, each with a numbered card placed at the top for identification.' Christina Giles made eye contact as she spoke to the assembled men as they stood around the long table.

'I will call out the name of the bank or company and the person signing. I will then indicate which documents are to be signed by number. If you have any questions, please speak right up.'

'What if we miss one?' A thickly accented member from the German banking syndicate asked. He smiled, trying to make it appear as if he really wasn't worried, but she could see he was quite concerned.

'Don't worry. The officers of the bank have assured me that they check every document before we leave here. Everything will be quite in order, I assure you.'

She was the only woman present, except for a bank stenographer, a small elderly woman who was unobtrusively taking notes in the corner. The stenographer also had a small tape recorder at her elbow to ensure the faithful recording of this significant transaction.

Christina had put together an intricate web of banks and companies, most interdependent on each others' assurances, all woven into a strong financial net for the ailing steel company. If business improved, everything would go well; if not, most of the institutions signing would take a loss, but not a great one.

It was a risk, but by being shared, Christina had spread it around so that none of the backers would be mortally hurt.

'Mr Carlton of Thompkins Steel I believe should go first.' She looked at her list. 'Please sign documents 1, 2, 3, 9, 17, 23, and 28, just above your name.'

She felt Kuragamo's appraising eyes upon her. She felt she had to perform or perhaps be disgraced. He didn't have to come, for although he owned several of the companies, he wasn't an officer. But he had escorted her, bringing her in as though she were some kind of prize animal that belonged to him. She resented his obviousness. No one present could doubt their relationship, seeing his pride of ownership.

Christina had already briefed everyone on the details of the arrangement, and the signing went smoothly. It was really only a formality. Like pilots, the London bank officials guided the signers through the documents on the table, carefully leading them through the maze of paper lying before them.

From the moment she had been escorted into the bank by Kuragamo, she finally understood why the closing had to be in London and why she had to be present. It had all been an elaborate ploy by Taro Kuragamo. He had used a billion-dollar transaction between multinational companies to arrange a meeting with her – for him, a very successful meeting. She was awed by the thought and by the fact that it had worked.

Wine was served by uniformed waiters and a quick toast was drunk by the assembled executives to the success of the plan. Harold Carlton, the president of Thompkins Steel, made a flowery speech, thanking Christina for conceiving the plan to save his company. He ended on a note of triumph and promise of greater days ahead.

Christina shook hands with everyone before departing. She thought she saw bemused looks on some faces, looks that seemed to hint at amused secret knowledge as the men glanced from the possessive Japanese to herself. She felt cheapened.

'You did well,' Kuragamo said as they descended in the bank's elevator.

'Tell me, did you arrange all this just to make a pass at me?'

His eyes were almost cold as he looked down at her. 'Arrange what?'

'The closing in London. My having to be here. I wasn't really needed, Taro. Any clerk could have done my job.'

He said nothing for a moment, then spoke softly but firmly. 'The financing concept was yours. It seemed only fair that you should be in at the conclusion. I must admit the closing in London was my idea. I like London. Since my companies were putting up most of the money, I thought it only fair that I select the location to complete the transaction.'

'But your main motivation was to get me here, away from New York. You arrange all this too — '

'Don't flatter yourself unduly,' he said, a ghost of a smile playing on his thin lips. 'What my intentions were has little to do with anything. It was a business transaction involving a great deal of money. Obviously it did enter my thoughts that it would be more pleasant if you were here.' His voice held a tone of faint scorn. 'And, as it turned out, it was most pleasant indeed.'

210

'You could have just as well made your pass in New York.'

His face remained immobile. 'To whom? The little career girl and wronged wife? The worried mother of an ungrateful son? No, you would have been charming, I'm sure, but nothing would have happened between us. London was better, especially after the break with your husband.'

The London weather had changed. It was colder and a promise of rain was in the air. They walked along the street; Kuragamo's limousine followed at a discreet distance.

'Why the walk?'

He had taken her arm, holding her firmly.

'You have no place to go when you get back home, is that not so?'

'There are hotels. I'll find an apartment soon.'

He nodded. 'You have seen my New York apartment. I'm not using it. It has a full complement of servants. You will use that until you find something else.'

'Taro, that's very generous, of course, but I can't.'

He kept walking leisurely, still holding her arm. 'It is not a matter of accepting it or not. I wish it. Besides, with you there it gives me an excuse to visit New York more often.'

'Aren't you supposed to buy me furs and jewels? That's the usual arrangement when a man puts a woman up in a New York penthouse, or so I've read.'

This time he did smile, but the smile held no real warmth. 'Jewels are mere babules. If you like them you can have them. But I think you're trying to say you see yourself as my whore, or something like that, correct?'

'Hardly your maiden aunt.'

For a moment the stern face flashed that boyish quality, but it was quickly gone. 'No, you are not my maiden aunt. However, you are my friend. You have no place to stay, no comfortable place, and I am offering you the use of my apartment. Surely that isn't so strange?'

'No, but — '

'You refuse me because I am your lover. That's somewhat illogical, Christina.'

She sighed, feeling the first of a rainy mist touching her cheek. 'Taro, my personal life is so chaotic. I can't make any decisions now. I surely can't — '

'I have called my servants,' he said, ignoring her. 'They are expecting you. My chauffeur will pick you up at Kennedy Airport.'

'Isn't that a bit presumptuous?'

He glanced down at her. 'Not at all. You need a place to stay, and I have one. It's logical.'

'But —'

'Christina.' He spoke firmly, as a loving father might counsel a child. 'It is arranged. I must leave in a few minutes for Heathrow to catch a plane to Tokyo. I fully appreciate your point of view, but I don't have the time for argument. The apartment is yours.'

'Taro, how would that look? I'm not thinking just of myself, but of my son, and Nelson and Clark for that matter. Any hint of scandal in a firm like ours is —'

'My apartment is unknown to all. The arrangement will be quite private. I assure you.'

'But —'

He stopped, took her hand as he looked down at her. His face was wet from the mist. 'I must hurry to the airport, Christina. My driver is instructed to pick you up at the Savoy at five and get you to your plane. My servants have my number in Tokyo if you need me.' He glanced at his watch. 'I must go. I'm afraid I don't have time to drop you at the Savoy.'

'Taro, I really can't accept all this.'

He climbed into the limousine and looked back. 'You can. Also, please give some thought to leaving Nelson and Clark. I have some companies where your talent can be put to greater use. This would please me.'

Before she could reply he was gone. The limousine pulled away, gliding smoothly into traffic.

She was confused. She wanted to accept his explanation that he was only a friend doing her a favour, but her instincts whispered that she was being quickly drawn into the world of Taro Kuragamo, a world in which she would become a possession, no more. His statement that he wanted her to leave Nelson and Clark was more of a command than a suggestion.

She continued to walk on, not noticing that the mist had turned into rain. Her thoughts were on the insolent eyes of the tall Japanese. Was it love, she wondered, or was it resentment she felt, perhaps even dislike.

But if he wasn't in New York, she reasoned, it would do no harm to stay at the apartment for a day or two. She could find another place as easily from there as from a hotel. And with things so hectic at the firm, it would be much more convenient.

But if he came to Manhattan, if this were just one more pretence, she told herself she would leave.

She felt like a whore, having given herself, but she was determined not to become one.

17

'It's been a long day,' Michael Collins said as they relaxed in his office. As a beginning associate his furnishings were of good quality but sparse. As he would advance in the firm, the significant symbols of his standing, such as a better rug and more wall pictures, would increase. Michael Collins' office was the firm's basic beginning law office.

Nancy Merriam pushed back an errant strand of hair and smiled. 'Hectic, too, but it all got done much faster than I had thought possible.'

Her green eyes regarded him thoughtfully before she spoke again. 'I imagine you had a prefixed idea about me.'

He was going to lie but thought better of it. She was intelligent. He knew she would appreciate a straight answer. 'You want the truth, Nancy?'

She did not appear apprehensive. 'Yes.'

He hesitated, trying to select just the right words. 'Frankly, after reading all the newspaper articles I thought you'd be a flashy, gum-chewing babe with an IQ to match your age.'

'Since you put that in the past tense, I hope you've formed a different opinion.'

Collins knew he was blushing. She was sitting across from him in such a way that her long legs were prominently displayed. He was very aware of how truly appealing she was.

'A very different opinion,' he said softly. 'I'm very impressed,

213

Nancy. You're intelligent, well organized, and I know Mr Scott was doing exactly the right thing when he named you as vice president.'

'Perhaps.' She smiled wryly. 'Time will tell, Mike. But I am very glad you changed your mind.'

'I'll never trust the newspapers again,' he said.

They looked at each other, locked unexpectedly in an awkward silence. Everything was quiet. The law office was deserted. The secretaries, pressed into overtime service, had long gone home. Everything was done. Collins wanted to ask her out, but wondered if he should risk it.

'Nancy, we're all done here. Can I buy you a drink before you go home?'

She did not reply at once, which caused his anxiety to become even more acute.

'Do you think that's wise, Mike? After all, I am, well, they say I am John Scott's girl, and he is a client of your firm.'

Collins sensed there was a feminine challenge beneath the logic of her words.

'I'm not interested in what the firm thinks,' he said, 'or even the powerful John Norman Scott. I'm interested in what *you* think, Nancy. Getting up in the morning is a risk. Will you have a drink with me?'

She giggled. 'After that, how could I possibly refuse.'

Michael Collins experienced a surge of triumph. She was a beautiful woman. His heart was pounding with excitement.

Emerson Becker prided himself that he wasn't cut from the same cloth as the other Wall Street lawyers. And his law firm reflected his driving basic nature. He had founded Becker, Sloan and Kettering with just that in mind.

The *New York Times* and even the *Wall Street Journal* habitually referred to him as the 'gunslinger of Wall Street'. It was a title he had earned. Most Wall Street law firms operated on a gentlemanly basis, doing little litigation except for discovery – that legal invention to get a peek at the other man's cards – and negotiation was usually conducted in a dignified club or in the quiet of walnut-panelled offices.

Emerson Becker was different. He didn't bring gentlemanly motions before the court, nor was peaceful settlement a fine art with him. Becker was a fighter by nature, and he loved battle for its own sake. He often frightened other lawyers into surrender just by his scowling aggressiveness.

He was a sharp-minded lawyer, unafraid of anything, and he had assembled a firm of men and women who knew only one tactic: attack. He was preparing a stunning move.

One of the senior associates in the firm, Carl Youngblood, resembled Becker both physically and in his warlike attitude. Young enough to be his son, the two had often been mistaken for father and devoted son. Becker liked Youngblood and had come to rely on the young lawyer as his right hand, a natural extension of himself.

Youngblood, a former clerk to an appellate judge, had been with the firm for over four years. He was up for partnership, a fait accompli as far as everyone else in the firm was concerned. A seething mass of aggression, Youngblood was fast becoming almost a clone of Becker's. His promotion seemed assured.

Emerson Becker accepted the steaming cup of coffee handed to him by Youngblood. He sipped at it, savouring it, remembering he hadn't eaten since lunch and it was almost midnight.

'Tomorrow will be a big day,' Becker said, rubbing the back of his neck. He hadn't realized just how tired he had become.

'Things are bound to get hot,' Youngblood replied, his white teeth catching the gleam from the office lamp, giving his smile an eerie glitter.

Becker sat back. 'You'll go into federal court tomorrow morning and get the temporary restraining order.'

'You sound very sure that the judge will give it to me.'

'You haven't seen the complete pleadings.' He patted the new file in front of him on the desk. 'No judge in his right mind could fail to issue a temporary injunction when he sees what's alleged.'

Youngblood accepted the explanation with blind faith. He was pleased that he had been selected as the point man, the lawyer who would spearhead Brown and Brown's attack.

Becker again sipped at the coffee. 'Do you know where I'll be when you're knocking on the courthouse door?'

'No.'

'I'll be right in the neighbourhood with you. I'm going to see the district attorney in the morning and publicly demand the arrest of John Norman Scott.'

'What?'

Becker again patted the file. 'It's all in here: how he has been robbing that company of his for years; his abuse of office to buy presents for that girlfriend of his, even to putting her on the payroll, and his scandalous abuse in the law in failing to file his Schedule 13-D in time.'

'Well, I know that he filed late, but can you prove he stole?' Youngblood asked.

Becker sneered. 'I don't have to prove anything. We'll use discovery to go over their books. Hell, Scott's a businessman. He'll have done just what every other businessman does: charge personal gifts to the company, jack up expense accounts, that sort of thing. Those executives, they're all jugglers when it comes to money. Maybe to us it's not theft, but to the guy in the street the facts will sound pretty crooked if presented correctly.'

'Do you expect to get a warrant?'

Becker put down the coffee and leaned back in his chair. 'Of course not. That would be the worse thing that could happen. The takeover fight would be killed and we couldn't charge any more fees to protect our little lamb.'

'You just want the publicity.'

'You bet your ass. Believe me, tomorrow when you go into federal civil court and get that order stopping Scott from buying stock or acquiring proxies, and at the same time I will take my little speech to the press in the district attorney's office about thieves in high places, the headlines will *be* the story. Everybody in town will believe our little Napoleon is a goddamned corporate gangster.' Becker's face grew sinister as he talked, his eyes narrowing. 'It will work like a charm.'

'It will make him mad,' Youngblood retorted. 'Maybe it could backfire.'

Becker shook his head. 'I know that little asshole. He's already mad as a hornet. Scott will offer to buy the stock for more than it appears to be worth. If everyone thinks he's a crook, a number of them won't trust him no matter what he offers. They'll be afraid of being burned.'

Youngblood touched a finger to his temple as in salute. 'An inspired manoeuvre, as always.'

'There's the old adage that nobody should get in a pissing contest with a skunk, and I'm the biggest skunk in this town. I think John Norman Scott will damn well rue the day he ever heard of Brown and Brown, or for that matter, Becker, Sloan and Kettering.'

'What about Nelson and Clark? Scott isn't exactly alone in this matter.'

Becker grimaced. 'The big deal Twelve Apostles. Listen, Carl, those tea dancers are nothing but a bunch of imbred candy-asses. When I get through with them, a fly-by-night collection company wouldn't hire 'em to collect small debts.' He laughed, sat up, and banged both fists against the desk. 'I honest-to-God can't wait for it to begin.'

Their brittle laughter seemed to harmonize in the empty office – they both shared the same motivation – hunters, ready and eager for the kill.

'How do you like it so far, Ainsworth?' Spencer had taken the managing partner on an inspection tour of the offices for the special task force.

Ainsworth Martin didn't like Greenwich Village, and despite the fact that it had become eminently fashionable, to him it remained an area to be avoided. 'This looks more like a garment hustler's office,' he said, giving words to his disdain.

'It's a working headquarters,' Spencer said, knowing he would have to keep Ainsworth happy if he were to get the equipment he deemed necessary. 'I'm not concerned that the walls are peeling or that the wood floors are bare. We're not here to be seeing clients. This is strictly utilitarian. I've rented everything from the best word processors to those old desks.'

'We had better desks than that in the combat zone during World War Two,' Ainsworth said, tentatively running his fingertips along the marred steel top of one of the desks.

'I think that's where the company got them – army surplus. It's a Spartan workplace,' Spencer said. 'The telephones are being installed now. By this evening I'll have everything in, including copying machines. We had to have two electricians run in special lines for some of the equipment.'

'Costly, seeing we'll only be using it a month or two,' Martin said.

'I hope all this proves to be worth it. If Brown and Brown simply folds without a fight, we'll have a devilish time trying to get Scott to pay for all this.'

'If I scrimp now, we're liable to go into battle with no equipment for the troops. Even if the chemical company gives up, all this is still preventive medicine. Come with me.'

Spencer guided him past rows of empty steel desks, desks to be used by lawyers yet to be assigned. The secretaries' section was located in another part of the former garment warehouse. 'Here it is.' He opened the warped wooden door and stepped into a long narrow room. Light streamed in from tall windows along one side. 'This was a former cutting room.' A cluster of unconnected telephones was massed at one end of a long table. An ancient high-backed chair served as a focal point behind the bank of telephones. Behind it was a large portable chalkboard.

'This is the war room, Ainsworth. I'll operate out of here, or someone whom I'll delegate. We'll have a lawyer on duty around the clock.'

'Nights, too?'

'You're worried about security, right?'

Martin nodded solemnly. 'If we have people in here, they will be natural targets for robbers. Also, I imagine even I could burgle this place without much effort.' He glanced at the old warped door.

'I'm ahead of you on that. I've contracted with a private guard service to have two men here, also around the clock. One will serve as a doorman downstairs, the other up here.'

A telephone bell sounded somewhere in the long, open office. 'The telephone men are installing the equipment,' Spencer said. 'They're probably testing it now.'

The door opened and a bored telephone installer looked in, his tool-festooned belt worn like a gunfighter's. 'One of you guys named Spencer?'

'I am.'

'You got a telephone call. We only got one instrument installed,' he said, leading the way. 'Wiring this old place is a bitch. Hey, you guys bookies or something? I'd of thought off-track betting would have put you out of business.'

'We're not bookies,' Spencer said as they passed rows of crated word processors.

'Must be a collection outfit or a boiler-shop operation, huh?'

'Something like that,' Spencer replied.

The man handed him the dusty receiver. 'Place is a mess in here,' he said, brushing it off.

'Spencer,' he said into the telephone.

'Morris Solomon here, Dan.'

'How did you get this number, Morris? Even I don't know it yet.'

'Old friend at the telephone company. Listen, Dan, things have blown apart this morning.'

'What do you mean?'

'Brown and Brown asked for a warrant charging John Norman Scott with a felony.'

'What charge?'

'A variety, fraud being the main one.'

'What happened?'

'The matter was taken under advisement by the district attorney. However, he flatly refused to issue a warrant at this time.'

'So it's made to look like Scott is guilty, but they don't have enough to pin something on him, is that it?'

'Precisely.'

'Good trick. Dirty, but good.'

'Unfortunately, that's not all,' Solomon said, sounding somewhat depressed.

'Go on.'

'Please keep this to yourself, Dan. A few minutes ago Jerry Groban called me.'

'The United States district judge?'

'Jerry and I are old friends, old classmates, as a matter of fact.'

'Go on.'

'Brown and Brown asked for a temporary restraining order to prevent Scott from buying stock or soliciting proxies in their company.'

'The judge didn't grant it?'

Solomon let out a long sigh. 'He says he had to. They have set a hearing on it for Friday. Jerry said he had no other choice. Brown and Brown alleged permanent damage, and the judge felt no one would get hurt by a few days' delay, so he signed the damn thing.'

'And he felt guilty about doing it, and he called you on the sly, right?'

'I suppose,' Solomon replied.

'I'll tell you one thing, Morris. Whoever thought this up is god-damned brilliant. This will get coverage on television, radio, even nationally. A brilliant setup.'

'And dirty,' Solomon said. 'He's known for those two qualities, if you count alley fighting as a quality. Brilliant, yes, ethical, no. That sums him up.'

'Who is it?' Dan Spencer asked, almost sure of what the answer would be.

'The gunslinger, who else? The rabid Emerson Becker himself and his little band of cut-throats.'

Spencer nodded, suddenly feeling threatened. Becker had a mean reputation. He was a winner. Gentlemen's agreements were not recognized by Becker, nor by the staff of aggressive lawyers he had formed.

It would be rough.

Spencer was controlling his anger. 'There's only one thing a prick like Emerson Becker respects, and that's a swift kick in the legal nuts – and that's what I'm going to give him.'

Solomon laughed. 'My, what rough language. And from a Bostonian, too.'

'It's more than language. Switch me over to my secretary.'

'Hang on.'

Dan Spencer's mind was racing, his competitive juices flowing just as in the days when he was tapped to go into a close basketball game. He completely forgot about Ainsworth Martin, who stood at his side, quietly listening.

When his secretary got on the line, Spencer rattled off a list of orders. 'Tell Bruno Chasen to draft a quick objection to a TRO against Lockwood and get his buns to federal court. I want him to file it and talk to Judge Groban. Got that?'

She replied that she had. 'If there's any question from any of the lawyers I assign, have them check with Morris Solomon until I get there.' He looked up at the ceiling, thinking. 'Tell Andy Perkins to draft a quick lawsuit in New York's Supreme Court asking that the annual meeting of Brown and Brown be postponed. Tell him to use any grounds he wants. The other side has made the rules. Tell him it has to be done before three o'clock today. That's important. Have him notify the newspapers and TV people and set up a quick press conference at the court after he files. Tell him to blast Becker and the offices of Brown and Brown. At least we'll have some counter at the six o'clock news and the newspapers' late editions.'

'Okay,' she said.

Spencer paused again, then a small smile played across his lips. 'Have young Mike Collins get in touch with his father. I need a real criminal expert, someone who knows the important people in criminal court and the district attorney's office. Ask Mike to have his father meet me at the office if he can for lunch. We'll have something sent in. Tell Mike it's terribly important and that we'll pay his dad top fee, okay?'

'Right.'

'One last thing. Have Charley Manning and Jeff Rowe start preparing pleadings for libel and defamation of character.'

'Against whom?'

'I don't know yet. Whoever signed the pleadings for Brown and Brown. I don't care if it's the company officers or their lawyers. Have Bruno call that information in when he gets down to court. I'll grab a cab and be back there in a half hour or so. But get this thing rolling. Time is our enemy, amongst others.'

'I'll get right on it.'

'One other thing. See who the resident state bar officer is this year in the firm. I might want to bring disbarment proceedings against a lawyer, maybe a whole firm. Have him meet me there when I arrive.'

'Boy, this all sounds exciting,' she said.

'It is,' he said tersely. 'I'll be there as quickly as possible.' Spencer hung up, and only then did he become aware of Ainsworth Martin.

'You're not over-reacting, are you, Dan?' he said coolly.

Spencer looked him directly in the eye. 'In one deft, brilliant swoop Becker has branded our client as a thief and a crook. If that sticks, the proxy fight, the takeover, are finished right now. But, by God, I'm not going to let that happen. I'm going to take the gun-slinger's pistol, use his own tactics, and run his legal pistol right up his' – he noticed the silent disapproval on Martin's face – 'his nose.' Spencer grinned.

'You're the litigator,' Martin said. 'Do what you think best. Just remember that if you lie down with dogs you get up with fleas. Alley fighting is all right for some, Dan, but at Nelson and Clark we really don't find it too efficacious.'

Spencer felt good; his adrenalin was running. 'Ainsworth, if this Becker wipes the floor with us, what good will our lofty reputations do us then? Does anybody want a prestigious firm that loses in order to justify its dignity? If you don't like my tactics, you can always assign someone else.'

Ainsworth Martin, who rarely smiled, did so then. 'Oh, there are a few people warming up. Andy Perkins, for one. If they start to get some hits off you, we might just take you out of the game. But until then you're our starting pitcher.' The smile quickly faded. 'Just be careful, Dan. For your sake and for ours.'

'There's a time to be careful and there's a time to take risks,' Spencer said.

'And a wise man knows the difference,' Martin replied. 'If you're taking a cab back uptown, I'll join you.'

Despite Ainsworth Martin's warning, for the first time in a long while Dan Spencer was thoroughly enjoying himself.

As usual, the hospital telephone operator sounded offended that she should be put to the trouble of paging a doctor. She let Christina know by her tone that it was done more as a personal favour for a family member than as some mundane duty she was employed to perform.

And, as had happened so many times before, Christina had to wait. The girl had checked surgery, but he wasn't there. He hadn't signed out, so it meant he was still in the hospital.

She stared at her baggage piled in a corner of her office. She was homeless, indeed, and although Taro Kuragamo had offered his incredible apartment, she felt reluctant to accept. The feeling of having been used, rather than loved, was inescapable, although she realized that in the emotional storm engulfing her, she couldn't really trust her personal judgements.

'Giles.' His voice startled her. Without meaning to, or intending it, the previous anger and rage seemed instantly awakened.

'Hank, it's me, Christina,' she said. 'I want to get some personal things out of the apartment. But I don't think it's a good idea if you're there at the time.'

There was a pause. 'Your fucking lawyer served me with the divorce papers yesterday,' he snarled. 'If you think you're going to get everything I own and little Hank, too, you're damned mistaken, bitch.'

'I want only what's mine.'

'Bullshit. You don't have to be a lawyer to read between the lines in those lousy legal papers. You want everything – my ass, my blood. Well, toots, you may be a fucking lawyer, but I ain't going to roll over. Whatever you get, you'll have to fight for.'

She tried to control her anger before speaking. 'It's best to let the lawyers do the fighting in these things, Hank.'

'Piss on it. I went out and got a lawyer, too. You'd think the son of a bitch had just discovered gold. Christ, the money he wants: God, and they complain about doctors' fees. Well, whatever it costs I'll pay it just to fuck you over. Get me?'

Her anger turned to cold rage. 'I take it, then, that I can't get my things?'

'My, you *are* bright. As a matter of fact, pursuant to my lawyer's advice, I had the locks changed in the apartment. And I instructed the management people, including the doormen, not to let you in. Does that tell you something?'

She wanted to scream at him, but she controlled herself. 'If you want it that way, Hank, that's the way it will be. Did you tell your attorney about your little hobby, the many, many times you were unfaithful, the drunkenness, the fact that you're a father in name only? Don't even reply. I know just what you did. You went in there and charmed the man. When you got through, he thought you were a saint and I was a miserable, grasping whore, right? Well, that's what courts are for, Hank; they bring out the truth. I really didn't want anything from you – my lawyer probably just used the standard divorce boilerplate language, nothing more. But by God, I'm going to take your little challenge. You may be good in the operating room, you bastard, but I shine in court, and that's where this is all going to be decided – remember that.'

She heard the click as he hung up.

Tears spilled down her cheeks and she couldn't stop shaking. He had got to her, much to her surprise. She felt a wave of nausea sweep over her.

She was alone now, and embattled.

Christina leaned back in the chair and forced herself to calm down. It had been a long plane trip. She was exhausted, and she knew that played a large part in the depression that was taking over. Her relationship with Taro Kuragamo bothered her, too. It had none of the joy she had often imagined a sexual fling might have. It only produced in her an unease, and a deep, instinctual fear.

She got up, went to the small bathroom, and repaired her makeup. The simple act of splashing cold water was soothing and restoring. She felt the nausea pass.

She needed a friend, someone in whom she had confidence, someone who could guide her. She knew her thinking was disjointed, out of perspective.

She left her office and walked through the hallway, passing offices, conference rooms, and the library until she got to the litigation section.

The fury of activity surprised her. It reminded her of old movies showing a newspaper at deadline, people were poring over papers, machines were clattering, verbal orders being given. It was a study in chaos. She found Dan Spencer's secretary in the middle of the action, her hair askew, her face haggard.

'Is Mr Spencer in?' Christina asked.

The woman looked up at her, irritated at first at having been called away from what she was doing. 'Oh . . . Mrs Giles.' She blinked in recognition. 'He's in conference with a visiting lawyer and one of the staff.' She took a deep breath as if dreading what she had to say next. 'If it's important, I'll let him know you're here.'

'No, nothing pressing. Perhaps he could drop by my office when he's through.'

The woman bit her lower lip. 'Mrs Giles, all hell has busted loose here. I know that Mr Spencer has to rush off to court as soon as he's finished with his conference. I'll leave the message, naturally, but I don't think he'll be able to find time to see you.' She paused. 'Of course, that is unless it's really very important.'

Christina looked around at the frantic activity. 'What's going on?'

The secretary brushed back a strand of hair from her eyes. 'Just about everything. Brown and Brown, the chemical company, is suing Lockwood Limited, our client, and we're suing them back. I don't understand it all, but it's obviously important. Almost every Apostle has been down here at one time or another today.' She softened. 'The problem, you see, is Mr Spencer is in charge of the

224

whole thing. That's why I don't think he can see you, well, unless it's desperate.' She smiled an apology.

'I understand,' Christina replied. 'Just leave a message that I dropped by.'

'If you like I can leave him your home phone number.'

Christina didn't know what to say. If she said she no longer had one, the choice gossip would fly through the office. She had to be discreet, although she really felt she had lost everything anyway.

'No, that's not necessary. Just leave word that I stopped by. I'll check again tomorrow.'

Before Christina had even turned from the desk, the woman was back at work, frenetically pounding away at a word processor, making it sound more like a rattling machine-gun than a sophisticated computer.

Christina returned to her office and quietly closed the door. She was tired, bone tired. A hotel would feel too transient; just a bed. She needed a place, a quiet place, where she could stay for a few days and contemplate what she had to do, formulate some kind of plan for the future.

She knew, reluctantly, there was only one place where she could find that kind of solitude. She dialled the number Taro Kuragamo had given her. The butler sounded reserved but pleasant. He said they had been expecting her.

She dictated a quick note to the file on the London closing. A law clerk helped her with her luggage, and they had no problem getting a cab.

It was a short trip through the gridlocked Manhattan streets, streets that seemed almost foreign to her although this was her home, her city. She felt a sense of dread, as if she were being pushed towards some terrible destiny.

She couldn't shake the dread from her mind. She hoped a bath and a good sleep would give her a fresh perspective.

At the moment, the world seemed a very lonely and threatening place.

18

Michael Collins ushered his father into Dan Spencer's office. The elder Collins, as usual, was dressed in a garish outfit, this time a russet polyester suit, tooled tan boots, and a white silk tie worn over a dark-brown shirt. The flashy suit was the type mostly seen at racetracks and criminal courts. His father, although heavy, was tall and carried his weight well. His great mop of white hair contrasted with the reddish tint of his delicate Irish skin. In contrast to the conservative men and women of Nelson and Clark, Patrick Collins stood out like a rodeo cowboy, or so it seemed to Michael Collins.

Michael introduced his father to Dan Spencer.

'Please sit down, Mr Collins,' Spencer said.

'Thank you. May I call you Dan?'

'Of course.'

'Then perhaps you could call me Pat. Most people do.'

'Certainly, Pat.'

Patrick Collins looked around the office. 'I've often wanted to see the inside of this firm, especially now that you people have been so foolish as to hire this ne'er-do-well son of mine.'

'He's hardly that.' Dan Spencer smiled. 'He's a great help to me.'

'Well, it is an age of miracles, after all.' Collins' pride was evident despite his denigrating words.

'Let's get right down to business, Mr Collins.'

'Pat.'

'Right, Pat. I'm told you are regarded as the number-one criminal lawyer in New York.'

Patrick Collins shrugged. 'I'm not number one. I'm very good, or so they say, but there are easily a dozen or more who are just as good. I don't need the flattery, Dan. Criminal law is my speciality and I presume you want to draw upon that expertise.'

'Yes. We represent Lockwood Limited. They are — '

Collins held up a large hand. To his son, his large diamond pinky ring suddenly seemed markedly vulgar, although he had never thought so before. 'I listened to the noon news at my office. According to the report, an attempt was made to get a warrant against John Norman Scott, the head of Lockwood. Fraud, I think they said.

Also, Judge Groban issued a TRO stopping any action by Scott against the chemical company, Brown and Brown.' He smiled. 'I've learned never to entirely trust the accuracy of the media, but that does seem to sum up the situation.'

'Exactly.'

'As I recall the story, the district attorney declined to issue the warrant, saying he needed additional evidence.'

'That's right. They have made it look as if Scott is nothing more than a crook.'

'So what do you want with me?'

'We need to offset this manoeuvre. This whole thing was started today by Emerson Becker. Do you know him?'

Collins grinned. 'I read the *New York Times*. I know of him, but he hardly swims in the same legal pool I inhabit. He has the reputation of being somewhat ruthless.'

'That's him, and ruthless is putting it mildly. That's why I've asked you to consult. We need to do something to offset this criminal-court ploy he's pulled.'

Patrick Collins never changed his expression. 'What did you have in mind?' His voice was friendly, but Michael Collins remembered that particular tone from when he was a boy. It had the sound of coming thunder and it was a signal that trouble was on the way. Michael hoped his father would remember his son's delicate position with the firm.

'Dan, are you implying that your client, Mr Scott, is innocent of these charges made by Becker.'

'Exactly. The accusations were false, intended only to splash some mud on Scott, to discredit him.'

'In other words, you're telling me that Emerson Becker perverted the law to obtain his unjust purpose, is that not so?' Collins asked softly.

'Right. The son of a bitch is clever.'

Collins nodded slowly. 'And now you'd like to use my services to do the same thing, as I understand it?'

Dan Spencer appeared flustered. 'Well, it's not quite like that. A wrong has been done and I want to undo it.'

Pat Collins sighed. 'Ah, there's no use my repeating the old adage that two wrongs don't make a . . . well, we all know that, don't we. Tell me, Dan, what did you have in mind? A charge of murder

227

perhaps? Carnal knowledge of a Boy Scout, maybe – that's always good for ruining a man's reputation. Rape seems to have lost some of its sting lately, and — '

'Look, I'm sorry. I realize how all this must sound to you. I don't want anything illegal or unethical, I just want to find a way to undo what happened to my client this morning.'

'Sue for defamation of character.'

'That's being done,' Spencer answered. 'But we both know that the case will take years to get into a courtroom. All this will be history by then.'

Collins glanced up at his son, who had elected to remain standing. 'You're fresh from law school, and you clerked for that fancy judge. Show off a bit. Tell the man what he should do.'

Michael Collins felt himself blushing. 'You're the criminal expert.'

'Wrong.' The word was spoken softly. 'I'm the criminal *law* expert. Don't confuse me with the poor people I defend. I don't mug old ladies and I'm much too fat to be an effective burglar.'

'I'm merely asking you for some suggestions. Is that unethical?' Spencer said.

'I think what you suggest is unethical, yes. But if it's viewed a different way, I think justice might be served.'

Spencer looked quizzical.

'What Mr Becker did this morning was to pervert the criminal law. By using the mechanics of the system, he made it appear that your Mr Scott was a criminal. By the way, did Becker actually demand a warrant in writing?'

Spencer nodded. 'I'm informed that he did.'

Collins nodded, his expression growing solemn. 'Well, if he did, and what he alleged has no basis in fact, you could ask the district attorney to charge him with malicious abuse of process. But you would have to show intent.'

'We have that. Becker wanted to stop Scott's takeover.'

Collins nodded. 'Now if you ask the district attorney for such a warrant, he'll do exactly as he did with the Scott charge; he'll duck and make pious sounds about additional proofs, and the fact that the warrant was never issued.'

'So then we're back to square one. There's nothing we can do?'

Collins shook his head. 'Give me your telephone. I'll make two calls. One is to Sid Irwin, the head of the business crime unit. I'll tell him my son is coming down with a request for a warrant against Becker. The second call will be to Herb Lewitt of the *Post*. Herb loves this sort of thing. He'll meet Michael there, get an interview, and if I know Herb he'll have some television people in tow. He trades stories with 'em.'

'That's great,' Spencer said. 'That's just what we need.'

Pat Collins was at ease as he made the calls, kidding both men as he skilfully persuaded them to agree to what he wanted.

'Thanks, Pat,' Spencer said when he was done. 'Be sure to bill us – that was just terrific.'

Patrick Collins stood up but did not extend his hand. 'I didn't do that for a fee. Nor did I do it for my son here. He will stand on his own two feet. And I didn't do it for myself. I have never needed the Twelve Apostles in the past, and I doubt that I ever will in the future. Do you know why I did that?'

Spencer shook his head.

Collins chuckled softly. 'I love the law. Oh, I bend it now and then myself, but I never break it. Your friend Becker broke it into little pieces this morning. What I've just done is to punch him on the nose, in a manner of speaking, for doing what he did. I don't hold with lawyers who prostitute the system. You people in these blue-blood firms seem to be able to get away with anything just so long as it's done with style and lots of money is involved.'

'Well, I don't think that is entirely true, Mr Collins . . .' Spencer began.

Pat Collins grinned. 'Oh, no? The lowly criminals at least know who and what they are. When all is said and done, they aren't fooling themselves. When they commit a crime at least they don't give it another name and pretend it isn't.'

'Dad, we're just trying to protect Scott,' his son protested. 'We must do whatever is necessary to serve our client.'

'I serve my clients, too. But I don't help them in their criminal activity. There is a difference.'

'Dad, this is a matter of business, big business.'

'Ah, situational ethics, is that it?' He turned to Spencer. 'Old men tend to pontificate. You're a bright young man and I hope everything works out well for you.'

Patrick Collins left. Michael elected to stay with Dan Spencer.

'I'm sorry about my father. I don't know what got into him.'

Spencer looked at Michael Collins for a moment before speaking. 'When you think about it, he may be right. Maybe big money does tend to obscure ethics. There are limits, even in this business.'

Abner Slocum had felt inept, even foolish. He had not filed an estate for probate for at least thirty years. He had forgotten everything. A surly clerk, filled with self-importance, had even demanded to see his bar association card. Slocum had forced himself to remain calm, suffering the indignities as part of the price he had to pay for securing his freedom.

Ordinarily, the estate and trust section of Nelson and Clark would have taken care of the matter. Francis X. Desmond and his lawyers were celebrated experts, knowing every cranny whereby estate assets could be concealed or protected from the ever-present taxman.

Slocum pulled his coat collar up against the sprinkle of autumn rain that had begun to fall. He was basically unfamiliar with the court complex of lower Manhattan. Court work was something others did. He was proud that he had managed to file Sylvia Winship's estate – at least the important preliminary papers establishing him as the executor with full power – all without being discovered by any of the lawyers from the firm.

What he had done, Slocum knew, didn't violate even firm policy. He was merely serving in a private capacity for an old friend. Others did the same thing. The only difference was that the firm's special probate section ordinarily handled such work. It was a matter of convenience as well as practice, but there was no rule to the contrary.

Slocum signalled for another cab.

It was nice to hold all the aces for a change.

Dan Spencer climbed out of a cab at Foley Square and raced up the steps of the federal courthouse. After clearing the metal detector, he half-ran through the halls, grabbed a packed elevator, and got off at Judge Groban's floor.

Judge Groban's courtroom was elegant, at least in comparison to state courtrooms. It reflected the availability of federal dollars. The walls were recently painted; the window drapes clean and crisp and carefully hung. The jury chairs were modern and new.

Bruno Chasen was standing at the lectern. Apparently he had been successful in getting Groban to hear their motion. Spencer guessed the threat to go to press had worked.

'Without the court's action, our client will suffer irreparable harm.' Chasen was speaking firmly but respectfully.

'What harm?' the judge asked, his question snappish. 'I don't see any harm to your client here at all.'

Spencer didn't take a seat at the counsel table. The uniformed officer frowned at him as he stood quietly by the door. Spencer recognized Tonny Vartan of the *New York Times*. There were other newsmen, but Vartan was the Cronkite of the print media where business matters were concerned. If he was covering the story, it would assuredly be given top priority by the *Times'* editors.

'Your honour,' Chasen continued, 'our client is under an order from this court stopping all efforts towards gathering proxies for the Brown and Brown annual meeting. But as of this moment, Brown and Brown is free to go ahead and obtain as many proxies as it may need.'

The judge held up a warning hand. 'The hearing is set for Friday morning. That's hardly much time to do anything. I still don't see what real harm can be done to Lockwood or its officers.' The judge emphasized the word officers. 'Remember, Brown and Brown is just proceeding in the normal course of corporate life in setting up its annual meeting. As far as I know – and all I have is your unsupported affidavit otherwise – they are doing nothing to gather proxies. I'd certainly jump in with both feet, Mr Chasen' – the judge looked out at the newsmen – 'if I thought any lasting harm was being done, but you have the burden of establishing that, and so far, I can't see — '

'Your honour, I wonder if I might add something?' Spencer stepped to the lectern. Chasen looked genuinely glad to see him.

The judge frowned. 'Mr Spencer, I realize you belong to the same distinguished firm as Mr Chasen, but you know the rules – only one lawyer is allowed to speak.' The judge smiled out at the press. 'This is not like football – we don't allow substitutions during play.'

Judge Groban seemed disappointed when his remark elicited no laughter. The faces of the newsmen remained as serious as before.

'I'm familiar with the rules, if the court please,' Spencer said, elbowing Chasen gently away. 'But those rules are surely discretionary, especially if they could result in a possible injustice. At least that was the decision in Foster versus Krauss.'

Groban's face became set. 'I'm familiar with the Foster case. It's entirely different from the matter at hand. Foster was a civil matter involving negligence. An exception to the hearsay rule was involved. There's nothing like that in this case.' The judge sounded self-satisfied and smug that he was able to remember the case Spencer cited.

'But the basic principle remains,' Spencer said, his voice clear and assertive. 'I have knowledge that Mr Chasen lacks. And this knowledge is crucial to the relief being asked of this court.'

Groban paused as if silently considering the matter. 'I'll hear you, Mr Spencer. But I hope for your sake you really have something of consequence.'

Spencer nodded, composed himself, and then proceeded in a good, loud voice, loud enough to carry to the group of newsmen behind him.

'This morning a warrant was requested against John Norman Scott, the president of Lockwood Limited, charging fraud.'

'I know that,' the judge snapped. 'And it was refused – at least until further investigation is done.'

Spencer nodded. 'That is quite correct. Now, based upon the scandalous and untrue statements made in that request to the district attorney, my office, acting on behalf of Mr Scott, has requested a warrant against the lawyer who made these grossly unjust and harmful allegations.' He saw that the judge looked startled. 'The matter has been taken for study by the business fraud division of the district attorney's office. Also, a formal complaint is to be made against the attorney who perpetrated this injustice, a request to bring disbarment proceedings against that lawyer for unethical conduct.'

The judge looked surprised and a little apprehensive. 'Even if true, what different does that make in this requested temporary restraining order? It doesn't bear on the question at all.'

Spencer felt confident. The judge had set it up nicely for him. 'It bears exactly on the question. A conspiracy, using the criminal justice system and this court, has been formed to defeat justice. In order to win in a corporate dispute, one side, Brown and Brown, has sunk to prostituting the courts for its own purpose. Judge, you and the district attorney have been used. There's no other way to put it.'

Judge Groban flushed. 'Watch yourself,' he growled.

Spencer was undaunted by the reaction. 'This morning, without giving my client a chance to reply, you signed an order stopping him from lawfully proceeding with a normal bid for proxies. I know the court's intentions were the best, but the result is the same. Brown and Brown has been given an enormous advantage over my client.'

'We're talking about a matter of only a couple of days,' the judge barked.

'No,' Spencer whipped back, 'we're talking about character assassination – a scheme to destroy a good name. Judge, if you don't grant our request to stop Brown and Brown, you've allowed a fight to go on but tied one of the fighter's hands. That's not fair under any standard.'

Groban's hands were clenched, his face red. 'Much more of this, Mr Spencer, and I'll be forced to find you in contempt of court.'

'I mean no disrespect, your honour,' Spencer said, although his tone was hardly conciliatory. 'This motion involves the same parties before you as in the injunction this morning. We had no choice to speak then. We ask only that this court do what is just. If Brown and Brown can get an injunction and Lockwood cannot, on almost the same set of facts and circumstances, then what conclusion can the public draw? It's obvious: they'll believe a learned judge has carefully reviewed the matter and has found for Brown and Brown.'

Spencer had turned as he gestured. He was pleased to see the reporters in the back of the courtroom all taking furious notes.

That circumstance had not been lost on Judge Groban.

His jaw was locked tight in anger. Then he spoke. 'I tend to disagree with you, Mr Spencer. I think you grossly overstate the problems here. However, since only a few days are involved, and in the interest of treating both parties fairly, I will sign a temporary restraining order stopping Brown and Brown from proceeding with gathering proxies or otherwise proceeding with the business of the annual meeting.'

'Thank you, your honour.'

The judge stood up. 'Don't thank me. You came very close to the edge, Mr Spencer. I'd be careful if I were you not to step over it.' He glared down at the now poker-faced Spencer. 'I will also order that both these matters, at least as far as injunctive relief, be joined. I will hear both matters first thing Friday morning.'

The judge swept from the bench. The clerk banged the gavel. 'All rise,' he snapped.

For the moment, Spencer had met the enemy and at least had battled him to a stalemate.

But it wasn't a victory, not totally, and it was only the first day.

'I thought you were on your way to the jailhouse,' Chasen said quietly.

Spencer wondered if jail really wouldn't be the best place to be after all.

Her desk phone rang.

'Merriam,' she said.

'Nancy, get your buns over to my office. There's something I want you to see.' Surprisingly, considering his stormy moods earlier in the day, John Norman Scott sounded rather relaxed, almost happy.

She looked at the many pages of financial projections that lay in front of her desktop computer. The figures, plus her projections, would play a large part in the tactics to be used against the chemical company. She didn't want to leave in the middle of the job, but he was still her boss.

'Can't it wait a few minutes? I'm right in the middle of something.'

'Can't wait. Come on, for Christ's sake.'

She put down the phone, smoothed her skirt, and walked down the hall to his large office. His secretary was gone, her vacant desk as neat as if it were for sale. She walked into the big office without knocking.

John Norman Scott was stretched out in one of his big leather club chairs. His shirt collar was loosened and his tie slack. He was in his stockinged feet, watching his large-screen television. The set was part of what he called his wall of pleasure. He had designed it himself, complete with stereo and a full bar, all concealed behind a movable wooden wall.

'It's the six o'clock news,' he said, grinning up at her. 'Pull over a chair. It's the local crew, and I think we'll be on after the business about the crap in the Middle East.'

234

She didn't want to waste precious time to catch an uninformative news show, but she reluctantly obeyed. She turned a matching armchair so it faced the screen. She sank into its soft cushions.

He glanced over at her, his half-hooded eyes giving her an easy once-over. 'Best fuckin' legs I've ever seen,' he said. He raised his nearly empty glass in salute.

She tugged down the hem of her skirt.

'Prude,' he said, laughing.

The local New York anchorman came on and made reference to Lockwood Limited and Brown and Brown. He then turned matters over to a newscaster, an older man who was wearing thick glasses, apparently the business reporter.

'Charge and countercharge flew down Wall Street like cannonballs as two of America's corporate giants squared off in what some observers see as the beginning of a titanic battle.' The newsman's eyes moved ever so slightly as he read the complex story off the teleprompter. As he talked, a film clip showed Emerson Becker entering the district attorney's office. The face of the commentator appeared again.

Another film clip showed Michael Collins striding through the same doorway belonging to the district attorney. 'This afternoon, attorneys from Nelson and Clark representing Lockwood appeared in Foley Square. They, too, demanded criminal charges be brought, but this time against the lawyers who had requested them in the morning. And Nelson and Clark, after a rather heated court fight, managed to get an injunction against Brown and Brown preventing any further proceedings concerning their stockholders' vote.' His face once again appeared on the screen. 'Remember, this isn't two next-door neighbours squabbling over the kids' bikes.' He grinned as if only he and the viewer knew the secret. 'This is war between two multinationals, and the stakes are in the billions. The beleaguered Judge Jeremiah Groban will hear arguments from both sides on the motions Friday morning. And all Wall Street is holding its breath.'

The camera returned to the anchorman. 'What seemed to have touched off this war, Cliff?' The anchorman sounded as concerned as if Moscow had just bombed London.

His eyebrows raised, the business commentator responded. 'It's only a guess, Bob,' he said, intimating it was a hell of a lot more than that, 'but informed insiders say John Norman Scott, the Napoleon of Wall Street, is after Brown and Brown. So far, when he's gone after a company, he's always succeeded in capturing it.'

Scott, using his hand-held remote control, flipped the set off, and the face of the anchorman faded into the dead television.

'Not bad, baby,' Scott chortled. 'This morning we looked like a combination of Fagin and Jack the Ripper. But, by God, between our lawyers and our PR men, we've at least broken even on the day.'

She was feeling uneasy. The fleeting sight of Michael Collins had made her heart jump. 'It still isn't the greatest publicity in the world, John.'

'Hell, we're lucky. It could have been a goddamned disaster. You have no idea, Nancy. I could have come off looking like an idiot, a crooked idiot. Brown and Brown could have ended everything with that one blow this morning. They damn near did.'

'What now?'

He drained the last of his drink and got up. He padded over to the bar and poured straight Bourbon into his glass. 'You want something?' he asked without turning.

'Not right now, thanks.'

He walked across to her, holding his drink so it wouldn't spill. He put one hand on her shoulder as he bent to kiss her cheek. As his lips touched her flesh, his hand slid down and his fingers gently manipulated her breast. 'Great tits, too,' he said.

She found herself discomfited by his attentions. She had been sleeping with him for almost a year, but now his touch was unwelcome.

Scott returned to his chair and sat down, taking a long gulp at the whiskey. He licked his lips. 'What's next, you ask? Well, I'll tell you, baby. I'm going to abandon the proxy fight. How about that?'

'You're giving up?' She was startled.

He grinned, his eyes dancing with secret amusement. 'Give up, my ass! No, I'm going to shift my attack, that's all. We'll make mouth music about the proxy fight, at least for a week or two, then I'll make my offer for the tender of their stock.'

She was puzzled. 'That's not the way you planned it in the beginning.'

He nodded. 'Right – it isn't. But a good field commander knows when to change his attack to take advantage of new conditions. Christ, with all this publicity the shareholders of Brown and Brown will be crapping in their pants. My God, they'll worry that they might lose everything. They'll jump at my offer. Most of 'em will think I'm a sucker to invest in a dying company.'

'Brown and Brown won't just lie back and let you rape them, John.'

He grinned. 'That's what makes it so good. The more they fight, the worse the whole thing will look to their stockholders. Christ, everything is working out perfectly for me.'

She nervously bit her lower lip. She remembered that he had made similar statements about the Boston and Des Moines Railroad, but that had blown up, costing the company millions. He never seemed to remember his mistakes.

'Have you talked to anybody about this, John? The attorneys. . .'

His smile immediately disappeared. 'Bullshit! If I floated everything past lawyers, I'd be running some mailroom in a mail order company in Chicago, not one of the world's largest companies. The bastards are only looking to make more fees off you anyway. They give advice that gives them more work.'

'Still, I think you should bounce the idea off someone.'

'I am.'

'Who?' she asked.

'You.'

She couldn't determine if he was kidding or not. She appreciated her own abilities, she was a good organizer, and her decisions were usually carefully thought out. But she wondered if he really respected her business acumen or whether it was just another ploy to get what he wanted – complete control over her.

'If you mean it, John,' she said quietly, 'I think you had better be more careful. We actually haven't laid out a complete plan for the takeover. I believe these things have to be planned out to the last detail.'

He snorted. 'You're really a bright broad, Nancy, honest to God you are, but all this elaborate planning business is your weak point. Look, no plan has ever been followed completely. Things come up and plans have to be changed.'

'John, you haven't even lined up the financing for the takeover. It will run into billions of dollars. Where are you going to get that money?'

He sipped his drink. 'The investment bankers are dying to lend cash. Christ, that's their thing. Don't worry, I'll have no trouble there.'

To oppose him would only serve to make his decision irrevocable. 'But you've always had the money, or at least the promise of money, before you started any of the other takeovers. Brown and Brown will come into the money market and try to stop you from getting loans.'

Scott snorted. 'They don't have a track record. They're just a bunch of pansy cough-syrup makers. The big-money boys know me, and they know I'm used to pitching in the major leagues.' He looked over at her. 'You worry too much, honey.'

'It's not worry, John. It's honest concern. Suppose — '

She stopped and gasped as he slowly unzipped himself. He took out his enormous cock, grinning at her all the time. 'Sort of gets your mind off things, doesn't it?'

'My God, John, not here!'

He was quickly becoming erect. 'The door's locked. No one would dare come in here, anyway. Come on over, Nancy.' He laughed. 'I've got something you like.'

'John, this is hardly the time. I don't feel like — '

The grin had turned into a leer. He put the glass down, got up, and began walking towards her.

'Ainsworth, I hope I haven't interrupted anything important?' John Crim's voice wasn't apologetic; his question was posed only for the sake of etiquette. His tone implied that what he had to say was much more important than anything Ainsworth Martin could possibly be doing.

'My wife and I are entertaining some people. The president of the Brazilian Banking Association, and John MacKenzie, the Canadian ambassador to the UN.' Martin spoke slowly and deliberately, as if he half expected Crim to write the names down. 'Oh, and their wives, of course,' he added.

Crim chuckled. 'It doesn't sound like an exciting time to me – but then you never know about those Latins, eh?'

Ainsworth didn't choose to dignify Crim's remark with a reply.

'The reason I called, Ainsworth' – Crim spoke in a low voice, almost a whisper – 'is that I'm out with Senator Mike August. The guy from Utah that all Washington is talking about as the probable vice-presidential candidate.'

'I'm delighted,' Martin said with a touch of disgust.

'This is business, Ainsworth. Senator August has a kid, a young guy, just out of law school. He wants me to hire him for the Washington office.'

'We have our full quota of associates,' Martin said, a fact also known by Crim.

'I want to hire him not as an associate, but as a participating partner.'

'Out of the question. Except for unusual expertise, we always pick from the associates, you know that.'

'If we get into a real battle over this Lockwood thing, Senator August could be a tremendous help. He's second man on the Banking Committee. They could step in on our side if it became necessary. I'd call that considerable expertise.'

Martin paused. 'John, where did this young man go to law school?'

'I'm not sure. Some city school in Chicago, I think.'

'The firm's policy' – Martin spoke as if it were gospel – 'is to hire only young people from leading law schools. We have made exceptions, of course, but again, the decision always reflected unusual circumstances. What kind of grades did the young man have?'

Crim's annoyance was reflected in his voice. 'How the hell should I know? I didn't have him fill out some kind of damn employment questionnaire. Look, by adding the kid we can pick up a really powerful ally on Capitol Hill. Jesus, Ainsworth, we've done it before.'

Martin shook his head, as if that action could somehow be projected over the telephone. 'John, if we hired every son of every powerful politician and businessman, the firm would be larger than the United States Army. Besides, you already have two participating partners in the Washington office. That's the number approved by the firm.'

At first there was only silence on the line. 'You know,' Crim finally said, his voice strained and angry, 'you're making a hell of a mistake. Oh, not just over this senator's son, but the whole policy towards the Washington office. This isn't some small outpost, Ainsworth, this is where the action is. I noticed when you people needed to straighten out the problems with John Norman Scott the other day , the first one you called was me.'

'Among the first,' Martin said dryly. 'As I recall, a paper needed to be filed. I don't think that called for walking on water – or adding a hundred staff members, for that matter.'

'Oh, that's typical. That attitude is going to cost the firm dearly one of these days, mark my words. I desperately need more people here. The firm needs them.'

Ainsworth Martin wished to end the debate. It was rude to be away so long from his guests. 'What you want, John, is tangible proof that you're important in the capital. You feel, God knows why, that your worth is judged by the number of lawyers and clerks you command.'

'That's not it at all!'

'Ah, but it is, John, in my humble opinion. I don't think you give enough credit to the fact that you are one of us, one of the twelve main partners in Nelson and Clark. Believe me, that's worth at least a battalion of young lawyers.'

'Not here it isn't.'

'John, I'm not going to continue the argument. If you like you can have Senator August's boy submit a résumé. He will be reviewed next year when we do the hiring. However, I wouldn't promise anything – he really doesn't sound like our cup of tea.'

There was silence. 'That's your last word?'

'You can bring the matter up at the monthly meeting, John. I'm not God, just the elected managing partner. If you're able to convince the others differently, then more power to you. But I do really have to go now.'

'You're making a mistake, Ainsworth.'

'It's possible. We'll have to wait and see. Goodnight, John.'

Martin heard the snort of anger as they hung up. John Crim had a short fuse, and his preoccupation with enlarging the Washington office was fast becoming an obsession. Crim, at least under the present firm rules, had only a few years of active practice before retirement. Martin couldn't understand why, under that circumstance, he was getting so excited.

*

Christina Giles' sleep was disturbed by dreams that reflected the past days' frustration. She had phoned some friends, one who was head of a real estate agency, an important one in Manhattan. The problem of trying to find an apartment that had at least two bedrooms seemed insurmountable. Because of the city's rent protection laws, there were two types of apartments available: those not under rent control laws, their inflated rents beyond any logic or reality. The other kind, where the rents were kept by law under market, were rarer than gold, with an underground throng desperately seeking them, a search not unlike the quest for illegal drugs or kinky sex.

She awoke several times while thrashing around in Taro Kuragamo's large bed. The panic of trying to orient herself was then followed by the battle to calm down and be able to go back to sleep again.

At first she thought it was another dream. The hand moved, just touching the skin of her shoulder. The hand was dry, with skin that seemed almost reptilian. Then she realized someone was sitting on the bed beside her.

A scream rising in her throat, Christina rolled away and slipped her feet to the floor.

'I'm sorry to have startled you,' Taro Kuragamo said quietly.

She flipped on the lamp on the nightstand.

'You were having a dream,' he said. 'Making little sounds as if someone was after you. I was merely trying to calm you, my dear.'

She pulled up the straps of her nightgown, trying hard to come fully awake. 'Taro, I don't understand. You said — '

His eyes were fixed on hers, his smile cold. 'My business was completed rather quickly – cancelled as a matter of fact.'

For the first time she realized he was clad only in his shorts. She pulled the sheet up closer around her breasts. 'What time is it?'

His expression didn't change. 'A little after three in the morning.'

She was confused. It was his apartment, his bedroom; she couldn't exactly order him out. But nevertheless she felt that he was an intruder.

'I'll get dressed and stay at a hotel.'

He laughed, although there was no humour in it. 'Don't be ridiculous. This is your place from now on, Christina.'

'It's your apartment. I can't — '

He calmly removed his shorts. He was fully erect.

'Taro, I can't — '

He smiled and slipped beneath the sheets, his eyes always on her.

She tried to leave the bed, but his hand snapped out and grabbed her. The hand gripping her wrist was like a band of steel. She attempted to pull away, but because she was off balance, fell backward, her head bouncing off his chest.

'This is absurd, Christina.' His voice was low and deep. He didn't release her, but instead leaned over and kissed the top of her shoulder.

'Taro, I'm sorry that I've given you the wrong idea.' There was smouldering anger and a hint of fear in her voice. 'You're a very nice man, but you caught me at a time . . . well . . . what happened never has happened before. It was more of a reaction than anything else. I hope you understand. You're a very attractive man, of course, but I — '

He maintained his vicelike grip. 'For a woman reputed to have brains, you seem rather slow, my dear. Of course I caught you at a terrible time, after that awful business with your husband and your son. Please remember that I did catch you, however. It was quite intentional on my part. Why you reacted is your business, but you did, and now you belong to me.'

She turned and looked at him with a penetrating gaze. Surely, she thought, he must be joking. But there was no change of expression, nor was there any laughter in his eyes.

'I have always been attracted by quality, Christina. As you can imagine, a man of my wealth can have almost any woman he wants. But I chose very carefully. You are a passionate woman, despite your denial of that. You are exceptionally lovely, stunning as a matter of fact, a good companion, and not merely for ornamentation.'

'Taro, please tell me this is some kind of joke.'

His eyes never wavered. 'In addition to that, you are sensitive, intelligent, and you are a successful lawyer. Of course I can't have you devoting all your time to that law firm, so we'll arrange a position for you with one of my companies. Nothing too taxing. Something stimulating, naturally, but a position that won't take too much of your time.'

242

She tried to pull away. 'Let me go.' This time she allowed the anger to show in her voice.

A hint of a smile now played across his wide, powerful face. 'There is no such thing as a modern woman, Christina. That is pure myth. Believe me, you will be happier with me than you have ever been in your life. You'll want for nothing, and the world will be at your feet.'

'Are you talking about marriage?'

The smile broadened, but again there was no humour in his eyes. 'Of course not. I told you why, I'm Japanese. My wife represents an extremely powerful house. I cannot dishonour her without losing valuable allies, not only for me, but more importantly, for my sons.'

Her arm hurt where he continued to hold her.

'This is really ridiculous, Taro. Let me go!'

'I think not. You know, my dear, after all is said and done, it's actually rather basic. The recent changes in society tend only to confuse the natural order. Woman was meant to be taken care of, provided for, protected. In turn, she is responsible for the comfort of her mate, his physical and mental well-being. When both sexes play their natural roles, there is harmony and happiness. If not, there is pain, and often, agony.'

'Taro, I'm going to tell you this for the last time. Let go of me. You're hurting me.'

'Christina, you are mine. It will save a great deal of pain if you will merely recognize that fact. Let us begin our life together on a note of mutual respect and devotion.'

She pulled hard, twisting and hitting at him with her other hand. 'Let me go!'

He caught her swinging hand and bent it back painfully.

She cried out.

'You see, it's useless. Come, let me kiss you.' He pulled her roughly to him.

'*Damn you, let go of me.*' She tried to bring her legs around to kick at him, but he only laughed.

'My dear, how foolish. We have been sleeping together. Isn't resisting now rather comical?'

'Help!' she shouted, startled at the panic in her own voice.

He jerked her to him hard, speaking to her through clenched

teeth. 'Luckily,' he hissed, 'my servants are all asleep. You will do well to pay me respect in my own home.' He released one of her hands, then smartly slapped her across the face.

The force of the blow seemed to clear her mind. 'Taro, are you drunk, are you on drugs?'

He hungrily pulled at her shoulder straps, ripping the nightgown away.

'Taro, stop!'

She tried to kick at him, but nothing seemed to work against his strength. She attempted to bite him, but was greeted by another sharp blow to her chin. She was struggling and short of breath as she tried to fight him.

He pulled himself up above her and forced one of his muscular legs between hers, using it like a pry bar. He grabbed her hair and jerked her head back, causing an explosion of pain to race through her scalp. At that moment he entered her.

Helpless to do anything else, she sobbed as he thrust against her.

As though she were almost a distant observer, she was forming the thought that rape hurts.

It hurt a great deal.

19

Emerson Becker's office, although spacious, with floor-to-ceiling windows and a great view of the city, was plain to the point of being sterile. There was no desk, only a long, polished table, clear of everything except a notepad. High-backed straight chairs were the only other furniture. There were no pictures, no couch, no bar, nothing that suggested comfort in any way. Except for the windows and the spectacular view, it could just as well have been an interviewing room in a prison.

Augustus Murray felt uncomfortable from the moment he entered.

Becker sat behind the refectory table, his chair no different from the others. He gestured at a chair opposite him.

Murray extended his hand, which Becker shook without getting up. His grasp was firm but cold.

'Have you seen Lockwood's proxy statement?' Becker asked.

Murray nodded. 'Yes. We are having our departments prepare answers to all the allegations.'

'Perhaps,' Becker said surprisingly softly, 'we can go over very briefly the main allegations raised in the proxy statement by John Norman Scott.'

'Certainly.'

Becker used no notes. He had nothing before him but the blank yellow legal pad. With a flourish, he uncapped an old-fashioned fountain pen.

'Mr Scott alleges that Brown and Brown manufactured a quantity of children's laxative but was unable to market it in the United States because the Food and Drug Administration wouldn't approve it. Is that true?'

'They didn't disapprove it. They wanted to do more testing. We felt we couldn't afford it. Little John, our competitor, had come out with a much better product. If we went ahead, all we'd accomplish would be to get approval of a drug that was inferior to the one being sold. It wasn't good business.'

Becker nodded without comment. 'And it's alleged you gave this drug to a child-care organization in Africa, where it was distributed.'

'Well, that's true enough. We couldn't salvage anything worthwhile from the batch. Our accountants advised sending it to these African organizations. It helped from a tax viewpoint. We still lost money, but it helped cut our losses a bit.'

'Scott's proxy statement says that almost one hundred children died as a result of taking the drug. True?'

Murray knew he was beginning to sweat. He could feel the beads of perspiration pop out on his forehead. 'Not entirely true, no.'

Becker's smile turned feral. 'Do you mean the children are only half dead?'

Murray decided it would be inappropriate to laugh. 'No. According to our records, there were ninety-two deaths in children who had taken the laxative. All were in backward Third World areas. There were few autopsies. So it really wasn't proven that the laxative was responsible for the deaths.'

Becker made a note, then his eyes glided up to meet Murray's. 'But there were a few autopsies, were there not?'

'Yes.'

'And what was found?'

'You must remember, Mr Becker, that these post-mortems were done in backward countries, many under Communist regimes. The doctors say anything just to make a large American company look bad.'

'Regardless, what did they determine to be the cause of death – officially, that is?'

Murray swallowed. 'They alleged, and this isn't proven, that an element in the laxative, when used to treat malnourished children, produced a serious spasm in the colon. Basically what they said was that the children died from shock, caused by the ingestion and resulting action of the laxative.'

'And you disagree.'

'Of course. It is regrettable that those children died, but nothing has actually been proven. There are lawsuits filed, as you probably know. In any event, we had no knowledge that the drug was potentially dangerous, if, in fact, it was.'

'Except the FDA warning.'

Murray knew he was colouring. The whole matter had been embarrassing. He wondered if it would ever go away. 'As I say, it wasn't exactly a warning. They just wanted more tests.'

Becker didn't reply immediately, but took time to make a number of notes.

He looked up. 'You know, of course, that the World Health Organization says your drug caused those deaths.'

'Politics,' Murray replied. It was his standard reply. 'It's all tied in with the whole Third World concept. We're a huge American company, therefore we're evil.'

'How about the allegations of mismanagement. Scott claims that although the company wasn't making money, the officers, including yourself, were being given enormous raises.'

'Enormous? I suppose if you were a clerk or a factory worker, you might consider the raises enormous, but in the corporate world the increases we received are considered to be quite normal. We pay our officers very well. We want to keep them with the company.'

'But the company wasn't showing a profit. Why keep officers if they aren't producing?'

Murray was always ready for that question. It was consistently asked at the annual stockholders' meeting by gadflies who, just because they'd purchased a few shares of stock, wanted to make pests of themselves. 'The company does make money. We have some highly profitable divisions. We also have some divisions which in the past have been very profitable, and will be again, although at the moment they are going through a development stage, a stage where their revenues are down. It balances out, you see.'

Becker sat back, clasping his hands over his trim waist. 'Good speech. You'll win the proxy fight, Mr Murray.'

'I'm glad to hear it.'

Becker's small, humourless smile looked painted on. 'Oh, not because of the merit of your case. You'll win the proxy fight, but in my humble estimation you will lose the takeover battle.'

'Why?'

Becker continued to stare at Murray. 'A takeover is a little like a poker game. You have to have enough money to stay in the betting in order to have the chance to win. Mr Scott, I believe, will shortly file and make a tender offer. He will offer to buy stock in your company for a dollar figure far exceeding its market value.'

'We'll match that.'

Becker paused a moment before speaking. The office seemed strangely quiet. 'With what?' he asked.

Murray felt even more uncomfortable. 'We have all that land. We can get a loan on that. We'll be able to match him dollar for dollar.'

Becker slowly shook his head. 'You have to have cash in hand, Mr Murray. You must make the offer and then pay cash for the stock when the stockholders let you know they'll sell at your price. It all has to be done within a matter of a few days. By law.'

'I'm in the process now of trying to raise the money.'

'I know, Mr Murray. You tried First of Boston and were turned down, isn't that correct?'

'That was my first stop.'

Becker cocked his head slightly. 'Do you know why they turned you down?'

Murray felt sure of himself in the answer. 'I was told there wasn't enough time to process title to the land, even as security for the loan.'

Becker nodded, again with that secretive smile. 'That was, indeed, what you were told. But the real reason is that First of Boston is contemplating backing Mr Scott. They have before. They want no conflict-of-interest issue to arise by any dealings with you.'

'There are other investment bankers.'

'Yes, there are. Many, but not that many with sufficient liquid assets to back a battle like this one.'

'So? What's your suggestion?'

Becker didn't reply at once. Murray found these delays not only uncomfortable but infuriating. 'Let's be frank, Mr Murray. Brown and Brown is run by Mr Teddy Edwards. He is the spokesman for the founding family, now numbered in the hundreds, but who still own a substantial slice of the company . He calls the shots, he elects the board members, he makes the key decisions.'

'He is chairman of the board, and as chairman — '

'Please.' Becker held up his hand. 'I don't want another speech. Mr Edwards and his family own approximately thirty per cent of all the outstanding stock in your company.'

Murray wondered if he was about to be fired.

'I suggested, and Mr Edwards agreed, that since you don't have the capital to see this fight through, and since Mr Edwards and his family could, in the long run, lose almost everything, that Brown and Brown consider looking about for a White Knight.'

'Mr Edwards agreed to that? I can't believe it.'

Becker was enjoying himself. 'Yes, he did agree. His primary duty is to protect the fortune of his family.'

'But a White Knight would come in and buy up the company?'

'Exactly. The White Knight – someone who did have sufficient resources – or the ability to get them – would come in, make a higher offer either for your company, or even the Lockwood company. In other words, if the right party came in, they could buy up Mr Scott's company and you would be saved. And even if the White Knight only bought your company to save it, at least Mr Edwards and his people could be assured of selling at a good profit.'

Murray knew that his days as president were numbered. And he had no golden parachute. He wondered if it might not be the right time to quit.

Becker nodded silently, as if reading Murray's mind. 'I have discussed everything with Mr Edwards. He realizes that if his officers are expected to cooperate fully in such a venture, they'll have to have some security. I am advised he will have the board approve a five-year contract at your present salaries in case any of you are let go as a result of this takeover business.'

Murray hoped his delight and relief couldn't be seen in his expression. It was like being reprieved from the executioner. 'That's reassuring,' he said, trying to sound casual.

'That's a miracle,' Becker replied, 'considering the mind-set of Mr Edwards. I did that for you, Mr Muray, because I will need your help and assistance. This takeover fight will test all of us. I don't want anyone quitting or running off to the other side. I want complete and absolute loyalty. This is the payment for that loyalty. It is agreed?'

'I would be loyal without the contract,' he said.

'No doubt, but this binds the bargain. Now, about the White Knight. Do you have any ideas?'

'We had a feeler from Germany's Verlag Chemicals last year. They might be interested.'

Becker shook his head. 'They're big enough, but I know them – they won't take such a risk. We need someone of immense wealth who is willing to take an enormous risk to make a possible profit, either in money or in power.'

'Who do you have in mind?'

'There are a few around,' Becker said. 'And my firm is making inquiries. We are baiting the hook a bit. If we get the right fish, we'll have a deal.'

'And if not?'

'We will continue to battle Mr Scott in the courts. We may win. I think he has chosen a law firm that suffers from having a reputation that is vastly overblown. But if we lose, you can expect no mercy from Mr Scott.'

'And if you find a White Knight?'

Becker snickered. His smile widened into an evil leer. 'We will destroy Scott.' He chuckled. 'And a certain well-known law firm as well.'

Dan Spencer had spent most of the night instructing each team he had formed in their duties. He stayed on, using the couch at the new office, but managed to get only a few hours' sleep.

He was more than slightly annoyed when Ainsworth Martin ordered him to leave his 'war room' and come to the firm's main offices. Although he tried to tell Ainsworth his problem, the managing partner insisted, without giving a reason.

Spencer felt the loss of sleep as he hailed a cab. He knew he'd have to watch his emotional outlook. He would need crystal-clear judgement, and exhausted men don't think clearly. He nearly fell asleep in the cab.

Spencer was ushered into the Apostles' main conference room. He'd been there before, but rarely. It was generally reserved for the original twelve themselves.

Ainsworth Martin sat at the head of the long, impressive table. Morris Solomon and John Crim sat on one side. Christina Giles and Abner Slocum sat on the other. The only non-Apostles were Dan and Christina.

She looked away when he glanced at her. She appeared drawn, tired.

'Sit down, Dan,' Ainsworth said. 'There's been a new development with Lockwood which I didn't want to talk about over the telephone.'

Spencer drew up a chair across from Christina.

'I discussed everything with John Norman Scott this morning,' Ainsworth Martin said. 'He met with me and Morris Solomon.'

Solomon grinned. 'At six o'clock, yet.'

Ainsworth Martin looked slightly annoyed at Morris' comment. 'Mr Scott informs me that he wishes to proceed at once with a takeover bid for Brown and Brown.'

'What about the proxy fight?' Spencer asked, his stomach sinking at the prospect that much of his work might be for nothing.

'He will keep that up, but only for the purposes of publicity. In other words, he won't even try to win at the stockholders' meeting. Perhaps, with luck, he may even own the company by that time. In any event, we have to shift our attack somewhat to suit the new circumstances. Do you agree, Dan?'

Spencer shook his head. 'Jesus, I've spent most of the night getting squads of lawyers ready for Friday. All their work is keyed on the proxy business. I think it's all been a damn waste of time if he really isn't going to make the fight.'

'I trust everyone's time has been appropriately billed?' Martin asked stiffly.

'Sure.'

'Then it's hardly a waste of time, is it? We can only follow a client's dictates. If he creates extra legal work, resulting in additional fees and charges, it's his problems, not ours.'

'So what's the plan now?' Crim asked.

'Simple, really,' Martin replied. 'We all knew there would be a takeover – we'll just have to accelerate our efforts in that regard, that's all.'

'I'll need more lawyers,' Spencer said.

'You have almost half the firm now,' Martin responded.

'This will be a full-scale battle, state and federal court. I'll need more, Ainsworth. I wish to hell I didn't, but I will.'

Martin pursed his lips. 'Well, I suppose you're right. We'll work it out as it goes along. Now, I've asked all of you here because you'll each serve a key roll in the takeover process.'

He paused. 'Morris will be in overall charge of the takeover. His responsibility will be to coordinate all aspects – the bid, investment bankers, and so forth. Abner is our banking expert, so he will run interference for whatever additional financing we'll need. After all these years, I expect you must know all the important bankers in the country, Abner.'

Slocum, who didn't look particularly enthusiastic, nodded. 'I know a few,' he said quietly.

'Crim, of course, will be in charge of the governmental aspects – the legality of the tender offer, the SEC process itself. We don't want to be stopped because of some damn dimestore bureaucrat. Right, John?'

'As I frequently point out,' Crim smiled, 'we in Washington office have saved this firm's bacon more than once during the past. We are prepared to do it again.'

Martin ignored the barb. 'Mrs Giles, our innovative lady in charge of financing, will be in charge of drafting the necessary security documents, and even schemes, to satisfy the evil-hearted bankers. Okay, Chris?'

Without even looking up, she nodded her assent.

Spencer wondered what Christina's trouble might be: They were competitors for Johnson's spot, but beyond that they were also friends. He was concerned.

'And you, Dan, will run the troops in our courtroom battles.' Martin looked a bit displeased. 'It appears this might amount to an actual battalion of lawyers.'

'More than a few,' Spencer said. 'We have to be prepared for anything, even an attack in the state courts. It could affect our federal actions. You all know that the federal courts like to step aside if a state court gets into the act.'

'What's wrong with that?' Crim asked.

'In this case, it's Delaware, the state where Brown and Brown is registered. Delaware doesn't like outsiders like Scott trying to break up businesses that pay taxes to the state. The state courts will tend to try to help Brown and Brown.'

'So what do you suggest?' Solomon asked.

'We get there first.' Spencer found the stimulation of the new challenge was washing away his fatigue. 'I had thought about this before. But now that the takeover is about to begin, I think I'll run a lawyer down to Delaware tomorrow morning with a request for an injunction against any state action until things are resolved in the federal court.'

'They won't do it if what you say is true,' Crim said.

Spencer nodded. 'But they won't even know that's what's happening. On paper it will look like a proxy fight, and the state doesn't care who pays the taxes; they just want to keep the corporation there. No judge would have any sleepless nights because of a proxy fight – that's internal. I know a judge, Judge Hastings, an old friend. He wouldn't do anything unethical, but this will be a run-of-the-mill ex-parte motion. He'll sign it.'

'And what happens when the other side finds out?' Crim asked.

'We'll have the advantage. We'll have a valid order. That, plus a win in federal court tomorrow before Judge Groban will keep things in the federal court. It's not much of a trick, but I think it'll work.'

'Well, we all have work to do,' Martin said, rising. 'This, as we know, is of extreme importance to the firm. Keep all this in confidence. Let's all do whatever we have to do to win.'

Solomon chuckled. 'Within reason, of course.'

Martin glared at him. 'Of course.'

*

After the meeting, Dan held back and waited for Christina.

She moved slowly, her eyes cast downward.

'Chris.'

She looked up. Her eyes, although heavily made up, appeared to be red and swollen. 'I stopped by to see you,' she said.

'I didn't know. I was tied up on his damn thing. Are you feeling all right?'

She managed a hesitant, tentative smile. 'I'm just fine, Dan. Thanks.'

She started to walk by him. He stopped her by taking her arm. She half-jerked from his touch. 'Why did you want to see me?' he asked.

At first he thought she was laughing, then he realized she was trying to keep from crying. This time he gripped her arm with authority. 'Come on,' he said. 'Let's get out of here for a few minutes.'

She didn't resist, nor did she talk as they went into the elevator. Spencer sensed her distress and didn't attempt conversation until he had seated her at a remote table at a small restaurant.

'Okay, what's the problem?' he asked after ordering coffee from the waitress.

'Private problems,' she said simply. There was a small sob in her voice.

'We'll be working together,' he said. 'Your performance will affect the team.' He didn't care about the firm, but he sensed she very badly needed an excuse to talk.

She bit her lower lip for a moment. 'You don't have to worry, Dan. I'm just a little down, but I can still do my job.'

'Problems with your husband?'

To his surprise, she laughed. 'I wish it were just that. My God, it's only a few days ago, but it seems like years. I've left Hank.'

'Sudden, although I knew you weren't happy.'

She nodded. 'Yes, very sudden. I left him, left my son, left everything, even my clothes. I had to go to London the next day, so I brought everything new. Now I've lost that, too.'

'Where are you staying?'

Her eyes met his. She looked desolate.

'At the moment, nowhere. I haven't even registered in a hotel.'

The waitress served the coffee.

'It's none of my business, but obviously something's happened, even more than leaving your husband. I think you may need a friend.' He looked at her more closely. 'Maybe even a lawyer. Suppose we put this on a professional basis. I'll be your lawyer, so anything you say will be confidential. It would be, anyway, but let's make it official.'

'I don't need a lawyer. I think I need a good psychiatrist, or a cop, or something.' She took a small sip at the coffee. Spencer noticed that her hand was shaking.

'Let's hear about it, Chris. Don't worry about how it'll sound to me. I may be able to help.'

She slowly shook her head. 'No one can help me.'

He reached across the small table and took her hand. 'Look, pal, why don't you try me? You might be surprised.'

She began to speak, hesitantly at first, forcing almost every word, as though the speaking itself were painful. Then she started to tell what had happened, as though the telling made her anguish less. At first she tried to conceal the fact that she had gone to bed with Taro Kuragamo, but then admitted it in a whisper, as if to a priest.

Dan didn't interrupt, but just listened. She told him of Kuragamo's forcing himself on her and her fear that he would find her and take her, despite the fact that they weren't in feudal Japan, in time or place.

She had to stop several times, crying into her napkin. The waitress was wise enough, had seen enough in her day, to stay away.

'So, here I am, Dan. Just like the most destitute prostitute on Eighth Avenue. I have no home, only the clothes on my back.' She took a deep breath, trying to control herself. 'And I'm afraid.'

As she had talked she had gripped his hand. After she realized that she was crushing it, she relaxed her fingers and patted his hand, smiling uncertainly. 'Oh, Dan, I'm sorry.'

He gently took both her hands in his. 'I told you I could help, and I will.'

She dabbed at her eyes. 'You must think me a whore. First I end up in your bed, drunk, then in Kuragamo's . . .' Her voice trailed off.

'You're a lady,' he said firmly. 'That Japanese son of a bitch set you up. Christ, he sounds like he's in the wrong century. You relax – I'll take care of everything.'

'How?'

'First, you need a safe place. After what happened with Kuragamo I know this suggestion can be taken in the wrong way, but I want you to go to my apartment and stay there.'

'Dan, this is no business of yours. I can't intrude . . .'

'Chris, you and I are friends. I think, based on past performance, you don't have to worry that I'll come climbing into bed in the middle of the night. You'll be safe. You need sleep, a chance to repair your nerves.'

'But all my things are at — '

'Leave them. In case you're worried about your Japanese friend, give me his address and telephone number. I'll take care of that end.'

'No. You've been kind to listen to my sordid little story, and you're right, I do feel better. But I'm perfectly capable of taking care of myself.'

'When you've had a chance to catch your breath. Come on, I'll take you to my place.'

'Dan, I know how busy you are with this Lockwood business. I can't ask you to do that. If I agree to go to your apartment, will you promise to go back to work?' She paused. 'We both have careers at stake here, Dan. I couldn't live with the thought that you had sacrificed yours because of me.'

Spencer knew they would be waiting for him back at the bunker. Everything had changed, and he would have to alter the marching orders. They had everything except time. 'If I do put you in a cab, you have to promise me you'll go to bed. I'll bunk on the couch tonight if I come in at all.' He looked at her. 'Let me call my doctor; he's a pal of mine. I'll get you something to help you sleep.'

She managed a weak smile. 'I won't need it.'

He got Kuragamo's address and telephone number. Spencer put Christina in a cab, gave her the keys, and told the cabdriver his address.

Before heading back downtown, he slipped into a telephone booth and dialled Kuragamo's number.

A professionally detached voice answered. 'Yes?'

'This is Mr Daniel Spencer.' He said his name very slowly. Please tell Mr Kuragamo that I am calling on behalf of Mrs Christina Giles.'

He waited, wondering why he felt no emotion, just an unpleasant coolness.

'This is Kuragamo.' He was surprised by the British accent.

'I am Daniel Spencer,' he again articulated carefully, wishing that every word be understood. 'I am an attorney representing Mrs Giles. She has informed me of everything that has happened, including your assault upon her. If you even think about contacting her again, Mr Kuragamo, I'll make life so hot for you, you'll think you've fallen into hell.'

At first there was no reply, then the deep, British-accented voice spoke smoothly. 'Daniel Spencer, is it? I shall remember the name, Mr Spencer. Please inform your client, if in fact she is your client, that I expect her here tonight for dinner. Failure to appear, Mr Spencer, will have very sad consequences, not only for Mrs Giles, but also for you, Mr Spencer.'

'Since you are unfamiliar with our law . . .'

'I am most familiar with your law. I have purchased enough lawyers, judges, and policemen to have earned a masters degree in your law. Don't get into these waters, Mr Spencer. I warn you. It could prove most unpleasant for you. Where is Mrs Giles?'

Now the anger came. Spencer felt the muscles in his neck tighten like drawn cords. 'You are to leave Mrs Giles alone,' he said, forcing himself to maintain control, speak coolly. 'Otherwise we'll find a judge you can't buy, and perhaps he'll find a policeman you can't buy, and just maybe between them they will teach you a little American law you haven't yet learned.'

'If you are a lawyer, I presume you have an office?'

'I'm with the firm of Nelson and Clark.'

Again there was a pause. 'Then Mrs Giles, if she is your client, is presumably your colleague, and perhaps your friend.' The emphasis Kuragamo put on the word 'friend' implied an illicit relationship.

'Stay away from her, Kuragamo,' Spencer snarled.

A soft chuckle was the initial response. 'You must be young, or exceedingly inexperienced in the ways of the world. My dear Mr Spencer, it will be a pleasure to add a little something to your general education.'

Kuragamo hung up. Spencer slammed the receiver into the wall of the telephone so hard he thought for a moment he'd broken it.

He stepped back, staring at the offending telephone.

He was angry, very angry. Yet, despite the anger, his instincts whispered that he should be careful. Something in the quality of that voice spelled danger. Real danger.

Taro Kuragamo placed the receiver back in its cradle, then looked at the telephone as if seeing it for the first time. No expression played on his smooth features. He was alone in his study, which, although in a New York penthouse, had the uncluttered, stark simplicity of a Japanese garden. He paused only a moment, then he returned to his visitor in the living room.

The old man had accepted the offered brandy, but Kuragamo noticed that it had remained at its original level. Teddy Edwards was too old a fox to let alcohol dull his mind's edge. Kuragamo's brandy glass was also nearly full. He had only sipped at it ceremoniously.

The tall Japanese sat down across the low coffee table from Edwards. 'Please excuse me, Mr Edwards. That was a matter of urgent business.'

The old man nodded. 'Considering the extent of your holdings, I'm surprised you aren't on the phone all the time.'

'Much of the time,' Kuragamo said, taking up his glass but not drinking. 'Please continue. I am greatly fascinated.'

Edwards looked like a wrinkled elf, his small form half-sinking into the luxurious chair's silk cushions. 'As I said, this fellow Scott is a bit of a buccaneer. We have checked. Most of the companies he's taken have been broken up and sold. They remain only a memory.'

Kuragamo smiled icily. 'But if the company is not profitable, of what use is it?'

'None!' Edwards snapped. 'Brown and Brown is profitable.'

'Barely.'

'On paper, I agree. We are in the process of chemical research that will turn the company into a bonanza.'

'Research . . . the term is so vague.'

'I can show you the things we are planning. Nothing pie-in-the-sky, but real products with very dramatic market potential.'

'And this is the reason Mr Scott and his people wish to take over Brown and Brown.'

Edwards shook his head. 'No. Actually, I think if they were going to keep the company together and continue with these innovations,

257

I'd welcome his tender offer. His money spends just as well as any other.'

'I presume,' Kuragamo said, this time not smiling, 'he is interested in your rather glittering land inventory. A most attractive bait, I must say.'

Edwards scowled. 'You're right, of course. And I can tell you exactly what he'll do if he gets his mitts on our firm. He'll sell off the land, make his profit, then break the company up like a scrap car, getting whatever he can for whatever is left.'

'And you wish to oppose him?'

'We do. We will.'

'Can you top his money offer? I would think that's the key question.'

Edwards seemed almost to age visibly. 'That's the rub. We are land rich. If we had time we could do a lot of things to repel the shark. We could sell the land and hide it by investing in long-term things. Or if we had the cash, we could even outbid him with our own stockholders' cash.'

'That could be illegal.'

'It's been done before.'

Kuragamo nodded. 'It has. But since you don't have the necessary time to convert the land into cash, what you propose is only the stuff of dreams.' Kuragamo smiled slightly, almost sadly.

'Let's quit beating around the bush!' Edwards snapped. 'You know why I'm here. We desperately need a White Knight.'

Pretending that the term was unfamiliar to him, Kuragamo raised an inquisitive eyebrow.

'You know as well as I what that means,' Edwards said, smiling now for the first time. 'We need someone with a lot of cash who can come along and outbid Scott – someone who will oppose him and defend us.'

'A White Knight – and I am familiar with the term – buys the target company. But that's no assurance that such a person would act any differently from Mr Scott would after buying your company.'

Edwards nodded. 'You're quite right. But it's my belief a man like yourself would see the long-range potential. Scott wouldn't look beyond immediate profit. Based on your track record, Mr Kuragamo, I believe you would keep the company intact.'

Kuragamo placed his brandy glass on the table. 'John Norman Scott is a potent force in the business world.'

'He's a fool. You read all that nonsense about his young bimbo. He's vastly over-rated.'

'Making a fool of oneself over a woman doesn't necessarily mean that all other judgements are tainted.'

'Does he have the capital to back up such a takeover?'

Edwards smiled wryly. 'That's a foolish question, Kuragamo. We both know that he can raise it.'

'Then you are in a rather dangerous position, are you not?'

'Not if you'll become our White Knight.'

'And why in the world should I do that?' Kuragamo's face became mask-like.

'Because you like profit. If you outbid Scott, you'll pick up the land – and that's worth billions – plus you'll have the largest chemical company in the world, one soon to become a regular gold mine.'

Kuragamo laughed. 'But I could lose, also. And if I lost, it wouldn't be just the money. I have a reputation, Mr Edwards. There is more risk for me here than is first apparent.'

Edwards looked Kuragamo directly in the eye. 'Look, this Scott is an asshole . . . a rough word, but entirely descriptive. He'll come in with too little preparation; he always does. He's just been lucky so far. He hired Nelson and Clark, hoping their reputation will scare the hell out of any opposition.'

'The Twelve Apostles?'

Edwards scowled. 'A bunch of pantywaists. We've got Emerson Becker. He's the real article, a genuine alley fighter. Nelson and Clark will fold just like Scott, believe me.'

Kuragamo's face remained immobile, his dark eyes betraying no hint of what he was thinking, as he lightly drummed his fingers on the table. 'I don't want to falsely raise your hopes, Mr Edwards. But I must say I am interested. Perhaps you could arrange to have your accountants and research people stand by. Just in case I change my mind.'

Impatience crept into Edwards' voice. 'This is an eleventh-hour thing, Kuragamo. If there's something more that you want, for God's sake tell me what it is and maybe I can help.'

'I will call you if I wish to talk further, Mr Edwards.'

Edwards forced his old body out of the chair. 'I'm searching for a White Knight. I will be approaching other people, too. Should you decide to come with us, it may be too late.'

Kuragamo bowed slightly. 'Time, my dear Mr Edwards, can be a friend or a foe.'

She had carefully selected the meeting place. She had always taken him to Rumpelmayer's for ice cream after dental and doctor visits, as a treat to take some of the sting out of any unpleasantness he might have gone through. She hoped some of the delight of childhood might still cling to the place for him. He had agreed over the telephone to come, but he was now almost a half-hour late. She experienced a growing hopelessness.

Her life had exploded into a thousand fragments, but despite everything she could not forsake her son, no matter how he might feel about her. He preferred to be called Henry, as a mark of his coming adulthood, but in her mind he was always her little boy, and to her he was always Little Hank.

She felt utter relief as she saw him come through the door, moving awkwardly, still uncomfortable with his newly sprouting height. His youthful face was beginning to fill out; soon he would be handsome. But now he had a complexion problem, and his features seemed almost out of balance because of his adolescent growth.

'I'm here,' he said, sitting down at the small table. His manner was petulant, as though he had been forced to come.

'I'm glad, Henry,' she replied. 'Do you want to order?'

She was heartened that he selected a banana split, his childhood favourite.

'I wanted to talk to you about what's happening between your father and me. I think it's important that you understand.'

'I understand,' he grumbled. 'I think most of my friends have had the same experience.' He sneered. 'Some of them have a hard time keeping track of who their parents are married to now. They don't know who they belong to.'

'Do you think that's going to happen to you?'

He shrugged. 'Why not? I'm no different to anyone else.'

She knew there was real pain hiding behind his casual indifference. 'Henry, you are important, very important, to your father and me. You have to realize that.'

He had avoided looking directly at her, but now his eyes sought hers. She thought she saw tears welling up.

'Dad says it's your fault.'

She sighed. It would do no good to force him to take sides. That would lead to his own self-destruction. 'Henry, this is no one's fault. Sometimes people, grown people, change. They grow apart. Your father is a doctor. I'm a lawyer. We both have demanding careers. Our interests are different now. You're almost grown. There's really very little to keep us together any more. I know it's difficult at your age to understand how these things happen, but — '

'That's bullshit,' he said quietly.

'Henry, I think you're capable of better expression.' She chose her words carefully.

He was served the giant ice cream concoction. He seemed to study it as though he had never seen one before, toying with his spoon. But he didn't eat.

'Why don't you tell me the truth,' he said without looking up.

'What's that supposed to mean?'

'I'm fourteen,' he said. 'Maybe things were different when you were young, but I know a great deal about people, whether you believe that or not.'

'You have a ways to go yet,' she said gently.

'Dad says you've been screwing around on him. That you have a boyfriend.'

'Do you think that's the truth?' Her heart was pounding in anticipation of his answer.

He used the spoon to roll the cherry around in the whipped cream. 'You know what I think?'

'I'd be very interested to know.'

'Dad's been screwing around and you're damn sick of it.'

'Henry, I — ' She was too surprised to talk.

He looked up at her again. 'I'm just a kid, but I know. I wondered just how long you'd put up with what he was doing.'

'Henry, I appreciate your concern, but you have to have respect for your father.'

'In what way? He's a big-deal doctor. I respect that. So what? He just wants me around so he can have someone applaud him.'

She started to speak, but stopped when she saw a tear tremble on the lip of one of his eyelids.

'I don't want this to happen,' he said. 'I'm scared, if you want the truth. I liked it when I was a little kid. I didn't know any of this shit existed. I had a home. I had parents. Things were okay, you understand?'

'Of course.'

'Now everything is going to change.'

'Life is like that, Henry. I suppose that's part of the growing process, finding out that nothing ever remains the same.'

He brushed away the tear with a quick, embarrassed motion. 'You're a lawyer, Ma' – he hadn't called her 'Ma' for years – 'what's going to happen to me now?'

His pain and fear struck like electricity into her very soul. 'Your father and I will live separate lives. I'll get an apartment. We'll both be as available to you as before – it's just that we won't be together.'

'Which one of you will get me?'

'Well, usually custody is shared when a boy is as old as you. The courts will do what's best for the child, but they will listen if there's a preference.'

'You mean I can pick which one I want to live with?'

'More or less.' Her heart was sinking. 'You'll be in school most of the year. Really, all that's at stake is holidays and the summer vacation. It isn't all that bad when you think about it. If you don't want to choose, no one will force you to do so.'

'But I *want* to choose.'

It was as though the world had stopped for her. All the love she had for her son seemed at risk. Even her own existence. She wanted to ask but feared the answer.

'I like Dad,' he said. 'We get along pretty good. He doesn't bother me and I don't bother him.'

She felt slightly faint. She watched as he aimlessly played with the ice cream.

'You're always after me about something – clothes, food, something.'

'I'm your mother, I have to — '

She was stopped by his sudden shy grin. 'You have to keep my act together,' he finished the statement for her. 'See, I like Dad, but I don't want to turn out like him. If you have no objection, I'd like to live with you.'

She wondered if she had heard him correctly. She was afraid to ask.

'Like you say, I'll be away at school most of the time so I wouldn't be too big a burden.'

He was asking her, asking that she take him. Suddenly the world had become a wonderful place.

'You can always live with me,' she said simply. 'I would like that very much.'

He began eating the ice cream. 'It wouldn't be forever, of course. When I get out of college I'll want a place of my own. It will be just until then, if that's all right, Ma.'

She reached across the table and took his hand. 'For as long as you like, Henry.'

He squeezed back, then, embarrassed, pulled away. 'Good ice cream, Ma,' he said.

20

Dan Spencer called and checked on Christina. He felt bad when he heard in her voice that he had awakened her, but was relieved that she sounded better. He told her he was needed to prepare for the surprise Delaware court action and wouldn't be home.

She protested, but he assured her that it really was work that kept him away. Unfortunately it was true. The state court action could be a key diversion. He would have to work through much of the night preparing the request for injunction.

Dan sipped at another cup of coffee. He tried to keep his thoughts on the Lockwood matter but found himself having a difficult time keeping the haunting image of Christina from his mind.

He was tempted to go back to his apartment, but he wondered at his real motivation. She had been through quite enough without his adding anything more to her burden.

Besides, he thought, he had no time to get involved.

Bruno Chasen rushed from the county courthouse. He knew he was flushed. His pounding pulse seemed almost audible; his stomach was churning. Jeffrey Rowe kept pace with him, his face set and angry.

Losing was a terrible experience, especially when it came as a surprise.

'There's a phone,' Rowe said.

'It's out in the open. We need a booth.' Chasen jerked his thumb behind him at the group of lawyers coming out of the courtroom. 'I don't want them listening in.'

They strode in silence to Chasen's car. He burned rubber as he pulled away from the parking space.

'Take it easy, Bruno,' Rowe said quietly. 'There'll be another day.'

Chasen didn't reply, his eyes searching the road for a telephone sign. He saw an outside, open booth, braked, causing the car to skid, then pulled up to the telephone.

'This is no-standing zone,' Rowe said.

'Fuck 'em!' Chasen snapped. 'Let 'em sue us.' He slammed the car door and pulled out his telephone charge card as he dialled the bunker. Spencer was waiting and took the call from the girl who answered.

'We've been had,' Chasen said, almost yelling. There was traffic noise behind him, and he found that a new irritation.

'What the hell do you mean?'

'They were waiting for us, Dan. The sons of bitches were right there when we arrived.'

'How could that be?' Spencer asked.

'And they had exactly the right pleadings to oppose us. I mean, they had everything – reply motion, affidavits, the works. It was as if we'd done the work for them ourselves.'

Spencer didn't reply for a moment, shocked at the news. 'It may have been luck,' he said. 'Myabe they just guessed what we might try to pull.'

'Bullshit,' Chasen said, using a word he hated. 'They were tipped off. They knew exactly what judge, when, and what we were going to ask for.'

'What happened?'

'What do you *think* happened?' Chasen replied angrily. 'Your old pal, Judge Hastings, took one look at the other side's paperwork and refused to issue the temporary restraining order. I don't blame him, given the circumstances. He refused to sign the order and set a hearing on our motion for a week from Friday. And you know what that means.'

'The whole thing has fallen through.'

'Right. Becker and his boys have beaten us completely. That judge of yours wouldn't rule now if Almighty God appeared to him in person and demanded it.'

'Bruno, did you or Jeff talk to anyone after you left?' Dan asked.

Chasen's lips set and he took a breath before replying. 'I thought you'd come up with something like that,' he snapped back in real anger. 'Look, we didn't even know where we were going this morning or what we were to do until you handed us that package of pleadings. And for the record, pal, we didn't even talk to a waitress or any other damn human being until we got to that court. Jeff and I were together the whole time. Neither he nor I made any telephone calls – nothing. So you know where that leaves you, don't you?'

'Take it easy, Bruno. You know I had to ask.'

'You've got a leak back there, Dan. A great big leak. I'd have the bunker checked for a tap. Jesus, it's either a tap or we have the biggest goddamned spy in history right in our midst. Maybe one of the girls, you think?'

Spencer felt sick. 'No. I took special pains that no one clerical knew what was happening. Everything was divided up between the girls downtown, the main office, and even some outside typing help. As far as preparing the pleadings, security was absolutely tight.'

'Besides you, who knew?' Chasen asked.

Spencer didn't reply. It was something he was already thinking about.

'I'll talk to you both when you get back.'

'Dan, these people made me look like a fool this morning. I don't care who it is that leaked us, but I want a piece of that damn fink.'

'We'll talk,' Spencer said, hanging up the telephone.

He sat quietly for a moment. A bug or tap was improbable. He had taken precautions when renting and outfitting the bunker that no one know who was moving in, or why.

As if in shock, he found it difficult to concentrate.

He forced himself to carefully review every step leading towards the Delaware court. It had seemed almost ridiculous at the time, and he had felt foolish, but he had clamped a very tight security lid on everything. None of the task force attorneys working with him in the bunker knew which court was the target or what specific action had been planned. They were like the blind man and the elephant, each knew only that part he could touch.

Spencer got up and walked to the small coffeepot. He poured a cup without even realizing he was doing so.

Only five people besides himself knew what had been planned. Four of the Apostles knew – Ainsworth Martin, John Crim, Abner Slocum, and Morris Solomon. That left himself and Christina Giles.

Like their original namesakes, the Twelve Apostles had among them a Judas.

Dan walked to the telephone and dialled Ainsworth Martin's private number at the office. Martin's secretary answered.

'This is Dan Spencer,' he said, forcing himself to remain calm. 'I have to contact Mr Martin. It's important.'

'I'm afraid he hasn't come in yet, Mr Spencer. He said he was going directly to a meeting, but I don't know where. I'll have him call you as soon as he comes in. Where are you?'

'Never mind,' Spencer said, controlling his annoyance. 'I'll be in the main office in about half an hour. If he gets there before I do, have him stay. Tell him it's an emergency.'

'I'll tell him. ' She paused. 'Could any of the other main partners help you?'

'I think not,' he said, putting down the receiver.

Someone had helped already, but they had helped the wrong side.

'Why?' was the key question. But that could only be answered when they had the answer to 'who'.

Ainsworth Martin approved of the meeting site. He was always comfortable in boardrooms. And he liked banking institutions. All New York banks respected Nelson and Clark.

Chauncey Fauxhaul, the bank's president and chief executive office, had received him, greeting Martin like a visiting ambassador. They had been friends for many years, sharing duties on a number of boards and charitable trusts.

Fauxhaul, like Martin, was in his middle sixties, tall and distinguished. He maintained a healthy tan by periodic visits to his seaside plantation in the Caribbean. He escorted Martin to the regally large boardroom.

As they entered, the man at the long, polished table stood up. Ainsworth Martin had read about him and had admired his business reputation. The tall Japanese, standing so straight and confident, seemed to radiate power.

'Mr Kuragamo, allow me to present Mr Ainsworth Martin.'

Kuragamo's grip was strong, almost to the point of pain.

'This is a pleasure indeed.' Kuragamo's words carried just the hint of a British inflection. 'Please sit down, Mr Martin.'

'I presume you gentlemen wish to do business in private,' Fauxhaul said as he withdrew. The tall Japanese merely nodded as if dismissing a servant.

Kuragamo directed his dark, expressionless gaze at Ainsworth Martin.

'I am informed you are the head partner of Nelson and Clark.'

'I am the managing partner,' Martin replied. 'As you may know, we have twelve main partners. Each of us is equal. I was elected as a somewhat overpaid office manager. The twelve of us operate the firm as a committee of the whole.'

'But you are in charge of personnel matters, correct?'

Martin hadn't the slightest idea what Kuragamo wanted. He knew only that the man seated next to him was one of the most powerful men in the world.

Martin smiled slightly. 'As far as the day-to-day operations are concerned, I suppose I am.'

Kuragamo said nothing for a moment. He was like a manikin, a wax figure; nothing changed in his face or in his eyes. 'I wish to hire one of your people away from you,' he said.

'That happens rather frequently. We select only the very best lawyers. Many are discovered and leave us for greener pastures. Since there are only twelve main partners, given the several hundred lawyers in the firm, the prospects for finally making the top are rather slim. Who is he?'

'He' – Kuragamo paused again – 'is Mrs Christina Giles.'

Martin tried to conceal his surprise. 'Mrs Giles is one of our top people. As a matter of fact, she's being considered for the existing vacancy as a main partner. I'm surprised that she would consider leaving, at least not until that selection had been made.'

'I don't think she has considered it.'

'But I presume you made her an offer?'

A cold smile played but briefly on Kuragamo's lips. 'No. I agree with you. I don't think she would leave your firm at the moment. Apparently, the chance to become one of the legendary Twelve Apostles is too strong a pull.'

'Then what's the purpose of this meeting?'

'I want you to discharge her.'

'Fire her?'

'Whatever is necessary,' Kuragamo nodded.

Ainsworth Martin had dealt with billionaires before, many times. He was aware that enormous fortunes often produced eccentricities, even madness. He was accustomed to the fact that the rich required different handling.

'As much as I respect you, Mr Kuragamo, I can't very well discharge an employee just because it would be convenient for you. I suggest you talk to Mrs Giles. It seems she is the one to make the essential decision.'

Kuragamo chuckled. 'I need a favour, my friend. At the moment, the lady isn't talking to me.'

'I will happily ask her to contact you.' Martin searched Kuragamo's face for some sign of emotion, anger, or even humour. There was no evidence of any human feeling.

'Mr Martin, this is a personal matter with me. Ordinarily I would never think of asking such a favour. However, I may be able to repay that favour many times over, and immediately.'

'In what way?'

Kuragamo sat back in his chair. He pursed his lips as if busy gathering his thoughts. 'I believe you represent Mr Scott, who is about to try a hostile takeover of Brown and Brown, the chemical firm. Is that not correct?'

'I cannot discuss a client's business unless the client approves. I presume you understand.'

Kuragamo nodded silently. 'I understand your legal ethics. Nevertheless, I know that the offer for stock is about to be made. The officers of Brown and Brown have asked me to enter the fray in the role of a White Knight.'

Ainsworth Martin forced himself to show no shock, although shock was exactly what he felt. If Kuragamo came in with his huge assets, Scott was doomed. He said nothing.

'I assume you realize that if I become such a White Knight, I have more than sufficient assets to destroy Mr John Norman Scott. I will buy Brown and Brown, then gobble up what's left of Lockwood Limited. A handsome profit is possible, and that's what I'm interested in.'

Ainsworth Martin attempted to make his expression mask-like as that of the Japanese. 'If that's what you want, then of course I suspect you'll do it. A businessman lives for profit.'

Kuragamo bowed in agreement. 'Yes, but sometimes there are other considerations. If I am successful in having Mrs Giles come to work for me, I think I can assure you I shall stay out of the takeover effort by Mr Scott. As I say, it's a quid pro quo.'

Martin felt a variety of conflicting emotions sweep through him. He felt revulsion that this stone-faced man could presume that Nelson and Clark would use its offices to further his lust. Yet he knew that Kuragamo could indeed smash John Norman Scott, and with him perhaps the law firm itself. Even the most basic form of life has survival instincts. He felt fear along with anger and confusion. He desperately needed the counsel of some of the other partners. This was far too weighty a matter to take on his shoulders alone.

'Please allow me to state my understanding.' Martin spoke softly, taking time to pronounce each word as if it alone had special meaning. 'If I discharge Mrs Giles, even though she's done nothing to merit such treatment, you will abstain from becoming Brown and Brown's White Knight, is that correct?'

'Exactly, Mr Martin. If you follow my suggestion I promise I will not involve myself or my companies in Brown and Brown's defence. You can draw up whatever papers you feel you need to ensure that I'm legally bound to my word.'

'May I discuss this with Mrs Giles?'

'No!' The word cracked out in the empty boardroom like a shot. 'Not one word of this must ever find its way to Mrs Giles.' He paused, then spoke calmly. 'My many businesses are represented by a number of law firms here in your country, Mr Martin. If you agree to my suggestion, I would be most happy to have Nelson and Clark handle all of my American interests.'

Ainsworth Martin could almost smell the money. The fees would be enormous.

'You can save a valuable client,' Kuragamo continued, 'bring in considerable legal business, and all for just a small favour.' He smiled coldly again. 'If you're worried about Mrs Giles, don't be. I will see that she is handsomely rewarded. I promise you she will make much more money by coming with me than she could ever earn at Nelson and Clark, even if she were to possess one of your glittering partnerships.'

'Still, it should be her decision.'

'I can't afford the time to allow that at the moment,' Kuragamo replied evenly. 'Because of Mr Scott's anticipated move, I must have a fast answer.'

'If I let Mrs Giles go – and I'm only speaking hypothetically – how can you be assured that she'd come to work for you?'

This time the smile was even colder, almost frightening. 'Pride is a marvellous thing. But it usually melts like ice before a furnace when you fan it with money. People are people, Mr Martin. They respond to economic reality. Oh, none of us likes to think that we do, but each of us will act, in the final event, in our economic interest, especially if the stakes are high.'

'You propose to buy her,' Martin said, regretting the bluntness instantly.

The mask was back in place. Kuragamo's dark eyes regarded him for a moment. 'A rather unfortunate choice of words. I intend to reward her, to advance her career. And, I think, when all is said and done, she will see it that way, too.'

'I wonder.'

'It is not your worry, Mr Martin, it is mine. You need merely follow my suggestion. What the lady does or doesn't do will have no bearing on my actions. I will stay out of the takeover and you will have my legal business, no matter what Mrs Giles does after leaving your firm. That seems fair to me.'

Martin nodded. 'Very fair.'

'Then you'll do it?'

Ainsworth Martin forced himself to relax. 'I wasn't prepared for this, as I'm sure you appreciate, Mr Kuragamo. I must have some consultation with the other partners.'

'Please keep this to yourself. Even if your partners are equal, they can talk. Part of this agreement is the silence that must enshroud it. You alone must make the decision, Mr Martin.'

'I will consider it, of course.'

Kuragamo stood up. 'I must have your answer by tomorrow afternoon.'

Now Ainsworth Martin stood up. They didn't shake hands. 'I will consider it and give you an answer by tomorrow.'

'Thank you,' Kuragamo bowed slightly. 'It's a pleasure to know you.'

Martin merely nodded, turned, and walked from the boardroom.

Chauncey Fauxhaul was waiting for him.

'Interesting chap, isn't he?' Fauxhaul asked.

'Most interesting. How did you come to know him?'

Fauxhaul laughed. 'I thought you knew. Mr Kuragamo owns this bank.'

Martin forced a smile as he said goodbye and stepped into the bank's private elevator.

Ainsworth Martin was disgusted. Clearly, Kuragamo wanted the woman, and he was prepated to buy out Nelson and Clark as if the law firm were some Eighth Avenue pimp.

He was disgusted, but he couldn't help but contemplate the benefits, not only to John Norman Scott, but also to the firm, if he agreed. And the dangers if he did not.

And it was all over a woman.

A Greek war had been fought over the possession of another woman long ago.

Now, like Troy, the Twelve Apostles had their own Helen, and a dangerous enemy was at their gates demanding her.

Martin reminded himself that such romantic thoughts had no place in law or in business. He knew he would have to reach his decision based on reality alone.

Ainsworth Martin, based on the experience of a lifetime, realized that reality could be very painful.

The Becker lawyers had been waiting not only in Judge Groban's courtroom, with printed answers exactly matching the paragraph numbers of Nelson and Clark's pleading, but they were also waiting in the Delaware courtroom.

It was much more than coincidence, or even brilliant anticipation. Despite the secrecy, and the few who knew what was to happen, the lawyers for Becker, Sloan and Kettering had been tipped off.

Dan Spencer was waiting when Ainsworth Martin arrived. Martin said nothing as Spencer detailed what had transpired in court and told of his suspicions. Dan laid out the facts quickly, then waited for Martin's reply.

'It doesn't necessarily mean one of our people has gone over to the other side,' Martin said, at last. 'There could have been a bug planted in your Village office. God knows, in these days of high technology such things are easily and often done.'

'Unlikely,' Spencer said. 'We kept the downtown location secret. Even the landlord down there doesn't know who we are or what we're doing.'

'Remote or not, it still is a possibility.'

'Perhaps. I've retained a firm that specializes in such things. They should be down there now going over the place for any kind of listening device.'

'From what I've read, if they use the right device, even someone as far away as across the street can listen in.'

'These people, the ones I've hired, have electronic equipment to pick up anything like that. They cost a great deal, but given the stakes, I didn't think you'd mind.'

Ainsworth Martin frowned. 'Perhaps in these rather unusual circumstances it is permissible, but otherwise I'd like you to check with me before laying out any substantial sums hereafter. No offence, Dan, but I am responsible to the other main partner for what goes on here. People sometimes have been known to get carried away.'

'I won't get carried away, Ainsworth. I presume my electronic detectives will give the bunker a clean bill of health. In that event, it still comes back to the people who knew the details of what was planned – you, me, Giles, Crim, Solomon, and Slocum. Each of us has a significant part in this whole takeover business. If one of us really has gone over, then we can expect to lose, no matter how careful or how good we are.'

Ainsworth Martin leaned back in his high-backed leather chair. 'It is very serious, Dan. However, it may be that one of us isn't being careful with vital information. A girlfriend, a wife, someone confided in who we don't suspect – it could be something like that. In fact, I rather think I know what happened.'

'You do?' Spencer was surprised.

Ainsworth Martin smiled. 'I have just returned from one of the most interesting and improbable meetings I think I've ever attended. Bizarre really doesn't cover it.'

'I don't understand.'

'As I said,' Martin continued, 'I think the problem is not disloyalty, but more probably just careless indiscretion. Do you know of the Japanese financier Taro Kuragamo?'

Dan Spencer felt his skin chill, as if a cold wind had suddenly blown over him. 'Yes.'

Martin smiled slowly, wryly. 'It seems he has a relationship with one of our people. It came as quite a surprise to me. Society and the times have changed so since I was a young man, I really shouldn't raise an eyebrow at anything any more. Nothing is the same.'

'Go on,' Spencer said, his heart pounding.

'It's quite simple, really. Apparently this chap Kuragamo has had a relationship with our Christina Giles. She's married, but that seems to count but little any more. I met with him this morning and he asked that I fire our redoubtable Mrs Giles, apparently the result of a lovers' squabble. He wants to hire her, or I hope he does, and she won't agree.' Martin chuckled. 'He believes, and he's probably right, that if she's unemployed and he dangles an enormous salary before her, she'll come around.'

'And you believe Christina may have inadvertently mentioned our tactics to Kuragamo?'

'It's possible. Lovers can be indiscreet; that's celebrated in song and story.'

'But what's Kuragamo's interest in this matter? Why should any of this be of concern to him?'

Ainsworth Martin shrugged. 'He's been approached to become Brown and Brown's White Knight. If Scott makes a bid to buy the company, Kuragamo has the resources to outbid him and preserve Brown and Brown. In fact, he could probably make a takeover bid for Lockwood Industries as well. He's rich and powerful enough to get the necessary loans.'

'Did he tell you this?'

'Yes. Interesting, isn't it? He says that if I fire Christina, he won't become anyone's White Knight. Moreover, he's pledged to throw his not inconsiderable legal business our way. Quite a plum, no matter how you view it.'

Spencer leaned back, his mind racing. 'Have you talked to Chris?'

Martin shook his head. 'I checked when I came in. She's been out sick, or so she claims, for the last few days. According to her secretary, no one knows where she is. She can't be reached. For all I know she may be with Kuragamo now.'

'Ainsworth, do you believe Christina has been feeding inside information to Kuragamo?'

'It's a possibility. Perhaps no disloyalty was intended; maybe she just failed to be tight-lipped.'

'I rather doubt that.'

'Why?'

'If, as you say, Kuragamo has a real interest in Brown and Brown, and Christina is his paramour, it would make more sense for him to keep her here, to continue as his inside source. I doubt very much if he'd ask you to let her go if that were the case.'

Martin nodded solemnly. 'I agree, if their relationship was continuing. But apparently, as I say, there's been a lovers' tiff. Perhaps he wishes to avoid having her as a source of information about him. Any number of possibilities exist.'

'Do you believe him – about staying out of the Brown and Brown takeover?'

Ainsworth Martin was no longer smiling. 'I think this firm is quite capable of preparing an agreement which will stand up in court. We can ensure that Mr Kuragamo keeps his word.'

'So it sounds as if you've decided to go along with what he wants.'

'No, not finally, although he demands an answer by tomorrow.'

'You'd sell her like a commodity? I really can't believe that, Ainsworth.'

Martin leaned back in his chair. He appeared quite at ease. 'Dan, this sort of thing happens in business every day. And for varying motives. The people who pay the piper get to dictate the tune. In publishing, a bestselling author can demand that an editor be fired. For any reason, good or not so good. Some do it.'

'But some don't. Not everyone is a prostitute.'

'Maybe, but economic reality is a great motivator. Retail kings can demand the firing of a manufacturer's representative. Advertisers dictate who they want to have in their commercials. It's all a question of money, Dan.'

'It's a question of ethics.'

Martin suddenly sat forward, his normally bland face colouring slightly. 'Then try this one on for size, as far as ethics are concerned. We, Nelson and Clark, represent Mr John Norman Scott and his company in his takeover bid for Brown and Brown, right?'

'Of course.'

'And, ethically, as lawyers we can do nothing, we should do nothing, that would be adverse to our client's interest, is that not so?'

'Ordinarily, yes, but —'

'But nothing,' Martin interrupted. 'Mr Scott is risking his business life, his company's future, not to mention billions of dollars. He expects us to act in his interest. If I keep an employee, out of some romantic concept of chivalry, and thereby set in motion forces I know will destroy him, have I acted ethically as a lawyer?'

'If you accept that premise. However —'

'This is not a debate, Dan. Nor is this a lifeboat question in some college ethics class. You remember them? In order to save the others in the lifeboat, one person must be sacrificed. Who is it? Those questions were an amusing way to challenge logic, but this is not a college quiz.'

'So you're going to fire her?'

Martin pursed his lips before answering. 'I have two basic choices. I can fire Mrs Giles and protect our client. Or I can keep her but inform Mr Scott we can no longer represent him. From the pure point of business, both present and future, I really can't see the second choice as being very practical. Since I would never ethically be able to make the reason public, the firm of Nelson and Clark would look as if it had been beaten before the battle even began. It would be seen as cowardly, as running away. I must protect the firm, as well as our client, Dan.'

'Are you going to talk to Christina before you decide?'

'I shall, if I can contact her. Otherwise —'

'You can reach her at my apartment,' Dan said quietly.

The sudden silence in the office was almost audible, as if the absence of sound had been converted into a solid, physical presence.

His eyes fixed on Spencer, Martin's expression gave no hint of his thoughts.

'It seems you have been in for a series of surprises,' Spencer said, finally breaking the silence.

'Yes.' Martin paused before going on. 'You realize I'm sure that this relationship with Mrs Giles, well, marks you as being under suspicion too.'

'Oh?'

'If you were to disclose something to Mrs Giles, and she in turn were to tell Kuragamo — '

Dan held up his hand. 'I think you had better know the complete truth, Ainsworth.' He then carefully detailed for Martin the history of the troubles between Christina and her husband, the quick fling with Kuragamo in London, the man's subsequent demands, and Spencer's protection of the besieged lady.

Martin seemed lost in thought. Then he looked at Spencer. 'You make my life rather difficult,' he said at last. 'As you may know, I generally disapprove of, well, relationships between members of the firm. They tend to be disruptive. Of course I've never quite been able to persuade Katherine Thurston to that position.' His smile was forced.

'There's been no relationship, at least not in that sense. Mrs Giles is my colleague and friend, that's all.'

Ainsworth Martin pushed himself out of his chair, then walked to the window overlooking the towers of Manhattan. He spoke as he surveyed the city. 'Are you sure that's all it is, Dan? You wouldn't be the first man to allow himself to become confused as to where friendship ended and something more began. Christina is a very attractive woman.'

Dan Spencer shifted in his chair. Ainsworth Martin had voiced his own thoughts. 'I'm reasonably sure, Ainsworth. But that really isn't the question, is it? It boils down to what you are going to do.'

Martin looked over at him. 'Will Mrs Giles talk to me?'

'I would think so.'

'Then I'd like to talk to her first. Once I've done so, I'll make my decision.'

Dan Spencer also stood up. 'Suppose it's one of the Apostles, Ainsworth? Suppose it is disloyalty, and it's one of your main partners. Firing Christina isn't going to solve that, is it?'

'It couldn't be one of us,' Martin replied, staring out at the city's skyline.

'And if I prove that it is?'

Ainsworth Martin turned from the window. 'There isn't time, I'm afraid. I have to have an answer to Kuragamo tomorrow.'

'But if I prove it before then?'

Martin looked troubled. 'If you could, which I doubt, it might change things, I suppose.'

Dan Spencer nodded. 'Well, I can take a shot at it, can't I?'

Martin shook his head slowly. 'The man has us between a rock and a hard place, Dan. Both ethically and in a business sense. I will defer my ultimate decision until tomorrow afternoon.'

'Ainsworth, you keep saying it's your decision. Christina is a participating partner and up for promotion to main partner. Doesn't firing her require a vote by all the main partners?'

Ainsworth Martin smiled. 'As managing partner I have absolute say in personnel matters. All the partners agreed to that. So I can act without taking a vote. Usually, just as a courtesy, I would consult the others. But time, plus the need for secrecy, dictates I operate on my own.'

Dan Spencer walked towards the door. 'God knows you've had your fill of threats today, Ainsworth, and I hate to add to your problems. But if you fire Christina, I think I'll have to reconsider my own position.'

'You mean you'd quit?'

'It's a possibility.'

'You're a key man around here, especially now, but a man does what he has to do.' He stopped for a moment, then continued. 'You know of course that you're being considered for Frank Johnson's vacancy.'

'I had heard.'

'Don't ruin your career just when you're about to reach the top, Dan.'

'As you say, Ainsworth, a man has to do some things.'

Ainsworth Martin walked over to join him. He extended his hand. 'Be careful, Dan.'

'I'll be careful. But I think that's good advice for us all, don't you?'

'Perhaps. Will you tell Mrs Giles I'd like to speak with her?'

'Of course.'

Dan Spencer walked down the long hallway, then took the stairs to his floor. He sat down in his own office, much smaller than one of the Apostles', although pleasant enough. He had always felt at home here. He hated the prospect of perhaps having to give it up.

Abner Slocum left his office about midday. He told his secretary he had some shopping to do. But when he reached the street he walked as fast as he could, his legs seeming stiffer than usual, and went to see his banker.

Over the years, Slocum had carefully marshalled his fortune; he was a rich man. His personal business was considerable, and that, together with his influential clients' business, made him beloved by the bank president, who was also an old classmate.

Slocum irritably brushed aside the usual polite banter and got right to the point. 'I need a fiduciary bond,' he said.

The banker put on his most professional smile, the one that was soothing and helpful. 'Of course, Abner. In what connection and for how much?'

'I'm executor of an estate,' he said. 'The will provides that I serve without bond, but I want to avoid any possible lawsuits. I'll need a bond, a substantial one, probably a half-billion.'

'Pardon me?'

Slocum abandoned his usual smoothness. 'Goddamn it, is your hearing going? I need a half-billion-dollar fiduciary bond.'

'Do you realize how much that will cost? If the will exempts you from being bonded as executor, I don't see — '

Slocum nearly barked his next words. 'I'm the lawyer, you're the banker. I know what is necessary and why I want that bond.'

The banker, a man who, like Slocum, didn't wear his age well, looked hurt. 'The fee will be substantial.'

'The estate pays for it, not me,' Slocum snapped. Then he paused, remembering that the man across from him was indeed a friend. 'Even if I had to pay for it myself, I'd want one. There may be a lawsuit to stop me from, well, performing my duties. If I'm serving without bond, a judge might question my motives. But with a bond . . . well, I think it's just a wise precaution.'

The banker looked troubled. 'Abner, a bond of that size . . .' He paused. 'It may be difficult to arrange.'

Slocum's eyes narrowed. 'I'll pledge every damn cent I have – stocks, bonds, everything. In addition, I will file an inventory, showing the assets of the estate.' He reached into his briefcase.

'Here's a copy. There are many assets that can't be stolen, even by a clever lawyer.'

The banker's eyes widened. 'This is the Winship estate!'

Slocum nodded. 'Right. And this has to be absolutely confidential, you understand.'

'But isn't your firm acting — '

'Everything that's being done is done by me.' Slocum smiled conspiratorially. 'In this case, for reasons I can't tell you, it's extremely important.'

The banker tried to hide his worry, but he was unsuccessful.

She watched him as a cat might watch a particularly succulent mouse.

Katherine Thurston had listened to Dan Spencer without once interrupting. She found his story as fascinating as she did the tall Daniel Spencer himself. She had made it a point to show her very good legs, but Spencer had been too intent to notice.

Such neglect usually would have annoyed her, but this time, considering the circumstances, she forgave him. And, she reasoned, there was always another time. 'Of all the Apostles, Dan, why did you select me?'

'One way or another, most of the main partners have had some connection with this case. You're sort of neutral, Katherine. You will be an objective witness, credible to the others.'

'I'm flattered.'

'It's true, Katherine.'

'You haven't heard all the office stories about me?'

He laughed, his eyes fixed on hers. 'There isn't a man in Nelson and Clark who hasn't heard those stories. And even if they were true, none of them reflect on your integrity.'

She smiled. 'Just my morals.'

He laughed nervously but didn't reply.

'I'll let you be the judge of those stories, Dan. But now tell me what you have up your sleeve.'

'A trap.'

'Go on.'

'I plan to tell each of the people under suspicion of a different legal action, each planned in a different court. Each of them will be told

279

separately, late in the day, probably telephoned at their home. That way they aren't likely to compare notes with each other.'

'So?'

'Early the following morning I will assign trial lawyers to go to each of the courts. Suitably prepared, by the way, with the appropriate pleadings. If there is no opposition, the lawyer is to wait a few minutes, then report to me. If the other side is waiting, they will have been tipped off and we'll know who the mole is.'

'So if you tell Abner Slocum, for instance, that you're bringing a motion before a certain judge in the federal court, and someone from Becker's office is there waiting, you'll know he's your man, right?'

'And if no one is there, we will know that he isn't.'

'I presume you'll do the same with Martin, Crim, Slocum, and Solomon, but what about Christina Giles?'

He took a deep breath. 'Christina too, although I may not.'

'You're in dangerous waters, Dan. I'm sure Ainsworth Martin will be incensed when he discovers you suspected him, and worse, that you didn't advise him of your little scheme. I trust you've considered the fact that the other Apostles will be damn angry to think you questioned their integrity. That's hardly the smart way to get yourself elected main partner, is it?'

'I can't wage a winning court fight if someone is giving my signals to the other team. This is something that has to be done.'

Katherine Thurston shifted in her chair, again allowing a generous expanse of thigh to show. 'And what about your Chris? She's living with you, after all. If she turns out to be the source, it could spoil a beautiful romance.'

Dan Spencer looked away, aware that she was an exciting woman. Her eyes and body language were challenging, even taunting. 'That brings up another request. Can she move in with you for a few days? I think it would be helpful, if it's not too much of a burden.'

She laughed. 'All this assistance you're asking may cost you something.'

He grinned. 'There's no romance between Chris and myself, by the way.'

'Just a pal?' Katherine raised an eyebrow.

'A colleague.'

'We'll see, Daniel. Men are so short-sighted about such things. However, if our little Christina has been trading with the enemy, I suspect you're the kind who would lose all interest in her anyway.'

'I doubt she is the one.'

'But if she *is*?'

'We'll cross that bridge when we get there.'

Katherine Thurston lit a cigarette. The act, done with a flourish, was a stylish bit of theatre. 'I'm taking a few risks myself,' she said. 'But I'll act as your impartial observer and witness, Dan. And, although I do find you charming and attractive, I am really doing this for the good of the firm. If one of the Apostles has gone bad, that must be known.' She expelled smoke through softly pursed lips. 'And I'll even take in our Chris for a few days. I rather doubt that you're the Boy Scout you would like us to believe. If you change your mind, I'll send her back.' She laughed throatily. 'And, if not, I may just come myself.'

'You're always welcome,' he replied, not knowing exactly what to say.

'I told you there might be a price to be paid.'

Christina Giles listened to Ainsworth Martin, much as an erring schoolgirl might listen to a stern but kindly principal.

'As I'm sure you appreciate much more than anyone else, Christina – you have such a fine feeling for business arrangements – I really have no choice in the matter. I must sacrifice either you or our client, to say nothing of the firm's interest.'

'And you chose to sacrifice me?' she asked icily.

Martin's bland face seemed entirely relaxed. 'Suppose I were your client, Christina, and found myself in a similar situation. Tell me, honestly now, what would your advice be, given these rather unusual circumstances?'

Christina Giles had thought of little else since Dan Spencer had called and asked if she were up to seeing Ainsworth Martin. Strangely, she felt quite calm, almost relieved.

'I'd advise you to fire me,' she said.

Martin nodded. 'I agree. It's a matter of priorities.' He sighed. 'However, there is one possibility we haven't tried.'

'What's that?'

'If Mr Kuragamo will call and ask me to keep you on, promising at the same time to stay out of the Brown and Brown business, it would solve all our problems.'

'Suppose, for argument's sake, he asked you to keep me on, but was going to plough ahead into the Brown and Brown matter anyway. What then?'

'In a manner of speaking, you are his hostage at the moment. Now, if he asked us to keep you on, the situation would reverse itself. I'd demand that he step aside in the takeover or we would fire you. Nothing personal, Chris, just a matter of good business.'

She forced a laugh. 'God, I wonder why I spent all that time going through law school and trying to build a career, when I should have known it would finally all come down to this – that I'd be nothing more than a female captive.' She looked directly at him. 'This is all quite bizarre, Ainsworth. More than anything else in life, I wanted to be an Apostle. I really did. Now just because some damn rich man has the hots for me I stand to lose everything I've worked for.' She felt tears welling up in her eyes as she tried to will them back again.

Martin retained his benign expression. 'Why don't you give Kuragamo a call, Christina? Perhaps he'll agree. You never know until you've tried.'

She shook her head and blinked. 'I'm a lawyer, and a good one. I don't need this firm, or Taro Kuragamo. I'd die before I'd sink so low as to do something like that.'

Martin nodded slowly. 'I understand. But when Mr Kuragamo calls tomorrow afternoon, I will be forced to tell him you have been discharged.'

'There are such things as sex-discrimination suits, Ainsworth.'

He smiled, almost kindly. 'Indeed, and more every day. However, my dear, if you sue, your relationship with Mr Kuragamo will of course be made public. I'm not being cruel Christina, just practical.'

'So I'm fired then?'

He shrugged. 'Not officially, not until tomorrow afternoon. If your Mr Kuragamo relents, or if you can work things out, you will continue to be a most welcome member of this firm. But, unless that happens, I'm afraid tomorrow is your last day.' He stood up and came around the desk. 'The firm will provide severance benefits, of course. And, if you decline Mr Kuragamo's offer, I'm sure we can get you a particularly handsome position with any number of our corporate clients. You are an excellent lawyer, as you say.'

She stood up but avoided his extended hand. 'Yes, I'm very good.

I won't need Nelson and Clark or anyone else. I have my own reputation.'

Despite her avoidance, he did manage to pat her on the back, a soft, paternal gesture. 'I don't like lectures, my dear. But you're about the same age as my daughter. In law, as in politics or business, one should keep one's private life separate. I know you don't need old Ainsworth Martin to give you a sermon on the benefits of being discreet. You've certainly learned enough.'

'I've learned a great deal in the past few days, perhaps more than I have ever learned before.'

He escorted her to the door. 'I'm glad, ' he said, as if purposely misunderstanding her statement. 'And I still hope things may work out.' He gave her a squeeze. 'We would all hate to lose you.'

21

It had been a nervous dinner. Although their hosts, Katherine Thurston and her husband, Noel, had been charming, even effervescent, there seemed to be a pall hanging over the whole meal.

Dan Spencer declined an after-dinner cocktail. 'I think it's time, Katherine,' he said. 'This may take a while, although I did alert everyone concerned to stand by. If you'll listen on an extension, I'll make the calls.'

Katherine Thurston gulped down her martini as if it were water. 'I honest-to-God think I'm going to enjoy this. This is better than reading a Dorothy Sayers mystery.'

'I feel left out,' Noel said, smiling. 'If you people return and find Christina and me gone, it means we couldn't control our mutual passion and have run off to a seedy midtown hotel.'

'I imagine you know a few,' Katherine said, but not unkindly.'

'Only those where you have a charge account, my love.'

They both laughed without hint of rancour or irritation. Christina was surprised. Katherine and Noel Thurston seemed to be a very odd married couple.

'Can't we do this telephone business in one bedroom?' Katherine asked with pretended coyness.

'Not unless you have two phones in one,' Spencer replied.

'Pity. I'll take up station in my bedroom and you can make the calls from Noel's. Shouldn't we record the conversations?'

'No, that violates federal law. You'll be my witness; that will be sufficient. Even if we smoke the culprit out, Katherine, this will never go to court. I'm sure everything will be handled quietly in-house.'

'I'm glad you took Christina off the suspects list,' she said so only he could hear.

Dan looked back. 'I think she's had trouble enough, don't you? Anyway, if this works, it will help to clear up a great many things.'

'And if not?'

He shrugged. 'That's a bridge we haven't come to yet.'

He found the telephoning surprisingly tiring. Spencer worked from his notes, giving each suspect a different plan of action. He had to be an actor, keeping his telephone excitement obvious while answering the searching questions asked. He liked each of the men he called, and he felt somewhat like a Judas himself. He was leading one of them into a trap. He had to remind himself that his little scheme might not work at all and none of them would be harmed.

But if it did work, one of them would be ruined.

And if it didn't work, he would be the one who was ruined.

He continued calling, performing his act, aware that Katherine Thurston was on the line, listening to every word.

It was a risk, and he wondered if it was really worth it.

John Norman Scott strode into the conference room looking like a conquering general. He stepped before the battery of television lights and nodded to the camera crews, photographers, and newspapermen. A pleasant, exciting sense of exhilaration coursed through him. It was a feeling he loved and wanted to remember, a memory to be savoured.

He glanced over at Nancy Merriam, who had set up the early morning press conference. There was some easy banter between Scott and the newsmen before everyone was ready. Then the television lights went on and he was given the signal to begin.

He glared at the television cameras as though trying to stare them down. 'Mediocrity has become the passion and trademark of today's business world,' he began, speaking quietly but forcefully. He knew only part of the tape would be used, so Nancy had written a short statement that had equally dramatic impact no matter what part the television people selected. 'However, in the open marketplace, competition usually corrects such regrettable circumstances. But competition seems to have failed concerning one company. I have watched with dismay as the world's largest chemical and medical producer has drifted not only into mediocrity but also into criminality. Americans are justifiably proud of their industrial giants, proud of America's heritage in making this world a safe and better place to live. Our largest chemical company, Brown and Brown, however, has become a mere shadow of its former self and has even spread poison throughout the world – killing children, leaving maimed bodies in its corporate wake. I had hoped the government would do something about this rogue-elephant corporation, but in vain. Lockwood Limited has reluctantly recognized its responsibility; we must do something ourselves.

'This morning members of the staff of Lockwood Limited, under my direction, are filing the necessary papers to make an offer to buy a majority of shares in Brown and Brown. We are doing this not only to protect the stockholders of Brown and Brown, but to protect the American people, and for that matter, all the people of this earth where Brown and Brown products are sold.'

The television crews turned off the lights and started packing, even as the newsmen began asking questions. The eye of the camera was only interested in a short few seconds of drama for the nightly TV news. Anything more than just the surface was of no real interest.

Scott had been briefed by his public relations people. He artfully dodged the traps set for him by some of the journalists, while expanding, to the pleasure of others, on the subject of corporate responsibility.

It was clearly a triumph.

John Norman Scott loved it. As he handled the questions he wondered whether his primary career might yet be ahead of him. Anyone as good as he, Scott decided, should be in politics. Something national, like perhaps running for the presidency.

While Scott was holding his press conference uptown, Dan Spencer nervously paced the wooden floor of the downtown office.

He had dispatched the lawyers like messengers earlier, each to a different court, each with a different task. Each attorney had been instructed separately; none had any idea of what the others were doing.

Each man had been instructed to call and check with Spencer before actually filing the papers he had in his briefcase or seeing the judge specified. Each was told to go to the courtroom or the court's chambers and see if any opposition lawyers were present. If not, a call was to be made to Spencer before the lawyer actually started anything.

The first call came at 9:45.

Bruno Chasen had visited the chambers of Judge Groban. No attorneys from the Becker firm were present. Chasen sounded excited, as if he now had the field all to himself. Spencer told him to scrub the operation and come back to the office. Chasen was angry, telling Spencer they were blowing a chance to steal an advantage.

Then the calls came, one after the other. There were no Becker attorneys at the federal court of appeals – Morris Solomon, who knew about that, was scratched from the suspect list. Ainsworth Martin was also cleared.

No action was reported at the federal district court clerk's office. Abner Slocum had been told what was being planned there. Abner Slocum was eliminated as a suspect.

Katherine Thurston was in the firm's main office, keeping her phone clear while awaiting Dan Spencer's call.

The only attorney yet to report was Jeff Rowe. He had been assigned to see Judge Warren Tudor, the Acting Chief Justice of the state Supreme Court's civil division. He had been told he was to try to get Judge Tudor to set up a quick hearing on a motion asking New York to step into the proxy matter. Not knowing his task was bogus, Rowe had doubted the wisdom of the motion.

Spencer felt the excitement of the morning turning into depression. If Rowe found no one waiting, then they were back to square one or worse.

Despite himself, he kept glancing at his wristwatch. The time seemed to be frozen, not moving. But it was moving, incredibly slowly, or so it seemed.

It was now 10:15. Spencer forced himself to make the effort to prepare a cup of coffee. He was just finishing when the telephone rang.

Hot coffee spilled over his hand as he grabbed for the receiver.

'Spencer,' he said.

'Jesus, you sent me into a hornet's nest!' Jeff Rowe sounded rattled and angry. 'Becker had a half-dozen lawyers there. Judge Tudor got sore at me when I tried to talk to him. I told you, Dan, that this wouldn't work. He's upset that nothing was filed with the clerk, and that we didn't give him the courtesy of a telephone call. I mean, he's damn mad. I thought I was going to end up in jail. Those Becker lawyers really egged the old guy on. I made an apology and escaped.'

'You didn't tell anyone where you were going this morning?'

'Of course not,' Rowe shot back. 'How the hell could I? I didn't know myself. ' He paused. 'I didn't know, the judge didn't know, the only people who knew were Becker, Sloan and Kettering. And they certainly knew. They had countermotions, even emergency appeal papers all ready to go. How come, Dan? How come they knew?'

'It's a long story, Jeff. Come on back to the office. I'm sorry you had to go through that.'

'You owe me at least a drink.'

Spencer depressed the telephone button, waited for the dial tone, and then called Katherine Thurston.

'Who is it?' She sounded genuinely excited, something exceptionally unusual for her.

'Guess,' he asked, feeling foolish for having said it.

'Abner Slocum.'

He was surprised by her choice. 'No cigar. It's John Crim.'

'You're kidding.'

'No, I'm afraid not. Our Washington ambassador seems to have become a mole. Crim's our Judas.'

'Well, that's it, Ainsworth,' Katherine Thurston said, her smile that of a freshly fed cat. 'It seems John Crim has gone over to the other side. I think our Mr Spencer here has done an exceptional job.'

Ainsworth Martin carefully scrutinized Dan Spencer. 'You actually suspected me?'

'You were treated the same as the others. It seemed quite impossible that any of the main partners would give secret information to a rival law firm, but if that were so, then I had to include everyone.'

'You played a risky game.'

'Perhaps. But it was successful. The question now is what do we do about it?'

'I think you should confront John Crim,' Katherine Thurston said. 'Let him know he's been caught with his fingers in the cookie jar. I should think he'd resign without much fuss.'

Ainsworth Martin nodded. 'I agree, considering what has happened. However, if he decides to deny it, we'll have to bring in all the partners — '

'Ainsworth,' Spencer interjected. 'I think I have a better idea.'

'Oh?'

'Don't tell him anything. We'll go on just as before. I'll feed him some things, information that won't harm us or which would be easily predictable anyway.'

'What for?' Katherine Thurston asked.

'We lull them into thinking they still have an accurate pipeline, then at just the right moment, we feed John false information – stuff that might kill them. He gives it to Becker's outfit and they act on it. In the right spot, it could be our key to victory.'

Martin slowly smiled. 'That's called "turning" an agent in the intelligence community, did you know that?'

Spencer shook his head.

'And what happens in the end?' Katherine Thurston asked. 'When all the smoke of legal battle blows away, what do we do then?'

Ainsworth Martin leaned back in his chair. 'That's when we ask good old John to resign. I would hope that at that time, if Dan's plan works, he should be regarded as a prime bubble head by Becker's people, thus any advantage all this might have had for him will be gone.'

'The traitor exposed,' Katherine said.

'Precisely.'

'What about Christina Giles?' Dan asked.

'I found it interesting that you didn't include her in the list of suspects,' Martin said. 'What about her?' He then looked at Katherine Thurston. 'This is a personal matter, Katherine, will you please excuse us?'

Katherine Thurston laughed. 'Don't worry about me. Chris is my houseguest. As the old saying goes, I know all.'

Martin emitted a dry chuckle. 'She does seem to get around, doesn't she?' He saw the quick anger in Spencer's eyes. 'A joke, poor perhaps, but only a joke.' He paused. 'The matter is entirely in the lady's hands. I asked her to contact Kuragamo and arrange some sort of compromise. If she's not successful, she's through as soon as he calls me. I must protect our client, and I must protect this firm.'

'I told you I'd pull the pin if that happens,' Dan Spencer said.

Martin nodded. 'Yes, you did tell me you would resign. That's your decision, of course. However, I think you underestimate Christina. She's handled some of the most delicate negotiations ever conducted by this law firm. Although this is a personal matter, and emotional, I still think she has the experience and the brains to work out something.'

Ainsworth Martin leaned forward and placed his elbows on the desk. 'I can see the disapproval in both your eyes. If left to my own inclinations I would tell that arrogant bastard to, well, to perform a physically impossible task. But the whole thing is tied in with the Lockwood matter. I have no other choice. You may not understand, but I think Christina does.'

'This will prove to be an especially interesting afternoon,' Spencer said, his tone carrying the unspoken threat.

Ainsworth Martin sighed. 'Dan, no one is indispensable, not you, not me, not John Crim. Let's just see what happens. As you say, it will indeed be an interesting afternoon.'

Christina had had little sleep and felt as if she were moving through invisible molasses. She was cleaning out her desk, and it seemed to be taking forever. She had packing cases sent up and was trying to sort out what she wanted to keep and what she wanted to discard. Each paper or file seemed to contain its own special memory of a case or a client. It was slow work. She wondered if she would get done in time.

Her secretary had refrained from asking the key question, but her eyes had pleaded for some kind of answer. Christina merely told her she was straightening up.

She wondered if her disinclination to tell her secretary what had happened might be an unconscious expression of her own deep desire to stay. She had lost her home, but that somehow didn't seem half as bad as leaving her second home, the office that had always been her refuge.

Her secretary appeared again in the door. 'I know you said to hold all calls, but that Mr Kuragamo is on the phone.'

Christina blinked up at the girl without replying.

'I can tell him you're out or in conference.'

Christina felt her heart leap, not with passion but with stark fear. 'I'll talk to him.'

'I'll put him through.' Her secretary discreetly closed the door behind her.

Christina stumbled over a packing box as she made her way around her desk. The telephone somehow looked menacing.

The sound of the telephone's bell, although expected, caused her to jump.

'Hello,' she said, forcing herself to sound calm.

'Christina, this is Taro.' His voice was deep, assured. 'Could we meet for lunch? I really must talk to you.'

'I have a luncheon appointment,' she said coldly.

'Break it.'

'I can't.'

'Christina, did your managing partner talk to you?'

'Ainsworth Martin?'

'Yes.'

'He talked to me.'

There was a pause. 'Someone told me you had been fired. I couldn't believe it.'

'I'm having lunch with some people who have offered me a partnership in another firm.'

'That's foolish, Christina. With your talent and experience you don't need to work in any law firm. My general counsel for the Sunrise Group has just resigned. We have over a hundred lawyers in the general counsel's office. It's an important job and it pays rather well.'

'How much?'

He chuckled. 'Everyone becomes very practical when they are job hunting. Three hundred thousand.'

'That's not enough,' she said. 'In a few years I can be earning

290

double that.'

He laughed. 'Then why wait a few years. Make it six now.'

'I could be fired.'

'You drive a hard bargain, my dear. I'll give you a five-year contract. How's that?'

'How about ten years?'

This time the pause was longer. 'Are you playing with me?'

'I don't want to be impolite, Taro. In a way, I'm flattered by your interest, although I truly find it offensive. What you want is a whore, high priced to be sure, but a whore nevertheless. But then you seem to manage to buy just about everything, don't you?'

'Christina, I'm just trying to be kind.'

She felt anger rising in her. It felt surprisingly good. 'Listen to me. I suppose you could ruin me, maybe even destroy me. But, by God, I will never have anything to do with you again, I hope you get the full impact of that. I doubt your father ever married your goddamned mother. You are a bastard in every way possible. You lie, you connive. You're one of the most rotten men I have ever met in my life. Now I want you to take your goddamned money and your little slant eyes and get the hell out of my life!'

'You'll see things differently. Believe me.'

'Listen, you damn — ' She sought through her memory for a racial insult. She didn't use them or even think them, but she wanted one now. 'You goddamn slopehead!'

'Christina . . .'

'You may have me fired from every job I ever get, but I'll become a bag lady before I ever have anything to do with you. You are nothing but filth.'

'Be careful, Christina.' His voice was suddenly cold and angry.

'Go back to Hong Kong and sell dope or whatever it is you really do. And take your fake Oxford accent along with you. You are — ' Again she sought something nasty, really vulgar, words she never used. Her memory, like a computer, tossed up a remembered insult: 'You flaming asshole!'

She trembled, but she felt relieved, as if she somehow had exorcised a deadly poison that was infecting her. She felt competent again, filled with a sense of self-esteem.

'Mrs Giles.' His voice was almost a whisper, a rasp of undiluted rage. 'I think you are going to be very sorry.'

'Flaming fucking asshole!' she said, carefully pronouncing each syllable. Then she slammed down the telephone.

She leaned back in her chair and for the first time in days burst out laughing. Her secretary hesitantly opened the door. 'Are you all right?'

Christina grinned at her. 'To tell you the truth, I've never felt better in my whole life.'

22

'Mr Martin, Mr Kuragamo is on the line.'

Ainsworth Martin felt old as he lifted the receiver. 'Good afternoon,' he said. He hated what he knew he must do.

'Martin.' Kuragamo's voice was angry. 'I don't give a damn what you do with that Giles bitch. Fire her, keep her, fuck her, I don't care!'

'Pardon me?'

'I am going to join Brown and Brown in fighting Scott's takeover. I will destroy Scott.' His voice became more menacing. 'And I will destroy your little law firm. I will crush it like an ant.'

Ainsworth Martin didn't reply at first. 'I take it by your rather hostile tone that things didn't go so very well with Mrs Giles.'

'Don't you listen? I said I don't care about her. I am coming after you people. You can hire her back – it makes no difference.'

'I can't hire her back, Mr Kuragamo.'

'What?'

'I can't hire her back, sir, because I didn't fire her.'

'She said — '

'Ah, my dear Kuragamo, I presume your wealth was inherited. Such naiveté. Christina was to pretend she was fired. Ah well, apparently the truth is out now, so it really doesn't matter.'

'You lawyers should all rot in hell.'

Ainsworth Martin laughed. 'What a delightful sense of humour – so rare in the Japanese, don't you agree?' Martin knew he should be conciliatory, but suddenly he was enjoying himself.

292

'You will regret this.'

'You are going to attack, then?'

'Count on it,' Kuragamo snapped.

Martin laughed again. 'Well, at least you people have learned a little about sportsmanship since Pearl Harbour. How very nice. We'll see you in court, Mr Kuragamo.'

Kuragamo swore and Martin heard the telephone connection break.

Ainsworth Martin buzzed his secretary. 'Please ask Mrs Giles to step into my office.'

'Yes, sir.'

'Oh, and call the florist we use. I'd like a dozen perfect long-stemmed red roses delivered to her office, at once. And I do mean at once, is that clear? Have the card read, "Nelson and Clark is enriched by your continuing presence. As ever, Ainsworth." Do you have that?'

'Yes, sir.'

Ainsworth Martin regretted the loss of the profits Kuragamo's business would have brought. But he had done nothing to lose it. He hated to admit it, but he was delighted that he had had a chance to twit Kuragamo.

Fun. It was expensive fun, and perhaps dangerous at that, he ruefully reminded himself. Still, no matter what the consequences, he felt a great deal better.

'Nancy, get in here!' His voice was strange, half-strangled.

Nancy Merriam walked fast, then ran. She rushed past John Norman Scott's startled secretary and burst through Scott's ornate office doors.

He sat behind his huge desk, his hands clasping the arms of his favourite leather chair. His face was rigid and white.

'My God,' she gasped, 'are you all right?'

His eyes, half staring, seemed to look through her. 'Come in.' His voice was just above a whisper. 'Close the door.'

She quickly closed the leather doors. 'What is it, John? You look terrible.'

'I'm worse than I look.' His attempt at a smile failed. 'I just got terrible news.'

Nancy Merriam knew Scott's mother was ill and in a nursing

home in Indiana. She presumed she had passed away.

'What news?' she asked, coming around the desk. Somehow he looked like a lost little boy. Perhaps he was human after all. Some of her old feelings for him surged within her.

'It's as good as over,' he mumbled. 'We're done for.'

'What are you talking about?'

He looked up at her, his eyes wide. 'Kuragamo is coming in; he's going to come to the aid of Brown and Brown.'

'My God, is that all? For a minute I thought someone had died.'

'I wish to Christ that was all. Death I can deal with.'

'John, you're white as a ghost. Tell me what this is all about.'

He sighed, leaning his head back on the chair, reminding her of an exhausted swan. 'Frank Lange, the vice president of United Northern, just called.'

'United Northern, the investment bankers?'

He made a feeble attempt at nodding. 'They'd promised me they would put up a billion dollars to help finance the takeover. Now they're pulling out.'

'Why?'

'Taro Kuragamo. He's announced he will be Brown and Brown's White Knight. He's warned all the big financial houses that he'll wreak vengeance on them if they lend money to me. He owns half the world's banks. United Northern doesn't want to risk bucking him.'

'Don't you have an agreement with them?'

Scott put his head into his hands. 'Oh, sure. But they drew it up. It's riddled with escape clauses. I can't hold them to it or even get damages.'

She frowned. 'I'd fire the lawyers who okayed that.' She hoped it wasn't Nelson and Clark, and especially she hoped it wasn't the appealing Michael Collins.

A wan smile played across his thin lips. 'I had our own lawyers look into it at the time. They sent me a memo saying it wasn't binding.'

'Then why did you agree to it?'

'Time. Christ, I didn't have the time to haggle, Nancy. I was moving too fast to get bogged down in details. It was a mistake, but hindsight's always best.'

'What about the other bankers? Will they pull out?'

He stared up at the ceiling melodramatically, his voice low as he replied. 'No, not all of them. The San Francisco people are too big to worry. Besides, they'll end up lending money to Kuragamo, too – that way they can't lose. They do it all the time in these things.'

'Then you still have money besides the company's to buy the tendered stock?'

'Sure, at the price I set.'

'Then why this hysteria?'

He sat up bolt straight. 'Hysteria? This is a disaster, but I'm far from hysterical.' As he said it, his face was shaking.

'Even if you don't succeed, you'll still end up owning a part of Brown and Brown. Sure, you will have paid too high a price, but Lockwood can absorb that loss. It's not the end of the world.'

He looked at her a moment before speaking. 'You don't understand. Lange tells me Kuragamo is going to use the Pac Man defence.'

'Pardon me?'

'The old arcade game where the little man eats up the monsters. Kuragamo is going to make a takeover offer for Lockwood.'

'How does that help Brown and Brown?'

'If Kuragamo can buy this company, he can negate anything we've done. He fires all the officers and the board of directors and puts his own people in. Even if we succeed in buying up Brown and Brown, it won't mean anything. He'll own everything – us and the chemical company.'

'Does he have that kind of money? You're talking about two of the largest corporations in America.'

Scott shook his head slowly. 'He's got half the money in the world, and he can get loans from the other half. 'It's over, Nancy. There's no use in going on. The end is inevitable.'

'Like Yogi Berra said about baseball games, John, it isn't over until it's over. We can still put up a hell of a fight.'

To her surprise, tears began to trickle down his cheeks. 'I'll look like a fool,' he said softly. 'The people on Wall Street will laugh at me.'

Nancy wondered what she had ever seen in him. He was like a whipped, childish bully, quite pathetic. She was disgusted by his attitude.

'If you want to resign, go ahead,' she snapped. 'As far as Lockwood Limited is concerned, we are going to put up a fight. I don't know this Kuragamo, and I don't give a damn about him. But I'll be damned if he's going to bluff us out of this. We're going to put up the toughest fight ever seen.'

Scott took out a monogrammed handkerchief and loudly blew his nose. A half-hearted smile ghosted upon his features. 'Maybe you're right,' he said softly.

'This is only the opening gun, John. We can't give up now.'

He thought about what she said, his face slowly taking on his old, arrogant expression. 'By God, Nancy, you're right! I don't know what I could have been thinking. Yes, we'll give him a fight.' Colour seemed to flow back into his cheeks. 'And I'll whip him, too.'

She looked at him and saw a weak but adult child. A child who had been caught playing at adult games. She realized he could no longer be trusted to run the show.

'I have some ideas, John,' she said softly but firmly. 'Let me take over for a while. You can rest and get prepared for what is to come. In the meantime I'll do what's necessary.'

His jaw had jutted out in its characteristic arrogant manner. 'Damn good idea, Nancy. I'll do the thinking, you do the running. We make a hell of a team.' Although the words were brave, his tone still carried with it an underlying insecurity.

Nancy Merriam knew her youth and inexperience wouldn't be accepted by the other company officers or by the stockholders – not to lead a major corporate war. She would have to bolster John Norman Scott, prop him up, and use him as a front.

But it was all up to her now. Although the thought should have been awesome, she felt a thrill of confidence and expectation.

She was determined to win.

Nancy put her determination into action. Acting under the name of the frightened and impotent John Norman Scott, she issued a call for a special meeting of Lockwood Limited stockholders. She proposed the passage of two shark-repellent changes in the corporate charter. The first provided that board members could not be removed until the end of their appointed term. A raider, even if successful, couldn't seize command of a company if the old board was still in power. Under her proposed provision, a raider couldn't exercise his voting majority for a number of years, thus delaying his ownership and possibly preventing the seizure of the property which was the real target of the takeover. Her second provision related to mandatory redemption provisions. In a takeover, a raider need buy only 51 per cent of the stock. Those stockholders who accepted the high dollar sold out and had coins jingling in their pockets, but those who chose to stick with the company were left holding the bag. The raider could sell off the assets of a company, devaluing the stock of those remaining. Nancy Merriam's change made it mandatory that the non-tendering stockholders get a price equal to the amount bid by the raider. This provision meant that a raider would have to buy a company totally, and usually for more than it was worth, making the whole thing chancy and possibly unprofitable.

Even Morris Solomon, Nelson and Clark's chief business lawyer, was impressed. The girl had a genius for quiet leadership.

Teddy Edwards was also impressed. Brown and Brown quickly added shark-repellent provisions to the agenda of their annual meeting, only a few days away, meeting the legal notice requirement by one day. It was all quite legal, not only the corporate charter, but also under the laws of the state of Delaware, where Brown and Brown, like so many large American companies, had chosen to incorporate their business. Delaware had a habit of looking the other way when it came to regulation of business. The little state prospered by carefully avoiding enacting any laws that big business found restrictive. If all the companies in America were required to physically move to Delaware, the *New York Times* had once commented, the little state would sink and the Atlantic would roll over it like it did the legendary Atlantis.

Brown and Brown used the same provisions Nancy Merriam had called for. In addition, they advocated a change whereby a majority of 80 per cent of the shareholders would have to approve any acquisition or merger. It was called a 'supermajority provision' in the business world, a legal way of stopping a hostile merger dead in its tracks.

It was Morris Solomon who pointed out the difference in the positions. Brown and Brown was relying on the regularly scheduled annual meeting. There was little possibility of successfully stopping or even delaying such a routine and legal proceeding. Besides, Delaware only required a simple majority – 51 per cent – to pass such a charter.

Lockwood was calling a special meeting, and courts always took a longer look at things out of the ordinary. Besides, Lockwood was a New York corporation, and the state of New York required a two-thirds vote for passage, a very difficult thing to obtain, especially when a takeover battle was raging. Lockwood Limited was on the long end of the odds.

Both sides attacked simultaneously in the courts.

Brown and Brown brought an action to enjoin the special stockholders' meeting called by Lockwood. Dan Spencer brought an almost identical motion against the chemical firm, asking for a hearing in federal court.

Bruno Chasen and a team of lawyers were sent to the New York Supreme Court to defend Lockwood's right to call the special meeting. The hearing was scheduled for Friday morning, the action taking place in the Manhattan complex of court buildings surrounding Foley Square.

Jeffrey Rowe and another battery of lawyers were dispatched to Delaware to ask the federal court there to strike the shark-repellent provisions from Brown and Brown's meeting agenda.

Michael Collins served as runner between Nancy Merriam at Lockwood headquarters and Dan Spencer's lower Manhattan bunker.

Both sides knew what was at stake. If one of the corporations was successful in setting up the shark repellents, it would be all over, the other side would be defeated, the purpose of the takeover completely demolished.

Although both court actions were key to the outcome, the newspapers didn't bother to cover the hearings. There was nothing dramatic about two dull motions for technical injunctions. The editors decided that the readers would be bored.

Dan Spencer considered the courtroom his natural habitat. Having to sit in his war room, waiting for the news of the others who were carrying the fight, was proving to be painfully frustrating. He had confidence in both Chasen and Rowe, although he did consider himself better, and someone had to do the court work. But he wished he were standing before the bar. Spencer was guzzling enormous amounts of coffee, waiting for some word of what was happening in the courts.

Michael Collins had come in from uptown. Nancy Merriam was

also waiting for word. She understood the implications of the legal actions.

'What are our chances?' Collins asked Dan Spencer.

'Not good.'

'If we lose, it's over,' Collins said.

'Not necessarily. We can try to delay the execution by appeal. If you can stay alive in these things you at least have the hope of a miracle. Delay is the name of this game.'

'And if we win?'

Spencer chuckled. 'Your Miss Merriam will be the toast of Wall Street.'

Collins shook his head. 'No one knows she's running the show. Everyone thinks Scott is still calling the shots. If we win, she'll get no credit despite everything she's done.'

'How is Scott, by the way?'

'I think they may cart him off to the loony bin before all this is over. He's either in that Hollywoodesque office of his, hiding – Nancy says he has crying spells – or he's out in the halls making speeches to frightened employees. He comes in early and goes home late, but he does nothing. Nancy's the only one who sees him.'

'Great leader.'

Collins laughed. 'Inspiring. I suppose when all this blows over, win or lose, he'll come out of it and start appearing on the talk shows, explaining how everything happened. Nancy says he's an egomaniac, that's why this is hitting him so hard. He can't stand the thought of losing.'

Spencer smiled wryly. 'There's a lot of that going around these days.'

They both jumped when the telephone rang.

'Hello, Jeff,' Spencer answered. He listened and asked a few quick questions, then replaced the receiver.

'Well, scratch Delaware,' Spencer said.

'What happened?'

Spencer looked out at the colourful old buildings across the street. 'The federal judge refused to make jurisdiction. He said it was a state matter at this point. So Brown and Brown are still on the track, going forward with their annual meeting, complete with shark repellents, as planned.'

'What about the state court. Shouldn't we bring an action in

Delaware?'

Spencer smiled humourlessly. 'I'm ahead of you. Rowe has the necessary papers in his briefcase. He's on his way to the state courts. But they may not give him a hearing in time. That annual meeting is less than a week away. Rowe will ask for an emergency hearing, but the Delaware courts favour the home companies. Even if we get it, I doubt we could possibly win.'

'And if they vote in those shark repellents?'

'Mr Scott's dream of raping Brown and Brown for its billions' worth of land dies. They can hold him off even if he owns them. The board can dispose of the land so he can't get his hands on it for years. He would owe all the money he borrowed to buy stock and not have a cent to pay it off. He would, in a business sense, be absolutely dead.'

'Jesus.'

They sat silently, except when one would make an unsuccessful attempt at conversation. Both their minds were on the state court building in lower Manhattan.

When the telephone did ring, Spencer seemed almost reluctant to pick it up.

'Tell me what happened, Bruno.'

Spencer again listened, asking only a few questions. He put the telephone down and looked up at Collins.

'Well, Bruno said it was nip and tuck, but the judge refused to issue the injunction against us. Lockwood can go ahead with the special meeting, at least for now.'

'We won, what do you mean "for now"?'

Spencer grinned. 'As we speak, lawyers from Becker's outfit will be filing an appeal of the judge's ruling in the state court. I imagine they are also starting a similar action in the federal district court. They only have to walk one block.'

'How do you know what they're going to do?'

Spencer laughed, but it had a hollow sound. 'Because we are doing the same thing in Delaware. And I imagine Becker's boys are in Washington asking the SEC to step in and stop us. John Crim's people filed our papers this morning. We're trying everything.'

Spencer continued. 'It will add up to a pretty penny. In our office computers are recording every minute spent, every mile travelled, and every telephone call made. Ainsworth Martin will be delighted – it's a little like striking gold.'

'Oh, he isn't interested in just the fees, not in a case like this,' Collins said.

Spencer arched an eyebrow. 'My, do you have a lot to learn. That's why we're in business, my young friend. It matters not a whit how the case comes out, except for our business reputation. What matters is the fees collected, or so it sometimes seems.'

'We're lawyers, not merchants,' Collins protested.

'I wonder at times, Michael.' Spencer stood up. 'You better give Nancy Merriam a call. She's the one who will eventually pay the bill. She's entitled to know what she's getting for her money.'

Abner Slocum walked into Ainsworth Martin's office.

'Make this fast, will you, Abner. Morris and myself have a meeting with an investment banker. We have to find a source of money for Lockwood, and quickly.'

'I heard we were unable to stop Brown and Brown from placing their shark-repellent proposals on the agenda for their annual meeting next week.'

Martin nodded. 'That's correct. It doesn't look too good for our side at the moment.'

'So it will be winner take all, at least as far as Lockwood is concerned.'

'I can't see any other result. We can put up a fight of course, but the end seems inevitable.'

Abner Slocum nodded. 'What about Brown and Brown? If they get those changes put in their charter it's all over but the shouting, isn't it?'

'It would seem that way.'

Abner Slocum chuckled. 'Seem? My dear friend, if those amendments pass – and they only need a simple majority in Delaware – your Mr Scott and his company will be only a memory. Brown and Brown, with the help of their Japanese saviour, will devour all.'

Ainsworth Martin sat up. 'Obviously you have a point to make, Abner. What's on your mind?'

'What's always on my mind, Ainsworth? I want the firm's rules changed to allow me to stay on as an active partner.'

Martin registered disgust. 'My God, Abner, we're in the middle of the biggest corporate war in America and you want to talk about firm business? It will have to wait.'

'I'm afraid it can't wait.' Slocum sat down and crossed his thin legs. His smile was sure and confident.

'You're up to something, Abner. What is it?'

'The late Sylvia Winship traced her ancestry from the original founders of Brown and Brown.'

'So?'

'I'm the executor of her estate. I have complete control of the assets, and I've even gone to the trouble of getting bonded, although that wasn't required by her will.'

Ainsworth Martin's eyes narrowed slightly. 'Is the estate being handled by our probate section?'

Slocum shook his head. 'No. I'm taking care of it personally, at least for the time being.'

'Again, what's your point?'

'The fellows at Brown and Brown have to get a majority of the outstanding shares to vote with them,' Slocum said. 'I rather imagine that Scott already has a large block of their stock. He's made his offer and the waiting period has run. And I suspect he'll probably pick up more in the next few days, although I think many shareholders will hold back to see if he'll raise his offer now that Kuragamo has come in on the other side.'

'I still don't understand how all this applies to you.'

Slocum seemed honestly amused. 'As we both know, Ainsworth, there is never an annual meeting where all the shares are voted, by proxy or otherwise. Some people just keep their shares and couldn't care less how the corporation is run, correct?'

'That's always true.'

'Yes,' Slocum said, 'it is. Now, as I figure it, Scott must own about fifteen to twenty per cent of Brown and Brown's voting stock. About right?'

'I suppose.'

Slocum paused as if savouring the moment. 'Well, the largest shareholder in Brown and Brown was Sylvia Winship, the late great-granddaughter of one of the founding brothers.'

Ainsworth Martin felt as if time had suddenly stopped. 'And you're the executor?'

'Yes.'

'How much of Brown and Brown stock is in the estate?' Martin asked.

'As I estimate it, and I could be off by several points, I think just a shade under twenty per cent.'

'Good God!'

Slocum smiled widely.

Ainsworth Martin rarely became excited, but he could feel the pulses in his neck throb. 'So, Abner, if you should choose to vote for the shark repellents, Lockwood Limited is lost.'

Slocum remained smiling broadly. 'That's how I see it. Interesting, isn't it, Ainsworth? If backing Brown and Brown is the most prudent course, my executor's oath requires that I do it. On the other hand, that would be detrimental to our firm's client, Mr Scott. As I see it, whatever I do could be considered unethical. A paradox, as Gilbert and Sullivan used to say, eh?'

Martin seemed to study him before speaking. 'You seem to hold all the aces, Abner. What do you want?'

'What do I always want, as I said before. My wishes haven't changed.'

'But we can't do — '

Slocum stopped smiling. 'Ainsworth, let me tell you what you are going to do. It's quite simple, and, honestly, I don't think you have any alternative. You will convene a meeting of the main partners, and I hope under the circumstances you can persuade them as to what must be done. The firm rules will be changed, allowing main partners like myself the election to stay on if they wish. Once that's done and official, I will take care of my end of things.'

'And even if we do that, an heir to the estate could stop you from acting. Becker could find one and sue to stop you.'

Slocum shrugged. 'Stop what? I plan to do nothing. I won't vote for or against the changes. As far as Scott is concerned, that's the same as voting against the proposals anyway. I will deny to the other side twenty per cent of the voting stock. How can any court enjoin that? Besides, I'm bonded. I doubt if a judge would step in when a bond already protects the heirs if I'm wrong.'

'You're a clever man, Abner, but then we've always known that.'

'And a good lawyer, Ainsworth. In all modesty, I am an asset to this law firm. I wish to continue to be an asset. I'm rather accustomed to being an Apostle, and I plan to remain one.'

'That's obvious.'

'I presume you'll call the meeting? And I further presume that the outcome will be favourable to my interests?'

'Abner, you have a gun to our heads. I'll call a meeting for tomorrow morning. I think it's unethical, but as a practical matter you leave us little choice.'

Slocum chuckled. 'And you've always been a practical man, Ainsworth.'

23

Michael Collins thought he was too excited to sleep, but he nodded off when the aeroplane was only an hour out of New York. He was gently awakened by the flight attendant.

'Good morning,' she said, her face reflecting fatigue. 'We're about to land. Please fasten your seat belt, Mr Collins.'

He nodded and pushed himself erect. It was a beautifully bright day below. The low hills of Ireland looked like soft, long fingers holding together the jigsaw pattern of the green fields below. His ears plugged up as the pilot began the final descent.

This was his second trip to Ireland. He had accompanied his parents two years before. Despite his heritage, he had found it too slow-moving; it lacked something, like a pie without salt.

Ainsworth Martin and Nancy Merriam decided he was the one to go. Telephone negotiations with the Irish financier Patrick Dowd had produced nothing. One of the richest men in the world, Dowd had the power to stop Kuragamo. Nancy told Collins over drinks that the situation was truly desperate. In order to survive, Lockwood Limited needed its own White Knight.

The firm wanted to send an older lawyer, but Nancy had insisted on Collins. She claimed that Dowd was partial to people of Irish background, and he liked the freshness of youth. Ainsworth Martin reluctantly agreed, although he expressed his opinion that success was unlikely no matter who contacted the Irish giant of finance.

While waiting for the plane, Collins had studied the background material Nancy had supplied. Dowd was apparently a bona fide eccentric who avoided publicity. *Fortune* had run a piece about his kingdom, which evidently extended to almost every country in the world. Dowd seldom left Dublin, and had no office, preferring to conduct his business out of his small home or in restaurants. A shadowy figure in world finance, there were few clues to Dowd's personal life – or to his thinking, for that matter.

Collins had no problem with Irish Customs, being waved through by a bored-looking customs officer. He took a cab to Dublin and registered in the Gresham Hotel. They provided him with a nice suite with a marble fireplace and raised bed. In the bath, the pipes were heated so that the towels were always warm. Old but well-kept, the hotel seemed to reflect the slow, almost majestic, pace of Irish life.

Dowd answered his own phone and agreed to meet Collins without any hesitation.

'I'll see you in an hour,' the gentle voice said. 'It's customary to meet at the foot of O'Connell's statue.'

'Where's that?'

'Your hotel is on O'Connell Street. As you come out of the Gresham, turn left. You can't miss the statue. It's right at the bridge over the Liffey River.'

'How will I know you?'

'I'll know you.' There was a little chuckle, then the man hung up.

Michael removed the personal reports on Dowd from his folder but kept the financial statements and other information Nancy Merriam said Dowd would require. He felt odd, knowing it was partly the jet lag. Still, this was pretty heady stuff for a fledgling lawyer. If he was able to persuade Dowd to rescue the Lockwood company from Kuragamo's clutches, his future would definitely be assured.

Lately, when thinking about his future, thoughts of Nancy Merriam always crept into his mind. She was Scott's girl, his mistress, or so they said. Ordinarily his interest would have been chilled by such knowledge, but Nancy was different. He was attracted to her in a way he had never felt for Mary Quinn.

O'Connell Street was Dublin's main street, very wide. He walked slowly towards the river, only a short distance away. The sidewalks were crowded, but unlike New York, here no one seemed in a hurry.

It was a pleasant day, crisp without being cold. He had decided against wearing a topcoat. The faces were typically Irish. Dark eyes and fair skin. Although he had found them irritating on the previous visit, he had to admit as he studied the faces that the Irish were, indeed, a handsome people.

He had hoped that only one man would be in the vicinity of the statue, but a long bench in front of it was occupied by a line of men and women, some obviously waiting and watching for someone, others just killing time.

A short, stout man in a rumpled jacket and badly knotted tie stood up. His old grey trousers were baggy and his black shoes were in need of a shine. His round face was almost cherubic. Hatless, his thinning reddish hair was uncombed. He ambled over, his eyes on Collins.

Michael Collins presumed the man was a bum and reached into his trouser pocket to get a coin ready.

'Michael Collins, is it?'

Collins recognized the soft voice.

'Mr Dowd?'

'Surprising, am I not? Well, I never was one for clothes. I'm built a bit like a pumpkin, and even the fanciest threads look shabby on me.' He extended a plump hand. 'How are you? You're a bit younger than the ones they usually send. Were they desperate or was it because of your name?' He chuckled. 'Michael Collins. It's the name, or was, of this country's sort of George Washington. Got killed. I take it you're Irish?'

'American. My father's folks, as well as my mother's, all came from Ireland.'

Dowd took Collins' arm and steered him back the way they had come. 'By law, since your grandparents were born here, you are an Irish citizen, did you know that?'

'No.'

'Well, you are, whether you wish to be or not. It's of small interest at the moment, of course. You're here to try to get me to part with some of my money, as I understand it?'

Collins was going to protest his terminology, but decided not to. 'Is there some place we can talk, Mr Dowd?'

Dowd gestured with his other hand. 'And what's wrong with these beautiful streets? God doesn't grant many days like this – let's take advantage of it. You tell me what it is you want as we walk along. Don't worry about privacy. Nobody here gives a damn about anything but politics. Finance bores 'em. Go on, young Michael Collins, let's hear what you've got to say.'

Collins ignored the crowds of strolling people and launched into reciting the information Nancy Merriam said Dowd would find interesting. He described in detail the war developing between Brown and Brown and the Lockwood forces. He noticed the round face showed some animation when he mentioned Taro Kuragamo. Dowd asked few questions but listened attentively. Finally, Collins was finished.

'I'll bet you're wondering why a man like me doesn't take on any of the accoutrements of wealth. It's a natural thing to be curious.'

Collins wanted to keep the conversation directly on the business at hand, but the man continued to speak as he held fast to Collins' elbow. 'I have a simple philosophy, young Mr Collins. Money means nothing to me. Does that surprise you? After all, you can only put your arse in one chair at a time. You can only be in one room at a time. I like to be comfortable, understand; a nice comfortable bed, good food, but beyond that, I want nothing much else. However, I want something that money can bring, but what it can't really buy. You know what that is?'

Collins shook his head.

'Power, my boy, power. If you have enough money you can play God. I've toppled governments, destroyed industries, which all has a rather negative sound, I admit. But on the other side of the coin, I have built cities and produced commerce in places you haven't even heard of. It's the power that I like. I don't need more money. I have all that is necessary. I play on a global board with only a few other players.' His voice seemed to grow even softer. 'It's a fascinating game. It's as if we few owned the world in a way. But we are fierce competitors. And in that kind of game, young Mr Collins, if a man's so foolish as to make a mistake, he is destroyed by the others. None of us takes any unnecessary risks. Do you understand me at all?'

'Well, generally. But I don't see what this has to do with Lockwood or Brown and Brown.'

The man chuckled; his eyes sparkled. 'Kuragamo is one of the players, my boy. You are asking that I pit myself against him. Even if I win, I don't gain anything except a chemical company. But if I lose, if I show weakness, then Kuragamo and the others will leap upon me like wolves killing a deer.'

'Then the answer is no?'

Collins steered him into the doorway of a small pub. They sat down at the bar.

'The answer is never no, my young friend. At the moment I have no reason to come into the fray. However, I will keep abreast of developments, and I'll rely upon you to let me know what you see happening. If my friend Taro Kuragamo should make a mistake, then I would be like the ravaging wolf myself.' He turned to the man behind the bar, who seemed to be ignoring them. 'How's that boy of yours, Jimmy? Was the leg broken after all?'

The bartender grunted. 'Like a matchstick. But the doctor says it will heal without complications. That'll teach him to stay off them damn motorbikes.'

'What are you drinking?' Dowd asked.

Collins shook his head. 'Nothing for me.'

He eyed him. 'You don't have a drinking problem or anything like that, do you?'

'No.'

'Good. Jimmy, I think we can use a couple of large whiskeys.' He chuckled again. 'My American friend here will pay. He's on one of them expense accounts.'

'Must be lovely,' Jimmy grinned, showing bad teeth.

'What do I tell my clients?'

'What did I just tell you? That's what to tell them. You tell them that if I see an advantage, I'll join the battle, but not before.'

'And if Lockwood Limited gets taken by Kuragamo?'

'Then he's got another company to add to his trophy case, hasn't he? No, I really don't care what happens to the savvy Mr Kuragamo. I respect him and I'm wary about tangling with him. But if he's down, I'll be happy to kick him, you see.'

Collins paid for the drinks, Dowd clinked glasses in salute, then tossed his down in one gulp. 'Well, young Michael Collins, I'm impressed by yourself. I think I'll probably be hearing a great deal about you. You have the mark of greatness on you. You know my number, please keep me up to date on what happens.'

'Then we may meet again?'

Dowd patted him on the shoulder. 'You never know what the

future holds.' He looked at him closely. 'With a fine name like yours, I'd advise you to study your Irish history. It might come in handy one day.'

Dowd left so quickly that he almost seemed to disappear. Collins sipped the whiskey slowly. He wasn't accustomed to drinking it straight.

He would have to go back to the hotel and call. He tried to figure the time difference, but was confused. He looked at his empty glass.

'Thanks,' he said to the bartender, who was reading the paper. The man did not respond.

Michael Collins, dressed in his expensive three-piece suit and carrying his polished leather breifcase, felt out of place on the Dublin streets, but he needed a brisk walk to clear his head before calling Ainsworth Martin and Nancy Merriam.

He turned several corners and was approaching a columned building. He recognized it from a travel book. It was the Pro Cathedral, one of the main Catholic churches in Dublin. It looked more like a bank than a church. Several women with small children stood in front of the church. They looked as if they were of another century, their heavy shoulders clothed in knitted, ragged shawls, their clothing tattered.

One of them stepped out and walked abreast of him. She was heavy and her face was bloated. 'Something for the child, sir?' she asked, poking a home-made cardboard cup before him.

As if bubbling up from his memory, he recalled a warning from his grandmother that a beggarwoman should never be denied. A terrible curse was promised those foolish enough to do so.

The fat woman grinned up at him, her smile exhibiting the few teeth left in her mouth. 'For the child,' she cooed.

Collins was about to reach into his pocket for a coin when in a different voice, a haunting voice, just above a whisper, she made a secret promise. 'Give me something, sir,' she repeated, 'and I'll go into the church and say a prayer for you. I'll pray that you get the woman you want, and that she'll do anything you want.'

It sounded more like a chant uttered by an evil priestess.

Collins stared at her for a moment, then he laughed. 'That's a bargain I can't refuse.' He reached into his pocket and pulled out a one-pound note, called a punt, and handed it to her.

She nodded, as if a contract had been made. 'The woman you

want, and she'll do anything you want,' she whispered.

He walked on, aware that he was being pursued by some of the other women who had seen the money exchanged. He outwalked them.

But the woman's words haunted him. All he could think of was the face and form of Nancy Merriam.

The smell of defeat seemed to be physically present in the bunker. Lawyers spoke in hushed voices in the hallways. There was little if any laughter.

Even the clericals who kept trying out reams of legal pleadings caught the feeling of doom. They worked, but with a mechanical quality. There was no animation, no gossip.

Nancy Merriam kept Dan Spencer up to date on what was happening. Lockwood Limited was buying Brown and Brown stock, but it wasn't coming in in sufficient quantities to ensure that Lockwood could take over, and the Lockwood money and lending sources were drying up.

On the other hand, business was brisk in the purchase of Lockwood shares. The word was out that Taro Kuragamo was Brown and Brown's White Knight. Lockwood shareholders were jumping at the high price offered, afraid they might get left behind.

Like a losing general, Dan was watching his army get chewed up, piece by piece. They had lost in every court.

Although Scott had called a special meeting of the stockholders, he cancelled it when Nancy Merriam proved that the other side already controlled more than one-third of the voting stock.

John Norman Scott was apparently having a nervous breakdown. He claimed he had chest pains, and quietly checked himself into Doctors Hospital under an assumed name. Dan Spencer wondered if it was only a ploy to escape responsibility for the corporate defeat about to take place. Scott had dictated an order that left Nancy Merriam in complete control of the takeover efforts. He had, in Spencer's judgement, made her the scapegoat.

But the scapegoat was showing fight, real fight. She battled for every inch, and a number of business leaders were being impressed by her wisdom and determination.

Michael Collins, who had had little rest since returning from his unsuccessful trip to Ireland, came into Spencer's war room.

'Nancy says the other side has planted an article in the dailies saying that she is Scott's girlfriend and that she really runs the place. She says they plan to run it tomorrow. I don't know how she found out. She wants to know if there's any way we can stop it.'

Spencer looked up at him. He was tired. 'Nothing that would work. If it's libellous, we can sue later. But the Constitution protects the right to speak. We could always ask to enjoin the article, but that would only serve to give it publicity and more importance. We couldn't stop it.'

'She's taking quite a beating in the press.'

'It's to be expected. The other side will use everything and anything.' Spencer laughed. 'We will too. It evens out.'

'But this article . . .'

'Look, Mike, she is Scott's girlfriend, and right now she is running Lockwood Limited. Those are facts. Unless you know of some way to show malice, the article isn't even libellous. The takeover is news; so is our Nancy. It's tough, but she seems to be taking it well.'

Collins looked troubled. 'She was.'

'Was what?'

'Scott's girlfriend. She isn't any more.'

'Oh, how do you know that?'

'She told me,' Collins said. 'I wish there was some way we could give her a little protection from these damn stories.'

Spencer shrugged. 'I should lecture you on getting emotionally involved with a client, but I won't. You're smart enough to know the dangers. Just don't screw up what little chance we have left.'

'How bad is it?'

Spencer leaned back and stretched his long form. 'Damn bad. Brown and Brown's annual meeting is set for Friday morning. If they get the changes in their charter, it's all over.'

'And if they don't?'

'Probably be all over anyway. I'm bringing another motion to enjoin them from the takeover bid on Friday. It's sort of our last hurrah.'

'You sound tired.'

Spencer slowly shook his head. 'I am. Well, win or lose, it will only be a few more days. Both companies will end up owning each other and then Kuragamo will spit out Brown and Brown but chew up our client.'

Collins sat down. 'Who's going to argue the motion on Friday?'

'I am.'

'Dan, is that a good idea? You're exhausted. Let one of the others do it.'

He laughed. 'Who?' Every one of our trial men has been battered in any number of courts during the past week. They are really pooped. No, Friday will be our last chance. I'll argue the motion.'

Collins looked at him. 'That's a little like a captain going down with his ship, isn't it?'

'A touch theatrical, but you got the gist of it.' He crumpled a piece of paper and expertly shot it into a wastebasket several yards away. 'I'm tired of being the button pusher. I need to get a chance to yell at somebody. I'll let it all hang out on Friday.'

Collins smiled. 'You'll end up in jail. Judges like quiet lawyers.'

'We'll see. It seems to me a drowning man is entitled to yell, at least a little.'

Christina stared out of her office window. She had work to do, but none of it was important or pressing. As if by magic, the type and quality of her assignments had suddenly changed. She was no longer trusted, that was obvious.

Given the firm's attitude, her chance of becoming an Apostle seemed just about dead. Ironically, she wondered what her abilities and experience might really command in the marketplace. Nelson and Clark always helped a losing participating partner obtain a secure and rewarding position. But her situation was different. She knew Ainsworth Martin was convinced that she was the pawn of Taro Kuragamo.

A pile of mortgage agreements sat on her desk. She read them, carefully combing them for drafting errors. But it was really a job for a clerk. Even her secretary seemed embarrassed for her.

In the tight world of Nelson and Clark, word had passed that Mrs Giles had done something to offend. As if she had a communicable disease, people seemed to go out of their way to avoid her.

Katherine Thurston remained her friend and ally, but she seemed to be the only Apostle interested in her fate. Dan Spencer was solidly behind her, but he was embroiled in leading the fight against Kuragamo. She felt guilty. If Taro Kuragamo hadn't come into her life, he would never have interested himself in the takeover battle.

But all that was history now. She could do nothing about the past.

She needed a friendly face. Despite misgivings, she called the special number to the bunker and was put through to Dan Spencer.

'I know you're busy, Dan, but I just wanted to see how things were going.'

'We are getting our asses beat off.' He sounded tired. 'Outside of that, things are just fine.'

'Really that bad?'

'Worse. How about you? What's happening?'

She sat down in her chair. 'I'm like the bastard at the family reunion. Everyone is polite, but I think there's an invisible leper bell tied around my neck. It feels that way.'

'Getting you down?'

'A little.'

'I'm really tired of this whole takeover business. I think I'm averaging less than four hours' sleep at night, if that. We figure out a strategy, draft the pleadings, go to court, lose, and then start the whole thing all over again. We work like hell, but we are accomplishing nothing.'

She hesitated asking, fearing rejection. 'Can we get together, Dan? Just to talk? You have to eat some time.'

He laughed. 'Sandwiches. I'm so damn sick of sandwiches. And I've had enough coffee to permanently stain my teeth.' He paused. 'I have to get out of here for a while or I'll go nuts. I have to pick up my laundry and stop by my apartment. Could we meet after that? But I'll have to come back here later.'

She had always liked the sound of his voice, but now it was like a healing balm to her.

'How about a home-cooked meal? But since I presently seem to have to rely upon the kindness of stranger, in the words of Blanche Dubois, I don't have my own kitchen. Could I use yours?'

'Sure. But I really don't have much time.'

'I'm pretty good in the kitchen, Dan. It wouldn't take more than a few minutes. I could shop and meet you there.' She felt herself colouring. 'I remember where it is.'

'Tell me what you want and I'll pick it up.'

'Never interfere with the cook. I'll take care of the shopping. What time should I get there?'

'I'll call the doorman and have him let you in the apartment if I'm not there. Make yourself at home, Chris. As you know, there's nothing but old cheese and stale bread in the place.'

'We'll change that.' There was a touch of sparkle in her voice.

'I should be there about seven. That okay?'

She felt better, much better. 'Just so long as you show up. I'll be there.'

'I'll pick up the wine,' he said. 'I really look forward to this.'

'Me too.'

After they hung up, Chrstina swung around in her chair and studied the city. Somehow it looked better, more cheerful, and much more friendly.

She occupied herself with the happy thoughts of what to make. It had to be fast, but she wanted it to be good, very good. But most of all, she wanted to see Dan Spencer again.

Spencer, accompanied by Bruno Chasen and several of the trial section associates, walked from the bunker. He had allowed plenty of time to get to court. He was prepared, perhaps overtrained, his head filled with facts, cases, arguments. The little group walked along without speaking.

A chill had come in, and everyone but Spencer had chosen to wear coats. Above him, glimpsed through the fluttering autumn leaves of the tree-lined street, he could see the dull grey sky, the low clouds ominous. The proper kind of day for a funeral or an execution, he thought as he strode along.

An ambulance wailed its way through the converging cars as they approached the court complex. The drivers of the cars, even the cabbies, seemed frozen by the sound of the whooping siren. It seemed impossible, but somehow the emergency vehicle made it through the jammed street.

They walked up the stairs of the federal courthouse, passing the giant Roman pillars, then into the building and through the metal detectors.

Becker himself was waiting in Judge Groban's courtroom. With him was a team of aggressive-looking young lawyers, including one young woman who arrogantly displayed an open hostility.

'Good morning, Dan,' Becker said, smiling from his counsel table.

'Good morning,' Dan replied. 'Looks like you brought your whole office.'

'Just an audience. I like applause.' Becker gestured at the four men from Nelson and Clark. 'You're not exactly alone either, I see.'

'I brought them along for training. I wanted them to see how to do things right.'

'Or otherwise,' Becker grinned.

'We'll see. You received our affidavits?'

Becker nodded. 'Yes. Of course I'm going to object to most of them. You seem to have something from everybody except the Pope.'

'His affidavit is coming.'

'It will be about as relevant as the others.'

'We'll see.'

Becker seemed to be basking in supreme self-confidence, his manner almost patronizing to Spencer. Spencer took it as a bad sign. He wondered if Becker, who did have excellent connections, might have been able to talk to the judge privately. It almost seemed that way, judging from Becker's attitude.

Judge Groban's clerk came out, a sign that the judge was about to make his appearance.

'Lockwood Limited here?' he asked, looking directly at Spencer.

'Yes.'

'And Brown and Brown?'

'Yes.'

'Kuragamo Group is a party defendant,' Dan said.

Becker nearly bowed. 'We represent that interest too. Everyone's all here and ready to go,' he said to the clerk.

The clerk, a busy, irritable-looking middle-aged man, glanced from Spencer to Becker. 'Good,' he said, as if they had personally passed his own rather critical test. 'Your motion is the first thing on the judge's docket this morning.'

The judge, his black robe swirling behind him, came out as the gavel cracked it's command for everyone to rise. The court officer, in a bored voice, intoned the usual litany stating the court was open, then sang out Judge Groban's full name.

'Okay.' Groban sat down and peered over his half-glasses. 'Let's get this thing on the road. Mr Spencer, you appear for Lockwood Limited, correct?'

Spencer walked to the lectern. 'That's correct, your honour.'

'And you want me to stop Brown and Brown from buying up your company, right?'

Spencer nodded. 'And for very good reason.'

The judge shrugged as if to show that the whole matter failed to impress him very much.

'Tell me about it, Mr Spencer,' he said.

'Michael, now that we're here, I'm scared.'

Michael Collins took Nancy Merriam's hand. 'It's natural,' he said. 'Everyone gets stage fright once in a while.'

They had taken seats near one of the aisleway microphones. Several newspapermen, covering the Brown and Brown annual meeting, had asked for statements when they had first entered the hall. Nancy had nervously repeated the litany of wrongs allegedly done by the management of the chemical company.

For the first time Michael realized just how young and inexperienced Nancy really was. She was brilliant, but she had had no training or preparation for the ordeal she faced now. She would have to lead the floor fight against the shark-repellent provisions. The hall was rapidly filling. The annual meeting had attracted not only the press but a number of stockholders who had been reading the papers and who came to enjoy a good show.

'Suppose I freeze?' she whispered to Collins.

'I'll be right alongside you,' he said quietly. 'You'll do just fine, believe me. If you freeze I just pinch your fanny. That should start you up again.'

She looked intently at him, then laughed. He had never been so personal with her before. 'You can't do that. We'll be on national television tonight.'

'Who knows?' He grinned. 'It might prove to be a whole new career for me, professional fanny pincher. After that fiasco in Ireland I may need another occupation.'

'Michael, that was only a thing done in desperation. No one really expected Patrick Dowd to come to our aid.'

'We'll see.' The crowd was quickly filling the hall. He saw a face he thought he recognized, then someone else got in the way. He searched the faces until he located the person he had seen. Abner Slocum was standing at the back of the hall near one of the doors.

Slocum saw him. Collins watched as the frail man made his way through the people crowding the aisle.

'How are you, Michael?' Slocum asked, as if they had been long-time friends. Collins recalled meeting the old man only once before, and that briefly. 'Please introduce me to this lovely lady.'

'Nancy Merriam,' Collins said, 'this is Mr Abner Slocum. He's one of the Apostles.' He felt himself colouring. 'I mean, one of the main partners at Nelson and Clark.'

Slocum smiled down at her. 'Are you worried, my dear?'

She looked up at him. 'A little.'

'Don't be.' He reached down and whispered something in her ear, in a voice much too low for Collins to catch any of it.

Nancy Merriam's face brightened. 'Oh God, that's fantastic!' she exclaimed.

'What?' Collins asked.

Abner Slocum smiled. 'I asked Miss Mirriam if she would marry me, and of course she accepted. Isn't that wonderful news?'

Panic swept through Collins until he realized Slocum was joking. 'Y-yes,' he stammered.

'I'll see you later,' Slocum said. 'I will be standing back by the exit. I hate crowds.' He bowed slightly, then began working his way back the way he had come.

'What the hell was that all about?'

She looked up at him, her eyes shining. 'He says we can't lose,' she whispered to Collins.

'Oh?'

'We have purchased thirty-four per cent of the voting stock, right?'

'Yes,' Collins said. 'So?'

'He has twenty per cent. It's part of an estate he's probating. We can block anything requiring a majority vote. The shark-repellent provisions are as good as dead. God, I'm excited!'

'You sure you didn't misunderstand him?'

She grinned. 'No, sir.'

The banging of the gavel signalled that the meeting was about to begin. The opening ceremony was followed by hours of routine business, all dull and uninteresting, slowed by the nagging questions of gadfly stockholders concerned over the nuts-and-bolts operation of the huge company. This was their moment in the sun. Being able to question allowed those stockholders their moment of glory, of importance, and that was all they really wanted.

Finally the shark-repellent provisions came up. Nancy Merriam fought her way to the aisle microphone and led the debate against them.

Cries of 'whore' and 'prostitute' crackled about her as she spoke, but she held herself with dignity and didn't surrender an inch. Collins was proud of her.

He resisted the temptation to punch out some of the more vicious hecklers, who he guessed were probably management plants. Their nasty comments were boomeranging in the face of Nancy's self-respecting coolness. The crowd was becoming sympathetic to her because of the attacks.

Collins was delighted. Taped clips of the meeting would highlight the nation's evening news programmes, and Nancy Merriam would look good, very good.

But Michael Collins had known that from the very first moment he had set eyes on her.

Spencer fidgeted impatiently in his chair. Emerson Becker was making another long reply to Spencer's arguments. Becker's manner seemed to say that this was all nonsense and not worth the court's time. He addressed the judge as one might a dull child, taking great pains to explain obvious points.

Dan was tired. Becker's cited cases were recent, on point, and powerful. Still, the pompous way in which they were presented seemed almost intentionally offensive. Groban was becoming angry with Becker's patronizing manner and his intonations that if Groban didn't rule his way the appellate court would pounce on the issue and reverse him. Becker didn't actually say that in so many words, but the insinuation was there, and strongly put.

Becker was once again coming to the end of his remarks. They had alternated all morning, and now, well past lunch, the judge still seemed indecisive.

The more the judge questioned Becker, the more arrogant and demanding the lawyer became. Spencer, on the other hand, was careful to be deferential, as if the universe itself was ruled by the all-powerful judge. It was a matter of tactics. If it had seemed a good idea to scream and shout, Dan Spencer could hold his own with the best. But in this matter it was better to play off against Becker's grating attitude.

'The court has only one choice here,' Becker said, his tone low and threatening. 'You can do only one thing. The law dictates that you must find for my client.'

'Are you through?' the judge snapped. He was leaning back in his chair, ill concealing his annoyance.

'I think the case well stated.'

'Mr Spencer, what have you to say?'

'I object,' Becker said, turning back towards the bench. 'He's had his say. My remarks were rebuttal. The matter is in your hands now.'

Groban's cold smile displayed more teeth than civility. 'Please sit down, Mr Becker,' he said, his voice dripping with false friendliness. 'As far as I know, I still run this courtroom. You have raised some interesting nuances in replying to Mr Spencer. I think he should be afforded the opportunity to reply.'

'This is most irregular,' Becker said, nearly snarling.

'I think not,' the judge shot back.

Spencer was trying to formulate his thoughts. He was on the losing side, and everyone including the judge knew it. It was only Becker's attitude that was keeping him alive.

He was about to step up to the lectern when one of the young lawyers who had been assigned as a member of his team came through the court's doorway. He held a note in his hand. The young man looked as though he were sneaking into the vault of a bank. The court officer glared at him, almost making him turn and run.

'I wonder if I might beg the court's indulgence for just a minute,' Spencer asked.

Groban preferred Spencer's treatment. 'Certainly.'

Although he was demoralized and tired, Spencer nevertheless was amused when the young lawyer actually tiptoed to the counsel table and handed him the note.

Spencer, like a good card player, opened the note carefully so that only he could see the contents.

The note was simple and direct. 'Brown and Brown's shark repellents defeated at annual meeting. Becker's outfit is suing, but

Brown and Brown are naked. Good luck.'

Morris Solmon had signed his name in a large scrawl.

Dan Spencer carefully folded the note, as if it were something quite precious. It didn't help his case. The court still wouldn't enjoin Brown and Brown or Kuragamo from buying up Lockwood. Still, perhaps if he could stall for a time, the parties now might negotiate something. Particularly if Brown and Brown thought there might be even a slight possibility of losing.

'If the court please,' Spencer began as he walked to the lectern. 'I have just received some information which may have a significant bearing on this motion. However, I must have some time to develop it. It may be determinant or it may be nothing. I know the court has been most gracious in giving us all this valuable time. But I really believe the interests of justice dictate that I ask for a recess until Monday. If the court can see fit to give us that time, I believe — '

'Objection!' Becker bawled. He shouldered Spencer away from the lectern. 'Look here, there is nothing to their motion, either factually or legally. I have shown that. I demand you depose of this matter now!'

'Demand?' The judge was smiling but his teeth were clenched.

'The existence of this motion casts a pall over my client's honest efforts to buy Lockwood stock. The stockholders are reluctant to sell, fearing that this court may eventually shut down the whole process. Demand is the proper word for this situation. Every minute that passes leaving this bogus motion alive robs my clients of precious time.'

'I will continue this matter on Monday, Mr Becker,' Groban said coolly.

'I object,' Becker said again, but not quite so loudly.

'I heard you the first time,' the judge said, snapping off the answer. 'We'll meet back here at two o'clock on Monday. I have some other matters in the morning.'

'My schedule doesn't permit me to appear Monday,' Becker protested, almost wailing. 'Couldn't we do this tomorrow? Or tonight?'

The judge grinned. 'No, we can't. You have a very large law firm, Mr Becker. If you can't rearrange your schedule to be here Monday afternoon, you have a regiment of capable attorneys who can more than adequately represent your client.'

'But — ' Becker began to renew his protest.

The gavel cracked and the judge flew off the bench like a black-caped spectre.

Jeff Rowe waited until they were alone in the courtroom. 'What was in that note?' he whispered, excitement in his voice.

'The shark-repellent provisions were defeated in the Brown and Brown meeting.'

'What else?'

'Nothing.'

'But you told the judge . . . I thought it would be something, well, something big.'

'It was nothing, at least as far as this case is concerned. I just wanted to buy some time.'

'Why?'

'We're licked, Jeff. Since Brown and Brown is naked, like Lockwood, and unprotected by shark repellents, they might agree to a negotiated peace over the weekend. I don't know if they'd even consider such a thing. But in any event we stay alive until Monday.'

'What are you going to tell the judge if we have to come back here, if there's no settlement?'

'I don't know.'

'Jesus, Dan.' Rowe's voice was a rasp. 'He's pissed off about Becker. He's spoiling to nail somebody. If he thinks you tricked him with the note bit today, he's liable to throw you into the can on Monday.'

'I just don't give a damn,' Dan said bitterly. 'They have beds in jail, maybe I'll finally get some sleep, some rest.'

Becker walked into the hotel room. Only Gus Murray, the president of Brown and Brown, Teddy Edwards, the ancient chairman of Brown and Brown's board, and Taro Kuragamo were present. Becker had been summoned soon after returning to his office from court.

'We have received a call from Nancy Merriam.' Gus Murray smiled at the name. 'The, ah, very pleasant-looking vice president at Lockwood. She wishes to discuss a negotiated settlement.'

'So would I, if I were in her shoes,' Becker said, sitting down in an armchair in the hotel's suite. 'They are beaten and they know it. She's just trying to save a few of the pieces.'

'You didn't win in court today,' Edwards growled.

Becker looked him squarely in the eye. 'I didn't lose, either. It's set over for Monday. The judge will throw the motion out; he has no other choice legally.'

'And if he doesn't?' Murray asked tentatively.

'The circuit court of appeals will. I guarantee it. Anyway, there is no injunction and everything is proceeding at full speed.'

'We were unable to get the shark-repellent provisions,' Teddy Edward said. 'We're still vulnerable.'

'So?'

'So perhaps we should see what Miss Merriam has to say,' Murray said. 'I know I'd like to meet her. She's becoming something of a celebrity.'

Edwards looked at Murray in obvious disgust. Murray continued. 'Perhaps something could be worked out. There's no use in taking unnecessary risks.'

'No.' Kuragamo spoke the single word quietly, but it was still clearly a command.

'Can't hurt to see what they offer,' Murray said uncertainly, like a schoolboy afraid that the teacher might strike him.

'You gentlemen asked me to come into this matter because you couldn't raise the money to defend yourselves,' Kuragamo said. 'You wanted me to buy a large enough block of stock to take over Lockwood. I have used my own money, plus that borrowed from investment bankers, to put up the sums necessary. I am the one at risk here. There will be no negotiation.'

Edwards' old but alert eyes sought some clue to Kuragamo's thinking. 'Suppose we say no and negotiate anyway.'

There was no expression on Kuragamo's face. 'I will exercise our agreement and buy your company. I always have that clause inserted any time I come to the aid of a distressed company. I have found it very peculiar how brave people become when an outside threat lessens.'

Becker hoped to gain some of Kuragamo's considerable business, so he took pains not to offend the tall Oriental. 'What can we lose by talking?' he asked. 'After all, we're not bound, and it might be helpful to see just what resources they have left to fight.'

The Japanese nodded 'Ordinarily, I would agree. However, I have risked much more than money in this venture. My reputation is at stake. The mere act of coming together to talk might be interpreted by some as weakness on my part. At the moment, I can't afford that. I suggest that we put such thoughts out of our heads.'

'But — ' Edwards began.

Kuragamo raised his hand to stop him. He frowned. 'I must insist on this. Believe me, if you should consider acting on your own, I will exercise my option and buy you out.'

'You seem to be taking this personally. It's merely a matter of business,' Edwards persisted.

Kuragamo smiled. 'To you, perhaps. Not to me. It is a matter of honour. Besides, I have taken certain risks. I cannot afford any sign of weakness now. I trust you will honour this?'

Edwards shrugged, then cackled. 'What other choice do we have? If we don't, you buy us out. That's what I didn't want to happen in the first place. We'll stick to our agreement.'

'Besides,' Murray said, 'we have an inside man on the other side. We don't need to test them – we know what they're going to do anyway.'

Becker scowled. 'Please – we also agreed not to talk about that arrangement. It's vital to the man's security and to our line of communication with him.'

'Sorry,' Murray said. 'What do we do now?'

'We buy their company.' Edwards cackled again. 'Then we humiliate them.'

'We will destroy them.' Kuragamo's words, though spoken softly and without apparent emotion, were deadly serious. They all looked at him and were glad they weren't John Norman Scott or his law firm.

24

Dan Spencer didn't return to the downtown office but stopped off at Igor's. It was still early in the afternoon, and only a few hearty drinkers occupied the bar, most of them too far gone to hold a reasonable conversation. Spencer and the bartender watched an old rerun as if it were some world-shaking news event.

After Igor's, he went on to O'Hagen's. Later in the evening an Irish band would come in and the place would be rocking with the shrill scream of pipes and the primitive beat of drums, the air pulsating with songs of war, death, and parting, all dear to the Irish and considered necessary for really serious drinking. But now O'Hagen's was quiet, and its television had on the same rerun. Spencer found no release from the depression that seemed to be engulfing him.

He hated to lose.

He thought about Christina and the dinner she had prepared. Why the fact that she was a good cook should surprise him he didn't know, but it had. They had talked long into the night, sometimes about the case but mostly about each other. He had wanted to make a pass at her, but somehow he couldn't bring himself to do it, as though such an act might drive her away from him forever.

The doorman at his apartment house, a genial and dignified Irishman, grinned at him as he walked into the lobby.

'Promises to be a fine evening, Dan,' he said.

'It will rain,' Spencer sharply responded, instantly regretting the uncivil reply, although it certainly did reflect his mood. 'But they've been wrong before,' he added, hoping to take the sting out of his first response.

The doorman didn't look offended, and seemed to grin even wider.

As he opened the door to his apartment, Dan was greeted by a variety of sensations. There was a delicious, spicy aroma in the air. A Frank Sinatra record was playing on his stereo, the music lilting and soothing. Fresh flowers were set in a bowl on the coffee table.

'I hope that's you, Dan.' Chris's voice came from the kitchen.

'Yeah, it's me.' The words carried his surprise.

She came out of the small kitchen and smiled up at him. 'I'm a trespasser. I hope you don't mind. I couldn't bear the office for another minute, and I really couldn't bring myself to go back to the Thurstons'. Your doorman thinks I'm your new lady. He came up himself and let me in when I brought in the groceries.'

Spencer laughed – that explained the doorman's wide grin and the business about the fine evening.

'Don't worry, Dan. I'm not moving in. I just needed a place to be by myself for a while. I didn't think you'd be home for hours yet.'

He laughed again. 'I'm not worried. This is the best thing that's happened to me today. What smells so good?'

'A casserole, a combination of Mexican and Italian. I thought I'd cook it and leave it for you for later.'

'You weren't going to stick around?'

She shook her head. 'No. In fact, I'm on my way as soon as I clean up your kitchen. I'm a pretty good cook, but messy.'

'Stick around, Chris. I could use the company. That is, if you don't mind?'

'I'll stay for a while. Can I fix you a drink?'

'Yeah. I've hit a couple of bars on the way here, so you'd better make it light or I won't last until dinner.'

She busied herself making the drinks. 'Dare I ask how it went in court today? You don't impress me as the kind who usually bar crawls.'

'I knew a trial lawyer, an old guy who I tried a long case with once. We were on the same side. I asked him what we'd do if we lost, and he said we'd go out and get drunk. Then I asked him what we'd do if we won. He said we'd go out and get drunk.'

'A profound philosophy.' She came out and handed him a Scotch, then, sitting opposite him, displayed her exceptional legs. 'What's the reason for this?' She held up the drink. 'Did you win or lose?'

'I managed to get the execution put off until Monday. Perhaps Nancy Merriam can work out some sort of equitable surrender in that time. If not, we are scheduled to die Monday afternoon.'

She sipped her drink, her eyes fixed on him. 'You're absolutely sure?'

Dan nodded. 'Yes. We have asked for an injunction to stop your old friend Kuragamo from buying up Lockwood stock, but we really can't back up any of our allegations. The only one that would work anyway would be the antitrust charges, and we can't back them up either.' He gulped half his drink. 'So, despite my oratorical brilliance, everything is going down the sluice on Monday.'

She put down her drink. 'Isn't there anything you can hang your hat on? Anyone who is as big as Kuragamo, or even Brown and Brown, must have some interest that would conflict with buying Lockwood. They must own some kind of similar company somewhere along the line.'

He shook his head. 'Right from the beginning, I went over everything with a fine-tooth comb. Just like you, I thought these industrial conglomerates must have some common type holdings, anything you could pinpoint as being in violation of the antitrust provisions. Hell, we wouldn't even have to win. If we were only able to show a probable conflict, the judge, the SEC, and maybe even the Justice Department, would need time to investigate. If that happened, we'd win. Kuragamo wouldn't be able to buy the necessary Lockwood stock in time and the whole takeover would collapse.' He downed his drink. 'I couldn't find a thing.'

'Who did you check with?'

'Scott. He built the whole thing; he should know.'

Christina frowned. 'He built much of the Lockwood company, that's true, but he doesn't impress me as knowing much about the details of his operation.'

'I checked with Nancy Merriam too.

'Before or after Scott fell apart?'

He held up his glass for a refill. 'I feel like a witness, counsellor. I refuse to answer another question until you feed my alcoholic habit.'

She made no move to get up. 'Dan, come on, I'm being serious. Nancy wouldn't have been in a position to do a complete survey, not at that time. And she has no way of knowing how important the information has become. I'll give her a call and we'll take another look.'

Dan Spencer kicked off his shoes. 'That's grasping at straws, lovely lady, no more, no less. There is a big hole in our boat and we will sink on Monday.'

She walked over to him, leaned down, and kissed the top of his head. 'I'll get you your drink, then you get some rest. I have things to do, counsellor.'

He reached out and caught her wrist. His grasp was firm but gentle. 'Chris.' He paused, his eyes looking up at her as if pleading. 'Could we . . .' He stopped speaking.

'Could we what?'

He released her. 'Oh, nothing. Forget it.' He coloured slightly.

She felt a rush of affection for him as she tousled his hair. 'How about a multiple-choice question. A. Could we go to a ballgame? B.

Could we do the laundry? C. Could we go to bed? D. All of the above? Which is it, Dan?'

He didn't look up at her, averting his eyes. 'C sounds like the best bet.' His words were barely audible.

Chrstina stroked his hair. 'How long is the offer good for, Dan? I have to go now, but I may be back.'

He stood up and turned. 'Chris. I feel very strongly about you.'

She placed her fingertips against his lips. 'Now now, Dan. Save it for later. I feel strongly too.' She stood on tiptoe and kissed him on the mouth. Then pushed away.

'I'll see you later,' she said, grabbing her coat and purse.

He stood there, looking as if he'd been hit, his eyes questioning.

She laughed. 'Later,' she repeated, as she blew him a kiss before she closed the door behind her.

The guard took her up to the executive offices where Nancy Merriam was waiting. Christina was surprised to see Michael Collins with her. They looked almost embarrassed.

'Michael has been helping me organize our forces,' Nancy said. 'He's been invaluable.'

Although she wasn't that much older than Nancy, Christina suddenly felt like a den mother who'd just caught two students in bed together.

'Well, Nelson and Clark always provides the very best,' she said. Then, as she realized her words could have two meanings, she regretted saying them. 'Let me explain what I need.'

Nancy Merriam listened attentively, occasionally glancing at Michael. Christina, though intent on her task, took feminine notice of the looks that passed between the two and realized that Mr John Norman Scott had lost out for good, at least on one front.

'My job with Nelson and Clark,' Christina continued, 'is to construct methods of business financing. Sometimes a company will stand as a kind of cosigner for another, pledging assets against a loan, usually with cross buy-out provision. Often there is a network of ownership by a number of companies, like a ladder, constructed carefully to get the maximum benefit from profits under a number of tax laws.'

Michael Collins looked puzzled. 'I don't quite understand your point, Mrs Giles.'

She smiled at him. Like Dan Spencer, there was an easy charm about him. 'What I'm saying, Michael, is that a company may own or have an interest in another without owning any of its stock as such. Stock options may constitute a kind of mortgage. But under the antitrust laws, this type of connection is as good as ownership.'

'So?' Collins was still puzzled.

'If one company, say chemicals, as in this case, tries to buy out another corporation which also owns a chemical company, that combination could very easily be an antitrust violation.'

'Suppose we could find such a conflict?' Nancy asked, now intensely interested.

'We would be able to enjoin Kuragamo's attempt to buy this company. Even a significant delay would defeat him.'

Collins grinned. 'We've been taking a hell of a beating in the last week or two. It would be fun to nail the other side for a change.'

'What do you want us to do?' Nancy asked.

'We need to go through the records of every company Lockwood owns or has an interest in. Also, if we can, we have to research Kuragamo's holdings. If we can come up with even the appearance of restraint of trade, we win the ball game.'

'And if we don't?' Nancy asked.

'I'm afraid we lose everything,' Christina replied. 'Kuragamo has a reputation for being totally without mercy.'

'I'll alert our office staff. Probably most of them have sneaked away for the weekend, but I'll catch a few. That, plus the use of our computer bank and the networks we subscribe to will give us at least a fighting chance. Can you stay and help?'

Christina thought of Dan Spencer. She wanted to go back to his apartment, but she knew how much winning meant to him.

'I'll stay,' she said. 'My knowledge of mortgaging devices may just come in handy.'

Collins grinned. 'Ladies, you do the work and I'll fetch the coffee.'

Abner Slocum returned to the office after a late dinner. Work was his hobby. He enjoyed late hours if the problem was difficult enough. He noticed that Ainsworth Martin's door was open and the light was on.

'You're working a bit late tonight,' Slocum said, looking in. He was surprised to see Ainsworth in his shirtsleeves. To the best of his recollection it was the first time he had seen the always-formal Martin without his coat.

Ainsworth looked up, his generally bland face showing signs of fatigue. 'What do you want, Abner? Some more concessions?'

Abner Slocum laughed as he sat down opposite Martin. 'Don't be bitter, Ainsworth.'

'Blackmail always has that effect upon me.'

Slocum shrugged. 'Such a strong word, blackmail. If we were discussing a client doing the same thing, both of us would describe it as merely exercising a strong bargaining position, and you know it.'

Martin smiled wryly. 'Perhaps.'

'Besides, everything worked out rather splendidly. I can stay and work as a full, active partner. Those Apostles who are aboard can still retire at age seventy with all the previous rights and privileges. Only the new main partners, whoever they may be, will lose those rather juicy retirement benefits. And they won't starve by any means. The changes will save the firm a great deal of money over the years, Ainsworth.'

'We'll see. Still, it wasn't quite the gentlemanly thing to do, Abner.'

'In my defence I'll cite that wise adage that nice guys finish last. No one got hurt and everyone's happy. If the tactics were a bit questionable, the results weren't bad. Now, what is keeping you here so late on a beautiful October evening? We won't have many more like this.'

Martin raised both of his long arms into the air and stretched. 'I had planned to go to the theatre tonight, but this damn Lockwood, Kuragamo war has me pinned down here. I'm trying to negotiate a settlement with Kuragamo.'

'Alone?'

'By telephone,' Martin said. 'This is just a pause between rounds. We have been on conference calls all evening, first one set of investment bankers, then another, and then contacts with London and Tokyo.'

'How does it look?'

Martin shook his head. 'Bad. Karagamo would like me to believe that they are really trying to work something out, but I know better.

They're playing with me.'

'Why do it, then?'

Martin shrugged. 'You never know, we just might accidentally stumble across a mutually agreeable understanding. And, in a way, I'm doing the same thing. I'm letting them think we're stalling, just playing at negotiation.'

'Why?'

'To worry them. This way they suspect we still may have something up our sleeve, even though that's impossible.'

'Sounds foolish to me, Ainsworth. If it's that bad, Scott should go to Kuragamo with hat in hand and beg table scraps.'

Martin frowned. 'We've offered just about everything, mainly to test the reception. No, they want the whole cake, and according to Dan Spencer, they'll get it, too.'

'How is Spencer doing? If we lose this thing, it will look very bad for the firm. Does he know that?'

'He knows, and he also knows his own future here depends on it. There's plenty of motivation, but we just don't have the cards. Spencer's doing a capable job. He's not responsible for the errors of that ass, Scott, but he knows he'll have to pay for them anyway if we lose.'

Abner Slocum stood up. 'I have a few things to do myself. Let me know if you need me on this Lockwood thing' – he smiled – 'even if only as a pallbearer.'

The telephone rang and Martin waited until the second ring, smiled at Slocum, then picked up the receiver.

Slocum left quietly as he heard Ainsworth talking in his usual smooth and persuasive way.

If anyone could settle this thing, it was Ainsworth Martin. And if it couldn't be settled, the firm would be hurt. A number of heads were bound to roll. Nice guys, thought Abner Slocum, really do finish last.

Michael Collins and Nancy Merriam wanted to buy Christina a drink to celebrate, but she was concerned. She had called Dan when they were sure of the data, but there had been no answer at his apartment.

Friday night had become Saturday morning, and although it was well past three o'clock in the morning, there were many people on the streets. New York was a night town.

Nancy and Michael, who were going to celebrate anyway, put Christina in a cab. The driver looked tired and made no response when she gave him Dan Spencer's address, but he did make the correct turn and they were quickly moving towards the apartment.

Christina checked her purse to see if she still had the key Dan had given her.

The night doorman was out under the canopy enjoying the fair, warm night when the cab pulled up. He took full advantage to look at Chris's legs as he helped her out of the cab.

She held up her key. 'I'm here to see Dan Spencer.'

The night man smiled lewdly. 'Lucky guy. You want me to call up and say you're here?'

'That won't be necessary.'

He looked her up and down. 'Whatever you say. Have a nice night,' he called after her as she walked across the lobby to the elevators.

After trying the bell, she knocked on the door, but there was still no response. Her hand was shaking as she found the lock with the metal key. She opened the door and was relieved to find the lights were on.

'Dan?'

There was no answer. A radio was playing softly in the living room. She glanced into the dark kitchen, the bath, then turned to the bedroom.

The light was on. Dan lay sprawled out on the bed, face down.

'Dan!' She moved to the bed and reached for him. Placing her hand against his cheek, she felt his warm flesh. He was breathing very easily, like a child in sleep.

'Dan, are you all right?' She went a step closer and knocked over a bottle. She stopped and picked it up. Half was gone. It was high-octane rum, over 151 percent according to the label.

She bent over and inhaled the rum-flavoured breath of the sleeper.

'Oh boy, will you regret this when you wake up.' She put the bottle on the nightstand. Then she began untying his shoes.

'Well, Dan Spencer, if nothing else, this evens up the score.' She began to undress him as best she could. He was completely dead weight.

When she had got most of his clothes off, he shifted a bit and began to snore.

Christina sat on the bed and watched him for a while. She really hadn't fully realized the depth of feeling she had developed for this man. He looked helpless, yet he was so strong. It was foolish; he hadn't shown the slightest interest that way in her, except for his inept pass earlier in the evening, more out of duty, she thought, than lust. Still, she was surprised that her own feelings were so intense.

She was proud of what she had accomplished. In her purse she had computer printouts that would be more valuable to him than any amount of gold. She felt like gift-wrapping them and presenting them as though they were a truly fine present. He was that kind of man, she thought, the kind that made you want to find wonderful things and give them to him. For her, he seemed more splendid than any knight out of a storybook.

She laid her hand on his muscular shoulder. It felt good to touch him.

Christina leaned over and gently kissed him. He mumbled something, despite his deep sleep. She smiled.

'I love you,' she whispered, knowing he could not hear.

Dan came awake several times. But the pain in his head and the rebellion of his aching body made him dive again into the escape of sleep.

Finally he blinked his eyes as if testing to see just how painful such a thing might be. His head pounded, but it was manageable. He tried to look at his wristwatch, but it had been taken off. That surprised him, for he usually slept with it on. He looked around to be sure he was in his own room.

Slowly he slid his legs over the edge of the bed and then made the effort to sit up.

There were no clothes strewn around the floor. Everything seemed rather neat. He had left his shorts on. Again he was surprised, since he had slept in the nude for years. Still, he reflected, there was no logic about drunks. And being neat was something definitely new.

He thought he imagined the smell of coffee brewing. He suddenly felt ravenously hungry. According to the digital clock on his bedside radio, it was just a few minutes after noon. He reached over and flicked on the radio.

'Are you awake?'

He was startled, and wondered for a moment if the voice had come from the radio.

Then Christina came into the bedroom.

'Last night I didn't know whether to call a doctor or an undertaker. Boy, you certainly go for the strong stuff. That rum could take off paint.'

Embarrassed, he tried to pull a sheet across his long, naked legs.

'It's a little bit late for that.' She smiled. 'I undressed you. Now you know how I felt.'

'Good God, Chris, I'm sorry.' His mouth felt like fur. 'I hope I didn't do anything, well, offensive.'

She laughed. 'How could you? I got back here after three o'clock and you were dead out. The world was quite safe from you last night. How do you feel, awful?'

'I have had better days. On the other hand, I think I may live. I may not particularly want to, but I will.'

'Can your stomach handle food or would that be asking too much?'

'As a matter of fact, I'm hungry, believe it or not. I seem to remember having lost most of that expensive booze at some time during the evening. Maybe that's what saved me.'

'I'll get you some aspirin and orange juice. How about eggs and toast? Do you think you can handle that?'

'I can try. Nothing's guaranteed, of course.'

'One hearty breakfast coming up.'

He stood up, his legs unsteady. He grabbed some clothes, then wobbled off into the bathroom.

The almost scalding water helped to revive him. He felt sore all over, as if he had been roughed up in a very tough game. And he felt foolish.

Dan shaved quickly, dressed, and came out in his bare feet.

Chris was preparing a tray.

'The dead have risen,' he said, admiring her figure. She hadn't changed clothes and her shirt was wrinkled, but somehow the total effect was quite sexy. 'I think I can sit up to eat.'

She handed him two aspirin and he gulped them down with orange juice. She set the eggs and toast before him, along with a steaming cup of coffee.

'You take it black, right?'

'Yes. The food looks good.' He bit into a piece of toast. 'Did you stay the night?'

'It was a reversal of the roles we played the first night I was here. This time it was my turn to sleep on the couch. It's comfortable enough for a small person like me, but I wonder how you got any sleep at all.'

'For the record, Chris, I don't get drunk very often. I think the last time I pulled something like this was the night after I got my divorce.'

'How sad.'

He laughed. 'Sad, hell, I was celebrating.'

'When you finish eating there's something I want to show you, Dan.'

'Oh?'

'I think it's something you'll like.'

He was wolfing down the eggs. 'Sounds like a present. What's the occasion?'

'I think we've come up with something that will elevate your mood a little bit.' She retrieved the computer printouts and handed them to him.

Spencer sipped his coffee as he tried to read the jumbled lines. Like most printouts, it made no sense to him. 'This is lost on me,' he said sheepishly.

She reached over, brushing his arm. 'Here, Dan, this is the main information. It shows that California Tech owns a small microchip research firm in Colorado.'

'So?'

'The Colorado company competes with one division of Lockwood Limited.' She rustled through several other sheets. 'The two companies bid against each other for a contract with Reynolds Electric just four months ago. Lockwood won.'

'I still don't see — '

'Another company, Cedra Steel, competes with Lockwood's steel division. They even share a government contract for some defence work.'

334

Dan looked at the pages. 'I see the entries, but I don't understand the relevance.'

'California Tech and Cedra Steel are both owned by Taro Kuragamo,' she said with elation.

'Are you sure?'

She nodded. 'Both companies are owned by Rising Sun Limited, a holding company owned entirely by Kuragamo. Both have loans outstanding from Kuragamo's bank.'

Spencer looked at her. 'Christina, are you absolutely positive?'

'We used the Lockwood computers to plug into a bank and investment firm network. There's nothing secret about that information; it's all on record in several places. We used several approaches to verify it.'

'My God.'

She was pleased at his reaction. 'At first we used the computers to scan everything Brown and Brown had ever done or owned. But we couldn't find anything that was in obvious conflict with Lockwood. When that failed, we tried Kuragamo, or at least his American companies. That's when we hit it.'

'Pure gold!' Spencer jumped up and kissed her full on the mouth. He held her face for a moment. 'I hope you know what you've done.'

'I have an idea. You can claim restraint of trade, right?'

Spencer laughed as he paced up and down the small room. 'The judge will have to grant an injunction until the basic question of antitrust is cleared up. Possible restraint of trade is a question that will have to be decided, not only in the courts but by the Justice Department and the Securities and Exchange Commission. And all of that takes time. Time is something Kuragamo doesn't have. If we delay him, he is finished. He can't finish buying Lockwood, while Lockwood can go right ahead and acquire Brown and Brown. We don't ever have to win the final decision.' He stopped and beamed at her. 'By God, this is wonderful. I was so tired of getting my ass whipped!' He kissed her again.

'Nancy Merriam is busy rounding up some more information. She should have quite a package ready for you when court opens on Monday.'

Spencer nodded. He stared at the printouts. 'Do you think she knows enough to keep her mouth shut about this?'

Christina nodded. 'The only people who know about this are Nancy, your Mike Collins, and myself. I think everyone understands the importance of keeping quiet.'

He grinned. 'I can hardly wait until Monday. It's going to be like coming from behind in the ninth and winning by one run.'

'Do you think the judge will grant the injunction?'

He picked up his coffee mug and gulped down the remainder. 'Judge Groban was looking for some way to stick it to Becker yesterday. I'm sure he'll go for it. And even if Becker tries to appeal, there are enough facts here to raise a good question. He won't get any relief in the appellate courts. If we play this just right, I think we might win the whole works.'

'What should we do?'

'First, we meet with Ainsworth Martin.'

'Now?'

'Why not?'

'I'll have to change. My clothes are at Katherine's.'

'If you looked like a bag lady, Ainsworth wouldn't care, not after digging up all this dynamite. Look, I'll take you out and you can buy anything you want to wear on me, okay?'

'That'll take time. Besides, I have my own money.'

'You may have money, but we don't have time.' He kissed her again. 'Besides, you look good to me.' He became suddenly quite serious. 'In fact, you look damn good,' he said quietly.

There was a silence in the room as they looked at each other.

'Well, I had better call Ainsworth,' he said, colouring slightly. 'This won't keep.'

Ainsworth Martin received them in his lavishly elegant apartment. Somewhere in its many rooms lived his wife, and also servants, but Ainsworth answered the door himself, dressed as usual as though he were going to a bank's board meeting, despite the fact that it was Saturday afternoon.

Dan showed him the printouts. Although Martin's face revealed little – Christina decided he wouldn't show emotion if his leg was being amputated – his eyes sparkled with enthusiasm.

'You've done an excellent job, Christina,' he said. 'It won't be forgotten.'

She made no reply, knowing he was talking about the vacancy as senior partner. She looked up at Dan, but he didn't seem to notice the reference or its meaning.

'Now's the time to use Crim,' Spencer said.

Ainsworth Martin looked surprised, but only for a fleeting moment. 'Does Christina know?'

Spencer shook his head. 'John Crim is a turncoat. He's been passing our plans to the other side. God knows why. We've been giving him good stuff, information that wouldn't really hurt us but would make him look good. Now is the time to give him something dead wrong.'

Christina was shocked. The fact that an Apostle had gone bad was unthinkable.

'What do you suppose?' Martin asked.

'Call him and tell him we are going to fold in court on Monday. Tell him we're going to beg a settlement.'

'How can you settle something you've lost?'

Spencer grinned. 'That's the point. Tell him we plan to withdraw our motion and ask the judge to mediate the takeover. Ask Crim to alert his contacts on the SEC that we are coming in with something for approval.'

'That sounds preposterous, Dan.'

'Perhaps. But it will also sound like the death throes of a dying animal. They'll come into court armed only to oppose a hopeless mediation request, legally improper on its face.'

'What good will that do?'

'They'll think we've given up. They won't be ready to do battle on the main issue of the injunction. This time they won't see it coming. We can use their confusion against them.'

'Crim may tumble,' Martin said. 'He's no fool.'

'Tell him we will propose selling Lockwood Limited to Kuragamo and withdrawing the Brown and Brown takeover offer on the condition that Scott can be kept on as Lockwood's president, or executive head, of whatever new corporation Kuragamo may form. It's happened before.'

'I suppose it might sound like something Scott thought up himself. A last-ditch effort to save himself.'

'Whatever,' Spencer laughed. 'Just so they aren't ready for the main battle.'

'I'll call Crim. What are you going to do?'

'I'll hit the office's law library. We probably have more stuff on antitrust litigation than the New York Bar Association.'

'The office computers have complete antitrust briefs in their memory banks,' Christina said.

Dan shook his head. 'I'm sure they do. But I don't want any of the computer operators to come in. It would be obvious what we're after. I don't want to risk any word slipping out, not at this point.'

'I can run the computers,' Christina said.

'You can?' Ainsworth Martin registered surprise.

She nodded. 'Sometimes I need data after hours. I had one of the operators teach me how to run our machines. I can probably find everything we have recorded on any antitrust case we have appeared in.'

Dan beamed. 'Damn it, Chris, you're a one-man task force.'

'Woman,' she corrected him.

'Whatever. I'm glad you're on our side. You're dangerous.' He looked up at Ainsworth. 'I'll use young Michael Collins. He knows what's happening. And he can be a great help in looking up the law.'

'What do you think of young Collins?' Martin asked.

'Excellent young man,' Spencer replied. 'A real comer.'

Christina recalled seeing Collins holding hands with Nancy Merriam. 'Good at client relations, too,' she added.

'I'm glad,' Martin said. 'He's one of mine. I picked him. Well, let's get at it. We have a busy weekend ahead.'

25

Michael Collins was surprised that he should think of Mary Quinn. In only a matter of days he had changed. His ambition had changed. It was an entirely new world and Mary Quinn was now only history.

'We can't win, not in any final sense,' Nancy Merriam said. She rolled over and studied Michael's naked form. He lay on his back, relaxed, looking not unlike a young god, at least in her eyes.

He glanced over at her. 'Why not? We'll stop Kuragamo cold. He can't move, and Brown and Brown doesn't have the resources to proceed on their own. Nancy, we can't lose.'

Tentatively she fingered the dark hair on his chest. 'Lockwood doesn't have the money to buy up fifty per cent of Brown and Brown.'

She noted his surprise. 'I'm afraid my leader, John Norman Scott, has alienated all the big-money people – those who weren't already scared away by Kuragamo. Even if Kuragamo is out of the picture, I can't see Scott raising the money to buy the stock within the law's time limits. We are just about broke, and no one will lend us the money we need.'

Michael sat up quickly. 'Does anyone else know about this?'

'You mean the financial world?'

'Whoever.'

She sat up. They had made love and had been quite relaxed until she had introduced the topic that had brought them together in the first place.

'Michael, I think most of the investment bankers and commercial houses suspect we have no other resources. But no one is absolutely sure.'

'How about our people? Dan, for instance. Does he know?'

'I don't think so. But Morris Solomon, one of the Apostles, does. He's been trying to raise the money. It's difficult for him because he has to keep our rather shaky position secret.'

'So what happens when Dan wins in court tomorrow? Good God – billions have been spent by both sides! It will be an empty victory.'

She pulled the sheet up around her. 'The usual thing is the settlement. We can meet with the board of Brown and Brown and see what we can work out. They will owe everyone, too. I think they'll listen to reason.'

'I suppose.'

'And if the money could be raised, then what?'

She shrugged. 'It can't, but if a miracle occurred we could buy out Brown and Brown. We could make back most of our losses by selling off that valuable land of theirs. That, plus the sale of some of their companies, might even give us a small profit.'

'All that money, and all that risk, and all for only a small profit?'

She smiled wryly. 'Don't blame me. It was John Norman Scott's grand plan. He wanted to conquer the business world. If he could have seized Brown and Brown, then all other companies would bow before him. It was all a matter of ego when you come right down to it.'

Collins hopped out of bed, completely at ease with his nakedness.

'What's the matter?'

He walked over to the large closet. 'I'm looking for my wallet – there's a telephone number I need.' He searched his suit coat and returned. 'You can charge this call up as business,' he said.

'What are you going to do?'

He sat on the side of the bed and gave his instructions to the overseas operator.

'What time is it, Nancy?

'A little after two in the afternoon, why?'

'That makes it about seven o'clock in the evening in Dublin. I hope I can catch him in.'

'Michael, what are you up to? You know Dan said all this was to be kept secret until tomorrow in court.'

'Dan didn't know that you guys were running out of money. If I get fired, I get fired.'

She reached across him and grasped him by the arm. 'Michael, there are billions of dollars at stake here. This is no joking matter.'

He laughed. 'You got that right. All life is risk, Nancy.'

She could hear noise coming from the receiver. 'Mr Dowd, this is Michael Collins in America. Do you remember me?'

She listened as he continued. 'Mr Dowd, what I'm about to tell you is in strict confidence. Can you hear me all right?' He put his hand over the receiver and spoke to Nancy. 'This is probably the most important phone call in my life and we have a bad connection.' He returned to the phone. 'I'll keep my voice up. Do you remember telling me you are always on the alert for a mistake committed by any of the world's financial powers? Good. I think I can show you a terrific mistake, one which you can use to destroy

Taro Kuragamo. Are you interested?'

Michael grinned at Nancy as he spoke. 'I thought you might be. I can't tell you what it is over the telephone, Mr Dowd. Can you come to New York? It's all going to happen tomorrow afternoon.'

He paused. 'I can't even hint. Except to say this is no half-baked scheme. If you're serious about what you said, I would think it worth a trip across the Atlantic if you can make it.'

Again Collins listened intently as the man on the other end talked. 'I can understand that. It's a gamble I'm asking you to take; it's as simple as that. All you have to lose is your time.'

He listened, then put his hand over the receiver and sighed in exasperation. 'He wants us to pay for the plane tickets. This is one of the richest men in the world, and he isn't willing to spend a few hundred bucks to make billions.'

'That's how he got rich,' Nancy said, excited now. 'Tell him Lockwood will arrange for American Express to pay his fare from Dublin to New York. We'll have a limo pick him up when he gets here.'

Collins relayed the information. 'Just a minute, I'll write that down.' He turned to Nancy. 'He's coming, but he insists on first class. It's having balls that makes you rich.'

She laughed and handed him a notepad and pen. 'Go ahead.'

Michael jotted down the time of arrival. 'We'll see you tomorrow,' he said. 'I'll have the driver bring you directly to the federal courthouse on Foley Square.' He paused. 'Yes, Mr Dowd, that is a good name for a square. We'll see you tomorrow.'

He hung up. 'Well, if that Irishman is a pal of Kuragamo's, I've blown the operation. But if not, he has the money to bail Lockwood out.' He lay back and reached for her. 'Either I'll be a hero tomorrow, or a bum. So I guess I better get what I can while I can.'

'I might still like you,' she said, 'even if you become a bum. You never know.'

He kissed her and pulled her to him. 'The difference between being a poor bum or a great businessman is often determined by the results of a gamble. It doesn't matter how you played the game, only if you won or lost.' He grinned. 'We'll see how this one comes out.'

Dan Spencer saw the newsmen as he approached the courtroom.

Christina walked with him, as did Jeffrey Rowe. Emerson Becker had tipped off the media. The big-name newswriters were out in force. Network television crews were assembling in the hall under the watchful eye of blue-jacketed federal marshals. John Crim had obviously passed the 'secret' information. Becker had turned out the media to bear witness to his great victory; he counted on seeing himself triumphant on television and extolled in the press. Spencer had known he would do it; it was predictable. And, this time, desirable.

Spencer looked for Michael Collins but didn't see him. Collins had told him he and Nancy Merriam would meet them in the courtroom.

Graciously fending off the questions of the newsmen, Spencer opened the door for Christina. She stopped and drew back.

Spencer looked past her at the rows of spectator chairs. In the back, sitting ramrod straight but nevertheless appearing to be at ease, sat Taro Kuragamo. He nodded to them almost imperceptibly, allowing a slight smile to play across his features.

Christina looked up at Spencer for reassurance.

'Relax,' he whispered. 'I'm glad he's here. It makes it even better.'

'Don't leave me.' He heard the real fear in her voice.

He squeezed her arm. 'Don't worry, I won't.'

Emerson Becker made a show of getting up from the counsel table, greeting Spencer as if they were long-lost friends.

'This should be the end of it today, Dan,' he said, smiling widely.

'I rather think it will be,' Spencer replied, keeping his voice low, as though saddened.

Becker patted his arm. 'Well, you did everything you could.'

Becker returned to his seat, the picture of a man enjoying the triumph of a lifetime.

Spencer fought to keep from smiling. He helped Christina to a chair at the counsel table and told the judge's clerk he was ready to argue.

'It's almost two, Michael,' Nancy said. 'Maybe I'd better go up to court. They may want me as a witness.'

The traffic was knotted, a mass of honking steel. Collins saw a silver limousine trying to get into a moving lane.

'This may be him.'

The limo stopped, stalled in traffic. A short, stout man struggled out. To Collins' surprise, Patrick Dowd was still wearing the same outfit he had worn in Dublin – worn jacket and baggy trousers. Dowd cautiously stepped between the cars, then began to climb the courthouse steps.

'Mr Dowd,' Michael greeted him as they met. The man's face broke out in a toothy smile.

'This is Nancy Merriam,' Collins said, introducing them.

The smile grew wider. 'Ah, the famous one, is it? My, you look like a lovely girl, not at all the mindless harpy the newspapers make you out.' He put his pudgy hand on her sleeve. 'Now, don't be taking offence, girl, I'm a plain-speaking man.'

'And I'm no harpy,' she said, trying to be angry. But there was something about the little man that was more charming than offensive.

'Now don't I know that by just lookin' at you? Michael Collins, what's afoot? I hope for your young career that whatever it is merits my loss of a night's sleep to cross the Atlantic.'

Collins nodded, weighing just how much he should tell, then glanced at his watch. It wouldn't hurt to tell him all; there was no time left. He quickly sketched out for Dowd what was about to happen in the courtroom above them.

The Irishman listened attentively, asking no questions.

Collins finished. 'That's it in a nutshell, leaving out the details.'

'And no one knows about this? None of the money people?'

'No.'

Dowd nodded to Collins. 'Well, let's go up and see what happens. If you're a reliable prophet, Michael Collins, my trip here will be worth it many times over.' He chuckled. 'I would hope for all of us, but most certainly for me. Let's go.'

Judge Groban, as usual, rushed into his courtroom. Everyone stood while the officer announced the opening of court. The gavel cracked and Groban sat down before any of the other people in the courtroom.

'As I recall, Mr Spencer, you promised you were going to present some kind of startling revelation when last we met?' The words were challenging, but the jduge was smiling, taking a bit of the sting out of them.

Spencer got up and walked to the lectern. He carried a file with him.

'If the court please,' he began, 'the history of antitrust legislation in this country started, in the main, with the Clayton Act. There has been a series of other laws passed by the Congress over the years, including the Williams Act of 1978, which strengthened the provisions of the original statute.'

The judge waved his hand as if brushing away an invisible fly. 'Please, Mr Spencer, spare us a history lesson if you can. I think Mr Becker and myself know the chronology of antitrust.'

Spencer bowed slightly. 'I'm sure you do. And, sparing the court a lecture, suffice it to say that all these laws had as their base the protection of free trade. It was made unlawful for any company to buy up their competitors in order to control the natural system of establishing price by open trade.'

The judge sighed. 'Please – I know all that. Get on with it.'

'I shall, your honour. In this case the chemical company, Brown and Brown, has formed an association with Rising Sun, an international corporation.' He turned and pointed towards the spectators. 'Owned by Mr Tao Kuragamo, who is in court today.'

'That's all in the pleadings, Mr Spencer. Brown and Brown make no secret that they are using the money and credit of Rising Sun to take over your client. Lockwood Limited. I thought you said you'd present something new?'

'I did,' Spencer said, smiling, 'and I will.' He reached into the file and produced the papers gathered and prepared by Nancy Merriam. 'I am presenting to the court today, to prove the allegations of antitrust in our motion, proof that Rising Sun is in direct competition with Lockwood Limited in two major areas.'

'Objection!' Becker shouted. 'I've had no opportunity to see those so-called proofs.'

Spencer handed the papers to Becker, who was becoming red in the face.

'This is manifestly unfair,' Becker sputtered. 'We were given to understand that Mr Spencer was going to concede defeat today. We aren't prepared to argue this issue.'

'And just who informed you of that?' the judge asked irritably, concerned that things might get away from his control if he didn't act quickly and decisively.

Becker was almost turning purple. 'A member of his firm.' He pointed indignantly at Spencer.

Spencer looked up at the judge and shrugged.

'You'll have to be more specific, Mr Becker.'

Becker paused as if weighing what he should do. He glanced over at Spencer, and that somehow seemed to make up his mind. 'One of the main partners of Nelson and Clark told me they would withdraw the motion this afternoon.'

'Mr Spencer?'

Dan Spencer slowly shook his head in bafflement. 'I certainly haven't talked to any partner who was going to contact Mr Becker. I'm sure he must be mistaken.' Spencer was careful that his words were correct, misleading perhaps, but correct.

'And just who is it who has misinformed you, Mr Becker?'

Becker's breath was coming in short snorts, his anger on the rise. 'I've obviously been had! We have been informed by Mr John Crim of Nelson and Clark just what to expect at each step of these proceedings. We thought we had an agreement with him. Evidently he was just stringing us along. In any event, because of that, I will need additional time to prepare.'

'Your honour,' Spencer interjected softly. 'The proofs I have handed to Mr Becker show beyond any doubt that Rising Sun and Lockwood are competing companies. We have alleged antitrust violations; we are in the position of being able to prove them now in detail.'

'Has your Mr Crim purposely misled Mr Becker?' the judge asked.

Spencer knew he was walking a tightrope. He had to protect the firm and avoid stepping into what could be extremely deep legal quicksand.

'If Mr Crim has done what Mr Becker alleges, it has been done entirely on his own. I know of no agreement. I suspect that all of this may be a rather shoddy effort to delay the ruling on this motion for a temporary restraining order.'

'Shoddy!' Becker shouted. 'This whole business has been shoddy — '

'Sit down!' The judge's words snapped out like rifle shots. 'Sit

345

down and allow Mr Spencer to address the court.'

'I made an objection,' Becker protested.

'Overruled,' the judge snarled. 'Sit down, sir!'

Becker once again opened his mouth to protest further, thought better of it, and resumed his seat at the counsel table.

'Allow me to take a look at those papers,' the judge said.

'Objection,' Becker said, rising.

Judge Groban's eyes narrowed. 'Overruled. I am not a jury, Mr Becker, and I am not going to rule on the truth of the exhibits. They are offered as part of the plaintiff's motion and I merely wish to see them.'

Spencer walked over, took the papers from Becker's unwilling hand, then passed them to the clerk, who handed them to the judge.

The judge turned sideways and read each paper, quickly flipping through the pages, his expression noncommittal. The courtroom was hushed as he read, with only an occasional nervous cough heard among the spectators. Finally he turned and looked down at Spencer.

'I see you have affadavits attached attesting to the veracity of this information.'

'Yes.'

The judge nodded thoughtfully. 'Well, Mr Spencer, you promised a surprise, and you were certainly as good as your word. I have examined the documents submitted. If true, there would appear to be several violations of federal antitrust provisions.' He looked over at Becker. 'Now, Mr Becker, you may favour us with your observations. But please keep them short, if at all possible.'

Becker half ran to the lectern. His face reflected his rage. 'I deny the truth of these worthless documents. My clients deny their truth. We demand to be heard on this issue.'

'And you need time to prepare, is that correct?' the judge asked.

'Indeed, we do,' Becker said, pausing to calculate the time needed to buy Lockwood's stock. 'At least two weeks at the very minimum. Possibly three.'

The judge's smile verged on the malicious. 'I agree, Mr Becker. This is a serious matter. I will grant you three weeks. We will set the hearing on these documents for three weeks from today, at this time.'

Becker turned and beamed at Kuragamo. He was facing away when the judge resumed speaking.

'However, the allegations, together with the information substantiated by affadavits, is quite compelling, at least on its face. I will issue a temporary restraining order prohibiting Rising Sun from taking any further action in the takeover action against Lockwood Limited – that includes lending of credit or assistance in any form.'

Becker snapped around. 'You can't do that!' he fairly screamed.

'Not only can I, Mr Becker, I just did.'

'That order will have the practical effect of destroying the stock offer made by Brown and Brown. We must have an earlier hearing, otherwise we can't meet the law's deadline on buying stock.'

The judge smiled down at him. 'You've just set the time, Mr Becker.'

'I'll appeal and I'll win.' Becker was almost insane with rage.

'Mr Spencer,' the judge said. 'I trust you have no objection?'

Spencer now stood up. 'None, your honour.'

Judge Groban nodded. 'I would also suggest that copies of what you showed me today be given to the Justice Department and the Securities and Exchange Commission. They may find it just as interesting as I have.'

'I will see that is done directly, your honour,' Spencer said.

Judge Groban stood up. 'You gentlemen have a half-hour to agree upon the language of the order. If you fail, I will draft it myself. I'll be in my chambers.'

As the judge left the courtroom, pandemonium erupted. Spencer found himself separated from Christina by a swarming horde of newsmen.

Becker and Kuragamo were shouting at each other.

Dan tried to push past the reporters. He saw Nancy Merriam and Michael Collins, also surrounded by the people of the press. With them was a short, almost bald man, dressed in rumpled clothing. He had one of the widest grins Spencer had ever seen.

'You've won, Dan.' Christina had fought her way to his side and she threw her arms around him. 'You've won.'

'We have won,' he said simply.

'Kuragamo is in a rather vulnerable poisition.' Patrick Dowd said, sipping his large glass of straight whiskey, served, to the horror of the waiter of the Ritz Carlton Hotel, without ice.

'So?' Dan had his arm around Christina. He was matching the balding Irishman drink for drink, happily celebrating the victory. His troops were busy preparing for Becker's anticipated appeal. Ainsworth Martin had been notified. Nancy Merriam and Michael Collins had rushed back to Lockwood headquarters to push the final stages of the Brown and Brown takeover. Spencer was more than pleasantly relaxed.

'Ah, all life is competition in one way of another, is it not?' Dowd said. 'Even the poor farmer competes with the elements for his crop, and later with the market people when he has reaped it. A man bargains his hours away for pay. It's all competition. I truly enjoy the thrust and parry of business on a somewhat larger scale than most.'

'What has all this to do with Kuragamo?'

'Everything. Taro Kuragamo has in the past tried to destroy me. Nothing personal, you understand, just a matter of business – that in addition to the thrill of beating a competitor. Now, the poor Japanese finds himself – excuse me, my dear – with his pants down. And here comes old Paddy Dowd with his kicking shoes on.'

'What do you plan to do?' Spencer asked.

The Irishman drained his drink as though it were a glass of water and winked at the waiter for another.

'Now, Mr Spencer, what kind of sly fox would I be if I confided my every move to two strangers, no matter how talented and charming? Mr K seems to have let his marbles get scattered – a very serious mistake. I will pick up the odd one here and there. Of course I won't be the only one. It will be a little like sharks hitting the carcass of a dying whale. We'll all manage to get a bite or two before the big fish disappears completely.'

Dan felt Christina tremble slightly. 'Do you think it will be that easy, Mr Dowd?' she asked. 'Taro Kuragamo seems a determined fighter. And he is powerful.'

Dowd took the glass from the waiter and gulped half of it. He wiped his mouth with the sleeve of his suit jacket. 'Was powerful is more accurate, Christina.' He grinned. 'As we speak, the international sharks are hitting his financial belly. The banks who loaned him the money for the Brown and Brown adventure are calling in the loans. He'll have to start selling off parts of Rising Sun just to pay them.'

'How do you know this?' Spencer asked.

Dowd winked. 'Ah, it's no mystery. I own a number of the banks who made the loans.'

'I thought you were a competitor.'

'Oh, I am,' Dowd replied easily. 'Money's money. The man came to my people for a loan, a straight business proposition. That's my bank's business, you see. Now, since I know he can't pay, we'll just see what choice part of his business hide we can chew off. That, plus a few other little things, will have turned all this into a very profitable business adventure for me.'

'And what will finally happen to Kuragamo?'

Dowd finished the whiskey. 'Oh, he'll be ruined. No question about that. And he is an arrogant bastard, don't you know, there won't be a bunch of pals hanging around helping him out. He made his bed; now he'll have to lie in it.'

'Are you going back to Ireland now?' Christina asked.

Dowd stood up. 'No. It will take a few days here to accomplish what I want. Perhaps we might meet again before I go back. If not, allow me to congratulate you on a masterful stroke. Sometimes I have the need of talented lawyers. We may be doing some business. Good luck to you both.'

He was gone before they could even reply.

'Dan, do you think he means it, about ruining Taro Kuragamo?'

'I'm not sure. But if I had to bet, I'd bet that he does. When we sent young Collins to Ireland we did some research on Dowd. He is a mystery man, but a dangerous one. He doesn't look particularly impressive, but based on his record, I'd sure hate like hell to have him coming after me.' He hugged her. 'I'm afraid Taro Kuragamo is a gone goose.' He paused. 'Are you sorry?'

She looked up at him. 'Do you mean do I have any feelings left for him? The answer is no, I certainly don't. Still, I sort of half feel sorry for him.'

'Don't. The bastard deserves everything he's going to get.'
Spencer tossed back his own drink. 'And if Dowd and company
doesn't do it, I may just go over there and bust him up myself.'

'It's all over, Dan. You did just that this afternoon, and he
knows it.'

Spencer grinned. 'That makes me feel better, Christina. Even if
Dowd did stiff me for the drinks.'

She giggled. 'I didn't realize.'

'See how fast he left? The man has perfected it to a fine art. I'll
bet he hasn't picked up a cheque in years. I just hope he's as sharp
in business.'

He was about to signal for another drink, but she restrained his
hand.

'Let's go back to your apartment, Dan,' she whispered. 'To the
victor belongs the spoils.'

Ainsworth Martin had hurriedly assembled the other Apostles,
except for Seaforth Russell, who was vacationing in Spain. They
were all there, John Crim had flown in and arrived late.

Ainsworth Martin presented the case like a prosecuting
attorney, a dispassionate prosecutor, keeping his words to a minimum, his facts succinct, his accusation simple and basic.

He had expected Crim to deny everything, to put up a fight, but
instead he quickly admitted what he had done, almost as though
he were somehow justified in his conduct.

'What do you propose to do, Ainsworth?' Crim glanced over at
the others, as if the question were on the same level of importance
as where to have lunch.

As usual, they were all seated around the long table, but this
time there were no drinks.

'We expect you to resign, John,' Martin replied evenly.

'That would cause me quite a financial hardship,' Crim said,
equally evenly. 'I could bring a lawsuit for dissolution and division
of the business.'

Martin nodded. 'We had discussed that, the others and I.
Despite your recent activities, you have done the firm a good
service in the past, John. We've taken that into consideration.'
Martin had shrewdly calculated just how much it would take under
the circumstances, to buy Crim out. 'We believe that a cash

payment of one million dollars would be more than fair. Upon resignation, that is, giving up all rights and benefits.'

Crim pursed his lips. 'A partnership here is worth a great deal more than that, Ainsworth, a great deal more.'

Looking around at the others to restrain them from entering into the discussion, Martin nodded. Several of the Apostles were red-faced with anger. 'I agree, John. However, if you do bring suit, a judge – upon hearing what you have done – may well decide you have forfeited all rights and benefits. Therefore, this settle-ment, given the circumstances, is, I believe more than generous.'

'A million and a half,' Crim responded. 'I have to pay income taxes.'

Martin, in anticipation, had already discussed the matter with the other partners. He was empowered to offer three million.

He sighed as though Crim's counterproposal was greatly dis-turbing. 'Do any of you have any great objection?' He looked at the others, all very serious, none of their expressions revealing that Crim was shafting himself.

'All right, John, it seems we have a deal. Morris Solomon and I took the liberty of drawing up your agreement to resign the firm. All that's needed is the amount.' He reached into the long, flat envelope in front of him and handed the papers over to Crim. 'Please read them, John. I think you'll find them in order. If you will sign them, I will issue a cheque for the amount you ask.'

Crim looked up from the papers. 'I don't mean to quibble, Ainsworth, but I'd like a cashier's cheque.' He smiled at the others. 'It's not that I don't trust you, of course – I'm simply being prudent.'

Ainsworth Martin's expression remained unchanged. 'I antici-pated that, of course. Eugene Cryderman, the president of the Manhattan Exchange Bank, is waiting for us. You can sign the resignation papers in his office if you like, and he'll then certify our cheque.'

'How did you know I'd agree to all this?'

Martin looked at him. 'Under the circumstances, the result was somewhat predictable, as I'm sure you agree.'

'As always, you've thought things out especially well.' Crim looked at the others as though he were about to say something further, then stopped.

'Why did you do it, John?' Asa Chamberlain asked.

Martin frowned. He didn't want the compromise upset by recriminations. 'That's quite immaterial, Asa.'

'No,' Crim said. 'I think I'd like to answer that. I owe you an explanation.' He looked at all of them, a wry smile upon his lips. 'Ambition is a terrible thing, isn't it? Here, in New York, Nelson and Clark is the top law firm, and each of us is regarded in our own world as something near to kings. But Washington is quite different. It's not nearly as sophisticated. It's like a small town, in a way. There, externals matter. They judge law firms, and lawyers, not by quality of reputation as much as by the numbers in the firm's Washington office. Big equals powerful. They even judge other countries by the size of their embassies and the sumptuousness of their parties.'

He paused for a moment, then continued. 'It's not much of a world, I suppose, but it is *my* world. Nelson and Clark is just a rumour there. We have only a handful of lawyers, therefore by Washington standards we aren't very important. I begged you people to enlarge the office, obviously to increase my own importance, but also to enhance the firm's power in the nation's capital. I am one of the Apostles, a powerful man in New York. But in Washington I am nothing. I found that galling.'

'So you sold out to Emerson Becker,' Francis Desmond growled.

'I don't think recriminations will do anyone any good,' Ainsworth Martin interjected quickly, hoping to keep the peace and preserve the settlement.

'Don't worry, Ainsworth,' Crim said. 'I take no offence. It's rather bluntly put, but true nevertheless. I did indeed sell out. Emerson Becker agreed to make me a full partner in his firm, obviously not as prestigious as Nelson and Clark, but almost as financially rewarding. But, like the rest of you, I really don't need the money. Becker promised to make his Washington office larger than any other firm. In other words, in my world I would then become the king.'

Crim laughed. 'Well, now Becker really believes that I was playing him for a fool, so I'm afraid that plan is finished forever. In case you're wondering what I'll do – which I rather suspect is low on your list of burning concerns – I will return to Washington and try to hook up with one of the larger firms. If not as a partner, than as a counsel. It may not be quite the same, but at least I won't be so frustrated.'

Martin stood up. 'Cryderman won't wait forever. We had better go.'

Crim slowly got up. 'Well, I'm truly sorry it all worked out this way.' He paused, looking from one face to the next. 'I shall miss you, despite what's happened.' He smiled. 'And, of course, if you're ever in Washington, do look me up.'

'Let's go,' Martin said quickly, watching Desmond colour even more deeply.

There was an uncomfortable silence in the room after they left.

'Damn Judas!' Desmond exploded.

Katherine Thurston smiled. 'Come on, Francis, what did you expect? As I recall, there was one in the original set of Apostles. This sort of confirms our, well, divinity.'

Even Frank Desmond started to laugh.

26

'We have nothing so grand as this in all of Ireland,' Dowd said, looking around at the delicate ferns gracefully set around the tables at the Palm Court of the Plaza Hotel. 'Mind you, we have some real castles, and some quite beautiful Georgian homes, but nothing at all like this.' He chuckled. 'Ah, it's just as well. If we had something like this, our dear friends the English would have stolen it anyway.'

'Why did you wish to see me?' The old man's face betrayed his suspicion. Teddy Edwards looked wary, like an animal caught in a trap.

'Do have some of the tea,' Dowd said. 'It's quite nice, really.'

'Mr Dowd, you are one of the most important men in the world. I'm sure you didn't invite me here merely to sample the tea.'

'I take mine with a touch of whiskey. It makes the world a

smoother place in which to exist.'

'I can't drink,' Teddy Edwards barked. 'My doctor won't allow it.'

'Good heavens, man, doctors kill people very day with foolish advice like that. But to each his own.'

'What's on your mind, Mr Dowd?'

'They're going to take your company, Mr Edwards. The courts have seen to that. You're quite defenceless without the financial assistance of Mr Kuragamo.'

'We're working towards another source of money.'

Dowd smiled and patted the old man's bony knee. 'Now, my dear man, I know everything that's going on. That's my business. You're done for. Lockwood will snap up the few shares remaining for control, break up Brown and Brown, sell off your valuable land and your profitable divisions, then close up the others. In a matter of weeks Brown and Brown will be but a memory. Ah, it's a shame, isn't it?'

'I trust this conversation has a purpose?' Edwards was becoming increasingly annoyed by the small Irishman's airy manner.

He was answered by an impish grin. 'It has a purpose, of course. Ah, you just don't understand the Irish. We like to caress a bit before we get to the actual fucking, don't you know.'

'Pardon me?'

'Crudely stated, and I apologize. Mr Edwards, I think I know what you want.'

'What's that?'

'You want Brown and Brown to continue as a viable company, not in name only, but as a profit-making entity, am I correct?'

Old Edwards studied the smiling, moon-shaped face for a moment. 'Yes. The company has been in my family for generations. Besides the sentiment, it provides most of my family with their main source of income.'

Dowd nodded as if hearing a great and irrefutable truth. 'Ah, yes. Tradition is so important to us all. May I be so bold as to make you a proposition?'

Edwards snorted. 'Go on.'

'Suppose I step in and take over where Mr Kuragamo left off. Suppose I buy Lockwood Limited?'

Edward's beady eyes narrowed. 'Suppose you did? What would you want in return?'

'Your soul.'

'Pardon me?'

'That's a bit of a joke. I can't help it; it's a national imperfection. We're always joking. It's like drinking, after a fashion. I would want ownership of Brown and Brown.'

Edwards scowled. 'You would do just the same thing: you'd sell the land and break up the company.'

Dowd signalled to a waiter. 'Ah, that's where you're wrong. True, I would sell the land. That would help me pay for the money I've expended. But I would give you a five-year agreement not to sell any of the other assets of the company.'

'We would stay as Brown and Brown?'

Dowd nodded. 'Yes, of course. I would merge you with Lockwood. I would sell many of Lockwood's divisions. I am, after all, in this for the profit. I would insist on replacing all your officers and your board with my own people. Except for you. You would stay on as chairman of the board.'

The old man's ancient face seemed to come alive as his muscles worked beneath the wrinkled facial skin. 'And if we refuse?'

Dowd chuckled as he gave his order to the waiter. 'Now, if you refuse, Lockwood and their Mr Scott will own you. He'll bust you up, and that's the end of your precious company. You'll also take a rather substantial loss. Scott's known to be an unforgiving fellow, I understand. Well, what do you say? Shall I step in to Kuragamo's empty shoes and save you, or shall you go down to certain destruction? Not much of a choice if I do say so myself.'

'What about Scott?'

'You mean if I acquire Lockwood?'

'Yes.'

Dowd smiled widely, reached over and again patted the old man's knobbly knee. 'Ah, don't worry your head about them small details. I'll attend to all that. Well, sir, now what do you say?'

'Do I have any choice?'

'Not that I can see.'

'All right. I'll have our attorneys draw up — '

Dowd laughed. 'No offence, of course, but my solicitors will do the job. They are, well, rather used to it.'

'Do I have to sign in blood?' Edwards growled.

Dowd roared with laughter. 'No, not now, Mr Edwards. Perhaps another day.' He stood up. 'I'll have the paperwork by this evening. Will you be at the office?'

'I'll be there.'

'No regrets about losing your officers?'

'None. They are, for the most part, a bunch of horses' asses.'

Dowd beamed. 'You see, we think very much alike.' He put his hands in his pockets. 'Oh, would you mind taking care of the bill? I left Ireland so quickly that I didn't have time to get much cash and forgot my credit cards.'

Teddy Edwards looked after the short, squat man as he walked through the aisles between the tables. He moved with the easy grace of a seaman, as though he were used to pitching decks.

Edwards knew he should feel jubilant, but he did not. He felt like a modern-day Faust who had, in reality, just sold his soul.

Nancy Merriam entered the lobby of the Lockwood Building. It was the first morning in some time that she allowed herself to sleep late. The battle had always kept her in the office well into the evening. Sometimes she'd had to settle for sleeping on her office couch.

The uniformed guard stepped up to her as she strode towards the elevator bank. 'I'm sorry, Miss Merriam,' he said, his voice kept low. 'I can't allow you up. Mr Scott's orders.'

At first she thought he was joking. 'What did you say?'

He looked uncomfortable. 'He gave written orders that you weren't to be allowed in the building. I'm very sorry, Miss Merriam, I truly am, but you'll have to leave.' His face jerked involuntarily. 'If it was up to me, there'd be no problem, but I'll get fired if I let you up.'

'Do you have a copy of the orders?' she asked, still in shock.

'Yes, ma'am.' He fished inside his uniform jacket, pulled out a folded paper, and handed it to her.

She read the short message. 'Miss Nancy K. Merriam is no longer an employee of this company. In order to safeguard the integrity of this organization, Miss Merriam, or any of her agents or associates, are not permitted access to any Lockwood Limited properties.'

356

John Norman Scott had signed it with his customary flourishing hand.

'Again, I'm awfully sorry,' the guard said. 'Didn't anyone tell you?'

She forced a smile and shook her head.

The guard frowned. 'Shitty way to do things.'

A television camera crew hurried by. One of them recognized her and called a greeting as they boarded an elevator.

'What's that all about?' she asked.

'Mr Scott has called a ten-thirty press conference. I understand he's blowing his own horn about this Brown and Brown thing. One of the executives said something about it earlier.'

'Is he in the building?'

He looked distressed, even a little fearful. 'Yes, he came in early. First time he's been in in a week. But you can't see him, Miss Merriam.'

She put the paper into her purse. 'I wouldn't want to,' she said, not knowing whether she was experiencing tears of fear or anger. She had never been fired before.

'I imagine they'll send your personal stuff to your apartment.'

She nodded and turned, walking quickly through the lobby, hoping she wouldn't see anyone she had to talk to.

The tears were flowing freely now, but at least she knew now what she felt. It was anger, it was rage.

The whole Nelson and Clark office, all six floors, was abuzz with the news.

The Apostles were to meet that afternoon to decide who would fill Frank Johnson's vacancy and the surprising vacancy created by the resignation of John Crim. He had been the first Apostle in the firm's long history ever to resign. No satisfactory reason was given for Crim's action. Office gossip had it that Crim was about to become a member of the President's cabinet, probably as Attorney General of the United States. But, except for raw gossip, no one seemed to possess any hard facts.

It was a tradition, when selecting main partners, for the Apostles to meet in their sacred dining room after lunch. The candidates were expected to wait in their own offices. If selected, they were invited

357

up to the dining room; the first time they would see it. After that they were full members, main partners, Apostles themselves.

The losers, who usually found out within minutes of the selection, were expected to put on a show of good sportsmanship, congratulate the winner, then hang around cheerfully for a few weeks or a month until they found something else. But on that day, selection day, the losers knew they were through forever with the firm of Nelson and Clark.

Christina came rushing into Dan's office. He looked quite relaxed, his feet up on the desk, a law book in his hands.

'Did you hear?' she asked.

He nodded. 'Yes. Everyone seems quite excited.'

'Oh, come on, Dan, don't tell me you aren't?'

He smiled. 'I don't know if you could call it excitement.'

'Well, I suppose you can afford to be calm. They couldn't deny you a spot, not after what you did in the Lockwood matter.'

'That would also apply to you, Chris. Ainsworth and the rest know it was your efforts that saved the day.'

She sat down opposite him. 'I don't know, Dan. They already have a woman Apostle. The betting is that they won't want two.'

'At least with two spots open, you and I aren't in head-to-head competition.'

'I know. It makes it much easier.'

'Chris, have you really thought about this main partner business? I wonder if it's worth all this fuss in the long run.'

'Dan, what are you saying? My God, as a main partner in Nelson and Clark a person would never have to worry about money agiain. And the prestige is at least double that. I know lawyers who would much rather be an Apostle than President of the United States. Really – I mean it.'

'I suppose.'

'Oh, you're just having last-minute butterflies.'

'Chris, what will you do if you don't get selected?'

'Isn't that bad luck? I mean talking about losing?'

'Luck is something you make yourself. Really, have you given the alternative any thought?'

She looked at him. He was very serious. 'I'd be a fool if I hadn't done so.' She paused. 'I have made some pretty good connections in the banking world. I suspect I might become a vice president in charge of business finance somewhere. It's what I do best. And, if all I hear is correct, the firm likes to see that the losers are helped out. I won't starve.'

'But would you be unhappy being something other than an Apostle?'

She frowned. 'Yes, very unhappy. Oh, if I'm not selected, I'll survive, but all I have ever wanted to do was to make it to the top here. And being a main partner at Nelson and Clark is the top, Dan. It's what I want.'

He studied her for a moment. 'You know, you and I have a serious relationship going on here.'

'Ah, what a poetic lover.'

He laughed. 'Hardly. Never claimed to be, but the fact remains.'

'So?'

'So, what if one of us makes it and the other doesn't?'

'What do you mean?'

'If you feel that strongly about becoming an Apostle, I think it could make a difference between us. One of us might be jealous of the other, or worse, patronizing. Have you considered what it might do to us?'

'No, to be truthful, I haven't. But I don't think it would really matter between us. Besides, I'm the only one who has to worry. The office hot line says you have it locked up.'

'We'll see. The world is full of surprises.'

Ainsworth Martin drew Morris Solomon aside before they entered the dining room. 'I just received a telephone call from Brown and Brown. They want to set up a meeting tonight. I'd like you to be in on it.'

'Where's the meeting?'

'Here. They want me to ask John Norman Scott to come. I talked to Teddy Edwards, the chairman of the board. You know him?'

'Yes. Crusty old bird. I doubt all this is going down very well for him.'

Ainsworth sighed. 'Obviously they want to talk settlement.'

'They lost; of course they do. Why meet with them, anyway? There's nothing to be done now. Scott holds the winning hand.'

'Maybe. Edwards says that Patrick Dowd will be there too.'

Solomon raised his eyebrows. 'That could make it an entirely new ball game.'

'That's why I think we should have the meeting. I called Scott and he's agreeable. He's going to push their faces into the dirt. He's the kind who enjoys that sort of thing.'

'Anybody else?'

'Yes. I thought we might ask the new Apostle who was responsible for our victory.'

'That makes sense.'

'Also, Edwards tells me Dowd would like young Michael Collins to attend. We sent him to Ireland to talk to Dowd in the first place.'

'I remember. It seems he must have made quite an impression on Dowd. He may be worth watching.'

Ainsworth allowed himself a small smile. 'He is. I selected and recruited him myself.'

Solomon chuckled. 'The young man will be in for a treat. He may witness financial history made tonight. Do you think?'

'Anything is possible,' Ainsworth Martin said. They proceeded into the dining room. The others were all there, and the room was filled with laughter and conversation. There would be no great battles this time over who was to be selected. Ainsworth Martin had polled all the Apostles during the morning and had found rare agreement.

Martin nodded to Roosevelt Smith. 'Roosevelt, you can begin to serve.' He turned to Solomon. 'We might as well get this little luncheon and ceremony over quickly. We have a lot to do.'

Christina had sent out for a turkey sandwich, but she was much too nervous to eat. Her floor had been filled with the sound of hushed voices as the baleful noon hour had come. Upstairs, the main partners were having their lunch and presumably making the selection. Additional word was out that Jeffrey Rowe and Andy Perkins had entered the race for the two slots. Both men were from good backgrounds, and were experienced trial men. If Dan Spencer didn't get it, either of them would be a logical candidate. The head of litigation had always been an Apostle.

She heard the elevator door open. That usually unnoticed noise had taken on a whole new meaning. It could announce the summons from on high. But so far it had been the staff and clericals coming on to the floor. No one had yet come from the dining room above.

She turned and looked out the window, trying to calm herself. It was tradition for candidates to stay alone in their offices on selection day, so she hadn't joined Dan Spencer. She wondered what he was thinking, whether or not he was nervous or was as cool as he appeared to be. She wondered if he thought about the possibility of losing.

She again heard the soft whooshing of the elevator. Win or lose, it wouldn't be long now. She remembered when Seaforth Russell and Philip Crawforth had been picked. Although the selection had been a few months apart, the timing had been the same.

'Christina.'

She jumped at the sound of her name, turned in her chair, and found Ainsworth Martin standing before her desk. 'Christina, I wonder if you could spare a few minutes and come upstairs.'

Her heart was beating wildly. 'Y-yes, of course,' she stammered.

She tried not to rush. They walked together in silence to the elevators. Ainsworth Martin continued to say nothing while they waited for the doors to open. He silently escorted her off the elevator, down the long hall, then into the sacrosanct dining room.

Everyone stood as she walked in. Katherine Thurston, usually so very regal, swept over to her, clasped her in a strong bear hug, and whispered, 'Congratulations.'

Ainsworth Martin indicated an empty chair at the long, gleaming table. She walked down towards it, past the smiling faces, and took that place.

'Mrs Giles, the main partners have voted to offer you a full partnership in Nelson and Clark.' Martin sounded like a preacher speaking in church. 'Do you accept?'

She was afraid she was going to cry, but fought against it. 'Yes, I do,' she managed to say.

The others all applauded.

'There are some rather mundane things that have to be taken care of – contracts and so forth,' Martin said. 'And as soon as we're through here, you and I can sit down and complete them. Is that agreeable?'

'Yes, of course.'

'Good. Please sit down.' Everyone was smiling, even old Asa

361

Chamberlain, whom she had never seen look even pleasant until this moment.

'Now, we are in a bit of a bind as far as established protocol is concerned, Christina,' Martin continued. 'We met and voted on the two people to be selected as main partners. There was some discussion, but we reached a unanimous agreement. That was when there were ten. Now we are eleven. We've never before had two vacancies at once. We think it proper that you have a chance to express your opinion of the other candidate. You are not a full-fledged Apostle. You can nominate anyone else, if you care to, but I would like to have your vote recorded. It makes everything legal,' he said, pausing for a laugh. But everyone remained serious.

'We have picked Jeffrey Rowe to be the other main partner.'

It was as though her heart had stopped beating. She wondered if in her excitement she had heard correctly.

'Basically, it was between Jeffrey and Andy Perkins, both exceptional men. I think, capsulizing our debate, the majority opinion was that Jeffrey, although of less seniority, would do a better job than Andy in projecting the qualities that we try to present to the public as main partners of Nelson and Clark. Andy seemed too preoccupied with office politics.'

She glanced from face to face. They were waiting for her to speak.

'What about Dan Spencer?' Her voice trembled. 'I thought he was a candidate?'

For only a moment did Ainsworth look surprised, then his face regained its normal, bland expression. 'Mr Spencer resigned from the firm this morning. I think it safe to say he would have been selected without exception, but he chose to leave the firm. Didn't he tell you?'

She shook her head. Again she felt close to tears.

'So, Christina, that's the choice upon which we've agreed, pending your approval. Is Jeffrey Rowe acceptable to you?'

She didn't even bother to think about it. She liked Jeffrey, but her thoughts were elsewhere.

'Yes, Jeffrey is an excellent lawyer,' she said, trying to keep her voice audible.

Ainsworth Martin again managed a slight smile. 'Well, that's settled, then. I'll get Mr Rowe, and if he accepts, which I think is probable' – this time there was a laugh – 'we'll break out the champagne. Please excuse me.'

She desperately wanted to rush to Dan, to find him, to ask why, but the others were around her, hands extended in congratulations, speaking words she hardly heard. She managed automatic responses, smiling and nodding, being gracious.

But there was only one thing on her mind.

Why had he done it? And, far more important to her, what effect would his decision have on them?

The same little ceremony introduced the newest Apostle, and Jeffrey Rowe glowed through his genuine delight. He came from money, and in his world being an Apostle was even sweeter than in any other social circle. His parents and their friends would know and appreciate just how important he had become.

Christina congratulated him. She sipped her champagne, trying to find an opportunity to slip away and find Dan.

'Oh, Christina,' Ainsworth Martin said, steering her away from the others. 'We are meeting here tonight with the principals of Lockwood and Brown and Brown. I would like you to sit in. This may result in a settlement, and we may have need of your expertise in drafting a financial section of the settlement terms, if one results.'

'Tonight?'

He chuckled. 'It's quite unfair to ask you to work your first night as a full-fledged Apostle, but I think it's necessary.' He grinned fully, a fact she found surprising. 'Before today you were expected to do what I asked, my dear. But I must inform you that as an equal partner you can tell me to go to hell if you like. It's one of the perks.'

'I would never do that, Ainsworth. Of course I'll be here.'

He patted her arm. 'Thank you.'

She finished her champagne, then quietly made her exit. Dan wasn't in his office. His secretary congratulated her, although there were tears in her eyes, then told her that Mr Spencer had taken the rest of the day off.

She suddenly found herself angry with him, as though he had somehow purposely ruined the jubilation she thought she should be feeling at gaining her life's ambition. Christina tried phoning his apartment, but there was no answer.

She kept trying to reach him right up until she was called to the conference room for the meeting.

Ainsworth Martin looked refreshed, and Christina marvelled at his apparently endless source of energy. John Norman Scott looked like his photographs – a small man with an arrogantly jutting lower jaw. He sat with one arm cocked over the back of his chair and irritably tapped the polished table with a gold fountain pen.

She was introduced to a very old man. He tried to stand up but found the effort too taxing, so he merely extended his arthritic hand. Teddy Edwards looked physically exhausted, but she noticed that his eyes were still amazingly sharp and lively.

The man from Ireland had the rough, unpolished look of a labourer. His wrinkled shirt still bore the faded stains of losing bouts with luncheons and dinner. He beamed out at her from a bloated, round red face. And she detected the strong aroma of whiskey as he spoke.

Morris Solomon sat next to Scott. As usual, it was impossible to even guess what Solomon was thinking. His features were as expressionless as those of a poker player.

Christina was surprised that they had included a mere associate in the meeting. She liked Michael Collins; they had worked well together. But he seemed preoccupied, even angry, his handsome young face stern and set.

'We have come together tonight at the request of Mr Edwards, the chairman of Brown and Brown's board. He asked that we invite Mr Scott. And he invited Mr Dowd. The rest of us are all from the firm of Nelson and Clark.'

Martin looked at the old man. 'Perhaps you'd like to begin, Mr Edwards?'

The old man nodded towards the Irishman. 'I defer to Patrick Dowd.'

Scott scowled. 'What's he got to do with all this? This is strictly between me and Brown and Brown.'

Dowd rose slowly and clasped his pudgy hands in front of his thick stomach. 'Ah, Mr Scott, where's the lovely young thing you have for vice president – Miss Merriam?'

'I fired her,' Scott snapped.

'It was my impression that she had led the rather successful fight put up by your company against Taro Kuragamo,' Dowd said.

Scott cracked his pen against the table a little more loudly. 'I ran the whole show. She was just a puppet. I pulled the string, she did the dance. But it went to her head. They were right, I never should have picked her for that job. She's much too young for that kind of responsibility.'

Dowd shrugged his shoulders as if it meant nothing to him one way or the other.

'I trust you people are here to surrender?' Scott asked, a vivid sneer on his thin face.

'Surrender? Such a warlike word among gentle businessmen, Mr Scott,' Dowd responded. 'I think it's time to come to an agreement between the parties.'

'I like the word surrender,' Scott persisted. 'Like old Ulysses S. Grant, I'm going to insist on unconditional surrender.'

Dowd reacted as though Scott's words were surprising. 'I think perhaps you've misunderstood the essential nature of this meeting. We would like to find out if there is any common ground for an agreement' – Dowd paused – 'between gentlemen.'

'Gentlemen, my ass,' Scott snapped. 'This is my show now. The courts have given me the green light. I'll own Brown and Brown by the day after tomorrow.'

Dowd slowly shook his head. 'I rather doubt that, sir,' he said softly. 'I bought the controlling interest in your company this afternoon. Brown and Brown weren't spopped from buying Lockwood stock. I have arranged to provide the money — '

Scott stopped tapping his pen. 'If Brown and Brown owns us, even if that's true, you haven't qualified under the SEC rules. In two days I'll own Brown and Brown. Your charter is different from mine. I'll toss out your board before you can mine.' He laughed. 'You wasted a great deal of money, Dowd. It's a shame.'

The Irishman's slight, ironic smile remained, but his eyes were like two ice-blue ball bearings, hard and unbreakable.

'I'm like a shopper – what do you call them over here, compulsives? When I start buying companies, I just can't seem to stop. This afternoon I also purchased fifty-one per cent of Brown and Brown. I paid a rather high price, but I bought it.'

'You aren't authorized to buy it!' Scott yelped. 'You have to go by the rules.'

'Oh, I'm doing just that, sir. I'm filing all those papers of which

365

you Americans seem to fuss over. I think everything's legal enough.'

Scott turned to Ainsworth Martin. 'You're my lawyers – tell this Irish son of a bitch where to get off.'

Ainsworth Martin sighed. 'Mr Dowd — ' he began, but the Irishman smiled and held up his hand to stop him.

'Do you represent Mr Scott individually or do you represent the Lockwood company?'

'We represent Lockwood Limited; that is our client. However, Mr Scott is the chief executive of that firm and we take our instructions from him.'

'Not any more,' Dowd said.

'What the hell are you talking about?' Scott demanded, half-rising from his chair.

'I took the liberty of contacting the members of your board,' Dowd said pleasantly. 'I'm afraid you don't have many loyal supporters there. I haven't been able to reach two of them, but I have contacted the majority. They agreed that you had become something of a liability to the company.' Dowd smiled at Scott. 'You have been ousted, I'm afraid.'

Dowd then turned to Ainsworth Martin. 'The board at Lockwood is meeting at the moment. I am given to understand a Mr Fred Hammerly will be named as interim chairman. You can telephone and verify. They'll be waiting for your call.'

Martin nodded, and Morris Solomon got up and left the room.

'You understand, Mr Dowd,' Martin said, 'we believe what you say, but we must be absolutely certain. In any event, unless informed otherwise, we will continue to represent Lockwood in this, ah, takeover matter.'

'Now look here!' Scott was standing now, his face almost purple. 'You represent me! I hired you.'

'Quite right, you did hire us – but as the attorneys for Lockwood Limited. Mr Dowd is quite correct on that point.'

'Well, I want you to represent me now,' Scott snapped. 'I *demand* it.'

Ainsworth Martin studied Scott for a moment before speaking. 'If what Mr Dowd says is true, and you have been ousted from the Lockwood board, we could not represent you in any matter concerning Lockwood Limited. It would be a conflict of interest for us and would be unethical. Lawyers cannot represent both sides.'

Scott was shaking with rage. 'Damn you – you and your ethics! It seems to me you lawyers only drag out those precious ethics of yours when they can do you some good. As far as I'm concerned, I'm still head of Lockwood and I'm firing Nelson and Clark right now.' He was shouting.

Morris Solomon came quickly back into the room. He looked at the enraged Scott, then took his seat once again.

'Well?' Ainsworth asked.

'The Lockwood board met just a few minutes ago. It's just as Mr Dowd said. They have fired Mr Scott from all his positions in the company, and Mr Hammerly is acting chairman. Hammerly said we are to take instructions from Mr Dowd.'

Ainsworth Martin glanced over at Scott. 'We will verify all this in writing, of course. However, I have no reason to disbelieve what I've just been told.'

'This is a goddamned sellout!' Scott yelled. 'This is a setup!' He turned and glowered at Dowd. 'Just who the hell do you think you're dealing with? I am John Norman Scott. They call me the Napoleon of Wall Street. You can't get away with this – I don't give a damn how much money you have!'

'Mr Scott' – Dowd's voice was friendly – 'win some, lose some, as the saying goes. I'm afraid you have lost.'

'You'll be damned sorry.'

'You are a fool who has been playing over your head for years,' Dowd said, no longer smiling. 'You have been a lucky gambler. But you went to the tables too often. Now get out of here.'

Scott's jaw was set. 'I will like hell.'

There was silence, and all eyes were on Dowd.

Then Michael Collins spoke, his voice low with restrained anger. 'If he needs any help getting out of here, I'll be happy to be of assistance.' He stood up, his body tense, on the ready.

'Well, I'm against violence myself,' Dowd laughed, 'unless it takes place in a proper setting, like a pub. Mr Martin, I'd be obliged if you'd call your building security and have Mr Scott escorted out.' He looked at Collins. 'Sit down and relax, Michael.'

Ainsworth Martin by nature abhorred emotional confrontations. 'Mr Scott, I would hate to call the security officers. It would be embarrassing for all of us. Please leave. We will double-check the information, I assure you. But it will serve no useful purpose if you stay now.'

John Norman Scott's lower lip began to tremble. He looked at each person in the room, defiantly at first, and then more like a beggar pleading for pity. He saw none.

Scott knocked over his chair, then silently stalked out of the conference room. He slammed the door behind him.

'Ah, I'm afraid I was a bit too harsh on him,' Dowd said. 'But then perhaps it will be instructive for the arrogant little son of a bitch.'

He smiled at Ainsworth Martin. 'I'm sure you must be harbouring at least the shadow of suspicion that somehow all this is a sham. Be assured that I held out an olive branch to every member of the Lockwood board. I think each found some, ah, profit from this evening's activities, in one way or another.' He paused. 'Besides, as far as I can tell, each of them thought Scott was about to ruin the company.' He looked over at Collins. 'They wanted me to have them name young Miss Merriam, your friend.'

'Didn't you?'

'No. For two reasons . . . well, really three. First, all that prior publicity would make that move unwise. Second, while I admire her abilities, she's still too young to take on the command of a company that size. She needs a little seasoning. Third, I want her to do another job for me.'

'As what?' Collins asked, knowing he was under Ainsworth Martin's disapproving eye. Demands weren't made of clients, especially rich ones.

Dowd seemed to take no offence. 'Michael, before this week is out I shall have control of Rising Sun. Mr Kuragamo's bankers are driving him from control of that conglomerate. I want your Nancy Merriam to be Rising Sun's chief financial officer. Actually, she will be presiding over the dismantling of Kuragamo's empire. It will give her further experience and an overview of international business that she could never get at Lockwood. She has accepted, by the way.' Dowd seemed concerned. 'I trust that meets with your approval?'

'If that's what she wants, sure.'

'Allow me to apologize,' Ainsworth Martin said. 'Mr Collins is new to the firm and — '

Dowd laughed heartily. 'Mr Collins is a friend of mine. I don't stand on formality with my friends and I don't expect it back. Besides, I want to make your Mr Collins an offer to come work with me.' He looked at Michael. 'You'll make a nice salary, Michael, a wee bit more than you do now. And you can watch what I do, invest, and become a rich man. Presuming, of course, that I know what I'm doing. How about it?'

Michael thought of his father. Patrick Collins had been bragging to his friends about his son, and the fact that he was on the staff of Nelson and Clark. More money wouldn't be sufficient reason to leave, at least in his father's eyes.

'Ah, Michael.' Ainsworth Martin interjected. 'We think a great deal of you, and while we wouldn't want you to miss an excellent opportunity, still we would — '

Dowd once again laughed. 'Don't waste your time. You can see the answer in his face. He won't leave. All right, if you won't come with me, Michael Collins, then I'll just have to hire your firm here to handle the Rising Sun matter and ask that you be assigned to head it up.' He turned to Martin. 'Is that unreasonable?'

Martin realized that the fees for such a major dismantling would run into many millions. He glanced over at Morris Solomon, who nodded his silent assent, as if reading his mind.

'As a matter of fact, we have an opening for a participating partner. I would have to ask for a vote for the other main partners, since Michael would be the youngest associate ever selected. But I believe we could count on their cooperation.'

Michael Collins' mouth popped open. He could almost hear his father's glee.

'Ah, you see, Michael,' Dowd said quietly. 'It's the power of money that makes it worthwhile.'

'What about the merger?' Teddy Edwards asked, anxious to have an agreement.

'I believe you're represented by Emerson Becker,' Martin said. 'He, or a member of his firm should be here.'

'Fired him,' Edwards cackled. 'Have to pay him a small fortune, though.' He glowered at Ainsworth Martin. 'You lawyers never do anything for free.'

Martin smiled benignly. 'Well, once in a while. But we never want it to become a habit.'

'Enough of this,' Dowd said suddenly. 'I want Nelson and Clark to complete the merger between my two companies. Mr Edwards will serve as the chairman of the new board. I shall be selling various components to pay off what I owe in buying their stock. As I figure it, I won't see very much of a profit from this whole encounter, but it has been rather fun.'

'Rather expensive fun,' Martin said.

'What does money mean to me?' Dowd leaned back in the large chair. 'I live in a small house. I eat plain food. Possessions mean nothing to me. I can only sit in one chair at a time. Right now I'm king of the world. Tomorrow, on the toss of fate, I can be back without a penny to my name. But I don't care, I live about the same either way. It's the game I like. Some men play tennis, others golf. This is my game. It's like your Monopoly, only with the real thing.' He chuckled. 'Oh, this sort of thing is a great joy. The action has been fast and furious. It usually is. We, people like myself, circle forever, then crash together for the kill. Oh, I tell you, I enjoy it all.' His eyes took in the others around the table. 'Does anyone have a cigar? I seem to be out.'

Ainsworth Martin offered one of his imported cigars from the case in his inside pocket.

Dowd made a little ceremony of sniffing the tobacco, snipping off the end, and lighting the cigar. He sat back and blew out a large cloud of smoke.

'Oh, it's a very beautiful thing to win. As one of your football people said, winning really is the only thing.'

He smiled slyly at the others and took a deep drag on the cigar.

Christina hurried from the meeting. Ainsworth Martin had invited everyone to the Four Seasons for a drink to celebrate but she had declined.

She took a cab to Dan's apartment. He answered the door in bare feet, dressed only in a scruffy pair of jeans. He held a large whiskey glass in his hand.

He grinned down at her. 'Ah, the working girl – heaven protect her. Well, does it feel any different now that you're an Apostle?'

She stepped past him into his living room. His stereo was playing a mournful Wagner dirge. She snapped it off.

'I think you owe me an explanation,' she said icily.

'Do I?'

'Dan, what on earth made you do it? Ainsworth told me you had it but turned it down.'

He raised his glass in mock salute. 'It's nice to be wanted. However, as Groucho Marx once said, I wouldn't want to belong to any club that would take me.'

'Damn it, Dan, this is serious. What made you do such a thing?'

He took up a bottle of Bourbon and poured a small measure into his glass. 'Can I get you a drink?'

'No!'

'Just asking.' He smiled. 'At least sit down. Or is that asking too much?'

She sat on the couch. 'Dan, please. After all we've been through together, you do owe me some kind of explanation.'

He slouched down in a chair and stretched his long legs before him. He held the glass in both hands and seemed to study it, twisting it in the light. 'I've been thinking about getting out for some time.'

'Why?'

'Well, it's simple really. I've been in the firm's litigation section for a number of years, doing just what I did in the Lockwood case. Usually on a smaller scale, but basically the same thing.'

'I don't understand.'

'How much money do you suppose was involved in that whole go-around?'

'Billions. Everyone knows that.'

'Right. Billions. But the money just got shoved around. It really didn't do any good for anybody. Nothing more got produced by it; no jobs were created; no industry aided. Just a couple of giant companies decided to have at one another, with the banks running in to finance the corporate war. Hell, if either one of those companies tried to borrow a few bucks to enlarge a plant or put some people to work, those same banks wouldn't have touched them. There wouldn't be any quick million-dollar profits in a straight loan. It seems that no one is interested in the final result any more Chris. All they want to do is play power games.'

'Even if you're right, what has all this got to do with you? Or for that matter, us?'

He sighed as he sipped the liquor. 'Everything. We fancy lawyers are the folks who make all this possible. We come in like hired gun crews to serve aboard pirate ships. We don't care who we shoot at just so long as we're paid. Like the bankers, we make a great deal of money, but nothing is contributed to society, or even commerce, by our services. I have merely served at the whim of the rich – or at least I did.'

'Is that your only reason? My God, you can't be serious?'

'I'm deadly serious. I've made arrangements to join a small negligence firm – plaintiff's work mostly.'

'You have to be kidding.'

He shook his head. 'That offends you, doesn't it? I'll be down among the unwashed, is that it?'

'It's sleazy work, Dan.'

He sipped the drink. 'But it's real. It will actually mean something to someone. I'll be asking a jury to place a price on Mr Smith's leg. Oh, the case won't make the pages of *The New York Times*, but to Mr Smith it will be pretty damned important. For a change, I'll be using my skill to do something beneficial in the world.'

'Dan . . . I can't believe this.'

'It's true enough. Oh, I won't make the money I'd have made as an Apostle, but I won't starve. And I'll admit the prestige won't be the same. My parents in Boston will probably disinherit me. Nevertheless, I'll be a working lawyer, not a pawn in some halfass game of giants. That's how I've spent my time in Nelson and Clark – acting as a legal muscle man for the big guys and grinding little companies into the dirt.'

'Dan, you sound like a Communist.'

He shook his head. 'No, Christ, not even a Fabian Socialist. The way I see it, our so-called blue blood law firms with their interlocking old-boy networks function like sleep parasites. They happily feed at the belly of American commerce. And what they do is always quite meaningless. All we ever seem to do in the big firms is manoeuvre and settle. You know, some of the lawyers in the litigation section have never even tried a jury case. They never get the chance. There's always the elaborate dance in the courts and then a negotiated settlement. I have no quarrel with the system. I can't change it. I just don't want to be a part of it any more.'

'You still haven't told me why.'

He looked at her. 'When I come home at night I would like to feel I had really accomplished something. At Nelson and Clark I never got that feeling. It was always like the Lockwood thing – I win by bringing a well-timed motion. I'm a lawyer, not some fop posturing in a French King's court. I'm tired of the empty pomp and show associated with serving the glittering clients of Nelson and Clark.'

'And the partners of Nelson and Clark – do you include us in on that?'

'You mean you.'

'Of course.'

He looked away. 'I'll have to think about that, Chris. I'm fed up with the old firm, to be frank.' He looked at her again. 'You apparently don't share any of my feelings about all this, do you?'

She sighed. 'You're right about that. I'm proud to be an Apostle. We handle the most important cases in America. You may think like some streetcorner anarchist, but I don't. You're wrong, Dan. You'll regret what you've done.'

'Those words have a rather harsh ring. Am I wrong or am I to find some kind of implication in them?'

She stood up. 'My husband sounds a lot like you. He always proclaims himself a great healer, at least to hear him tell it. According to him, he got into medicine for the sole purpose of benefiting mankind. But he only fools himself. He is a child, Dan, a child in a man's body. This is the real world. Frankly, I've had all I can take of adult children. I don't think you honestly yet realize what you've kicked away.'

He poured a bit more liquor into his glass. 'Chris, I think the world of you,' he said slowly. 'But apparently there exists a great gulf between us that we really didn't know was there. Perhaps we both had better try straightening out our lives before we end up really hurting each other.'

She hoped she wouldn't cry. He was different from Hank, very different. She knew that. Still he was wrong, foolishly wrong. 'I'm sorry, Dan,' was all she managed to say.

'It would have been a dreadful life.' He spoke softly. 'We would have been together every day at the office, then at home, and with nothing more lively to talk about than the latest market fluctuations, mergers, or petty firm gossip. We would have been locked together forever, feeding on ourselves.'

'It wouldn't have been awful for me. But perhaps you're right.' She turned and then stopped. 'I'm still your friend, you know that.'

'And I am yours, Christina.' He started to stand up, but she was quickly gone, slamming the door behind her.

He sat back in the chair and downed the rest of his drink.

'It would have never worked out,' he said aloud. But even to his own ear his words sounded hollow.

Patrick Collins sat in his darkened law office, without thought, just enjoying the sense of elation. Below, the people on Broadway were hurrying towards the theatres. The street was alive, pulsating.

He sighed happily. The news was nothing a man wanted to keep secret. The weather had turned cool, so he put on his topcoat and left the building.

The cab dropped him off at the small bar. It was a favourite hangout of police court lawyers, cops, and the flotsam and jetsam who drifted in and out of the American criminal justice system. The bar was like a watering hole in the jungle; the creatures, although natural enemies elsewhere, allowed each other to drink here unmolested. It was a place of truce, informal but real.

Two lawyers were sitting at the bar. They greeted Pat Collins by name.

Collins took off his coat and pulled up a stool.

'Drinks are on me,' he said, peeling a large bill from his wallet.

'What's the occasion?' Jack Dolan, a lawyer specializing in defending prostitutes asked.

'My kid was just made a partner at Nelson and Clark – one of the disciples.'

Dolan's eyebrows shot up. 'He's only been a lawyer for a year now, right?'

Collins beamed. 'Right.'

Dolan looked at him strangely, as if seeing him for the first time.

'Jesus, Pat, that's unbelievable.'

'Not bad, eh?'

Dolan laughed. 'Put your money away. Shit, it's an honour and all that, but I'll buy. You just lost a son – that kid of yours will never again speak to a bum like you, you know that.'

'Would you?'

'Hell, no,' Dolan laughed.

Patrick Collins could never remember being quite so happy.

27

The recessed lighting seemed to make the gold and copper-coloured panelling glow. The huge, starkly modern office was more in keeping with the image of a movie mogul than a practising lawyer.

The client sat across from Dan Spencer. He told his story but continued to look around, impressed with the gleaming office and large desk.

'And what did you do then?' Spencer asked.

'I looked to see what was going on. You know, I heard the guy shout, "Watch out!" So I turned around to see who he was yelling at.'

Spencer looked at the man's face. It had been badly torn up; his left eye was still patched. He had been hit by a swinging cable while at work on a construction job in Manhattan.

'And he was yelling at you,' Spencer added.

The wind and sun had reduced the man's skin to a brown, crinkled leather. He grinned, exhibiting a gold tooth. 'Not me in particular – the whole bunch of us working near the sand.'

'Was anybody else hit?'

'Just me. I didn't know what had happened. I didn't even get knocked out. The next thing I knew I was on my knees. At first it didn't even hurt.'

'The cable was broken?'

The man shook his head. 'Nope. A restraining screw pulled loose. The thing came out of there like a steel snake. Sort of like cracking the whip. Somebody had put the screws in wrong.'

'How do you know that?'

The man fingered the fresh scar along the side of his face. 'The guy running the rig told me. He was mad as hell. They had a young millwright working that day who didn't know his ass from third base. He had screwed up a couple of times.'

'Will this operator testify to that? We have to have him say it, not you. In court it's called the Hearsay Rule.'

'Sure. He's the one who sent me to the union. They sent me here. I guess you guys handle all the union's legal work, eh?'

'Just the suits for personal injury. Another firm handles workmen's compensation.'

The man chuckled. 'You guys must do a pretty good business, huh? We're a bunch of klutzes. Half the guys I work with are drunks. Somebody's getting hurt all the time.'

'Business isn't bad,' Spencer said, making a note. 'What do they say about your eye?'

'Too early to tell. A specialist at the hospital told me I might lose it. He said they'd have to wait and see. I go back to the eye doctor next week.'

Dan went over the details of the accident with the man, taking careful notes and getting what names the man could remember. If a mistake had been made by a workman, especially one who had proven himself incompetent, liability looked good. The company was on notice as to the possible danger. The man's face could be repaired, almost as good as new. Spencer had doctors' reports to that effect. But if he lost the eye, or lost effective vision, then the measure of damages would be increased greatly.

'When can I expect this thing to go to trial?' the man asked.

'It might take years. It depends on what happens to you medically and how open the company might be to a decent settlement.'

The man expertly fished a cigarette from his shirt jacket and lit up. 'Well, take your time – the only thing I ask is that I come out rich.' He laughed.

'You're taking all this pretty well.'

'Tell me some other way to take it. Shit, I can't half see. I look like a movie monster. If it wasn't for my old lady, I couldn't ever get laid. My head hurts and I'm bored sitting around at home. I got two choices, as I see it: I can feel sorry for myself and jump off a bridge or I can laugh. I sure can't do anything about it otherwise.'

Spencer nodded. Mentally he made a note that if the case did go to trial, he would have to prepare the man to be less offhanded about his pain, especially if it came down to a jury trial.

'Okay,' Spencer said. 'We'll check all this out and be in touch.'

The man's hand was calloused and strong. His good eye looked around Spencer's office. 'Damn, I sure wish I had gone to school,' he said. 'It must be nice.'

'Beats stealing,' Spencer said, escorting him to the door.

The man grinned at him. 'Some say with you lawyers it's really the same thing.' He laughed as he walked away.

'There's an attorney named Giles here to šee you,' his young secretary said. 'She's waiting out in the reception room.'

Dan was surprised at his own reaction. His heart seemed to leap at her name. 'Christina Giles?'

'Yes. She said it was personal. I told her you were in with a client. She said she'd wait.'

Dan restrained himself from running into the reception area. Instead he turned back towards his office.

'Ask her to come in,' he said.

He looked out his window. It was snowing. The new year had come and gone. It had been almost three months since he had seen Christina. He suddenly felt nervous. He turned as she came in.

She was even more beautiful than he remembered.

'Come in, Chris,' he said.

'Thank you, Dan.' She sounded like a nervous schoolgirl instead of one of the Twelve Apostles.

'Let me take your coat.' She slipped it off and he hung it up in the small concealed closet.

She sat down and looked around. 'Very Hollywoodish.'

He laughed. It was just that – garish, with a long, curved desk and coloured wall panelling. 'It's all part of the business. We have to impress the clients. They feel better if we conform more to their idea of high-powered lawyers, the kind you see in the movies. It's slightly more ostentatious than my old digs at Nelson and Clark.'

'Yes, it is that.' She smiled. 'I received your office announcement, Dan. I happened to be in the neighbourhood so I thought I'd drop by and see how you were doing.'

'That's very nice. They're letting me do office work and take depositions until I get a feel for the medical terms and the price lists for limbs. Then it'll be back into the pit. How are you doing?'

'May I smoke?'

'That's new. How come?'

'It's not new, just a return to an old habit. Things have been a little nervous-making for me lately. Smoking helps. When everything gets straightened out, I'll quit again.'

'Well, you're on the top floor now, Chris. How's the view?'

She inhaled on the cigarette before replying. 'One floor higher. I have almost the same duties as before. The only real difference is I can eat in the Apostles' dining room.'

'Nice?'

She laughed. 'The very best, just as rumoured.'

'Are you still staying with Katherine Thurston?'

'No. I was offered an apartment by a friend who's moving to the Coast for six months. It's fully furnished. I'm just apartment sitting, but at least it gives me a place to hang my hat. I was wearing out my welcome with the Thurstons, anyway. None of us shed great tears when I finally left.'

'How about your family?'

'The divorce will be completed quickly. Henry has the hots for a little nurse who luckily has herpes. It is – and I know I'm being catty – a match made in heaven. He's taking a teaching position at a Nevada hospital to establish residence and get one of those famous quick divorces.'

'And your son?'

'I have custody. Henry's back at school now, but he stayed with me over the holidays. Perhaps my motherly charms are becoming more apparent. I actually think we're becoming friends.'

'That's good. I know that whole business hurt you terribly.'

'And you, Dan. How about your personal life? Anything new?'

'You mean anyone, don't you?'

She smiled and inhaled on the cigarette. 'Perhaps.'

He leaned back in his chair. 'Nothing, or no one, new with me. As predicted, my family went berserk when they found out I left Nelson and Clark. I think they believe I'm keeping something hideous from them, that I'm a coke fiend or worse.'

'And do you like this?' She gestured at his office.

'So far. It's different, but it seems to scratch my particular itch. And it's a different bunch here. We don't have any diplomats, just hard-eyed, hungry lawyers looking to bite someone or something. I sort of enjoy them.'

'That doesn't sound like you. Do you think you actually fit in here?'

He grinned. 'I love it, to tell the truth. This is a wild bunch, and I don't have to worry about being underdressed or overdressed. As long as I'm hitting the ball, they don't give a damn.'

'Definitely not Nelson and Clark.'

'How's young Michael Collins getting on over there? I meant to call when I saw the announcement that he had made participating partner. Do you see him much?'

She crushed out the cigarette into his desk ashtray. 'He spends most of his time travelling to the Orient. He handles almost all of the Rising Sun business.'

'With Nancy Merriam? I read where she's doing a bang-up job.'

'Still read the *Wall Street Journal*?'

'Old habits are hard to break.'

'Well, everything seems to have worked out quite well. Taro Kuragamo has been broken. I understand most of his personal holdings are being challenged by creditors and they expect him to go bankrupt.'

'Couldn't happen to a nicer guy. How about the White Knight, Patrick Dowd? Anything new with him?'

'Who knows?' He's still a mystery man. As far as I know he still runs his empire from the foot of that statue in Dublin. We see the awesome power of his money, but we never see him.'

'Does anyone ever ask about me?'

She looked at him directly. 'No. You know how it is, Dan. If someone leaves the firm, that person just drops from sight and mind. Your secretary asked me a few times if I had seen you, but I'm afraid that's it.'

'How soon they forget.'

'I haven't.'

He looked at her, studied her serious eyes for a moment. 'I haven't forgotten you, either. I haven't thought of any other woman but you, Christina.'

'This whole thing is rather silly, isn't it?'

'In what way?'

'We love each other but we're letting our careers ruin our lives.'

'Perhaps.'

'No perhaps about it, Dan, and you know it. I can't stand being away from you. That's why I'm here.'

He didn't reply at first, aware that a great sense of relief was sweeping through every part of him. 'I find being without you painful, too,' he said slowly.

'Dan, I'll do anything you want me to do. If you want me to quit the firm, I will. If you want me to quit the practice of law, I will. I'm not ashamed to come to you like this. Frankly, life without you is unthinkable for me.' Her voice cracked slightly. 'Just tell me what you want me to do.'

'You'd quit Nelson and Clark?'

'If that stood between us.'

'I know how much being an Apostle means to you, darling.'

'I like it, but I'm not going to let it ruin my life.'

He smiled. 'Are you proposing to me?'

Her lower lip trembled. 'Dan, if you want me to live with you, I will. If you want me to marry you, I will. I don't care what or how – I just want to be with you.'

A tear slowly trickled down her right cheek.

Dan Spencer got up and walked around the desk. 'If you stay with the firm, don't you think you'll be ashamed to introduce me at parties? After all, I'm hardly in the Nelson and Clark league any more.'

The tears were coming now in little rivulets. 'I wouldn't be ashamed of you ever, under any circumstances.'

He held out his hand and pulled her to him. 'Tell you what. We'll live together until you get your divorce. Then we'll get married. You can stay a member of Nelson and Clark if you like. It won't bother me if it doesn't bother you.' He cupped her chin with his hand. 'And, what the hell, we can always use a spare million or two. Is it a deal, counsellor?'

She squeezed him tightly and sobbed into his chest.

He turned her face towards him and looked down at her. 'Well, do we have a deal?'

'Oh, God, yes!'

He kissed her hand, hungrily, suddenly realizing how very much he had missed her and how desperately he wanted her.

Roosevelt Smith was fussing at the busboy. 'Now you got to be faster, boy. When they gets through eating, you got to clear the table. They are in a hurry. They wants to get to business. This is a good job you got, boy, don't mess it up.'

'They do the same thing every month,' the busboy protested. 'Don't they ever get tired of this? I mean, it ain't no party or nothing. Hell, they don't even look like they're having a good time.'

'They ain't here for a good time,' Smith said in exasperation. 'This here is business. I hear some of them are up in arms about the bonuses to be paid to the participating partners. Some wants them to get more, some wants 'em to get less.'

'You know, I ain't been here but a couple of months, but it seems these here rich folks are always arguing about something. They don't get angry or nothin' like that, but they's always pushin' or pulling at one another. The faces have changed some, but that's about all around here that really changes.'

Roosevelt Smith looked over at the dignified, elegant Ainsworth Martin sitting at the head of the long table, delicately sipping his coffee. 'You see, boy, that's the magic of this here law firm. The whole damn world may change, everything in every way, but they don't. They never change, and that's what makes them great.'

His dark face split into a proprietary grin. 'Them's the Twelve Apostles, boy. They'll outlast everything and everybody. Nelson and Clark's got a life of its own.'

He chuckled. 'The Twelve Apostles, boy, they goin' to live forever.'

Fiction

☐	**The Chains of Fate**	Pamela Belle	£2.95p
☐	**Options**	Freda Bright	£1.50p
☐	**The Thirty-nine Steps**	John Buchan	£1.50p
☐	**Secret of Blackoaks**	Ashley Carter	£1.50p
☐	**Hercule Poirot's Christmas**	Agatha Christie	£1.50p
☐	**Dupe**	Liza Cody	£1.25p
☐	**Lovers and Gamblers**	Jackie Collins	£2.50p
☐	**Sphinx**	Robin Cook	£1.25p
☐	**My Cousin Rachel**	Daphne du Maurier	£1.95p
☐	**Flashman and the Redskins**	George Macdonald Fraser	£1.95p
☐	**The Moneychangers**	Arthur Hailey	£2.50p
☐	**Secrets**	Unity Hall	£1.75p
☐	**Black Sheep**	Georgette Heyer	£1.75p
☐	**The Eagle Has Landed**	Jack Higgins	£1.95p
☐	**Sins of the Fathers**	Susan Howatch	£3.50p
☐	**Smiley's People**	John le Carré	£1.95p
☐	**To Kill a Mockingbird**	Harper Lee	£1.95p
☐	**Ghosts**	Ed McBain	£1.75p
☐	**The Silent People**	Walter Macken	£1.95p
☐	**Gone with the Wind**	Margaret Mitchell	£3.50p
☐	**Blood Oath**	David Morrell	£1.75p
☐	**The Night of Morningstar**	Peter O'Donnell	£1.75p
☐	**Wilt**	Tom Sharpe	£1.75p
☐	**Rage of Angels**	Sidney Sheldon	£1.95p
☐	**The Unborn**	David Shobin	£1.50p
☐	**A Town Like Alice**	Nevile Shute	£1.75p
☐	**Gorky Park**	Martin Cruz Smith	£1.95p
☐	**A Falcon Flies**	Wilbur Smith	£2.50p
☐	**The Grapes of Wrath**	John Steinbeck	£2.50p
☐	**The Deep Well at Noon**	Jessica Stirling	£2.50p
☐	**The Ironmaster**	Jean Stubbs	£1.75p
☐	**The Music Makers**	E. V. Thompson	£1.95p

Non-fiction

☐	**The First Christian**	Karen Armstrong	£2.50p
☐	**Pregnancy**	Gordon Bourne	£3.50p
☐	**The Law is an Ass**	Gyles Brandreth	£1.75p
☐	**The 35mm Photographer's Handbook**	Julian Calder and John Garrett	£5.95p
☐	**London at its Best**	Hunter Davies	£2.95p
☐	**Back from the Brink**	Michael Edwardes	£2.95p

☐	**Travellers' Britain**	} Arthur Eperon	£2.95p
☐	**Travellers' Italy**		£2.95p
☐	**The Complete Calorie Counter**	Eileen Fowler	80p
☐	**The Diary of Anne Frank**	Anne Frank	£1.75p
☐	**And the Walls Came Tumbling Down**	Jack Fishman	£1.95p
☐	**Linda Goodman's Sun Signs**	Linda Goodman	£2.50p
☐	**Scott and Amundsen**	Roland Huntford	£3.95p
☐	**Victoria RI**	Elizabeth Longford	£4.95p
☐	**Symptoms**	Sigmund Stephen Miller	£2.50p
☐	**Book of Worries**	Robert Morley	£1.50p
☐	**Airport International**	Brian Moynahan	£1.75p
☐	**Pan Book of Card Games**	Hubert Phillips	£1.95p
☐	**Keep Taking the Tabloids**	Fritz Spiegl	£1.75p
☐	**An Unfinished History of the World**	Hugh Thomas	£3.95p
☐	**The Baby and Child Book**	Penny and Andrew Stanway	£4.95p
☐	**The Third Wave**	Alvin Toffler	£2.95p
☐	**Pauper's Paris**	Miles Turner	£2.50p
☐	**The Psychic Detectives**	Colin Wilson	£2.50p
☐	**The Flier's Handbook**		£5.95p

All these books are available at your local bookshop or newsagent, or can be ordered direct from the publisher. Indicate the number of copies required and fill in the form below   11

....

Name_____
(Block letters please)

Address_____

_____

Send to CS Department, Pan Books Ltd, PO Box 40, Basingstoke, Hants
Please enclose remittance to the value of the cover price plus:
35p for the first book plus 15p per copy for each additional book ordered
to a maximum charge of £1.25 to cover postage and packing
Applicable only in the UK

While every effort is made to keep prices low, it is sometimes
necessary to increase prices at short notice. Pan Books reserve
the right to show on covers and charge new retail prices which
may differ from those advertised in the text or elsewhere